The Banners of Enid

Enid (EE-nid) - The origin is Middle Welsh eneit, meaning "spirit, life."

THE BANNERS OF ENID

THE KINGDOM STORIES

Raymond G. Dennis

Forgetful Farm Press
Susquehanna, PA

Forgetful Farm Press

THE BANNERS OF ENID: THE KINGDOM STORIES
Copyright © 2020 by Raymond G Dennis

https://raymondgdennis.com/

Forgetful Farm Press
9351 SR 547, Susquehanna, PA 18847

Publisher's Note: This is a work of fiction.
Names, characters, places, and incidents are a product
of the author's imagination. Locales and public names
are sometimes used for atmospheric purposes.
Any resemblance to actual people, living or dead,
or to businesses, companies, events, institutions,
or locales is completely coincidental.

Cover and map illustrations by Mary Rose Sorenson

Book design by Ryan Forsythe

First Forgetful Farm Press edition
February 2021

Hardcover ISBN - 978-1-953251-01-5
Ebook, EPUB ISBN - 978-1-953251-06-0
Ebook, Mobi ISBN - 978-1-953251-02-2
Paperback ISBN - 978-1-953251-00-8
Audio, Downloadable ISBN - 978-1-953251-03-9

Dedication

For my grandchildren, great grandchildren,
great-great grandchildren, etc.

Acknowledgement

Thank you Nanc, for your patience,
the proof reading and supporting my crazy ideas.

Prologue

ood evening and welcome to the Tavern Hall. Make yourself comfortable. Pull your chair up close to the fireplace. Or if you like, take a seat on the floor next to the children. I'm sure they'll make room for you.

Let me introduce myself. I am known as the Raconteur, a storyteller from a long lineage of storytellers who have entertained in this Kingdom's tavern for generations.

Make yourself at home. It's of no matter whether you are a Noble or commoner or a stranger seeking respite from your travels. All are welcome. We appreciate your visit to the Kingdom. A different landscape than yours, I'm sure, but recognizable despite the peculiar aspects and some uncommon characters.

It's my pleasure this evening to present one of the Kingdom Stories, a narration of lives lived, and stories told of kings, queens, battles, quests, magic, and mystery. I enjoy a good story, don't you? All stories are valid, of course, worth a hearing; everybody has one. Stories told here convey the consequential fabric of life so often neglected outside the Tavern Hall.

Settle in this evening, out of the storm, with your back to the door. Gaze upon the fire and the glowing coals; enjoy the warmth caressing your face. Those prowling drafts slipping through the window cracks that lick the back of your neck will soon be overcome by the heat of this ancient stone hearth. Don't be concerned with those dark dancing shadows on the wall. They are but the creation of the comforting flames.

Listen to the crackling of the fire mix with my words as I guide you into the realm of the Kingdom stories, an apparent foreign place, yet one you may find familiar.

ENID AND SURROUNDS

ENID

SAMIS' FARM
TARIFF STATION
HOUSE of LOWE ESTATE
MINER'S VILLAGE
FORGES
HOUSE of CONOR ESTATE
WILDS
NORTH ROAD
HORSE CLAN
QUARRIES
BANGA ROAD
HOUSE of HIRSCH ESTATE
STAGG ROAD
SAW MILL
LOGGING VILLAGE
SHEEP CLAN
WESTERN HUNTING GROUNDS
HOUSE of BARIN ESTATE
WARDEN
HUNTING CAMP
TRAINING GROUNDS
CHURCH
NOBLE'S FARM
CASTLE
OLD MILL
CALDER RIVER
TARIFF STATION
VILLAGE
MORODON
TARIFF HOUSE
SOUTH RIDGE
MILL ROAD
FREE FARMERS
EAST ROAD
HARBOR
MILL AND POND
ARMY GARRISON
SHEEP MEADOW
TANNERY
SWAMP ROAD
DARK FOREST

Introduction

The Reign of King Drake
1021 to 1054

The tale that occupies us, on which we shall dwell, unfolds in the Kingdom of Enid, in a time and place outside of our realm. This particular episode portrays an eventful period in the life of King Drake.

The records of Enid's royal lineage testify that Drake was the father of Prince Bardolf, grandfather of Prince Broderick, and the son of a king whose name has been forgotten.

The Kingdom of Enid was of average size in territory and population as compared to the surrounding kingdoms. Enid belonged to the Northern Alliance, a group of kingdoms, those on or close to Enid's boundaries. Cooperation and assistance were expected from the other kingdoms, but not always assured.

The census at the time (1034) of this story reported 1,932 souls, including Nobles, servants, free persons, and children. The Kingdom's territory boosted abundant variation and more than adequate resources. Contained within its borders were a seaport trading village, a mining community, timberlands, lowland farmlands, western and northern hunting grounds, a castle village, and more.

The populace was divided between the Nobles and the commoners. The Nobles lived upon and controlled their modest estates, which included various enterprises; farming, lumber, raising cattle, import/export, tool manufacture, and the like. The commoners were identified in census documents as unbound farmers, servants, village tradesmen, sheep clansmen, horse clansmen, and peasants (individuals of self-determination engaged in scores of occupations).

The King's residence was a primitive stone castle located in the very center of the Kingdom. The castle sat atop a flat-topped hill, the bottom of which was ringed by a rampart wall.

As documented in Church records, King Drake was born in the millennium year, 1000, an auspicious date, a harbinger of grand things, an expectation of a destiny to be fulfilled.

He lived during the time known as the Dragon War. In fact, in church records and the tales of storytellers, he is known as the hero of the Dragon War.

Sky Full
of Dragons

King Drake placed his palms on the cold granite stones, leaned out between the keep's parapets, and gazed earthward into the darkness of the castle-hold. Within a short time, on this chilly spring morning, the courtyard would erupt with activity, the bustle of castle-life. Drake straightened up and pulled his arms into the warmth of his long, heavy robe. He looked out across the courtyard and over the castle-house roof to the glow on the eastern horizon. While Drake watched, moment by unappreciated moment, the dawn light steadily erased the field of stars that had kept him company throughout the night. Around midnight, he had been awoken from a brief and restless sleep by a recurring and vexing nightmare.

In his dream, the sky is full of dragons, shooting fire, scorching the earth, destroying crops, and burning villages. They swoop down, lifting cattle and sheep away with the long claws of their sturdy hind legs. The King, atop a hill, flails his useless sword above his head.

The nightmare had propelled Drake out of his bed and up to the castle keep's roof for a night of worried pacing beneath a dark sky, brimming with a display of unhurried rotating stars.

Exhausted from the long torturous dark hours, Drake laboriously climbed the ladder to the top of the keep's watchtower. Only four paces square, the watchtower was a wooden framework that occupied the middle of the keep roof. The tower roof provided an excellent vantage point, four stories above the ground. One story above the keep roof, the keep, a stone tower, was three stories in height. From this elevation, the King's view was unobstructed in every direction.

Now at rest, Drake sat in the center of the watchtower floor with his back against the flagpole, his arms wrapped around his knees like a child. Above his head, the royal family flag, red and white, rested limply against the pole. Simple strips of the same colors trimmed the edges of the hood and sleeves of his dark brown robe.

Since childhood, the keep's roof had been one of Drake's favorite places, a perch from which to view the Kingdom. He spent many hours there envisioning his future, leading the army on heroic exploits, and conducting the Kingdom's business. But now, in middle age, he suffered the fate of being seen as the childless monarch; he had no heir to the throne. And to add insult, this dragon invasion loomed as an immediate problem that he must deal with, decisively and swiftly. Dragons, confounding creatures of myth, had appeared in the Kingdom for the first time in recent history, an event contrary to reason.

Nevertheless, Drake had confronted challenges before, head-on, without restraint, in wartime, and in peace. He was confident there was a solution to the dragon problem, and given the time, he would envision it. But did he have time? If so, how much time?

The dragons were first sighted a month ago, in the northern reaches of the Kingdom. Sightings were reported a few weeks later in the Western Hunting Grounds (near the Kingdom of Enid's center). And then, only a week ago, Drake and two of his Knights confronted one of the beasts in a short-lived skirmish.

Stiff and cramping, his body begged for a change of position. Drake rose and limped two steps to the wooden hand-railing that ringed the top of the watchtower roof. He raised his arms over his head and arched his back. A breathy gasp escaped his lips. He clasped his hands behind his back and twisted from side to side. As the dawn's glow took command of the entire sky, Drake stood witness as his Kingdom, moment by moment, appeared before his eyes. Although this was a vision he normally relished, now, the possibility of dragons swooping in over the horizon haunted him.

From the lofty height of the watchtower's roof, Drake scanned each direction, taking in the farmlands to the east, the castle village to the south (the Dark Forest just beyond), the western foothills with the hunting grounds, and to the north, the snow-covered mountain peaks. He was responsible for it all—the governance, the commerce, and the welfare of his people. As a child, he had welcomed the morning light, a messenger with the promise of a bright day of adventure and play. As King, especially these days, the sunshine could not dispel the gloom of another day of responsibility and worry.

Stories and rumors were spreading through the Kingdom. The recent arrival of the dreadful beasts was taking its toll and infecting the minds of his people, commoner and Noble alike, with anxiety and dread.

When the rumors first surfaced a month ago, Drake was inclined to discount them as nonsensical stories of mythical beasts. There was the talk of dragons snatching up sheep, taking horses, and attacking merchants on the Braga Road. Drake and sensible men dismissed them, yet the stories flourished, demanding attention. The stories of sightings in the hunting grounds were more credible, more recent, and there was physical evidence (animal carcass remains and tracks in the snow) to support them.

His back to the castle, he looked out over the castle wall to the western hill country, still held in darkness. Drake brooded over an insuppressible image. The look of the beast, those sinister eyes dominated his mind, chilling him even more than the biting morning air.

Drake had concluded that the threat of dragons could not be dismissed or ignored. He deliberated with Sir Feargus and Sir Boetius, his trusted Knights, friends since childhood. They arranged a hunting trip into the Western Hunting Grounds, just the three of them. It was not uncommon, something they had done regularly since they were young boys. Drake did not want to raise alarm or the concern of his subjects; the hunting party was a subterfuge to hide his true intent to investigate the dragon sightings for himself.

Drake preferred to have a solution for the problem of dragons appearing in the Kingdom before he declared it a problem. Boetius and Feargus both argued for patrols to scour the Western Hunting Grounds in search of the beasts. Drake had wanted firsthand knowledge, which he now had; the image of the dragon was seared in his mind. The monster had been so close he could have almost touched it.

On the day they set out, fresh snow blanketed the ground, laid down by a spring squall the night before. It wasn't long before they were following the recently made tracks of three deer. Drake reasoned that following them might lead them to dragons. Evidence suggested that deer were one of the dragons' prey.

The sky was clear, and the sun was not up yet. The leafless woodlot of new-growth trees they were hiking through was lit pale. Feargus was in the lead when they reached a broad clearing. Three does were feeding at the far end at a distance just out of effective archery range, which did not stop Feargus from taking a shot.

One animal dropped to its knees, hesitated a moment, and then bounded up and away, followed by the other two into the forest. The men trotted across the clearing to the spot where the deer had been feeding. It was marked by dabbled blood in the snow and tracks leading away into the woods. Drake, out of breath, took notice of his lack of fitness, something to be expected, no doubt, for a man in his 32nd year. In their youth, they would have run down the wounded animal, but now they were content with an unhurried walk.

As usual, Boetius was in the lead, following the blood trail through a stand of old beech trees. The under-story of beech-brush that still held dead leaves limited their vision. "A cleaner shot, and we'd be back at the tavern eating roasted venison by now."

A comment directed at Feargus likely meant to taunt him, as his arrow had only wounded the deer, having struck behind and high on the shoulder. Ideally, a hunter's goal is to take the animal with a shot in the ribs that penetrates the heart.

"Are you having any trouble following the blood in the snow?" Feargus leveled a retaliatory barb, a reference to Boetius' own high opinion of his tracking skills.

"Gentlemen, less talk. Hunting is a silent sport," Drake said, hoping to head off another squabble.

Boetius came to a quick halt, the flat of his hand extending back toward his companions. "Something in the field ahead," he whispered.

The three men, crouching low, moved through the brush toward the edge of the field like prey animals, the prey animals they were. They settled in behind a laurel thicket, its umbrella of oval evergreen leaves concealing them.

The hunters looked to each other, communicating silently, the way they had done since they were children. They froze in place; their expressions betrayed their shock and disbelief.

The blood trail in the snow marked a path out of the thicket into the clearing. It ended at a tattered deer carcass, crushed in the claws of a dragon's hind legs. The dragon was sitting up like a trained bear. Its serpentine tail slowly undulated on the snow like that of a cat. The long neck arched downward. Its head, reaching to its forelegs which held a haunch of dear flesh, lurched from side to side. Four dagger-like fangs (two top and two bottom) shredded flesh before the dragon raised its head to swallow.

Drake had never seen such a fearsome beast. When they were boys, he and his friends had listened to the stories of dragons (legends, myths), tales meant to frighten children. But there, standing in a clearing, not over 20 paces from them, was a dragon, a real and most startling creature.

It was at least twice the size of a warhorse. The body appeared to be covered with scales, in shades of green, darker on the back, lighter on the sides, with a mottled amber underbelly. Along the spine, from the top of the head to the tip of the tail, small triangular fins projected like yellow-stained saw-teeth.

Suddenly, the beast stopped its feast and swiveled its head in the men's direction, adopting an alert posture. Had it sensed the men's presence? Was it sniffing the air? No, Drake noted that their position was downwind. Had it detected movement? Not likely, they had satisfactory cover. In a state of awareness, the dragon's eyes were scanning the edge of the wood-line. Strips of bloody flesh dangled from its teeth.

It dropped the flesh it held in its front legs, dropped to all fours, and took a few halting steps in their direction. The dragon paused, rose on its hind legs again. It had found them, direct eye contact, bright yellow eyes with black vertical slits for pupils.

In their childhood sign language, Feargus signaled for retreat.

But before Drake, who was in agreement, could give the command, Boetius stood, stepped into the clearing, and let an arrow fly. It shattered on the dragon's chest. The beast dropped to all fours and took a few more steps in the men's direction.

"Retreat!" Drake called out.

As Drake and Feargus backed out of the thicket into the woods, Feargus grabbed the back of Boetius' cloak and pulled him with them. They backpedaled into the forest. The dragon closed the gap from its position in the field to the laurel thicket with only a few lumbering strides. It stopped in the thicket. Their hiding place, just a moment before, was now trampled under its hind legs. The dragon rose once again, now only ten paces from Drake.

The dragon's head high above, Drake's gaze locked with those eyes, yellow orbs, sinister and unnerving.

Smoke curling out of its nostrils, the dragon tilted its head back, and a blue fireball shot from its mouth. The flames skirted over the men's heads and into the treetops, igniting the dry limbs. Embers cascaded around the three men like glowing snowflakes.

Still facing the dragon, Drake, bow in hand, instinctively pulled an arrow from his quiver to mount a defense. "Fall back!" he commanded.

Feargus and Boetius sprinted toward a position ten paces behind Drake.

As he notched an arrow, Drake took a knee. He released the string. The arrow bounced off the side of the dragon's head. Leaping up, he ran toward a position ten paces behind his Knights. As he ran past them, he shouted, "Aim for the eyes!"

They released their arrows. Feargus' arrow went wide; Boetius' arrow struck an eye but bounced off.

Drake took up a defensive position again behind Boetius and Feargus as they turned to run. Drake let loose another useless arrow to no effect.

"Retreat," Drake cried out.

All three men were now running headlong through the trees and brush. Drakes bow hung from his left hand. His right arm was extended in front of him in an effort to deflect low-hanging branches and brush, which nonetheless stung his face.

Drake heard a few crushing footfalls and a gravelly roar. He glanced over his shoulder but collided with a tree trunk before he could get a glimpse of the dragon's position. As he stumbled to the ground, Drake dropped his bow and threw out his hands to break his fall. He got up on one knee but collapsed back to the ground when he put weight on his forward foot. Suddenly, Feargus was behind him, his arms under Drake's armpits, lifting Drake to his feet. Drake threw one arm over Feargus' shoulder, and they hobbled forward for many long moments.

"Halt." It was Boetius' voice.

Drake and Feargus turned around just in time to catch a glimpse of the dragon in flight above the treetops. It was already in the distance, beyond the edge of the woods. Boetius was only a few steps away, leaning against a tree, gazing at the sky.

They had attempted an orderly retreat by falling back in leapfrog succession, to no real effect since their arrows were useless.

"I'm alright." Drake withdrew his arm from Feargus' shoulder. He took a few tentative limping steps. "Probably a sprained ankle."

Cuts on Drake's face were stinging and warm with blood. He was breathing hard, as were Boetius and Feargus.

"Sire." Boetius was pointing to Drake's left hand.

His arm at his side, blood was dripping from Drake's fingertips, splattering the snow and his boot.

Drake noted the gash in the palm. "I must have landed on something sharp."

From his waist bag, Feargus pulled out a piece of cloth and wrapped it around the wound. Drake curled his fingers to put pressure on the bandage and felt the pain in his palm for the first time.

"The scales are like armor plate," Boetius said.

"I saw your arrow bounce off its eye." Feargus slumped to the ground, his back against a tree trunk.

"Its eyes got duller," Boetius said. "I think the beast may have clear eyelids. Hard to tell, but I believe it's what I saw."

After a few minutes passed, and they had caught their

breath, the men, Drake hobbling, made their way back to the clearing. The deer carcass was gone; the dragon had taken the time to recover it.

Drake saw himself as a pragmatic and grounded man, but this apparition had shaken him to his core.

The sun was peaking over the castle-house roof; rays struck the top of the keep tower. Drake glanced back over his shoulder and was blinded for a moment, jarred out of his memories and bad dream, back to the present.

Dragons in the land. What to do about it? Drake turned back toward the castle and took inventory of the castle's defenses from his perch on the watchtower roof. Below him, the three-story stone keep was attached to the center of the western courtyard wall. The west, north, and south courtyard walls were two stories in height, as was the castle-house building, which made up the eastern wall. The castle-house and courtyard walls were all topped with periodically spaced short-walls with archery slots. Parapets, shoulder height, filled the space between the short-walls. The walkways on top of the walls were accessed from the courtyard interior by stone stairways attached to the south and north courtyard walls. An excellent and proven defense against armies of men, but Drake feared the fortress to be of little value against a dragon attack.

The castle, built of quarried, mortared stone, sat on a small flattop hill, the bottom of which was ringed by an earthen rampart at the bottom of the hill, 100 paces from the castle. The outer wall of the rampart was vertical, a story high, surfaced with laid flagstone. Its inner side tapered off into an earthen gutter where the first defenders would stand their ground. The rampart had served its purpose in the war King Drake's grandfather waged against the Kingdom of Chambold. The Chambold army reached the rampart and attempted a breach with ladders but was repelled. However, the rampart and the castle walls would be of no value against an enemy capable of flight. And besides, arrows were useless against a foe covered with impenetrable armor.

In Drake's mind's eye, scanning the castle, he envisioned his army in their defensive positions, at first organized and prepared, and then in disarray and defeat.

"Here, you are again." A familiar voice interrupted his thoughts. A figure, dressed in the same basic brown garb with colored stripes the same as his, was standing at the base of the watchtower. Queen Ramona had caught him unaware; she moved like a hunter. The way the finely woven coat was cut revealed her attractive feminine form. A tall woman, equal to Drake in height, wearing trousers and laced knee-high leggings, Ramona was imposing. Drake wished she would dress like the other Noblewomen, not in men's clothing. How she dressed was just one of their running topics of argument.

"You can't spend every night on the keep roof. Come down now. You're not going to solve anything staring up at the night sky." Walking toward him, she put up her hood against the chill air.

She was right about that; every night for a week since the encounter with the dragon had been dominated by the nightmare. Nothing good would come from lack of sleep.

Drake hurried down the ladder and glanced to his Queen as he walked by her. Not in any way wanting to be seen as dutiful, Drake's voice had a harsh edge. "I was just about to come down."

Ramona recoiled.

He strode to the keep doorway, stopped, and looked back at her. "I am meeting with my advisers this afternoon to discuss my plans to put an end to this dragon problem." Drake passed through the keep doorway, leaving Ramona standing alone on the keep roof. Drake plunged into the dimly lit keep interior, skipping steps, hurrying away from the Queen, her opinions, and another inevitable argument.

The Queen's View

"Plans, what plans?" Queen Ramona whispered as Drake disappeared in the darkness of the doorway. She knew her husband, and she knew he had no plans. What he had were worries. Couldn't blame him. The people of the Kingdom were in a panic. Dragons, dragons, dragons, it was all they talked about.

It was the same in the surrounding lands. Talk and rumor of dragons consumed everyone, the Nobles and the commoners. The dragons had appeared in the Kingdom of Enid and the two most northern principalities of the alliance, Braga and Duren. The news of their arrival had spread to the other kingdoms of the alliance, Evora and Brives in the east, Chambold and Dacian in the south. None of those kingdoms had sightings as yet.

Everyone would be counting on King Drake for a solution, his subjects, and the other Monarchs. He was well respected, known as resourceful and capable, a problem solver, and valiant in battle. The other Monarchs will undoubtedly call him to leadership now. There was a plan to convene a council to discuss the dragons. If anyone could unify the always squabbling Rulers to support a common cause, it would be Drake.

Drake was a man of average height, average build, and average looks, but nonetheless stood out and above other men. He was a prince by nature, not only by birthright. Ramona had always been attracted to him but had not always admitted it, not even to herself. As a girl, she feigned interest in Boetius, who was virile and charismatic, and in turn, Feargus, who was handsome and tall. Thinking back, she did it instinctively to elicit Drake's jealousy.

Ramona's mother told her there was not a better man to marry than Drake. When reproving Ramona's less than feminine ways, her mother warned that Drake was likely the only man available to her.

"Oh, the young men will have you," her mother said, "But not their mothers."

The Noblewomen arranged the marriages for their sons, through a convoluted social network within Enid and the other kingdoms. They went about their scheming in quilting circles, at banquets, in covert meetings, and through secret correspondence, wherein proposed matches were considered and debated, all laced with gossip and intrigues. The appraisal of Ramona was, although modestly attractive and likely a good child-bearer, that she was too headstrong, uncontrollable, and would be a headache for any man and his family.

At one time, Ramona's mother had considered Boetius as a possible match, but his mother was not likely to ever find any woman worthy of her golden boy.

A union with Feargus, also unlikely. His parents died young. He was raised by a bachelor uncle, who himself found no comfort in marriage and did not press it on Feargus. Feargus, himself, was content with the procession of women who found his company alone enough to meet their needs.

To Ramona's dismay, a rumor had circulated that Drake's mother was trying to arrange a marriage for him with a princess of another kingdom. But Drake, the only person in the Kingdom more headstrong than Ramona, overcame his mother's plans. He wanted Ramona and would accept no other.

"What do I need a man for?" Ramona said to her mother, "I can do everything they can do."

"Not everything. You will want children, and I certainly want grandchildren. And Drake is a fine man to supply them."

She did want children, as did Drake, but their desires had been thwarted, the greatest disappointment they had suffered in their lives. Ramona couldn't imagine anything worse; except maybe a dragon war with the couple on opposite sides.

The way Ramona saw it, there were two different views one could take concerning the dragons, a dangerous threat to the Kingdom, or only a passing curiosity with no malicious intent. Which viewpoint would prevail and be acted on would eventually be arbitrated and decided by Drake.

When the first accounts of dragons came to her, Ramona assumed they were false; there must be some reasonable explanation. She first heard the gossip from Drake, who relied on the Noble Council for his information, always a mistake in her opinion. Those men only confided what served their interests.

But then the rumors were confirmed through her sources, the common people she trusted (her network of informants) and also her confidant, Amalia, her maid. Ramona and Amalia had become fast friends the first day they met, in their teen years, before Ramona became the Queen and Amalia became the Queen's maid.

Now, dragons were not merely in the tales of storytellers; dragons were in the Kingdom. Drake, Feargus, and Boetius had seen one, fought one. Drake's and Boetius' account of the fight put the dragon on the offensive. Feargus disclosed that Boetius initiated the conflict and that the dragon could have easily killed them, but instead flew off.

She wished she had been there, to have seen it for herself,

the actual event. To see such a creature, a creature of tall tales and dreams, how fantastic. Drake's account and description weren't enough for her; she wanted to see one.

The flapping of the tower flag against the pole and a sudden chilly gust of wind brought Ramona back to the present. Awoken from her thoughts, Ramona realized she was pacing the keep roof, the same aimless path Drake likely followed. She made another pass around the roof along the parapet edge. The sun hung in the sky well above the horizon. She surveyed the Kingdom from the same vantage point as the King, but now, it was illuminated by full morning light. The spring sun would soon provide the welcome warmth to melt away those last lingering patches of snow in the fields.

Ramona left the roof and descended into the keep's core. Her hard-soled boots clattered on the wooden stairs and landings as she made her way to the bottom, where she exited the ground level passage door. As she strode across the courtyard in the direction of the castle proper, she took note of the birdsong. Flocks were returning in late winter in anticipation of spring. She couldn't identify them, not like Boetius, like he did when they were children. She always relied on him and never learned the songs herself. He was always in the forests, hunting and tracking. He could identify every bird and every animal by sound or track.

Upon reaching the castle-house, Ramona entered through the kitchen door and into the clamor of the servants wrapping up their breakfast duties. Gerda, the head cook, was elbow deep in dishwater at the far end of the room. Over a week ago, Gerda imparted a story that came from her family, the Northern Sheep Clan. It was said that dragons were seen flying over the North Woods in a southerly direction, and the next day, a small flock of sheep was found missing. Ramona exchanged nods with Gerda as she passed through the kitchen into the great-hall.

At one table, a few guardsmen were finishing up their

breakfast, and several servants were moving about, gathering up dinnerware.

At the far end of the great-hall by the castle gatehouse door, the guardsman, Dunstan, sat resting his bad back. Dunstan, an old veteran, had earned the right to sit. As a young man, he had fought in the wars with Drake's father and returned with disabling wounds. Now an old man, he was delegated to guarding the door to the great-hall, a door that did not need guarding.

Because of his age, people assumed he was hard of hearing, which he was not. The presumption provided opportunities for eavesdropping and to gather information that he would then pass on to his Queen. Ramona relied on him to furnish the latest gossip, usually intermixed with war stories, both of which she was eager to hear. Recently, he had picked up an account from the quarrymen who lived in the North Woods, a similar story to that of Gerda's. The only difference was, it was horses that had disappeared.

To Ramona's left, in front of the fireplace on the east wall, Amalia sat knitting. Both the east and west sides of the great-hall offered fireplaces that provided warmth to those near them but only the cheer of the flame to those distant. The hearths now held the coals of the morning's consequential fires, having earlier done their duty of dispelling the chill from the chamber.

"Morning to you, Amalia." Ramona stepped up behind her.

"Morning, Ma'am." Amalia stood. She was a head shorter than Ramona, and her timid nature reduced her statue even more.

"Please sit." Ramona pulled up a chair opposite Amalia. "What have you heard?"

Amalia recounted several stories received from Elsa, a barmaid at the tavern.

A free-holder farmer in the eastern reaches of the Kingdom had reported a fire in his winter wheat field, the destruction attributed to dragon flame. In addition, recently, the hunting troop, whose custom was to gather at the tavern in the evening, had concluded that the remains of animal carcasses they found in the Western Hunting Grounds were the work of dragons.

Ramona nodded slowly, then made eye contact. "I need to know more about these dragons, and if stories coming to us are true. The King is on the verge of doing something rash. I know it. I fear his worried mind will lead him to some sort of foolishness."

Ramona was aware of the questions Drake was wrestling with. How dangerous were the dragons? What were they capable of? How could one fight them?

Ramona, on the other hand, entertained her own questions regarding the dragons. What were their true intentions? What brought them to the Kingdom? Is it possible to get close enough to observe them safely?

The members of the royal court, who were feeding Drake the dragon stories, were good at acquiring and spreading rumors. The courtiers were as talented as magicians, sometimes making stories appear out of thin air. Many times, what the court entertained as truth was later exposed as sheer nonsense. Ramona needed to learn the truth about the dragons. She had a plan even if the King didn't, a logical course of action, to track down the source of the stories and determine what risk, if any, the dragons brought to the Kingdom.

"By all accounts, these creatures seem to be truly dangerous, Ma'am." Amalia focused on her knitting, her needles rhythmically clacking.

"I'm not convinced. From Feargus' account of the men's encounter, it doesn't seem the dragon intended any harm. And from Drake's description of the creature, it certainly could have."

"It may have been just luck that the dragon wasn't successful in its attack."

"Maybe, but Amalia, wouldn't it have been fantastic to have

been there? To have seen the beast? How amazing, to be in the presence of a mythical beast."

Amalia's needles went silent. Her bright eyes held Ramona's.

"I hope I get to see one soon. Drake's description was amazing." Ramona needed to find a way to at least get a glimpse of a dragon.

"According to rumor, the dragons are terrifying. Shouldn't something be done about them? Won't the King find a way to deal with them?"

"What my husband might decide to do about it, that's what worries me."

Although Drake was not likely to appreciate it, Ramona hoped to find a way to help him make the right decision. Ramona feared that the appearance of dragons in the Kingdom would lead to another contentious dispute between herself and Drake.

King in the Middle

As Drake sat in his chambers behind his massive wooden desk, he pivoted back and forth from Feargus to Boetius as they stood before him arguing. It was later in the afternoon, after the morning confrontation with Ramona on the keep roof. Drake was regretting having brought these men together. Letting them play out their debate seemed like the best course, but as usual, it was dragging on. He had told Ramona he would seek advice, and he was committed to hearing them out, no matter how long it took. Hopefully, this meeting would produce results and also appease the Queen.

"It's time to take action, deal with the beasts. Confront them with all our forces. We can't wait," Boetius proclaimed.

Turning his head sharply toward Boetius, Feargus replied, "But there's no actual evidence that the dragons pose a threat. It's only ..."

"No threat? No threat!" Boetius shuddered. "How can you say that?"

"I advise caution. We need to think things through." Feargus was addressing Drake.

"While you're thinking things through, the dragons will

overrun the Kingdom."

"A few dragons, overrun the Kingdom?"

"A few?" Boetius said, "There could be hundreds."

"No one has reported seeing hundreds. Not more than four or five at a time." The mocking tone in Feargus' voice was surely meant to infuriate Boetius.

"That doesn't mean there aren't hundreds out there, or hundreds coming."

"You see things that aren't there." Feargus and Boetius were face to face.

"You can't see things that are right in front of your face."

Drake lost track of the argument as his thoughts drifted back to childhood, reminded of the many times he had spent as the mediator between his two boyhood friends. Feargus and Boetius could always find their way to opposite sides of any issue, leaving Drake in the middle, the final arbitrator. If Boetius wanted to go swimming, Feargus wanted to hike. If Feargus said it would rain, Boetius commanded the sun to come out. Drake longed for those simpler times and simpler problems.

"Your information comes from stories that are only rumor and gossip." Feargus' growl brought Drake back to the moment.

Drake was aware of the reports of dragon sightings. Everything got back to him, one way or another, by those who sought to curry his favor. Since their arrival, the dragons were being blamed for almost every troubling incident in the Kingdom. It was a generally held opinion that creatures of such ugly appearance, things of nightmares, could be nothing but a source of trouble. This belief was compelling Drake to provide a remedy for the situation.

"You're wrong there. I heard the accounts firsthand from those who witnessed the dragon's crimes," said Boetius.

"Where did you pick up these stories, the tavern hall?" Feargus was smirking.

The tavern hall was referred to by some as 'the gossip hall.'

The hall, the central room of the village tavern where food and drink were served to locals and travelers, was used as a meeting room by Nobles and common folk alike. It was where Drake, Boetius, Feargus, and his other childhood friends had spent many an evening sitting on the floor in front of the fireplace listening to the Raconteur tell stories. He treasured those childhood times in the tavern hall, one of the few times that Boetius and Feargus were not arguing.

Drake interrupted. "Hold. Has either of you seen a dragon since our encounter? Or have any of your men?" He pointed to each man in turn.

After a slight hesitation, "No," they both replied simultaneously.

"Do we have any idea where they are coming from? Do we know that, at least?" Both Knights were silent. "Only stories, second-hand information, that's all you bring me?"

"That time with the dragon, it tried to kill us," Boetius asserted, "That's proof enough for me."

"Tried to kill us?" Feargus replied, "Only after you shot an arrow at it. Even then, I don't think it meant to harm us."

Boetius uttered a disgusted grunt. "Rubbish."

On becoming king, Drake had selected these men, his closest friends, to be his advisers and the commanders of his army. Following tradition, Drake's father had abdicated the throne as he approached old age, his commanders retiring with him, leaving the new King to select his candidates. Charismatic, a natural leader, and an archer champion, Boetius was the obvious choice to be the commander of the archers. On the other hand, appointing Feargus as field commander and commander of the Knights and soldiers had raised concerns with the Nobles' Council, an advisory body to the King. The council members were selected from the Kingdom's Eminent Nobles, high-ranking men, the primary contributors to the coffers of the Kingdom. A magnificent horseman, able-bodied with a lance and sword, Feargus was also a champion, but some said he lacked the tenacity to command. But despite his cautious temperament, his men were as loyal and committed to his leadership as Boetius' men were to him, maybe more so.

Feargus continued, "At this point, it would be a waste of our time and resources to attack the dragons. And a dangerous enterprise."

"We need to defend the Kingdom at all costs. The dragons are a threat to our food supply; they're taking game in our hunting grounds."

"Ah-ha. Now there's the heart of the matter, the hunting grounds," Feargus said, "Now we know what you are about."

Boetius was a renowned hunter; some said the greatest hunter of all time. Drake, having spent many hours hunting with Boetius, supported that assertion. There wasn't an animal he couldn't track and kill.

"So what's your solution, what's your plan? Talk with them?" Boetius was smiling and shaking his head.

"I propose we investigate, study the problem, and then devise a plan based on the facts."

"Nonsense. We need to get in the field and confront the creatures," Boetius said, looking to Drake.

"A decision to go to war with the dragons hasn't been made yet. Even so, we would need to prepare." Feargus focused on Drake.

Yes, preparation. Drake's thoughts turned to the state of his army. Were they prepared to mount an attack or even a defense? The standing army comprised the King's guard (24 swordsmen), 24 archers under Boetius, 30 mounted Knights, and 20 men-at-arms under Feargus and the eight guardsmen stationed at Morodon. And if needed, the first company reserves could be called up, 34 archers, and 60 men-at-arms.

"I agree with Feargus," Drake said, "The reserves' training is scheduled for a month from now. Advance the training to this week."

Feargus was visibly pleased, Boetius stoic.

"Our usual training exercises, Sire?" Feargus asked.

It was a leading question, a troublesome question. How will his troops train to fight the dragons? Drake didn't like not having the answer.

"For now, yes. Unless you have something else in mind?" Drake eyed Feargus and then glanced to Boetius. Neither man responded. "We need to understand the nature of the problem we're facing."

"If there is a problem," Feargus interrupted, "The dragons . . ."

"I will determine that," Drake asserted, "I want patrols sent out immediately." He was not pleased with Feargus' interruption. "I want as much information as possible about these dragons. Our best option is to use the hunting troop and tracking dogs. Boetius, arrange it." Then directed to Feargus, "You are also free to send out patrols."

"I will do so at once, Sire," Boetius said, clearly pleased, "I will determine the threat and report back."

"If there really is a threat," Feargus said with a scoff, shaking his head.

"There's a threat alright, it's obvious," Boetius declared, "You just can't see it. Never could see what's right in front of your face. Always looking for a way around a fight."

Feargus pivoted toward Boetius. His right hand crossed his body and grasped the hilt of his sword. Boetius stiffened.

Drake stood, leaned forward, and slammed his hands down on his desk. "Enough!" he yelled.

Feargus and Boetius both retreated to a relaxed stance and stood silent as King Drake settled back into his chair.

"As you both know, the Kings of the Alliance have called for a war council. We will meet in Evora in two weeks' time."

Evora, the kingdom that borders Enid on the east, unusual compared to the other kingdoms of the alliance, had monarchs of maternal lineage, Queens in charge rather than Kings. Queen Saskia, the current monarch, had proposed to host the

War Council, and the other monarchs agreed. The opportunity to visit Evora and Queen Saskia, Drake's first cousin, five years his senior, pleased him. He did not see her often. He enjoyed her company, always had, despite her reputation for being headstrong and domineering. Her irreverence and use of profanity, which made men blush and flustered, Drake found entertaining. As a teen, he loved to watch the older men squirm in their seats.

"Although I don't think there is much to be gained from the meeting, I intend to go. I will take one adviser with me."

"I am ready and at your service, Sire." Boetius promptly stepped forward and made a quick bow at the waist.

"Likewise, I am at your service, Sire," said Feargus.

"I am taking Reynard." Not wanting to listen to another argument, Drake raised the flat of his hand in front of his Knights.

Feargus and Boetius stood glaring at each other for a moment.

"That will be all." Drake waved his arm as he turned his attention to the papers on his desk.

His commanders turned away and left the room. Drake knew they weren't happy with his choice, but so be it.

The Invitation

Reynard had been summoned for a meeting with the King, not an unusual occurrence. As the King's Weapons Master for the last 12 years, they had an untold number of meetings. This time, though, he had a knot in his stomach as he stepped into the castle's great-hall.

The sentry at the door called out, "Master Reynard, Sire." He then pushed the heavy wooden door closed behind Reynard, its hinges creaking in complaint. At the far end of the hall, with his back to Reynard, the King sat at the central dining table that was located in front of the royal throne. On the wall behind and above the throne was the royal crest, a red shield with a silhouette of a white mountain-lion in the center. It was flanked by weapon displays on both sides; on the right, two standing crossed lances; on the left, a horizontal bow with an arrow pointing to the ceiling. To Reynard's right, morning light flooded in from the hall's eastern second-level clerestory windows, illuminating the table and the King. Sparkling dust floated in the sun's rays.

Reynard advanced across the cavernous room. King Drake stood and walked toward him. A quick halt and a bow as the

King neared, "Your servant, Sire."

Stopping short in front of Reynard, the King announced, "Reynard, I have decided that you will accompany me to the war council in Evora."

Boetius had told Reynard of the meeting between himself, the King, and Feargus the day before. Reynard had anticipated the King's announcement but was not entirely prepared for it. He did not want hard feelings between himself and Boetius or Feargus. Better if the King had chosen one of them.

"You look surprised, Reynard."

"Oh, no ... It's an honor, Sire."

"You expected me to select Boetius or Feargus. Everyone did. But you are my Weapons Master, and you will have an important part to play in implementing our strategy to defeat the dragons."

"You've decided then. War?" Despite his employment as a designer and builder of weapons, Reynard did not relish combat as some did. He enjoyed the craft of making armaments, but not the craft they were used for. He preferred to put his abilities to work as a blacksmith. His talent, though, was well-known to the King, and he had been thrust into the role of Kingdom's Weapons Master.

"No, not as yet. But I need to be prepared," the King said. "I intend to hear everyone out on all sides of the matter before I decide."

The King took Reynard by the elbow and directed him toward the dining table. "Take a seat." Occasionally, King Drake slipped into the casual manner they had shared in their childhood friendship.

Reynard waited until the King took his seat and then slid, uncomfortably, into a tall straight-back chair across from him.

Once seated, King Drake continued, "I want you to tell me what you know of the dragons. Specifically, do you have any idea where they came from?"

"Legends say somewhere beyond the North Mountains."

Reynard thought the statement might hold a truth. His grandfather believed that dragons (part of his storytelling lore) lived in the far north. And like his grandfather before him, he was a hunter who trapped black bears in the North Mountains and beyond. Reynard's grandfather had brought back a wife from one of the native tribes in that region. She brought with her the folklore of her clan, including the stories of dragons.

"Yes, the legends. Yet I have been told that the dragons may have come from the Dark Forest. A possibility, don't you think?"

"Not likely, Sire." Anything and everything malevolent was said to come from that forest.

"But the colored lights that people have reported seeing in the forest treetops could that not be the dragons, their yellow eyes, as they fly in the forest?" the King asked.

"The flickering lights in the Dark Forest treetops sometimes do pop up in the Raconteur's stories. Usually blamed on witches, ghosts, or the like."

King Drake leaned forward, raised his eyebrows, and lowered his voice. "I understand it's more than just a story or a legend for you. It's rumored that you've seen the lights yourself."

Reynard and the King were silent for a moment. Reynard was searching his mind for an answer, not wanting to be entirely truthful. He didn't want to lie to the King. He never had, although he may have omitted things on occasion. Even when they were children, it was best not to divulge everything to Drake. When presented with a problem, Drake became consumed with the challenge of fixing it—as quickly as possible.

An enjoyable day at the swimming hole could be ruined by Drake leading them off to settle some petty injustice. Like the time Ramona let it slip that a village boy called her a tomboy. Despite the truth of the allegation, Drake's gang was off to avenge the slight to Ramona's honor. And once Drake started down a path, there would be no change in direction.

When confronted about his rash behavior (usually by Ramona), his stock retort was 'He who hesitates is lost.' To which, her routine reply was, 'Look before you leap.' To which, Drake would return a scowl and then do as he damned well pleased.

"Let me be blunt," the King said, "I know that in your youth, you and Amalia had secret rendezvous on the South Ridge Trail."

The castle village and the seaport town of Morodon were connected by the well-traveled Morodon Road, which tracked in close proximity to the deep and wide Morodon River. The road lay on the north side of the river; the Dark Forest edge bordered the south side of the river. In addition to the Morodon Road, a shortcut trail ran over the top of South Ridge, a series of rugged hills to the road's north. Steep and rough going in spots, the trail was not passable for carts and wagons. The trail cut a winding path along the ridge. At its midpoint, a rock outcropping overlooked the Dark Forest.

King Drake dropped his hands to his hips and smiled. "Not to worry, Reynard. South Ridge has a long history of romantic rendezvous between village boys and seaport girls. Tell me what you saw. I can be trusted with a secret."

Many years had passed since Reynard first met Amalia, a merchant's daughter. Her family lived in Morodon and imported textiles (linens and fine broadcloth). Amalia's father was also a tailor and her mother a seamstress. Amalia became a skilled seamstress as well, one of the reason's Ramona's mother selected her as Ramona's handmaid. Not an appointment Reynard was happy with since it put Amalia in lifetime service to the Queen. He couldn't help but be resentful of Amalia's loyalty to Ramona, but she always countered any argument against the arrangement by criticizing his loyalty to King Drake.

Reynard was reluctant to talk about his experience of the Dark Forest, one he preferred to keep secret, but the King's friendly manner put him at ease. "We would meet at the lookout point. From there, you can see down into the treetops of the forest. Most of the time, there's only darkness. But one time, and only one time, we ... I saw the lights." Reynard paused.

"Go on." King Drake leaned in.

The King's attentive expression drew the story out. "The lights were mesmerizing to watch. Sometimes they flickered, hanging in place. And sometimes they flashed brightly like signal lanterns, and then abruptly streak through the treetops like shooting stars."

"So it could be dragons flying in the treetops?" the King interrupted.

"I don't think so. The lights were small and many-colored, red, green, purple, not only yellow." Reynard and Amalia talked of the experience often but did not share it carelessly. Amalia may have told Ramona. She and the Queen were very close, and of course, Ramona could be trusted. Reynard didn't want this story spread, to be the subject of rumor or bad jokes. His business was his business.

"I see," the King rocked back in his chair, disappointment on his face. "I had hoped to have something to offer at the council. Be that as it may, prepare yourself for the trip. I want you to be my eyes and ears with the commoners and the men-at-arms, here and at the council."

"Yes, Sire."

Reynard didn't want to disappoint the King; he would ready himself for the trip and his tasks. He believed the King respected his loyalty and reasoned, that was why he was chosen (despite his lack of Noble blood) to attend the war council.

"Thank you. You may go." The King did not look up but sat brooding.

"Yes, Sire." Reynard bowed, turned, and left the great-hall. A fleeting sense of honor, his selection by the King, was taken over by the dread of war. A war with the dragons, a most likely undefeatable foe.

Reminiscing

eturning from the castle, Reynard was on his way to his village shop. As he walked the village street, his mind wandered in its own landscape, focusing on this or that; memories of childhood awakened.

His relationships with his boyhood friends had changed. It had been a long time since he had punched Drake in the arm or pulled Ramona's braid. When they were young, there was little distinction between a commoner's child and the Noble children. Not that they didn't have a hierarchy, they just didn't rely on bloodline or wealth to ordain it. Friendship bonds didn't accommodate social boundaries. And competitions were decided by skill, intelligence, talent, or charm. Drake was a prince; Boetius, Feargus, and Ramona were from Noble families; and Reynard was a son of a blacksmith. Still, they were, all together, a gang of inseparable companions.

Nevertheless, at a young age, Reynard realized their childhood solidarity would not hold. He was well aware of the colored stripes on his friend's clothing: royal family colors, markings he didn't wear. As a commoner, companionship with Nobles and the prince had its drawbacks. His brothers teased him, and his mother warned him not to get too big for his britches.

As Reynard continued along the village street, passing familiar shops and cottages, a memory took hold. A winter day, he and his friends were following Drake down this street on their way to the Mill Pond.

The five of them, Drake, Ramona, Feargus, Boetius, and Reynard, had just emerged from Reynard's father's blacksmith shop. In Reynard's hand, pressed to his chest, he clinched the straps that crossed over his shoulder. Three new pairs of ice skates rhythmically bounced on his back. Feargus and Boetius, ahead of him, each carried a pair of skates as well.

Through the village, tromping in the slush, the troop threw snowballs at unsuspecting villagers, laughed, and ran. At the end of town, they turned onto Mill Road, chattering, shoving, and tumbling as they went. As they reached the last bend in the road before the Mill Pond, Drake lifted his arm that ordered halt.

"What's the matter?" Ramona asked.

Reynard, who was in the rear, didn't hear or see anything.

"Quiet!" Drake's voice was emphatic but hushed. He held out his arm in Ramona's direction.

About to reply to the affront, Ramona opened her mouth but hesitated. In the silence, they could hear the distant voices of children, distressed voices, shouting.

Without a word, Drake took off at a run. Everyone followed.

Drake and company rounded a corner, left the road, sprinted through a stand of trees, and arrived at the edge of the Mill Pond. On the bank of the pond, a gang of children stood shouting and pointing to the middle. Some fool had taken a dare and ventured out on the thin ice, where now only his head and flaying arms were visible above the black hole he had created.

"I'll get him." Boetius slid down the bank and started out on the ice.

In an instant, Drake was right behind him. Drake's hand caught the collar of Boetius' coat. Boetius' legs flew out in front as he went down on the ice, flat of his back.

From his prostrate position, Boetius looked up at Drake. "What the heck."

"Thin ice, dummy."

"We gotta do something," Boetius said.

"Yeah, you're the heaviest. Stay where you are."

Boetius started to get up.

"Lay down, I said." Drake spoke with enough force to pin him there.

"Feargus, you're next," Drake commanded, "Reynard then you."

They all grasped the plan now. Boetius flipped over, wiggled on his belly out as far as felt safe. Feargus, also on his belly, wiggled past, and Boetius grabbed his feet, then Reynard the same, then Drake, forming a human chain.

"Ramona, you're the lightest." Drake, head up, was looking back over his shoulder.

"I won't be able to reach," Ramona said.

"Pick out a skinny kid."

Ramona scanned the now quiet crowd standing on the pond bank. Some adults were also there now.

"You. Yeah, you." Ramona was pointing at a tall, thin lad, who looked like he would do. He hesitated, but then joined the chain.

Ramona, the last link, got the victim by the hands. Two men on the shore grabbed Boetius by the legs and pulled. The ice gave way, and Ramona's head went under. She kept her grip; the men pulled; the links in the chain held, and the almost drowned boy was out. The chain separated, and the links slithered like snakes across the ice until they all were on solid ground.

The memory had accompanied Reynard on his walk all the way to the tavern. Reynard had followed Drake that day, and he would follow him again.

The squeaking of the Black Horse tavern's sign drew Reynard's attention as it swayed in a gentle breeze. A magnet for children, the tavern enticed them like moths to a flame.

Under the sign, the main doors opened into the tavern hall, the center and common room, the heart of the tavern. There were three other ground-floor rooms, the Royal Hall on the north-side, the commoner's hall on the south-side, and the kitchen at the back. The kitchen was a favored destination, a portal into the tavern. Many days, a childhood romp led to the kitchen back door.

"What's you kids do'en hang'en round here?" the bulky cook asked, knowing the answer. He stood looming, showing as stern a face as he could.

The boys pushed Ramona forward toward the cook, who filled the doorway.

"We were wondering if, maybe, you know, you had some bread with jam, extra, maybe we could have?" Despite her wobbling words, Ramona stood straight and tall in front of the burly, towering man.

Continuing the weekly ritual, "Ain't got no extra bread, short on jam."

The children held their ground. He waited an appropriate amount of time and then stroking his chin said. "Ta think of it; I do have a batch a cookies; I dont's knows what to do with. Guess you could have em."

He stepped back as the children burst into the kitchen. The gang surveyed the counters, searching for the prize.

"Hold on, hold on. Not likes a pack a animals. Where's your manners?"

The children came to attention, shoulder to shoulder. "May we have some cookies, please?" Ramona asked.

The cook waited.

Ramona elbowed Drake. "Please?" he said.

Then the other boys in turn. "Please. Please. Please."

The cook pointed to the tabletop near the hearth.

In a flash, in a scramble, gathering cookies like they were gold, it was a moment of turmoil. With cookies in their hands, pockets, and mouths, the children headed for the doorway where the cook again loomed. "Manners?"

"Thank you. Thank you. Thank you. Thank you. Thank you." Then out the door, the mob went.

Other days, the kitchen became their secret eavesdropping spot. They huddled under the serving window and around the doorway that opened from the kitchen into the tavern hall. It was an ideal place from which to listen in on conversations and spy on the adult's meetings in the hall. The kitchen staff didn't seem to mind the children's intrusion and mostly enjoyed the subterfuge except on those occasions when they got rowdy, in which case, they got the boot.

On select evenings when troubadours or jesters provided entertainment, they tempted fate, staying as late as possible. The cook looked out for them, though, and sent them home on time.

But the best of times at the tavern hall were those spent listening to stories told by the Raconteur, a traveling Bard who visited Enid twice a month. Children were only allowed in the hall on those storytelling evenings, a day near the full moon, and then one day around the new moon. Storytelling didn't begin until nightfall. Bedtimes for children were suspended.

On those nights at sunset, a tension built in Drake's group that pulled them toward the storytelling. At a breaking point, unable to resist, someone took off running for the tavern. The race always ended with Boetius and Feargus arriving at the tavern door before the others, in most likely a tie, but with them standing on the flagstone walk under the sign (Black Horse Tavern) arguing over who got there first. In any case, they were always early.

After a few moments of focus on the dispute, the children, like a pack of dogs being released from a pen, bolted through the door, jostling each other as they passed into the tavern hall. With a sudden flash of attention from the adults, the group quieted respectfully and proceeded peacefully across the room to their customary place on the floor in front of the fireplace. In winter, the children slid near and away from the warmth of the crackling fire to adjust their comfort. In summer, the scent of cold ash in the hearth mixed with the aromas of food coming from the kitchen.

As he waited for the storytelling to begin, Reynard sat quietly, ignoring the other kids who were talking, wrestling, pushing, and being told to 'Be quiet' or 'Sit still.' It wasn't just the storytelling that made the tavern special in Reynard's mind; everything about this forbidden room was interesting. His attention was drawn to the trappings, the furnishings, and the design of the hall. Fascination guided Reynard's eyes around the room. His back to the fireplace and his comrades, this vantage point, and the wait allowed Reynard to survey his surroundings.

The fireplace, behind him, was located in mid-wall opposite from the main entrance. The kitchen door and serving window were on the same wall to the left of the fireplace. To the right, stairs led to the upper-level sleeping quarters. Also to the right, on the north wall midway down, was the passage door to the Royal Hall, the meeting room and dining hall for the Nobles. To the left and on the south wall was the passageway to the commoner's hall, a place for the commoners use. The space between that doorway and the kitchen was filled by the serving bar, a focal point of the children's attention. From it emanated the smell of stale beer and sour wine. Pewter mugs hung above, small wine barrels were stacked on the shelves, and beer kegs rested on the bar. Barmaids served drinks to locals, merchants, and travelers, who sat on tall stools that lined the length of the table. Men drinking their wine or beer spoke in slurred low voices that could, at any time, erupt in boisterous laughter or angry shouting.

In the early evening, the room was lit by the orange glow of sunset radiating from the windows, later to be replaced by flickering ambers of wall sconces and table candles. The light of the flames created shadows, dancing on the walls, adding a haunting character to any story.

During a storytelling, Nobles, commoners, and travelers alike congregated together in the tavern hall, regardless of rank or age. On other days they passed through the tavern hall and those defining doorways, either into the Royal Hall if they were Nobles or into the commoner's hall if they were commoners. Reynard knew that, despite their close friendship, someday he would follow his father's path to the commoner's hall. Boetius, Feargus, Drake, and Ramona would follow their parent's path into the Royal Hall.

Paths did cross in the tavern hall where some Nobles and some commoners met and lingered at the four long tables that occupied the center of the room. The men gathered in packs, driven by shared interest. They claimed their places at tables like churchgoers, claiming seats in their lifelong pews and engaged in unrestrained conversation. Although, the language, alluring to children, was not likely to be heard in church.

In contrast to the long, center tables, for those desiring intimacy, small round tables were located along the walls, offering opportunities for more discreet conversations.

One way or another, the tavern accommodated all, from all walks of life; travelers, merchants, peasants, farmers, tradesmen, soldiers, Knights, and Nobles. It sustained all the gossip, rumor and intrigue that, at any time, may be flourishing in the Kingdom of Enid.

But of all the characters that frequented the tavern, it was the traveling men that intrigued Reynard the most. They were men of mystery, from faraway places, who spoke with accents, and wore unfamiliar clothing. And in the imagination of a child, their whispered conversations, possibly, were meant to conceal their secret identities and secret missions.

Now, he was to become a traveler with a mission. Reynard would soon be leaving with the King for the war council, a harder reality than his youthful daydreaming. He had been selected to attend because of his talent, not rank, not his childhood friendship with King Drake. It was just good fortune, due to his talent for metalwork, to have risen in status to become the King's Weapons Master.

His other village friends had not been so lucky. As adults now, they lived in a world where rank and wealth determined prospects, not talent or skill.

However, it appeared that an equality was about to emerge, an equal opportunity to fight in a war.

Another Confrontation

eargus ducked his head as he passed through the doorway from the tavern hall into the Royal Hall. As he straightened up, he was confronted with a much larger gathering than usual. If it weren't for those damn dragons, he wouldn't have to be here, and not have to confront Boetius in public. Feargus hadn't been sleeping well or eating well, not since the dragon problem had arisen.

The hair on his arms bristled. He felt the urge to abandon his plan. He had discussed it with his uncle, who predicted failure. "Can't reason with a mob, especially Nobles, and certainly not Boetius. When are you going to learn, son? You just got to learn to accept things you can't change." But as uncomfortable and ill-fated as this confrontation portended to be, Feargus was committed to it.

Frozen in place, a step from the doorway, Feargus took in the room. It glowed in the orange of the setting sun that radiated from the distorting, flawed window glass. Recently lit oil wall lanterns and table candles provided a token of light and their disagreeable but familiar odors. The curtains on the private booths that lined both sides of the room were drawn back; every booth was occupied. The six banquet tables (two rows of three) in the center of the hall were full. In addition, men were standing throughout the room in packs, exchanging gossip with gaping mouths and nodding heads. Feargus saw no friendly faces.

He wished that Cenhelm was here tonight, his friend since childhood, two years his younger. He had shared his plan with Cenhelm, who was at his home estate (the House of Coner) in the North Woods on business, the family stone quarry. Feargus' family estate (the House of Hirsch) bordered that of Cenhelm's.

In childhood, they had spent many a long day filled with adventures, roaming the North Woods, swimming in the quarry pits, or taking riding lessons with Eachan, the Horse Clan leader. If Cenhelm were here tonight, he could be counted on to support Feargus. But just as well, it was too much to ask. It was best not to involve him. Despite the minimal hope of success, Feargus was compelled to try. At least he would be remembered as being on the right side of history.

Feargus hoped to influence Drake's decision concerning the dragons. He wanted to be the one to go with the King to the war council, an opportunity missed. Reynard was going, at least that was better than Boetius. He was sure Reynard shared his position that the dragons were not a threat, and a war was not necessary. Unfortunately, Reynard would not press the matter with Drake. As always, he would follow Drake, anywhere, into hell without a word for that matter.

A roar of laughter went up, startling Feargus. For a moment, he thought it was directed at him. But no one was looking his way; everyone was focused on the center banquet table. The chairs around the table were occupied by men that Feargus knew well: the King's Knights and Noblemen. Seated in the middle of the central, long table was Boetius, the actual orchestrator of the laughter.

Feargus walked up behind a cluster of men that were

standing across the table from Boetius.

"Excuse me," he said, but not loud enough to be heard over the chattering voices. Louder this time, "Excuse me." He placed his hand on the shoulder of the man who stood in front of him, one of Boetius' archers. He looked back over his shoulder to Feargus. Surprised, the man stepped aside, opening a pathway through the knot of men. Feargus wound through them until he was on the opposite side of the table from Boetius. One of the King's Knights, who was seated there, surrendered his chair to Feargus with a respectful nod.

The ensuing silence, encapsulating the table, allowed the screech of the chair legs to dominate as Feargus pulled himself up to the table edge. "Don't let me interrupt; go on."

"Sir Boetius just finished telling us one of his hunting tales," an archer captain, Sir Hartmann, seated next to Boetius, offered, "The one where an apprentice archer shot a farmer's goose by mistake and ..." Making eye contact with Feargus, his voice trailed off, and his wide grin faded.

"Telling any tales of dragon hunting?" Feargus asked. It was if a ray of sunlight had pierced the clouds and was illuminating the center of the table. Quiet spread through the entire room. Faces tensed with attention. Persons in the booths leaned out.

"Yes, we were talking of our success, tracking the beasts," Boetius seemed to be unaffected by the heat that Feargus was feeling, "My patrols with the hunting dogs are having no trouble finding their trails or feeding spots."

"We knows em like the backs of our hands," Boetius' hunter captain, Berengar, seated to Boetius' right said, "Knows their habits, their trails, their feed'en spots, everythin about em." He was leaning in toward Feargus over his crossed arms resting on the table. Despite Berengar being a commoner, Boetius had given him the title of Hunter Captain. Due to his talents, Berengar was the one responsible for organizing and leading the hunting troop. Besides running the hunts, he was responsible for rationing the game meat for the village, primarily supplying the needy. No one objected to his presence in the Royal Hall.

"You know everything except their intent and their true nature." The force of Feargus' voice sent Berengar to the back of his chair.

"Their nature, they have nothing to do with nature. Their nature is unholy," Boetius erupted.

"How can you possibly know their nature?" Feargus said.

"It's obvious. You've seen them yourself. They have the look of the devil."

"Their look? They're unholy? What would you know about holy or not? When did you get religion?"

"In the meadow that day with the King. We were face to face with a fire-breathing monster. It almost burnt us alive. Meant to do us in."

"The dragon didn't make a move until you antagonized it by bouncing an arrow off its chest."

Boetius looked confused for a moment. "That was my plan to show what the beasts are capable of. And the beast showed its true nature, its evil intent."

"Nonsense."

"Nonsense? You're the one who talks nonsense. You want to let these beasts have their way. Who knows what they will do next?" Boetius sat back in his chair and scanned the room.

"I believe the dragons are merely in search of food. There's no real evidence of anything else." Feargus forced a calm response.

"Yes, they are. They're taking game in our hunting grounds, OUR hunting grounds, OURS," Boetius was tapping his fingers on his chest, "taking our game, our food. They're a threat to our food supply. They're also taking cattle, sheep, and horses."

"I don't believe they're taking any of our livestock. Taking game yes, but they can't be taking that much; and besides, game is plentiful." Feargus looked away from Boetius to the faces around the room, hoping for acceptance. "And besides, there aren't that many dragons."

"You don't know how many there are, where they're from, or how many more are coming," Boetius said, "What did our good people do to deserve this invasion by those horrible creatures?" Boetius paused for effect, "Nothing I say, NOTHING!"

"Here, Here." A muffled chant spread through the crowd. Men struck the table with the flat of their hands, Noblemen and their ladies in the booths were nodding in agreement: the crowd was with Boetius. Time to change tack.

"Even if what you say is true, that they pose a threat, better to drive them away than an outright attack."

"If we attack and kill a few of them, that's the best way to drive them back to where they came from." The crowd murmured in accord with Boetius.

"Yesterday, one of my patrols encountered a group of dragons. My Knights approached them, encircled them at a safe distance. After a few minutes, the dragons flew off," Feargus said, "Harassment may be enough to force them out of the Kingdom. We could station small platoons around the hunting grounds near their feeding places, which you have so conveniently found. Then use harassing tactics to disrupt their feeding. Rid ourselves of the dragons without a war."

"How long will that take, if it even works? What's to say that when harassed, they won't fight back? A solitary patrol would be vulnerable. Attack with a full complement, it's the only way."

More affirming murmur from the crowd.

Feargus knew he was losing the argument. He considered it flawed himself, but he still felt it better to test the dragons than attack them. He waited for the room to quiet and pressed still another argument.

"So then, these evil beasts you describe with such terrible powers, of untold numbers and unknown origin, are the ones you want to war with? You sure war with them is the intelligent course of action?"

"How can you ask that? It's the only course, the only course for righteous men. We must defend the Kingdom." More cheers and hand thumping followed Boetius' words.

"But how will you wage this war? With what weapons? With what number of men? What strategy will defeat them?"

"I will put my all into the effort. I will spend as much time as it takes to find a way to kill them, to defeat the dragons. We have our weapons—swords, lances, and arrows," Boetius paused, "And we have overwhelming numbers."

"Our standing army does not present overwhelming numbers. At best, we can muster 40 men between your archers, the Knights, and my men-at-arms," Feargus said, "Against several dragons without effective weaponry, I doubt our victory."

"This is not just a fight for the Nobles. With an army of commoners, over 100 strong, led by the Knights, we will overwhelm them, destroy them, or drive them from the Kingdom."

"So you think you have the commoner's support? Or do you expect the King to order them into service?" Not waiting for an answer, Feargus continued, "I would prefer to enter battle with comrades rather than conscripts." Feargus knew that Ramona was of the same mind, to avoid an all-out war. He hoped that the commoners would be influenced by their affection for their Queen.

"I am sure they can be swayed to our cause. The commoners face the same evil threat from the dragons as we do." Boetius' voice grew louder to overcome the hum of voices.

"Swayed by rumors and lies," Feargus was near shouting.

"With the facts. With the truth about the beasts." Boetius stood, violently pushing himself from the table. His chair toppled to the floor with a thud that wasn't noticed. "I will stand against the threat. Who will stand with me?" Within a few moments, all the men in the room, except Feargus, were on their feet as well.

Someone at the far end of the table called out, "WAR!"

The chant was taken up by the entire room. "WAR, WAR, WAR"

Feargus pushed himself away from the table. As he walked calmly through the growling crowd, an invisible man, he looked into angry, jubilant faces. At the doorway, he heard Boetius' voice intertwined in a chorus of laughter. His jaw clenched. He didn't turn; he had seen and heard enough.

Feargus passed into the tavern hall. He snaked his way through the tables, not acknowledging the men who spoke to him, not making eye contact. Reaching the bar, he placed both hands on it and looked down at nothing. To the barmaid who stood directly in front of him, he said, "Meade, a bottle."

He glanced into a smiling face, "NOW!" Her smile disappeared, and she jumped away. Feargus' fingers curled into fists.

The maid returned and placed the bottle on the bar. He took up the bottle and turned to leave.

"Sir." The maid's voice faint.

He turned back to face her. "What?"

She did not speak, but the fear on her face brought Feargus out of his angry trance.

"Sorry," he said as he returned to the bar. He reached into his waist pouch and placed a coin on the bar top. Embarrassment overtook his anger.

He turned away and walked slowly across the room toward the exit. Upon reaching the main doors, he again became aware of the raucous voices coming from the Royal Hall and Boetius' annoying laugh. "Someday, someday," he muttered. And with a sudden tension that filled his core, he flung the door open, which swung back and struck him in the shoulder as he passed out of the tavern.

Queen at Tavern Hall

It had only been a few days since Ramona's brief encounter with the King on the keep's roof. She and Amalia were ready to leave the castle on her after-dinner walk. A daily custom, it was a convenient routine to conceal covert meetings, intrigues, and avenues of subterfuge, her business, of which she wanted the King kept unaware.

Drake tried to keep track of her and her activities, but even he did not have the audacity to have her followed, but watched he did. Could be jealousy, though she had never given him reason. More likely, he wanted to keep tabs on her activities, assuming correctly that her pursuits were not always in line with his goals. The couple hardly ever agreed on anything, being at cross purposes on most issues.

Ramona and Amalia strode out across the great-hall to the main doors where Dunstan, after a quick bow, pushed a door open for them. The women passed on through the castle's gatehouse and out under the portcullis, raised as usual. The sentry stationed there bowed, acknowledged by Ramona's nod. As they stepped into the coolness of the late evening air, the inner door clunked closed behind them. In front of them, only a dim lingering glow on the horizon brightened the otherwise dark southern sky.

The women walked down the hill on the cobblestone castle road. On the ground before them, a circle of light jumped forward and back, moving with the rhythm of the lantern swinging in Amalia's hand. When Ramona and Amalia reached the rampart gate at the bottom of the castle hill, two sentries sprung forward to put one of the massive wooden doors in motion, which groaned in resistance. Nodding her appreciation to the sentries, Ramona and Amalia passed through the gate, turned right onto the dirt road that led to the castle village and their destination, the Black Horse tavern.

The Queen's evening strolls were presented to King Drake as a matter of health and exercise. The night air was argued to be a primary contributor in maintaining the Queen's health and well-being, thwarting illness, and dark spirits. Like many other disagreements that focused on her activities, Ramona's persistence eventually overturned the King's objections to the practice.

"I hope to find out as much as I can about the 'dragon problem' this evening," Ramona said, "I will need your help."

"Yes, Ma'am." Amalia could be so formal and distant, despite Ramona's overtures of friendship.

"There are lots of stories out there concerning the dragons, none of them good. But I don't accept it. We need to uncover the truth."

Ramona had heard much of the dragon gossip that raged through the Kingdom. Everything that went wrong in the Kingdom was being blamed on dragons. A horse disappeared, a sheep was taken—a dragon was responsible—those thieving dragons. What will they take next? Are our children safe?

Were any of these stories true? Ramona needed to know.

"What can I do to help?" Amalia asked.

As they walked along the dirt road, the only light they had was Amalia's lantern and the brightness of the cloudless new moon sky. This route, traveled since Ramona was a child, was so familiar that the lantern light wasn't necessary.

"Encourage your friends and contacts to share what they know of the dragons. Try to discern if there's any truth in what they say. Ask for corroboration—discreetly. Report what you learn." The best place to monitor gossip was the village tavern.

"I'm afraid the King is being influenced by gossip and doesn't know the truth of the matter."

Ramona was keenly aware of Drake's concern for his people and the effect the 'Dragon Problem' was having on the Kingdom. She determined to help him, provide the help he never wanted, at least not openly.

Most people considered dragons to be mythical creatures of legends; their existence kept alive in the storytelling of the Raconteur. A few of those stories, Ramona remembered, featured dragons that frequented the Kingdom in the distant past. The Raconteur's tales were full of all kinds of magic, fanciful ideas, and strange beings to be dismissed as fantasy. But now, stories were circulating about real, live dragons. Some of them, at least, were likely true.

"He may act without careful consideration, without really knowing if the dragons are a threat."

"It sounds like you're convinced that the dragons mean no harm," Amalia said, "Despite all the stories?"

"Just intuition, the stories don't ring true."

It wasn't long before Ramona and Amalia were in the village, standing at the tavern door.

Ramona knew Drake relied on a few trusted advisers, Boetius and Feargus, along with Reynard. Assuming she could influence Feargus and Reynard, they, in turn, would influence the King. She knew them all since childhood.

"When we get inside, see Reynard first and find out what he knows," Ramona said, "I will meet with Feargus." Reynard and Feargus were reliable sources.

"Yes, Ma'am."

Ramona pulled up her hood, putting her face in shadow, hiding her uncommon hair braid. Her mother called it the archer's braid because Ramona wanted it that way for archery practice. It kept her long hair out of the way as she rampaged around the Kingdom. It was a temptation for the boys, though, who couldn't help grasping it from time to time.

Still, her custom as an adult, the long braid made Ramona recognizable from a distance, distinguishing her from the other ladies of the court, who wore their hair long, loose, with colored ribbons. Also a disparity, Ramona wore trousers, shirts, and tunics, much like a man's, although Amalia did her best to tailor them for a women's form. In contrast, the Noblewomen wore dresses of imported linen, dyed in various shades of tan, brown, green, and blue, trimmed with family colors. As for the peasant women, they had to content themselves with homespun fabric, only in dark green or brown, to make their skirts and blouses. All in all, Ramona did not conform to any of the Kingdom's norms of dress or convention, a distinction that created yet another issue of contention between Queen and King.

Tonight, Ramona was wearing an ankle-length oiled raincoat. There was no rain, but it had no family markings.

Ramona peered at Amalia through her hood's vertical slit and smiled. They both knew the disguise to be a charade, as did most everyone else in the Kingdom. It was, of course, not proper for any respectable Noblewoman, let alone the Queen, to be seen in the tavern unaccompanied by a man. The Queen's secret visits to the tavern hall were a widespread conspiracy, with King Drake one of the few left unaware. The commoners loved their Queen and kept her secrets, and the Nobles feared to cross her and kept her secrets.

After passing through the main door into the tavern hall, Ramona stepped to her right, taking up her habitual place at a small table in the corner near the door. Murmurs stirred the room for a few moments; side glances came the Queen's way.

Amalia headed off for the doorway to the commoner's hall, the annex on the north side of the tavern. The spring in Amalia's stride betrayed her enthusiasm to meet with Reynard. Ramona, through Amalia, had gotten word to Reynard days ago that she wanted him to seek out what honest information he could about the dragons.

Ramona sat facing out into the room, her hood still up. She took note of several women, commoners, scattered in amongst the groups of men. These common women, mugs in their hands, laughing, appeared to have more freedom of movement than the Queen of the Kingdom.

A barmaid hurried across the room with a pewter goblet in her hand. After she placed it on Ramona's table, she started to curtsy but stiffened instead.

"Sir Feargus, please." Ramona nodded in the direction of the Royal Hall.

The barmaid retreated without saying a word. She made her way across the room and passed through the doorway that led into the Royal Hall, the annex on the south side of the tavern.

It wasn't long before Feargus appeared, his tall figure ducking through the doorway.

With a fluid gait, he wove his way through the center tables, toward Ramona. Men that tall were generally awkward, but Feargus' moved with ease and grace, also true on horseback. A quiet man, he had his appeal; many women thought so.

Feargus took a seat next to her, his back to the wall, facing out into the room.

"Good evening, Ma'am. A pleasant evening and a pleasant stroll?" Feargus looked straight ahead.

"Yes, a pleasant evening. But not pleasant times. Not with all the talk of dragons."

"True. They are the focus of attention. An annoyance, at least."

"Do you have any idea why the dragons have suddenly

appeared in the Kingdom?"

"No one knows. Most thought them to be the stuff of legends. But they have truly arrived. And we don't know from where. Although, I have a theory."

"Go on."

"It may have to do with the severe winter, the bitter cold. I have heard stories from the northern kingdoms that their winter was even worse than ours. There were times the temperature dropped so low and so fast that cattle and goats died were they stood."

Feargus had ties, family and friends, in the Kingdom of Braga, the kingdom directly north of Enid. In fact, his sister was married to a Noble merchant who controlled the import/export trade in Braga's seaport town, Braganca. All the gossip available from Braga and the other northern Kingdom of Duren found its way to Feargus.

"Really, how terrible," Ramona said.

"Yes. And if the dragons were from the northern wilds out beyond Duren, which I expect to be the case, they could be suffering from a food shortage. The animals they normally feed on may also have died off because of the bad weather."

"Sounds plausible," Ramona said, "That could explain why there have been sightings in our hunting grounds."

The barmaid, the same one who served Ramona, approached the table. Feargus, raising his hand, signaled he had no need of a drink.

"The dragon sightings in the hunting grounds are reliable. The warden and members of the hunting troop have seen them on several occasions."

"What of the other rumors?" Ramona asked, "The stories of dragon mischief?"

"I have no firsthand accounts. Only gossip."

"The northern Sheep Clan has been complaining that they are missing sheep. They blame the southern clan, and the southern clan blames the dragons." Ramona rubbed her clasped hands together to generate warmth.

"If the northern clan is missing sheep, it's probably the southern clan that's responsible. Those clans have been stealing each other's sheep for years, a feud that goes back for generations."

"But, they claim more than usual."

"I spoke with my squire. He has a friend in the northern clan," Feargus said, "There's no evidence of kills by dragons. They didn't find any carcasses."

"What of the stories of disappearing horses? Dragons responsible?"

"Probably the same story, an opportunity for horse thieves to pin the blame on someone else, divert suspicion." Feargus leaned back, crossed his arms, and stretched out his long legs.

"And the other stories; the farmer's wheat field that burned, or the merchant from Morodon who claims he and his men were attacked on the Braga Road and they fought off a dragon. What do you think? They sound like nonsense to me."

"I would agree. People like nothing more than to hear themselves talk. They enjoy the attention an intriguing story brings," Feargus said.

"Amalia reports that the farmer's field was an accidental fire."

"Most likely. And those merchants may have seen a dragon, but a fight unlikely, a tall tale. I've seen a dragon. No merchant band fought one of them off."

"I suppose gossip is inevitable. It has its use, but these dragon stories are out of hand and spreading like wildfire." Ramona's attention was on the table candle, its flame flickering near extinction every time the tavern door opened.

"I wouldn't be surprised if Boetius weren't the source of it, or at least encouraging it," Feargus said.

Boetius had his faults, boasting and exaggeration for sure, but straight out lying didn't seem likely. He was too single-minded to be dishonest, made him easily manipulated, but not a liar.

While Ramona and Feargus sat in discussion, Boetius entered the tavern hall through the main entrance door. He paused for a moment, turning his head in their direction. Boetius and Feargus acknowledged each other with a nod.

Boetius was dressed in hunters' green, his long black hair pulled back into his customary short ponytail. His natural good looks and charm always held sway; he at once dominated the room.

Boetius continued across the hall, followed closely by his hunting dog, Riley. As he approached the long table in the center of the room, a clamor went up from the group of men seated around it. Boetius took a seat at the head of the table; the dog laid down next to his chair. Roars of laughter punctuated the rumble of conversation. Serving-maids hustled around the table with pewter mugs as other men closed in, surrounding the table.

"Why would he encourage such stories?" Ramona asked.

"He sees the dragons as disgusting creatures, hideous and evil. He advocates for their destruction because they threaten our food supply."

"Does he think that because of a few missing sheep and because the dragons are taking game from the hunting grounds?" Ramona was looking to Boetius' table. "Does he really believe that the dragons could cause a food shortage?"

"The meat supplied by the hunting troop is not a mainstay of our diet at present. During an actual famine, yes, it has in the past, but not now. I don't understand how he could speak with such conviction about something that isn't true." Agitation flashed in Feargus' eyes.

The Kingdom was self-sufficient regarding food. The eastern farmers produced all the grain, fruits, and vegetables needed plus a surplus to export. Cattle and sheep were plentiful as well. Only luxury or exotic foodstuffs and medicines were imported.

"People believe what they want to believe and look for support of what they believe. That's just the way it is."

"Maybe so, but he has the King's ear, and we don't want Drake falling for the same line of rubbish."

"Does anyone speak against the rumors?" Ramona asked.

"Besides myself, no one. I'm sure that some Knights and even a few members of the Noble Council support my view, but they are not taking sides publicly. They are waiting to see what the King decides."

"I don't understand why Boetius is so afraid of the dragons, but it must be so." A sigh escaped Ramona's lips. "Thank you for the information. Something must be done to counteract these lies and rumors. I can't let them influence Drake. I feel that I should talk with Boetius."

"Good luck with him. It's a waste of your time, but if you must. I, myself, am tired of arguing with him." Feargus rose to his feet. "Ma'am."

"You have patrols going out?"

"Yes."

"Keep me informed."

"I will." A nod, and he left the tavern hall.

It wasn't long after Feargus left when Amalia returned to the Queen's table, bringing Reynard with her. "I thought you should hear for yourself what Reynard has to say."

"Ma'am," Reynard said, taking the seat Feargus had vacated. Amalia sat across from Ramona.

"Go on, Reynard."

"I have talked with several people who have actually had encounters with dragons."

"Have you talked with Boetius' men?"

"Yes, they tell their leader what he wants to hear and what he wants told, but I got the stories without exaggeration from an honest man," Reynard gestured with a nod of his head to the center table.

"Go on," Ramona encouraged.

"The stories they tell about destruction or ill deeds caused by dragons are events linked by circumstance, not actual evidence or witnessed," Reynard said.

"Are there any stories you find credible?"

"Yes. The wife of the warden at the hunting grounds, she has a story to tell. She was in the yard behind her cottage with her oldest child, a toddler. She ducked into the cottage for a moment to check on her baby, who had started to cry. She was only gone for a minute. When she came out, she saw that the boy had wandered out into the field, 40 paces or so from the house. To her horror, a dragon was hovering over the child. She screamed and ran forward, but tripped and fell. When she looked up, thinking the worst, she saw the dragon had become distracted by movement at the edge of the woods. When it flew off in that direction, she took advantage, raced to her child, and returned him safely to the cottage."

"A frightening account, but no harm done. What else?"

"Two shepherds, Ald and his grandson were tending their sheep in the pastures in the northern foothills. They were herding them onto the road when a dragon landed right in front of them. Ald said its eyes were glowing. He wouldn't admit to it, but I think the old man was paralyzed with fear. But the boy had the presence of mind to use his signal horn to call for help, three long blasts. It scared the dragon off."

"Odd that a mere horn blast would scare off such an intimidating beast."

"I thought so too."

"What about the commoners? Do they believe the rumored stories? Do they follow Boetius?

"Mostly yes," Reynard replied, "They are desperately afraid of the dragons. They see them as a threat."

"There must be some people that aren't convinced of the threat?" Ramona asked.

"Yes, but they keep quiet. If they express their doubts about the dragon rumors, people attack them. They're made fun of, shunned, put down as stupid, and their loyalty to the Kingdom is questioned. Only Feargus continues to speak out against Boetius, but that's his nature, to argue with Boetius."

"Thank you, Reynard," Ramona said.

"I'll take my leave, Ma'am," Reynard stood, bowed to Ramona, gave Amalia a glance and quick smile. He left the tavern hall, returning to the commoner's hall.

"I want to present what I've learned to the King when we go out for our evening ride in two days' time," Ramona said, "I will need time to think this over. We should go."

Amalia looked down at the floor.

Noticing, Ramona added, "This time, I have to make him listen."

Heads turned as Ramona and Amalia left the tavern hall.

Outside the door, Ramona scanned the area. "We won't meet here again. It's too public. I must find a better place, a secret place.

King vs. Queen

"What more can I say to convince you?" Ramona was clearly agitated. Drake was familiar with the tone.

"I don't know how ANYONE could say more," Drake rose in his saddle and thought to ride away from her, but thought better of it.

Better to let her talk herself out. He hated to think of all the time he had spent listening to Ramona's opinions and recommendations. It was on afternoons like this, during their long rides in the countryside, that Ramona took the opportunity to express herself.

Even these days, he still enjoyed their rides, the cool evening air, the beauty of the Kingdom's landscape. It was pleasant, riding along, nodding, not always listening.

When had things changed? Ten years of marriage, ten years of religiously following this practice, when had it lost its passion?

In his memory, it had been his idea, on their wedding day, to go out for that first evening's ride. It was a hot summer day with a ripple of clouds on the horizon, promising a sunset worthy of the royal wedding. Coincidentally, a full moon was expected, an event that portended a royal tradition. As they rode, side by side, along the East Road, the moon, a pale ghost in the still blue sky, escaped to freedom from the hills in front of them. Behind, the sky was a theater of clouds, lit orange and red. Satisfied with the moon's performance, they headed back home, riding west into the sunset, wrapped quiet, although there should have been applause. The castle atop its hill held steady in silhouette in the still bright sky. Finally, as they rode up the castle road, the darkness brought down the curtain on the day and invited them into the night.

From that day forward, a monthly ride on a full moon evening became an unbreakable romantic tradition. They made a game of trying to pick the best day around the date of the full moon, a clear night to see the moon, the best weather. In the summer, it was a late evening ride, past the heat of the day. In the winter, it was a late afternoon, still holding remnants of the sun's warmth.

They had missed a few rides this winter, too cold. They cut a few outings short as well. Even their sheepskin vests and bearskin robes, which normally provided comfort, couldn't repel the icy cold. Day in and day out, the Kingdom suffered in constant frigid temperatures of a long winter. Ramona and Drake, losing their sensual ritual, suffered disagreeable moods.

Drake welcomed the relative pleasantness of this early spring day. It was a relief when they could resume their customary rides, gratifying outings. Despite the topic or matter of conversation, there was always the night to look forward to.

"Clearly, you haven't been listening."

"Of course I'm listening," Drake said, "I just don't agree with you."

Ramona had been quiet for the first half of this late afternoon ride. They had ridden halfway to Morodon before turning back. On the return trip, she began making her opinion known; that the dragon stories were gossip and exaggerations.

He listened, somewhat, with one ear. She didn't say how she knew or where she got her information. Her information may just as well be gossip.

"I wish I could believe that you're listening and will at least consider my point of view."

"Of course, I will." Granted, Drake was inattentive, but he had reason; the landscape troubled him.

His horse, in her nervous tremors, was affected as well. He could claim it as a distraction, a reason for neglecting her conversation, but he wasn't about to reveal his unfounded anxiety to Ramona. She didn't seem to be affected by the ill-ease, and he wondered why.

It was Ramona who selected the Morodon Road for their travels that day. Drake always allowed her to choose the route, a concession he felt contributed to an agreeable mood. Riding along the Morodon Road at dusk, with darkness closing in, had always made him edgy. He avoided it, scheduling his trips on this route for daylight hours. Foolishness from childhood memories had control of him, and he resented it. Those stories of the Dark Forest, probably the source, or maybe there was a real malevolent spirit that was plaguing him.

Now riding east toward home, on their right, the river's edge was their constant companion. The Morodon River flowed innocently in the opposite direction toward the Maran Sea. Just across the river, always present, the Dark Forest loomed. In some stretches, it crept up to the edge of the river's far bank.

On the opposite side of the road, to the north, a ridge of hills (the South Ridge), rose abruptly. The hillside, in effect a wall, provided a sense of entrapment, nowhere to go, no escape from whatever might release itself from the forest.

Drake's bothersome childish fears took their comfort from the river, wide and deep, between him and the forest, between him and whatever evil resided there.

Thankfully, they were nearing the castle village, the ride

almost over.

As they reached the edge of the village, the light was abandoning the sky. Drake was relieved that the Morodon Road and Dark Forest were behind them.

As the royal couple rode past, villagers stopped what they were doing and bowed. Ramona nodded in return. Drake speculated on what they might be thinking, their concerns, what they expected of him.

Through the village and along the road toward the rampart gate, the couple was quiet. At the end of the ride and the end of the conversation, Drake hoped.

It was best to listen to Ramona, to at least know her positions, even if he didn't accept them. She was highly respected in the Kingdom, mostly by the commoners. And sometimes in her ramblings, a point was well-made, something of value, but not this evening.

When they reached the rampart gate, Ramona pulled her horse to a halt; Drake also did in response. She pivoted in her saddle and again launched into her arguments.

"There's no valid reason to start a war with the dragons," said the Queen, "From what he has learned from his patrols, Feargus tells me he believes there are probably only 20 to 25 dragons in the Kingdom. He thinks the small groups his men have come across are families with three to five members. And each time they made contact, the dragons fled."

Feargus. Drake did not approve of him sharing information with Ramona. He didn't appreciate the thought of them together at all, not even when they were children. It seemed as if everyone had a crush on Ramona then, Boetius too, maybe even Reynard. Probably still do. Perhaps that's why none of them are married. Reynard has Amalia, though. Too bad she's the Queen's maid and can't marry. She would never leave Ramona, not even for Reynard. He wished Ramona was more like Amalia, dutiful, less bold.

"Boetius tells a different story. He assures me what the

people have been reporting is true, and the threat is real. If something is not done, our hunting grounds could be depleted by the dragons in a very short time." Drake pulled back on the reins of his horse. The animal was eager to get back to the barn. "Boetius is the best hunter we have, probably the best ever. He knows the hunting ground and its carrying capacity. And need I remind you how popular he is with the people?"

"Yes, I know. He's extremely popular, very generous, sharing his game's meat and pelts with those in need."

"That's right; the people sing his praises. His hunting feats are legend in the tavern hall."

"No one sings his praises more than he does himself," Ramona said.

"You never liked Boetius. Not since we were children," Drake said.

Ramona's father had been too lenient with her, allowing her to roam the Kingdom with the boys. She should have been at home learning woman's work, in a woman's place, not challenging boys to archery contests and horse races. It wasn't until their late teens that Feargus bested her in horse racing, and Boetius became the better archer. If she only would accept her place, Queen of the Kingdom, and fulfill her duties as his wife. The memories of childhood stirred a disappointment; he should have children of his own running throughout the Kingdom by now.

"It's not that I didn't like him; we got along fine. I just get tired of his bragging. He has been a good friend over the years-for both of us."

"He has, and he deserves respect," Drake said. They were riding up the castle road now, their ride near its end.

He pushed his horse into a trot and held it the short ride up the castle hill until he reached the gatehouse. He dismounted. Ramona was still in saddle.

"That doesn't make him right about the dragons. That doesn't mean you have to start a war," Ramona said, raising her voice in an apparent attempt to regain his attention.

Drake dismounted so quickly his groom fumbled, trying to take control of the reins. Drake marched through the castle gatehouse. The Queen was right behind him. He felt her presence as he passed through the main castle door into the great-hall.

"You need to consider his prejudices. He fears anything unfamiliar, anything different." Ramona was talking to Drake's back as he strode through the great-hall, attempting to dislodge her.

Drake, reaching the front of the hall, stopped abruptly and pivoted to face Ramona, who stopped up short to avoid colliding with him. They stood nose to nose. "Nonsense. Boetius fears nothing. We have fought side by side. I trust him and his sources."

"My sources have a completely different view of the dragons and their intent."

Looking over Ramona's shoulder off to his left, Drake noticed Amalia sitting at the servant's table under the stairs. She was likely one of Ramona's sources. She was busy with some needlework, one of those things Ramona should have learned as a child. Ramona shared too much with Amalia, a maid and commoner, treated her more like an equal than a servant. He could challenge her on that, but he remembered a saying of his father's, 'Pick your battles.' He had enough conflict with Ramona to deal with at the moment.

"I am not interested in what your sources have to say. I need to do something," Drake shouted. "I have a duty to my subjects. They're terrified of the dragons."

"But, their fears are unfounded."

"The threat the dragons pose to the Kingdom is real."

"There's no real evidence, only gossip."

The servants in attendance shifted nervously.

"The Kings of Braga and Duren have already taken action, engaged the dragons in combat."

"Without success, I understand."

"I'm not going to the war council without something to contribute."

"You don't need to take some rash action to impress the other Kings."

"I cannot do NOTHING." Drake leaned close to Ramona's face. Suddenly overcome with the idea that he was being observed and not acting in a dignified manner, Drake pivoted and collided with one of the tall back chairs. He reached for the chair as it fell, but missed.

A boom echoed into the silence of the cavernous room. The guard at the entrance door jumped to attention, and the serving maid standing by the kitchen door dropped a metal serving bowl, adding a clatter to the echoing.

With long strides, Drake headed back for the main door. As he approached the door, he turned back toward the Queen. "I will issue a proclamation of war tomorrow. I will authorize Boetius and Feargus to prepare for battle. We will attack the dragons before they attack us."

Drake, who was looking back at Ramona, collided with the guard, who had flattened himself against the wall. The King, nose to nose with the guard, glaring at him, turned, stepped away, and opened the great-hall's door himself.

It should have been a pleasurable ride, followed by a pleasurable evening if only Ramona had allowed it. Walking away from her would have its cost, but he was committed now, no looking back, no turning back.

Drake felt a need to hesitate as he stepped through the doorway, but overcame it, reached back and grasped the door handle. He caught a glimpse of Ramona, at the far side of the great-hall, looking to him. And making his point, he slammed the door behind him, leaving Queen Ramona standing in still another booming echo.

War Preparations

The church tower clock rang out nine peals, faintly heard in the castle's great-hall. Feargus crossed his arms and rocked his chair back for a moment.

Boetius was looking back over his shoulder to the great-hall's main door. "Where is he? Always late. We should send someone after him."

"He'll be along," Feargus said. Reynard will show; he wouldn't disappoint the King.

"He installed that blasted clock," Boetius said, "I know he can hear it in the village."

The King had purchased a striking clock last summer, and Reynard had installed it. A tower was built alongside the church, and a sluice trough constructed to channel water from the Calder River. A water wheel was installed, and a mechanism designed to connect the striking clock to the water that powered it. Ironic and humorous, a joke pervasive in the Kingdom, Reynard, the man always late, was the man to install the clock. Before it was put in place to announce the hours, Reynard used to blame his tardiness on cloudy days and sundials. The ancient timepieces were located throughout the

Kingdom, the stables, castle gate, church, and village corners, installed by an earlier king with a penchant for punctuality. In the presence of a sunny day, the same as he was a master of inventions, Reynard was the master of manufacturing excuses. The truth be told, when involved with a project, he lost all track of time, and he was always involved with something, tinkering with this or that.

"It's not right he holds us waiting," Boetius said, "We have important matters at hand. We need to finalize our war plan, get our men into the field against the dragons."

It was only yesterday the King had given the order to develop a plan to deal with the dragons. He demanded the beasts out of his Kingdom and tranquility restored. All of his army leaders were assembled with the burden to comply. Besides Feargus and Boetius, the others present were Hartmann (the archer captain), Cenhelm (the Men-at-Arms captain), and Berengar (the hunting troop leader). They fidgeted in their chairs, like men planning their escape.

"I've seen no plan, no plan with a chance of success, at least." Seated at the center table across from Boetius, Feargus considered reopening his argument. It would undoubtedly be better to drive the dragons out of the Kingdom than engage them head-on in combat. He knew, though, that the dragons couldn't merely be driven away. It was true they retreated when harassed, but the dragons had no reason to fear the King's men. But Boetius' call for a frontal attack on the dragons, Feargus foresaw as disastrous.

Boetius spoke as if addressing a child. "The plan, as I see it, and explained before, is this! We will set up a base camp in the west hunting grounds, in the fields just west of the warden's cabin, where we will station the 1st regiment, its two platoons of archers and two platoons of men-at-arms, a full cadre of Knights and the hunting troop. From there, the hunters and their tracking dogs will go out on patrols. When they find a group of dragons, they will signal with a trumpet, and then march our men to the area and attack."

"So, you've confirmed that the dragons are deaf and won't react to a trumpet-call?" Feargus leaned in toward Boetius. Boetius and his foolhardy ideas were like a plague, Feargus' entire life, testing his patience and his temper. Always attack, move forward, no thinking, no actual plan. Study and preparation were vital. Find a method, develop a strategy, organize for it, and train for it; that's what leads to success. Feargus hoped Drake appreciated his approach. He was sure that is why Drake selected him to lead the army over Boetius. But sometimes Drake suffered from the same rash impulses as Boetius; he might take Boetius' side.

"If not a trumpet, then, each patrol will have a horseman that will report back to camp. One of your fastest men."

The creaking of the main door caught the group's attention. Reynard passed through the door into the room.

"Sorry I'm late. What did I miss?" Reynard took the seat at the head of the table.

"Just the beginnings of another argument," Cenhelm said.

Feargus and Boetius both turned a scowl on him. Not to be intimidated, he returned a smug grin. Cenhelm was a bold Knight, fearless on horseback, a leader, second in skills only to Feargus.

"Fill me in," Reynard said.

"The plan." Feargus motioned with upturned hands for Boetius to proceed. Why not hear it one more time, for Reynard's sake. He hoped Reynard would see the flaws in Boetius' plan, if you could call it that, no real strategy, no foresight, no damn sense of caution.

Boetius reiterated his strategy with a respectful tone, now addressing Reynard.

Boetius finished; Reynard said nothing.

Feargus glanced at Reynard. "He has nothing more. Find the dragons and attack them with a full compliment."

Feargus glanced at the paper that lay before him on the

table, the army census. The army comprised two regiments, the first regiment of the standing army divided into two companies, one of men-at-arms, led by Cenhelm and one of archers led by Hartmann. Each company was divided into two platoons, each platoon with an attachment of Knights. The second regiment was all call-ups with a similar structure. Feargus had command of the overall army, the Knights and soldiers directly. Boetius commanded the archers.

"I don't understand why you're so reluctant to attack the dragons. You show more concern for them, the enemy, than the Kingdom," Boetius was addressing Feargus, "Something has to be done about the beasts."

Feargus' hands braced against the tabletop. His arms straightened as he rose from his chair, his voice rising as well. Leaning across the table, he was face to face with Boetius. "I'm not saying to do nothing. I want them gone just as much as anyone, but some other way than war. A way without bloodshed, ours or theirs. It will be mostly ours if we engage them in a fight."

"What is that, this other way?" Boetius was smug as usual.

"I don't know as yet!" Feargus collapsed back to his seat, arms across his chest.

After a few moments of silence, Boetius continued, "So then, we should prepare for our engagement with the dragons." Turning to Cenhelm, "I expect you to have a full company ready for battle in a few days."

"Only the regulars are ready for immediate combat," Cenhelm asserted, "The call-ups will need time to train and prepare."

In Cenhelm's men-at-arms company, each platoon, of which there were two, was made up of 24 men, ten regular full-time soldiers, and 14 were call-ups who came from the ranks of laborers, tradesmen, and farmers.

"We conducted our monthly training yesterday," Boetius said, "I don't see the need for more training."

"Our normal training exercises, not training to fight dragons," Feargus said.

"What equipment will they carry, swords, lances, and shields, chest armor?" Cenhelm asked, "What weaponry suits a dragon war?"

"A full complement, of course," Boetius said.

"Once we decide on the tactics needed to fight dragons, the men-at-arms will need at least several weeks of training, maybe a month." The longer Feargus could delay this venture, the longer he had to find a nonmilitary solution. He had an ally in Ramona; he knew she was casting for an alternative to outright war.

"I don't see it that way," Boetius said.

"Hartmann, how long will it take you to form up the 1st archer company and have them ready to fight dragons?" Feargus was putting the archer captain on the spot. Hartmann reported to Boetius.

After a hesitation, a look, checking with Boetius, Hartmann replied, "I could have a full complement ready by the end of the week, Sir."

Boetius smiled broadly.

"Ready to fight Dragons?" Feargus asked.

Hartmann did not respond.

"Assembling the 1st regiment will take time, time to train, training to fight dragons, training we haven't yet determined or designed," Feargus said.

"We have assembled quickly before, in emergencies," Boetius said.

"This isn't an emergency."

"To hell, it isn't," Boetius responded.

"Why not bring up the second regiment as well?" Feargus intended sarcasm; it always agitated Boetius.

The second regiment, structured the same as the first, with lancers, Knights, and archers organized into two platoons, was composed of old men and young boys, along with a few women who disguised themselves.

It was quiet for a moment; Boetius did not rise to the bait.

"I say we need to prepare before we engage the dragons." Feargus continued.

"Preparation, planning, it's procrastination," Boetius said, "Who knows what ill fate awaits us if we delay. We don't need training in a new way to fight. We fight as we always have. The Knights will circle the dragons, harass them with their lances. You said yourself that the horses are getting more accustomed to the dragons."

"Only for the men who have been out on patrols. Only at a distance, no one has gotten close enough to use a lance."

"They will be enough to start," Boetius said, "And the men-at-arms can carry lances as well and form up an encirclement formation. My archers will take up positions on high ground and shower the creatures with a deadly volley."

"And what of the dragons' fire?" Cenhelm asked.

"Carry shields," Boetius replied.

"Long lances and shields?" Cenhelm said, "I have my doubts."

"There's never more than a few dragons," Boetius continued, "An archer company, a lancer company against a small group of dragons. The Knights and the lancers confront the enemy, contain them, and keep them occupied and distracted. Then my archers will have their way with the beasts." Boetius glanced to Feargus and then to Reynard. "It's how we fight. How we always have and won."

"You forget that the one time you released an arrow," Feargus said, "It bounced off the dragon. That day none of our arrows penetrated the dragons hide."

Feargus waited a moment for a response and then continued.

"I have reports from the northern kingdoms. Both Braga and Duren engaged with the dragons. They say the dragons hides are impenetrable, neither arrows nor lances are effective. The Knights from Braga even struck a dragon with a spear from a small frame catapult. It shattered."

The kingdoms of Braga and Duren had also been invaded by dragons, by what seemed to be a lesser number, on account of fewer reported sightings. Feargus' sister kept him informed of the dragon's activities in the northern kingdoms. The northerner's encounters, of which there had been only three, were brief and fruitless, with only a few minor injuries.

"Neither Braga nor Duren have our numbers. Nor do their men match the character and bravery of our troops," Boetius said.

"I don't see how our numbers will do us any good," Feargus said, "To what advantage?"

"We won't know for sure what's possible until we try. Something must be done," Boetius said, "We are under King Drake's orders."

"Orders to develop a plan for success."

"I say we move immediately with the first regiment." Boetius scanned the faces around the table for affirmation.

"I recommend a month of training, our regulars, no conscripts," Feargus replied.

"I agree with Feargus," Cenhelm said.

"Berengar, you have a voice," Boetius said, "What do you say?"

The hunter leader did not respond. He looked aghast. Berengar most likely did not want to become entangled, not take a side. For a commoner, taking a side could be a grave error, the right side or not.

"Hold," Reynard said, "King Drake expects a consensus. Unless one of you wants to tell him, we are deadlocked."

No one responded.

"What about tactics, strategy, weaponry?" Reynard continued with the apparent intent to redirect the heated conversation to the practicalities.

"That's why it's necessary to train for a new strategy," Feargus gave Reynard a grateful nod.

"A strategy we don't have?" Cenhelm said, "My troops are prepared to fight MEN, not dragons."

"I find some merit in what Boetius proposes," Reynard said, "There may be value in engaging the dragons straight away. We need to test our enemy, explore, look for weaknesses. The knowledge we gain may afford a strategy, and I may be able to develop an effective weapon once we know more about the dragons."

"Yes, Reynard, exactly my point. Who else is with me?" Boetius asked as he scanned the faces of the men around the table.

"I said explore, not a full-fledged attack. There we differ," Reynard asserted, "I too have been communicating with friends in the northern kingdoms, and they also report they have no effective strategy or weapon."

"An exploratory force then, not the full regiment. What are your thoughts, Reynard?" Feargus hoped to find an ally. Reynard was practical, cautious.

"A small exploratory force. Lancers, Knights, and archers, regulars only. Station our men near the warden cabin and then send the hunting troop out in search of dragons. When we find the dragons and engage, we will test them with varied attacks. The archers with volleys of arrows, the men-at-arms to prod them with lances, and the Knights on horseback with lances." Reynard spoke without confidence or enthusiasm, but with resignation.

"One platoon from 1st company, 12 archers, 15 Knights, ten lancers." Feargus ran his finger across his census.

"And the hunt'en troop?" Berengar asked.

"Yes, of course," Feargus replied.

"Not enough," Boetius asserted, "We can't fight the dragons with such limited numbers. I insist on at least a full company."

"There's no need to engage them fully, just test them to determine the level of threat," Feargus said.

"Probe for a weakness," Cenhelm nodded to Reynard.

"I won't risk my men in such a weak force. It's not much larger than a patrol." Boetius was leaning back with his hands at his hips.

"Both platoons from the first company then." Reynard checked with Feargus, offering a compromise. "24 archers, 20 lancers, and 30 Knights, all regulars."

The other men were quiet, waiting for either Boetius or Feargus to erupt.

Cenhelm intervened in the silence. "I don't see how we can stalk dragons with such a large force."

"I agree. A small troop, one platoon, will be more nimble, quicker to respond to a sighting," Hartmann said, "Station both platoons at the warden's field, one in reserve, one on duty. Rotate their duty. We can call on the reserve platoon if needed."

"With a small force, we can test the dragons. See what they're capable of and not risk so many men," Cenhelm added.

"I suggest the red platoon take the lead. They are more experienced, better archers." Boetius, plainly not happy, seemed prepared to aqueous to the compromise.

"Do we have a consensus?" Reynard jumped at the opportunity for agreement.

He looked to each man, in turn, each of who nodded assent, Boetius, last, withheld for a moment but then also nodded.

"We will assemble the men this afternoon at the training grounds and make our preparations for tomorrow morning's expedition," Reynard said.

"I'll inform the King of our plans." Feargus rose to his feet.

The rest remained seated, all eyes on Boetius, who, with a dramatic flair, slowly stood up.

"Sirs," from both Hartmann and Cenhelm as they stood, bowed, and backed away from the table.

Berengar stumbled to his feet. "Sirs." He turned and fled for the door, joining Hartmann and Cenhelm as they passed out of the great-hall.

Reynard stood. Boetius, without a word, strode across the

great-hall.

The creak and thud of the door left Feargus and Reynard alone.

"I can't believe you sided with Boetius." Feargus took the opportunity to chastise Reynard. He couldn't resist; he knew he would regret it later.

"I'm not on anyone's side," Reynard said.

"Well, because of you, we will be in a fight with the dragons very soon. You could have supported my argument for a long training period."

"Train for what? How do we train to fight dragons? Drake will insist on action. An exploratory force is our best option. It's possible that by engaging the dragons, we may find a way to drive them out of the Kingdom. Which is what you prefer, correct?" Reynard said, "Consider that."

After a pause, wanting to change the topic, Feargus offered, "My thoughts are that the dragons came from the far north. What do you think?"

"I agree. My grandmother told stories, handed down from her grandmother, that place dragons in the northern territories well beyond the North Mountains," Reynard said.

"Your grandmother was from the native tribes, am I right?"

"Yes, Grandpa Samis used to say that he went hunt'en bear in the northern wilds and brought her back by mistake."

"So what we thought were tall tales and legends are now coming to life."

"Looks that way," Reynard replied.

"We should keep our thoughts about the dragons' home to ourselves for now."

Reynard nodded in agreement.

"Who'd ever thought we would have to confront dragons, fight beasts from legends," Feargus said.

"Yes, hard to believe," Reynard replied, "Hopefully we can find a practical way to rid ourselves of the dragons without a war. But if not, I want to be prepared for a fight, one I hope we could win. One with minimal casualties."

"I don't see how; the dragons appear invincible. I fear disaster."

"Tomorrow we shall see," Reynard said, "Good fortune Sir Feargus."

"Good fortune, Reynard." Feargus headed off for the King's chambers.

Conversations in Confidence

Amalia took a seat at the corner of the table across from Ramona, her back to the throne and royal wall displays.

Ramona glanced up from her paperwork. "Foolish men, off on a fool's errand."

The King's troops had left to hunt dragons that morning.

"Maybe they won't be able to find the dragons."

"We can't count on that. They do have their talents—hunting, tracking, and fighting. Unfortunately, clear thinking isn't one of them." Ramona rolled her eyes. "I'm afraid this venture will come to no good." She returned her attention to note-taking.

Certainly, Feargus was providing Ramona with information concerning the plans for the dragon hunt. Amalia had her source as well in Reynard.

Time passed, Ramona focused on her papers, Amalia diligently knitting.

From her seat at the central dining table, a seat that commoner like herself was not usually allowed to take, Amalia scanned the great-hall. Behind her was the throne chair resting in front of the royal throne wall with a display representing

Drake's royal family (the House of Lowe). In the center of the presentation was a red shield with the royal crest, the white outline of a mountain-lion in the middle. Above that, hung a banner with the red and white royal colors. Both were flanked by mounted weapons (lances, swords, bows) and various animal trophies (skins, horns, antlers, and tusks). Both sidewalls of the great-hall were lined with simpler displays of other Noble families, a shield with the family crest, sided by weapons of choice, and a banner with the family colors above. The first family display on the east wall was that of Sir Feargus (the House of Hirsch), a blue and white colored pendant, a shield with a stag on the crest, and crossed lances. On the west wall, the first display, appropriately but coincidently, opposite Sir Feargus' family display, was that of the family of Sir Boetius (the House of Eber), presenting a green and white flag, a shield with a wild boar in the emblem and an arrangement of bows and arrows. Other family displays continued along each wall, with Ramona's (the House of Barin) on the west side near the end of the hall with a banner of yellow and white, a crest with a bear in the emblem and crossed swords. Only the Eminent Nobles, members of the Noble Council, had these presentations of status in the great-hall, the displays changing from time to time as Noble families rose and fell from grace.

"I don't know where they get their ideas," Ramona said, shaking her head. "The King thinks the dragons might have come from the Dark Forest." She seemed to be asking for an opinion.

Despite the many times it was expressed, Amalia was always taken aback when Queen Ramona confided in her. Ramona shared her feelings, her worries, and her plans with Amalia, only a commoner, the Queen's handmaid.

"Boetius has taken up that thinking as well." Amalia took up a ball of red yarn from her bag.

"How do you know?" Ramona asked.

"He sometimes shares his thoughts and ideas with Reynard."

"And you, of course, have access to Reynard's thoughts." Ramona was showing a sly smile.

Amalia's face felt hot.

"Sorry, didn't mean to tease," Ramona said, "Reynard is probably the only commoner, besides Berengar, that Boetius has any respect for, their relationship since childhood, probably the root of it."

"Reynard often speaks of the bond you and the others had as children." Amalia regretted the statement as soon as she said it; she shouldn't have brought up Ramona's childhood. The contrast between past to the present troubled Ramona. When she and Drake were children, they shared a special friendship, one with an edge of romance. Into adolescence, the romance bloomed. Their early years of marriage were an extended honeymoon, not marked with conflict as their relationship was now.

"Yes, we were very happy as children." Ramona looked past Amalia at the throne wall, sadness in her eyes. "Happy children is what's missing today." Ramona dropped her gaze back to her papers.

No heir to the throne is what the Queen meant. Amalia felt Ramona's heartache. The royal couple had been married for ten years, but no children; a fruitless marriage, the people called it.

An uncomfortable quiet filled the great-hall; no one else was present.

"What are you working on?" Amalia nodded to the Queen's papers, trying to restart the conversation.

It looked as if Ramona was making a map with blocks of notes, and another paper appeared to be a list of names.

"Oh, just some ideas I need to sketch out."

The two women sat in the stillness of their thoughts.

"It seems that Boetius has the ear of the commoners as well as the Nobles." Ramona returned to the original line of conversation. "That's worrisome."

"He's an odd man. Sometimes he's so snobbish, and other times he's just one of the boys in the tavern hall."

"He gets the high and mighty attitude from his parents. As a child, I remember Boetius' father at gatherings in the great-hall, espousing his views on bloodlines and inherited traits. He was a frightening man. He looked down from his lofty, noble perch on what he called the underclasses. My father tolerated him but avoided him when he could."

"Why does Boetius hate the dragons so? He seems to see them as more than just a threat to the Kingdom's food supply."

"He was born to hate dragons. It's in his blood."

"What do you mean?"

"He gets his inclinations from his father and his mother as well."

"They have both passed. There were no dragons in the Kingdom in their time."

"They taught him to be suspicious and disdainful of anyone or anything different. He's not alone in that sentiment. A lot of people are like that."

"But he's so generous with people. It doesn't seem to line up with his prejudice."

Sir Boetius was the Noble in charge of the hunting troop that supplied food to those in need during lean times.

"He profits by it. It enhances his status. He doesn't shun the praise," countered Ramona, "But maybe I'm too harsh, maybe there is a generous heart in that big chest."

"You know him better than me."

Sansa, one of the kitchen maids, approached the table. "May I take your dishes, Ma'am?"

"Yes, thank you, Sansa." Ramona flashed a smile. Sansa gathered up the tableware, curtsied, and hurried away.

"The appearance of the dragons has stirred up the men's childhood fantasies; I think." Ramona put down her pen, sat back, laid her hands on the edge of the table. "The storytelling of the Raconteur included all manner of fantastical ingredients—

witches, beasts, fairies, monsters, the Dark Forest, and of course, dragons.

"After an evening of storytelling, the next day, the boys started planning expeditions, gathering weapons and supplies, making up their stories of conquests and adventures. It could go on for hours, sometimes days. But they were only children and didn't have the where-with-all to carry out their plans, except in their imaginations. In any case, bored, I'd go off by myself for a while, take an archery lesson, go horseback riding, wait till they played out their fantasies, and exhausted themselves."

"We don't have a storyteller tradition in Morodon, nor do we live so close to the Dark Forest."

Amalia grew up in the seaport town of Morodon, a good ten miles from the castle village.

"Yes, the Dark Forest, it was a fascination for them as well, although no one was brave enough to go near it. Thankfully."

"Most adults seem to have this ability to ignore its presence, except for occasional gossiping."

"Its allure can take hold of a man. In past times as well, at least according to the Raconteur's stories. No one has ventured into that dark place in our lifetime."

"What could possess someone to even think of entering the forest?"

"You've got it right, a possession."

"How does the Dark Forest cast such a powerful spell over a person?"

"It's the promise, the promise the Dark Forest holds," replied Ramona.

"The promise?"

"The promise of adventure, the promise of reward. They picture themselves coming back as heroes from a glorious quest, or they find fortune, and become the stuff of legends themselves."

"I don't understand. Why chance going into the forest? In

the Dark Forest stories, it doesn't end well for the fools who enter. There's no story I've ever heard where any mortal comes back. I thought the point of storytelling was to teach a lesson, pass on wisdom." Amalia stated the obvious. A mystery why others didn't see it.

"In their minds, just because someone else wasn't able to accomplish the feat, doesn't mean that they can't. Some people do hold a rather high opinion of themselves."

"It may be that witches have done it, past in and out of the gate in the Sheep Meadow." Amalia remembered a story regarding the forest. "The Witches Gate's story says that in ancient times, the witches escaped into the forest to avoid persecution. Many people suspect they still live there to this day and can go back and forth at will."

"I know that story as well," Ramona said, "But I trust it's just superstition."

"But there are people who say they've seen witches in the Sheep Meadow on nights with a full moon." The Sheep Meadow Amalia was referring to was a common use area, bordering the castle village to the south.

"Yes, people say. People say a lot of things," Ramona countered with an edge of sarcasm in her voice, "People give those clandestine witches credit for all kinds of things, good and bad. They get blamed for various misfortunes; crop failure, illnesses, or just bad luck, and credited for mysterious acts of goodwill, like healing potions left on a doorstep during the night."

A good thing too, since the people of the village shunned the sick and ill. They thought them contagious at best or possessed by evil spirits at worst. Amalia had no respect for the head priest or his teachings. Especially, his nonsense preaching that misfortune was something people brought on themselves. Contempt swelled in her chest. What a ridiculous idea that some people were inherently wicked, or that they were paying for their sins. Who could help what situation they were born into or the circumstances life delivered? Of course, the priest had the cure for their ills, the potions he sold, the idea of which soured in her stomach.

Those medicines from the priest had not done her mother any good. If only mother had listened to Aunt Florence and gone to see Renilda, the healer woman in the village. After her mother died when Amalia was just ten years old, Amalia spent summer months with her Aunt Florence, who lived in the village. Amalia got to know Renilda very well. Even though Renilda couldn't have cured Amalia's mother's condition, the wasting disease, she could have made her comfortable at the end.

"Speaking of stories, there's one circulating that says the lights of the Dark Forest might be caused by dragons." Ramona continued. "But it is said, as well, that the flickering lights in the forest treetops are caused by witches casting spells, sparks, and flames of magic. What nonsense, what people say!"

"But you believe me, don't you, that Reynard and I saw the lights," Many years ago, Amalia had confided her account of her and Reynard's experience on South Ridge. Amalia's concern added tension to her voice. She wondered if Ramona was making fun of her. Ramona didn't put stock in anything supernatural. Shouldn't the appearance of dragons make her reconsider?

"Of course," Ramona said, "I don't doubt you. There just must be other explanations for the lights besides witches or dragons."

"I hope the men don't do something foolish, a Dark Forest expedition or something?"

"We don't have to worry about any of them going off into the forest anytime soon," Ramona answered, "They have enough to keep them busy, arguing over the dragon problem and planning a war. Foolishness seems to be in their nature. They always seem to find some folly to pursue."

Amalia opened her mouth to contradict the Queen on that

last point but stopped.

"Sorry, I should speak for myself. I have Drake to contend with. You have Reynard. I admit not all men are fools, or at least, not all the time." Ramona grinned. "You do have Reynard, don't you?"

Amalia, again, felt her face flush with heat.

"We're not girls anymore, but I can still make you blush. Can't seem to help myself." Ramona laughed softly. "What were you, 16, when you started meeting with Reynard on the South Ridge?"

"Yes," Amalia's face was cooling, she returned Ramona's smile.

"Remember, I was the one that used to cover for Reynard, so his father didn't know what he was up to," Ramona said.

"You lied about Reynard doing chores for your father."

"IMPLIED, not lied, there's a difference. Misleading, Amalia, is not the same as lying." Ramona's voice was adamant, and she showed a mix of distress and feigned hurt.

"Really."

"Yes, the sin of commission is a real sin, the sin of omission, not so much," Ramona said, "If it weren't for me, you and Reynard wouldn't have gotten away with your secret meetings. The boys couldn't do it; they're not skilled in the art of deception."

Amalia was taken aback by Ramona's pride in her "art of deception" as she called it, but that was how Ramona had mostly gotten her way throughout life. She'd bend a rule rather than break it, create confusion, leave out details and fabricate only as a last resort; it was her code of honor.

"The boys were too straightforward, single-minded: Boetius the hero, Feargus the planner, Drake the caretaker, and Reynard the—the what? The lover?" Ramona asked.

"Ramona!" Amalia scolded in as adamant a voice as she could muster, trying to discourage Ramona.

"Just marry the man already," Ramona's tone matched her

rolling eyes.

"Married women don't serve as maids in court." Her voice so low, Amalia was afraid that Ramona did not hear her.

"Oh. I'm sorry." Ramona held Amalia's gaze, visibly dismayed. "I'm so thoughtless." Her eyes dropped, a slight shake of her head.

Amalia didn't understand why this topic had never come up before. She had never broached the subject, of course. Her relationship with Reynard was an open book; she assumed the Queen was aware of the conflict in Amalia's heart.

"That needs to change," Ramona said, now with a calm, assured voice. "I believe I can make that happen."

"If it were only possible, I would love that. Reynard and I would want to have children right away." Amalia saw a pulse of sadness appear in the Queen's eyes. Children, the word slipped out again? Why couldn't she have kept her concerns to herself? She was good at staying quiet most of the time.

"It's only right," Ramona said, "What are you knitting there, a scarf? You should be knitting baby clothes," not waiting for an answer, "How old are you now?"

"Twenty-eight."

"It's past time you got a family started. You don't want to end up old and barren like me."

Ramona's words struck Amalia with force. "You're only four years older than me."

"Seems like yesterday I was a young girl, teasing the boys and planning my future."

The flash of her own youthful memories of her courtship with Reynard warmed Amalia.

"But time has passed. Things don't always work out as you hope. Ten years of marriage and no children."

With that remark, the warmth of her memories was driven out of Amalia's heart.

"No. No. It's not too late for you. You could still have a child."

"The King thinks it's too late," Ramona said, "He's seriously considering his younger brother's petition to designate his oldest son as the heir to the throne. He's just a little boy now, but . . ."

Amalia was silent. She didn't know how to console her friend. It was likely that the King blamed Ramona for their infertility, although it was never voiced as far as Amalia knew.

"Enough about me," Ramona said, "We need to focus on you and your future, your children, your first daughter."

"You think my first will be a girl?"

"Yes, of course. I would be her godmother. If you'd have me." Ramona was biting her bottom lip, a telltale trait that showed when her mind was scheming.

"Really?"

"Yes. I could teach her how to shoot and ride a horse." Ramona smiled broadly. "Teach all kinds of things. Things girls need to know to get along in this world."

Although this was just speculation on the future, Amalia felt a bit uneasy with the Queen's offer.

"Your first may also be a girl." Amalia was going to insist on hope.

Ramona produced a sad smile. "I hope so. If it were ever to happen," she said with softness, and then with conviction, "Got enough males in the Kingdom causing problems; should be a woman in charge."

"You really think a Queen will rule as Monarch someday?"

"Of course. Men in charge. That should change. I can see a daughter of mine as queen. Yes, definitely."

Coming back to her personal concern, Amalia said, "Wouldn't the King and the court object to having a married woman as your maid? It's customary for maids to be unmarried. I wouldn't want to leave your service."

"That's what's holding you back, your loyalty to me?"

Amalia looked down at her knitting. She owed Ramona a lot: the offer to become a Queen's maid had facilitated her escape from her father's dominance.

"That can't be an obstacle to your happiness. I won't allow it."

"I don't think the King likes me already. It's likely, the Nobles' Council will be against it. I don't want to cause any trouble." Amalia did not want to get her hopes up, but couldn't resist a sense of rising excitement.

"I know how to get my way," Ramona declared, "I'll organize a rebellion if I have to."

"Too bad you couldn't do that to avoid a dragon war." The commoners following Boetius and not Ramona was a serious disappointment for Ramona, one also felt deeply by Amalia. But people overcome by fear can't make rational choices, not even choices in their own self-interest.

"We will have to resort to more devious methods," Ramona responded.

Amalia was sure that would be the case. Ramona could be counted on to do what she could for Amalia and for the dragons as well.

The Telling
of a Battle

Amalia stepped up on the boards of the sidewalk in front of Reynard's blacksmith shop and strode past the doorway. At the corner, she turned into the broad alleyway between Reynard's shop and the tailor's.

Back at the castle, as she left, she had controlled her pace and maintained her composure despite her desire to get to Reynard as soon as she could. But as she cleared the rampart, her gait quickened. Propelling herself along the village road, she nearly broke into a jog.

Reynard had sent a boy from the village with a message; he needed to talk with her. It was unexpected. An urgency plagued her as she made her rounds caring for the wounded. Busy in the great-hall, she hadn't seen Reynard since the battle.

A few moments of striding down the dirt path and Amalia stopped to catch her halting breath. Ahead of her, set in behind the blacksmith shop, was her destination, Reynard's cottage, illuminated by the late morning sun.

Amalia knocked, opened the door, not waiting for a response from within. She stepped into the cottage with one familiar motion without a stitch of hesitation. The front common room was sparse with minimal furniture, adjusted to Reynard's liking from the abundantly decorated family home it had been when his mother was in charge. This cottage, inherited from his father, contained his family memories, the home where Reynard and his two brothers were raised. A solidly built structure with a wooden floor and glass windows, features not found in a commoner's house, were evidence of Reynard's father's high status. And now the cottage reflected Reynard's similar high standing in the Kingdom, the village blacksmith and King's Weapons Master.

Reynard looked up with a forced, awkward smile and remained seated at the dining table. No genuine smile, no warm reception was expected, not today. Amalia had heard the cursory reports of yesterday's battle. Everyone was talking about it.

Only three days ago, the King's men, from their bivouac in the Western Hunting Grounds, began their hunt for dragons. The tracking dogs quickly found the dragon's trails and feeding places amongst the old logging roads and clearings. Timbered many years ago, a mix of fields and young growth forest, the territory was an ideal habitat for game animals. Late yesterday afternoon, a platoon engaged with a group of four dragons, unsuccessfully from what Amalia had heard. The accounts circulating at the castle were varied, conflicted. But Reynard had been there, Amalia would learn the truth from him.

She crossed the room and pulled a chair up to the table. Amalia positioned it, so she was within reach of Reynard, who remained still except for the slow shake of his head that answered a question she had not yet asked. It must have been awful. She sat waiting for him to compose himself.

"I can't believe no one was killed," Reynard began, "only minor injuries. It was chaos."

"I'm glad you're safe."

"I was out of harm's way with no part to play. I was a helpless observer."

"I'm sorry I couldn't come to you last night." Amalia had spent the night with the wounded that were being cared for in the castle's great-hall.

Amalia reached out and placed her hand on top Reynard's that was resting on the tabletop. Reynard had never actually seen a battle before, the results of it for sure. His experience of previous wars was limited to the casualties coming home, the wounded and the dead. He had created and manufactured the weapons, but not used them or seen them used.

"The dogs found the dragons just south of our encampment. Berengar returned and led us to them. We—only the red platoon—followed his lead up a logging road just past the warden's cottage. The dragons, four of them, were in a clearing, feasting on a catch of turkeys. We approached from the higher ground, a low rise at the edge of the road. They saw us but paid no mind. We were only 50 paces from them."

He leaned in closer with a slight shrug of his shoulders.

"Without warning or consultation with Feargus, Boetius ordered his archers into formation just in front of the rise. From their hastily formed crooked line, they let fly a volley of arrows. The arrows either bounced off the dragon's hide or missed their target, falling to no effect."

Amalia gently squeezed his hand. She was biting and releasing her bottom lip.

"The four dragons then turned their attention on us. Their head's low, like geese when they attack, they lumbered forward toward the archer's position." Reynard grimaced and paused.

Amalia nodded for Reynard to continue.

"Feargus had no choice; he released his Knights. He sent five forward to defend the archers. They formed up a line in front of the archers, lances aimed at the oncoming dragons. Five others rode left, and the remaining six went right, flanking the dragons on both sides, intending to encircle them.

"An effective tactic, often used, a standard advancement in battle. But the dragons had stopped their slow march toward the defenseless archers and formed up in flanks themselves, pivoting to face the Knights on their left and right. Then, extending their necks, the dragons issued growling trumpet-calls. Quiet, muffled, and unearthly. The horses panicked, reared up, spun, the Knights lost control, several men and horses fell to the ground. Others just froze in place; their riders couldn't move them forward, or at all. The looks of beasts scared the horses, maybe, or it was the noise or maybe the smell of dragons.

"The Knights train their horses well for battle, conditioning them for the chaos and the sounds of combat. Feargus insists his Knights spend many hours in training, desensitizing their horses not to react to the clash of swords and lances, and getting them accustomed to close combat, body to body contact with other horses."

Under Amalia's hand, Reynard's hand clenched to a fist.

"But, this was more, much more, than they were trained for. Dragons. We should have known, been prepared for it. How could you expect a horse to approach a dragon? How could you even train a horse to approach a dragon?"

Reynard paused, looked up for a moment. "Who could blame them for panicking? Only the horses had the sense to be terrified. It happened so fast. Everyone was acting on instinct." Another pause.

"Cenhelm and his men, only ten men carrying lances, rushed in to protect the fallen Knights who had unsheathed their useless swords in defense.

"The dragons ignored them and pivoted back toward the archers and our position on the hill. We were backing away in retreat. Boetius reassembled a small cadre of archers, and they shot again. The largest dragon, ahead of the rest, lowered its head, roared a trumpet-call and . . ." Reynard stopped; his face conveyed that dreadful moment in time.

"What is it?"

"A fireball shot from its mouth. I swear, a fireball, a blue stream of flame. It flew just above our heads. Ash floated down around us; it smelled of rotten eggs. I know that Drake, Feargus, and Boetius had described it in their encounter with a dragon, but I guess I didn't really believe them. You had to see it."

"Then what?" Amalia was in high suspense. She wanted a quick answer. How did this fight end without significant casualties?

"The lead dragon called out again, a lower tone, a gravely sound. The dragons extended their wings, came right at us. And as they were almost upon us with a swift downbeat of their wings, they lifted off. They flew right over us, only a few yards above our heads. Boetius was still commanding his archers to shoot. Some men on their knees, others falling to their backs, firing arrows that struck and deflected off the underbellies of the dragons.

"The dragons only had to stand their ground and fight. Our complement would have been devastated. I don't think one man would have survived. If all the dragons can shoot fire? God.

"The archers had no shields; foolish, but Hartmann had allowed it. They were defenseless against the flame. Men-at-arms tried to put their shields in front of themselves and the archers. A hopeless gesture."

Amalia wanted to console him. She slid her chair around the table next to his and put her arm around his shoulders.

He didn't seem to notice, staring at the tabletop, lost in his thoughts, nightmarish thoughts most likely.

Reynard returned his attention to Amalia, "You just came from the castle. The men, the casualties, how are they?"

Queen Ramona had converted the castle's great-hall into an infirmary, using the dining tables as beds. The injured were attended by the healer-priest. Each of the wounded had a dedicated nurse, arranged by Ramona. Amalia spelled each nurse for brief periods, rotating from patient to patient.

"The priest says all the men will recover from their injuries, but I'm concerned with Sir Amalric. His head injury is serious."

"He was thrown from his horse into a stone wall and struck his head."

"He has a concussion at least, maybe a skull fracture. He keeps going in and out of consciousness."

"And the others?"

"Another Knight with a broken leg, two soldiers with arrow wounds, not serious. They're expected to heal well."

"In the chaos, the archers shooting volley after volley, arrows ricocheted, struck our own men."

"It seems hopeless to engage the dragons," Amalia said, "Surely the King will call off the hunt."

"Not likely. I know Drake. He won't accept defeat, neither will Boetius. The two of them together are a dangerous combination. But Feargus will argue for suspension, another way, not another battle."

"Maybe the King will listen to reason. You could talk to him. He respects you."

"We are beyond that now. I've known these men since we were boys. Boetius' pride and Drakes' reputation are involved. They will have to play this out.

"The King has called for a meeting at noon to discuss the battle. He expects a new plan, wants new ideas on how to defeat the dragons."

"What of Feargus' idea of driving the dragons out of the Kingdom?"

"How? They don't fear us. We were merely an annoyance." Reynard was suddenly angry.

Amalia drew back.

"I'm sorry. I'm just frustrated."

Amalia, looking into Reynard's eyes, thought she saw guilt.

"At the meeting, support Feargus," Amalia said.

"No." His response was harsh.

Reynard leaned back; both hands rested on the table

edge, fists clenched, his eyes drifted back and forth. Amalia had watched this play out many times. Reynard's mind was working, like a searchlight methodically scanning a room, looking into the hidden corners of the problem.

He leaped up, walked toward the far wall, talking at it or to himself. "The lancers shields were too heavy and too small, designed to protect just the torso—a modification, I could add—no, a new design."

Reynard took a paper and pen from a cupboard and returned to the table.

He was lost to her now, deep in thought, the search for a solution to become an addiction. She would be of more value at the great-hall, tending the wounded. Ramona was expecting a report, an accurate report of the battle.

Amalia rose from her chair. "I'm needed at the castle. I'll come by later this evening."

"Yes, yes," he said, not looking up.

As she was grasping the door latch, he said, "Sorry, I'm sorry, I just need to . . ."

"It's alright. I'll see you later. We can talk more then."

She passed through the doorway, looked back. Reynard was huddled over his papers, already sketching and making notes. "Don't forget your meeting."

He did not respond.

Confrontation
& Blame

After Amalia left, Reynard procrastinated. He had quit his attempt to design a new shield, and the idea for a catapult lacked inspiration. Instead, he tinkered with this and that, wandered around his blacksmith shop, his father's shop before him, and his father's father before him. Tools of all types hung on the walls, ancient and precious. The forge and bellows, how many hours had the fire burned, shaping, twisting, sculpting metal to conform to a man's imagination? This sacred place, smoke and ash and heat, Reynard wanted to be here, not in a meeting, and certainly not in another hopeless battle.

King Drake was expecting him for the meeting with Boetius and Feargus at noon in the great-hall. The evening before, immediately after the army returned from its late afternoon fight with the dragons, Boetius had gone to report to the King. Reynard and Feargus stayed with the troops, for an inspection and to arrange for the care and transportation of the wounded. Boetius was eager to discuss the battle and pressed the King to immediately call a planning meeting.

With reluctance, Reynard left his shop and followed

the well-traveled route down the village street, through the rampart gate, up the castle hill road, into the castle, and the great-hall.

Reynard was the last to arrive; often accused of habitual lateness, he was actually on time. Reluctant to attend any meeting, he intensely did not want to attend this one. No good will come from a session to discuss the failed assault on the dragons that involved Boetius and Feargus. Argument was guaranteed, agreement unlikely, even the account of events will likely differ.

Drake wanted a plan of action, a strategy, methods, a way to fight the dragons. Reynard expected Boetius to call for a full assault, Feargus for caution, and he, despite his full attention and effort this morning, had nothing of substance to offer.

Reynard stepped through the doorway into the great-hall. At the far end of the hall, King Drake, facing Reynard's direction, was seated in the middle of the central table in front of the throne wall. Boetius and Feargus, with their backs to Reynard and an empty chair between them, were sitting across from the King. No one noticed or acknowledged Reynard's entry. He hesitated for a moment, stopped by the ridicules idea that he could turn around and leave, and no one would notice.

Reynard drew a long breath and crossed the room to the table.

"Sire," Reynard said with a bow.

The King gave him the 'why are you always late' look, which was totally unfair, this time at least. The church clock was announcing the hour of noon, the meeting time. Everyone else was early. A moment before the last clock strike, Reynard took a seat at the end of the table to Feargus' left, not the one in between the rivals. Feargus and Boetius each nodded.

"I will be leaving in four days for the war council. I am putting you two in charge of developing a battle plan while I'm gone." King Drake looked across to Feargus and Boetius, who nodded assent. "Reynard, when we return, I expect you to provide support for their plan."

"Yes, Sire." A battle plan, it was settled, they would fight the dragons again. Feargus will need to give up his ideas of driving the dragons out of the Kingdom by harassment. Feargus and he will be compelled to commit to a strategy they did not yet have, a plan Reynard was not able to imagine.

"From Boetius' report, it's obvious that we need to do better than yesterday's encounter," Drake said.

"We need a new strategy," Boetius said.

"I didn't realize you even had a strategy yesterday," Feargus said, smirking, "Unless finding dragons and breaking arrows and lances on them is a strategy."

Reynard found no humor in the remark. The encounter was terrifying. The archers were ineffective, lances of no use, the Knights waving their swords, all puny in front of the dragons.

"If we had taken a full company into the field like I recommended, we would have fared better." Boetius was already near shouting.

"Better? The more men, the more casualties," Feargus said, "How's that better? More injured or possibly killed."

"I agree with Feargus," Drake said, "No large-scale frontal assault. No engagement until we have a strategy, and not until I approve it."

Boetius began, "But if I had more archers, I could have . . ."

"Why did you order your archers to attack?" Feargus tensed his shoulders. He sounded like he was going to erupt.

"I was testing the dragons as we agreed."

"Enough talk of yesterday," Drake barked, "I'm interested in the future, the next time we engage."

Ignoring or maybe not hearing the King, Feargus was not ready to abandon his angry discourse. "If you had shown restraint, we could have taken the opportunity to test the dragons, learned something about them."

Boetius pivoted in his chair to face Feargus. "Restraint?

You don't hold back when confronted by this kind of threat. You attack."

An empty chair between them was good, and also that Reynard was not in it.

In childhood, Reynard had witnessed many of these arguments degrade into a scuffle. They sat side-by-side today. It would be difficult to intervene if they got physical. As kids, just a wrestling match, as men, a brawl between them was too dangerous to contemplate.

Sometimes Reynard wondered if these two would someday push Drake to the limit of his patience and force the King to select other men to lead his army. Although they argued and fought over the planning of a fight, there were no other men in the Kingdom equal to them in a fight. Strangely, their extreme positions brought balance to the planning and the outcomes. Reynard remembered a time as young men when he had questioned Drake about the contentious relationship between Feargus and Boetius. His answer, the highest compliment he ever heard Drake issue, was, 'If I'm ever in a fight, I want them on my side.'

Twice in King Drake's reign, Drake had that opportunity, to fight side by side with his friends. Both times, the Kingdom of Enid had come to the aid Evora, Enid's sister kingdom, bonded by an alliance and the blood relations of the royal families. Both wars were fought over territorial disputes between Evora, which bordered Enid on the east and the Kingdom of Nendos, a domain that lay farther east yet of Evora. Nendos and Evora both laid claim to rich timberlands in the Northern Wilds that adjoined Evora's northern border.

"Gentlemen, compose yourselves." Drake inserted himself like a wedge between two storms. "Fixing blame for yesterday is not helpful. Consider the future, the next time we do battle. How do we defeat the dragons? How do we kill them?"

Drake was emphatic and somber. After a moment, he stood. Their chairs screeched as the other men hastily rose to their feet.

"I have other business," Drake said, "I will leave you to your deliberations. You all witnessed the encounter. You have scouted the dragons with your patrols. I expect you to use that knowledge to find a weakness, a way to defeat the dragons." With that, King Drake stepped away from the table. He strode across the room and out the main door. He could be heard calling to the groom stationed outside the gate for his horse.

Boetius got up and glared at Feargus as he walked around to the other side of the table and took a seat across from Feargus, putting Reynard between them. Reynard did not appreciate this position, in the middle, the mediator.

After a few moments of stilted silence, Reynard slid his chair back, better to see both men as he spoke. "We're charged with devising a battle plan. The King is expecting results. We need to work together on this. Let's discuss what happened yesterday. What do we know about the dragons?"

"That they are the superior force. That we were lucky to have had only minor casualties, and no fatalities," Feargus said. "And we didn't even injure a dragon. No success at all."

"No success, the dragons retreated from our attack," Boetius countered.

"Yes, and a good thing too. If they stood and fought, they could have destroyed us. We don't have a weapon that can touch them. They breathe fire. Their claws could crush a man."

The lifelong opponents had immediately retreated into their bickering, subverting any constructive conversation.

Reynard knew Feargus had no stomach for this fight and preferred it abandoned or at least postponed until they had a semblance of a plan. Reynard felt the same. But it was unlikely that Boetius or King Drake would give it up, their egos and pride governing their actions. A path to conflict was inevitable.

Addressing Boetius in an effort to interrupt the bickering, Reynard said, "Feargus is right. At this point, I don't see any possible way to defeat the dragons."

"You must have something to contribute. A modification of our weapons to make them effective. Some new weapon," Boetius said, "We need something that gives us an advantage."

"No, I don't. I have been working on it. I've sketched out a few things, new shields, for a better defense against fire, a catapult design. But I have nothing concrete as yet," Reynard said.

Visions of the battle flashed in Reynard's mind; the chaos that lasted only moments, but long moments; lances breaking on the dragon's hide; arrows of no value; Knights on horseback twisting and falling; shields useless against flame.

A new shield was a priority. A soldier's shield was wooden, clad with metal, oval-shaped, two feet in height, with a strap to suspend it from a shoulder. In addition, it could be strapped to an arm, light enough to be wheeled by one arm in a sword fight, but of no value against dragon fire.

Even though he didn't favor this enterprise, Reynard didn't want the King's men to come to harm. He truly wished he had more to offer, but he needed more time. Although there were no deaths so far, it was inevitable, if only by accident.

"We need to find a way," Boetius echoed Reynard's thoughts.

"We're not going to accomplish anything by recklessly charging into a battle without a strategy, no effective weaponry, and no training," Feargus said, "I won't press my men into a battle again. Not until there's a plan in place."

"We should continue the patrols," Reynard said, "Keep track of the dragons and their movements."

"Yes," Boetius replied, "My archer platoons and the hunting troop will remain at hunting ground's camp. They will go out on morning and afternoon patrols, scout the area and report back."

"I will send out horsemen on patrols as well," Feargus said, "Cenhelm and ten of his best riders, their horses are steadier around the dragons. They can take the opportunity if they find dragons to condition the horses. So if we engage again, the horses will be less likely to panic.

"Also, Reynard, the horse armor is too heavy, it impairs movement. We need something lighter, something to protect against fire. If it's possible, and the men too, light armor."

Feargus was asking for the impossible. Reynard had no idea how to proceed.

Placing his hands on the table, Feargus extended his arms and pushed himself back in his chair. "I have nothing else to offer." Looking to Boetius. "And you?"

No response from Boetius, he looked to Reynard. "At this point, you have nothing to offer either?" Reynard nodded agreement. "Well then, there is nothing more to discuss. We will meet again in three days." Feargus rose and quickly exited the hall.

A moment later, Boetius, growling his disgust, stood and left.

Reynard was left sitting alone. The encounter had fared better than expected. At least it was a short argument, not the usual drawn-out affair of stating and restating their opposing positions.

Clearly, Feargus was going to use the lack of ideas or a plan as a justification to delay and not engage the dragons, which of course, would infuriate Boetius.

The problem was left unsolved, how to defeat the dragons in battles that loomed on the horizon.

A Death

Drake held his position on the Morodon Road Bridge in sight of the Castle Village's southern boundary. He and two members of the royal guard waited for the third guardsman who Drake had sent to investigate and report back about the commotion ahead. Drake stood up high in his stirrups for a better view. At the village stable gate, in the distance, the guardsman, leaning out of his saddle, was conversing with a man standing beside his horse. Seated again, Drake twisted around, scanned the landscape, and checked in with his men behind him. On horseback, 20 paces away with the pack mule between them, they shook their heads in response, no concerns.

Although the possibility of encountering trouble in his own Kingdom was unlikely, better to err on the side of caution. The disturbance in the village was unusual. Groups of people were in the street. Others were exiting their cottages and shops to join in. The setting sun, to Drake's left, hovered over the ridge behind him; he estimated an hour of daylight remaining.

Members of the Noble Council advised against the King making these monthly trips to the Morodon Tariff House. A tax was levied on all goods, passing through the Port of Morodon on the Maran Sea. The tax was one of the Kingdom's profitable revenue streams. Council members considered it beneath the King's station to collect the tariff money, but Drake insisted. He had other motives for a trip with an overnight stay in Morodon, a long day's ride from the castle. The visit provided the opportunity to inspect the army garrison and to call on old friends. Besides, he enjoyed the sea, the beaches, and the salt air. It was an opportunity to be on Kingdom business and also to be away from Kingdom business.

Morodon had been one of Drake's assignments as a young man, apprenticeships his father called them, a time spent learning the family business. Posted at the Morodon Tariff House, he learned the ins and outs of tax collecting. Taxes were collected at the entry points on the three primary roads that led into the Kingdom of Enid, the Morodon Road, the Braga Road, and the East Road. One other road led out of the Kingdom, the North Road. No taxes were collected there. A king in the past tried it, but the wild clans and native tribes, the only people who lived in the northern reaches, displayed their displeasure by raiding and by burning cottages. Not worth the trouble, the practice of tax collection on the North Road was abandoned.

Time spent at Morodon, living in the garrison with the guardsmen, despite the lack of comfort, was not without its rewards. In rotations, four men manned the tariff gate on the road, and four men patrolled the town of Morodon. To be on patrol in a seaport town was a pleasure for a young man away from home, feeling his oats.

Drake also pulled assignments at the other tariff stations. The worst of which was duty at the East Road tariff station. It was just a guard shack at the road edge with a meager hut for lodging the four men stationed there. There were no distractions, no village, nothing for miles. Day after day, evening after evening, Drake watched his three companions drink too much, gamble too much, and then argue too much. The month there was the longest month he had spent anywhere.

Despite lacking the charms of Morodon, the Braga Tariff Station also had its special place in Drake's memory, a rough and tumble place of adventure. Only two guards manned the station. Only one in winter, as the road was impassible most days. The station was managed full time by one man (by his choice), an old army veteran named Samis. A second guard rotated in from the castle garrison. Besides managing the tariff station, Samis ran a small dairy operation that supplied milk to the castle village. His home and farm were a stone's throw from the Braga Road tariff station gatehouse. One summer, Drake was assigned to the Braga station for a month but volunteered for a second and then a third.

A flash of movement at the village caught Drake's eye. Another man, standing by the guardsman, waving his arms, had joined the conversation. Drake settled back into his patient waiting.

At the Braga Station, besides his honest work of tax collection, Samis had side arrangements with his favorite merchants. It became apparent to Drake right away that not all merchants were being taxed equally. From some wagons that stopped at the gate, cases of wine, beer kegs, or whiskey casks were clandestinely left at the side of the road before their departure.

Drake thought of reporting Samis and his less than honest activities to his father, but Samis had drawn him into an awkward position, snared him. Early on, Feargus and Cenhelm, who both had family nearby, came to visit Drake. They dropped in each morning, sometimes sharing breakfast before they left to explore the countryside on horseback. Drake was left behind and to his duties, sitting at the guard shack, numbed by boredom. One morning, in his second week, his friends appeared with an extra horse, a temptation. Drake thought it Feargus' idea but later came to believe that Samis had something to do with it. Drake had a vivid memory of Samis standing at the gate, eyeballing him as he mounted the horse.

"Far as I can see, you was here at your post all day, your prince-ness."

An insubordinate remark Drake felt a need to correct, but not as much as he wished to spend the day riding with Feargus and Cenhelm. The daily rides became a habit of minor dishonesty, one that paralleled Samis' activities; a secret Samis kept to this day.

The memories of youth entertained Drake as he waited. And he didn't forget that Samis was Reynard's maternal grandfather. He needed to remember to inquire of Samis the next time he saw Reynard.

At a lope, the guard rode back to the King. He pulled up his horse to a quick stop. "Sire."

"Report. Who were you speaking with?"

"The stable owner and his hired hand. They tell me, that's about two hours ago, one of Sir Boetius' men arrived to get a horse and cart from the stables."

"Does he know why?"

"No. Boetius' man was real agitated, they say. Yell'en and holler'en at em, some-thin about a dragon. They didn't even get a chance to ask what's it all about. Boetius' man jumped in the cart and took off."

"Anything else?"

"There's word spread'en in the village that Boetius and his men are come'en down from their encampment in the hunt'en ground."

"Do they say why?"

"They say'en there was another fight with the dragons."

"I can't believe it." Drake motioned with his arm. "Forward." He trotted down the road toward the village. His guardsmen and the pack mule loaded with coin fell in behind.

When Drake arrived at the village, he had a clear view of the main street. People, in packs like wild dogs, were running away from Drake's position toward the north end of the village in the castle's direction. They were calling to each other, stopping momentarily, calling into shops and cottages, drawing more people into the frenzy like bees swarming out of a hive. Their attention to the north, they were unaware of the King and his guardsmen trailing behind them, focused on whatever was drawing them forward.

Drake and his men rode up behind and through the pulsing throng. Then at a pacing trot, they passed through the village and on up the Village Road until they arrived at the base of the castle hill, just outside the rampart wall. There a sizable crowd was gathering. Its attention focused on Braga Road; most were unaware of the King's presence.

One guardsman rode ahead into the crowd, issuing commands that separated the people, making way for the King.

Drake positioned himself on the roadside on a knoll in front of the crowd. From horseback, he had a better view of a band of men, 20 or more, coming down the road from the north. Drake recognized Boetius, dressed in hunter green, the only one on horseback, leading the group of men and a horse-drawn cart.

When Boetius came within 30 paces of the gathering, the crowd surged toward him. They engulfed the cart and his entourage (men of the hunting troop and an archer squad). Boetius had been leading these men on patrols in the Western Hunting Grounds. Those who arrived first at the cart gasped and pushed back against the crowd. A moment later, a cheer went up.

Drake held his position. Villagers were shaking hands with Boetius' men, slapping backs. A man next to Boetius' horse stretched up to grasp Boetius' hand in congratulations.

On Drake's order, a guard rode up behind the crowd, announcing the King. The people quieted, opened a path, and bowed. Drake rode through to Boetius, who bowed his head.

"Great news, Sire, a dragon kill." Boetius spoke in a voice louder than needed for Drake to hear. A cheer went up. Boetius swept his arm back toward the cart behind him. "And in the cart, the hide of the beast." Another cheer.

Drake rode around to the side of the cart. "This is great news. Excellent Sir Boetius, excellent."

"Show the King our trophy," Boetius said.

From the opposite side, Berengar stepped up on the spoked wheel into the cart. Now standing in the cart, the old man tugged and struggled and nearly toppled over as he tried to raise the dragon skin for examination. A second man, commanded by a wave of Boetius' arm, jumped in to help him. Between the two men, they managed to display the skin at chest height.

Boetius drew his sword and, with the tip, touched the hide at a yellow splotch in a sea of shaded greens.

"There, there is their weakness, this spot on the back of their neck, a crease just below the head that scales don't cover. It gets larger the farther they lower their head. That's where I placed my arrow."

"An arrow, just one arrow brought down a dragon?"

"Yes, a penetration into the spine at their neck. We can kill them with one well-placed arrow." Boetius slid his sword tip into a small hole to demonstrate and for obvious dramatic effect.

"Amazing, a great turn of events. Just what we needed. But, how did you manage to skin it?"

"It was a bear, al tell ya," Berengar said.

"Show the King," Boetius commanded.

Reaching into his pouch, Berengar retrieved a handful of dragon scales, displaying them in his outstretched hands.

The scales were a little larger than the size of a man's extended hand and translucent, not as thick as Drake had imagined. A dragon's colors must come from the skin under these see-through protective plates.

Berengar placed the scales on display on the cart fender and drew his short sword and slid the tip under one of the scales.

"What's ya got's to do is slide a sturdy blade under this pointed tip. Slide it deep in and sever the connecting tendon. Pops em right off, with a bit a work at it a course."

"The scale is tougher than anything, even steel," Boetius said, "Can't cut or dent it. The men have been having a try at it."

"We shall hang the skin on the throne wall in the great-hall," the King announced. Drake was picturing it hanging behind the throne, next to his royal family crest.

"It would be an honor, Sire," Boetius replied.

Drake stood in his stirrups and made a sweeping gesture with his outstretched arm, "Tomorrow night, we will have a banquet in the great-hall to honor this momentous occasion." More cheering erupted. None of the peasants standing before the King would be there, of course, but he would have Ramona set up a celebratory feast in the courtyard for the commoners.

Leaning from his saddle toward Drake, Boetius began, "Sire. I must be telling you how it happened. We were on our morning patrol and one of the . . ."

"No, not here," Drake interrupted, "Of course I want to hear all about it, a full report, but back at the castle, a private audience." Undoubtedly a disappointment for Boetius, but Drake wanted as accurate an account of the kill as possible without the exaggerations and embellishments a public telling before a crowd was sure to inspire.

An aside, as a consolation, "Over a goblet of celebratory wine, the Chambold red you enjoy so much."

Drake moved into position in front of the cart and started toward the castle. With a wave of his arm, he assembled the crowd into a spontaneous parade. Boetius trotted up alongside.

The two men led a raucous plodding procession through the rampart gate and up the castle hill road to the castle gatehouse door.

It was essential to know the real story, not the one Boetius was sure to spin. He would ask Reynard to connect with his hunter friends to learn what truly happened.

Pleased with this turn of events, Drake now had something of substance to present at the war council. For a moment, he considered taking Boetius instead of Reynard, but that wouldn't do. No need for a distraction (which Boetius could be) from the critical deliberations. To placate Boetius, Drake would put him in charge of the war preparations, make it his responsibility to develop a battle strategy. That might antagonize Feargus, but so be it; he's easier to deal with. He would present it to Boetius as an honor and a duty. Surely, it will be feasible to take advantage of the newfound dragon vulnerability.

Only two days before his departure to the war council, Drake had commanded that a plan be in place when he returned. The dragons could be killed; the Kingdom will be rid of them, gone for good.

The Killing Story

"I heard Boetius' version of the killing last evening," Drake said, "It sounded plausible at first, but after the wine flowed, so did the story, more crooked than the Calder River. Have you found a reliable source?"

Reynard had. On the King's request, he searched out men who were with Boetius at the kill, specifically, those he trusted to provide an honest report. Boyhood friends, one a member of the archer company and one of the hunting troop, both told a consistent account, an accurate tale for the King's ear this morning.

"Yes, Sire, I believe I have found the truth of the matter."

The telling of the dragon kill hadn't hesitated; it wove and spun its way throughout the Kingdom, from castle folk to stable hands, through the village shops, and from cottage to cottage. Inevitably, like a fly to honey, the tale found its way to the tavern hall where Boetius held court.

Reynard believed his story more factual than the tavern version. At the tavern, Boetius was the center of attention, but each hunter and archer had their part to play. Boetius, like a conductor directing an orchestra, called on each man for his solo part that his particular vantage point of the events provided. In each telling, the story stretched a bit, grew some, but never left out any of the courageous, brave, and bold deeds.

"I appreciate your efforts," Drake said, "I wanted to have the truth before the banquet this evening. And I want it to get back to Boetius that I know the true story. Could you make that happen?"

"Yes, Sire." That knowledge might help control Boetius' boasting and exaggeration.

Seated behind his desk in his study, Drake rocked back in his chair and raised a hand, a signal for Reynard to proceed.

Reynard, always slightly uncomfortable in the chair opposite the King across that vast desktop, took a breath and recounted his story.

✿✿✿✿✿✿

In the West Woods, Boetius and his hunting troop had continued to track the dragons and observe their habits. On their patrol yesterday morning, the trackers and a squad of archers found three dragons feeding at the base of a high-walled ravine.

Because the men were in a lower position and downwind, the dragons were unaware of their approach. Boetius sent two groups of archers, five in each, to the left and right in a flanking move. Boetius and the remaining archers positioned themselves behind boulders at the wide end of the ravine. The far end of the ravine presented a vertical cliff face. The dragons were boxed in, trapped.

Boetius assumed that when surprised by an attack, the dragons would attempt an escape by turning toward his position.

After waiting until the archers were in position atop both sides of the ravine, he gave the signal to attack with a shrill whistle. Startled, two of the dragons, as expected, lumbered toward Boetius' position, and lifted off into the air.

The bowmen on the higher ground targeted the tops and flanks of the dragons without success, their arrows deflecting off. Likewise, the arrows from Boetius and his archers bounced off the underbelly of the dragons as they flew over.

The third smaller dragon, apparently confused and panicked, turned the opposite way toward the cliff face. The target of every archer, struggling, climbing, and beating its wings against the cliff wall, a torrent of arrows showered over and around the dragon. As it reached the summit, an arrow, later discovered to be one of Boetius', struck the back of the dragon's neck. It was the sole vulnerable spot on a dragon, a crease without scales between the head and neck.

❁❁❁❁❁❁

Finishing, Reynard relaxed into his chair.

"So what we have is a lucky arrow," the King said, "not a well-placed arrow?"

"That is the case, I'm sure."

"Good to know. Thank you," Drake said, "Another favor?"

"Yes, Sire."

"I am having a hard time impressing on Ramona the importance of the banquet. She's dragging her feet with the preparations. Would you have a word with Amalia? Maybe she could get Ramona moving. Let her know how disappointed I will be if things aren't perfect."

"Yes, Sire. I'm sure she'd be glad to help." Reynard understood the women's reluctance. They didn't see a killing as an occasion for celebration. Reynard stood to leave.

"Reynard, wait. I meant to ask about your grandfather. How is Samis?"

"Not well, he's quite feeble these days."

"Sorry to hear. How old is he now?"

"Seventy-nine last month."

"Amazing. And his mind?"

"He can still hold his own telling stories. He can tell you

what and when and how things happened years ago, when he was young, his time in the army, and his hunt'en trips in the Northern Wilds. His memory for the past is remarkable. It's the present day he struggles with. Can't remember if he ate breakfast or not or where he put things. He knows people, though. He'd recognize you if he saw you."

"I could tell you some stories myself about my times in the North Woods with your grandfather. Did you know I was stationed there one summer?"

"Yes, Grandpa spoke of it."

Samis' farm in the North Woods was Reynard's favorite place to visit when he was a child. A man of many talents, Samis was a veteran of the King's army, a dairy farmer, a bear hunter, and a master storyteller. He rivaled the Raconteur when it came to telling stories.

"Fergus, Cenhelm, and myself had some good times in those days," Drake said, "Did Samis ever take you to a Van-Du?"

"Yes, when I was ten." Reynard was sure he had stories to match Drake's.

Besides exploring the North Woods area around the farm, Reynard and his brothers, Drake and his friends, in their turn, were taken by Grandpa Samis to a Van-Du. A Van-Du was a raucous gathering every full moon night during the summer.

Grandpa Samis, a popular man in his neck of the woods, had connections with the wild and the undomesticated men that lived in or frequented the North Woods; the quarrymen from Cenhelm's estate, the lumberjacks who worked for Feargus' family, the Northern Shepherd's Clan, the men of the Horse Clan, and native tribesmen from the far northern reaches.

At a Van Du, around a tremendous bonfire, all day and into the night, games of chance were played, contests contested, arguments argued, fights started and finished, and Samis' stash of alcohol liberally dispensed, lubricated relationships and promoted friendships.

"That must have been something for you, that young. Even us young men were intimidated the first time."

"Sure was."

The first time Grandpa had taken Reynard to the Van-Du, Reynard had to admit that the ruckus was unnerving. The stories the men told were outlandish and wild; he couldn't tell truth from a tall tale. However, it was the ride home in the darkened woods that frighten him most. Reynard fretted the whole way, his grandfather sitting next to him asleep on the wagon seat. What good was a drunken old man if they were attacked by bears or wolves?

"That's something I should do, visit old Samis and swap stories." Drake was smiling, a rarity these last several weeks.

"I wouldn't mind going with you. It would be good to spend time listening to his stories again. Me and my brothers had good times on the farm."

"I'd like that. We'll do just that," Drake said, "after we get our present problems behind us."

"Sounds good."

It had been a while since he had such a familiar conversation with Drake.

"And your uncle Munson, how's he. I know he took over the station duties. Does he still run the dairy sideline?"

"He brings their surplus milk and butter into town some evenings. Drops it off at my brothers' place. They keep it cold in their spring overnight. In the morning, one of my cousins that lives in the village peddles it the next morning to the bakers and the cook at the tavern."

"Does he still have those bad habits?"

"Unfortunately," Reynard replied, "After he drops off the milk, he heads straight for the tavern. Stays there till just after dark. The innkeeper makes sure he gets into the wagon, looses the horses, and points them in the right direction. Uncle Munc sleeps sitting up, head bobbing the entire way home. The horses know their way up Braga Road and don't stop till they're at the barnyard gate, which is when Munc wakes up."

"This reminiscing is making me long for the good old days. We can take this up again at the banquet. Let's get Feargus and Cenhelm involved as well—over some of my best wine."

"Yes, that sounds good too." Reynard stood up as he spoke. "I'll take my leave Sire."

"Yes, that will be all. And don't forget to speak with Amalia."

"I'll do it on my way out."

As Reynard left, he looked back over his shoulder at the King, who was sitting back in his chair, his hands behind his neck, smiling. Drake was in a pleasant mood, but it won't last, not with what Reynard saw looming on the horizon.

The Queen's Ride

Amalia had been knitting by candlelight in the darkened hall for the last hour. From her place, seated at the servant's table under the stairs, she could hear the King and Queen arguing. Their voices emanated from the balcony above Amalia's head. King Drake loud enough to be understood; Ramona's voice was muffled. The door to the royal chambers must be open.

Amalia had listened, off and on, to the arguments since the couple rose at sunrise. It was the same argument; Ramona was pressing her points against war with the dragons, the King in opposition. The dragon kill, two days ago, had bolstered the men's confidence. What seemed impossible before, winning a battle against the dragons, was now something they could envision, something attainable.

A door slammed, and above Amalia's head, the King's heavy boots clunked on the creaking balcony floorboards. A moment later, he was descending the stairs into the great-hall. Amalia moved quickly to the foot of the stairs and bowed as the King passed. He did not acknowledge her, but Ramona, who was right behind him, glanced Amalia's way and rolled her eyes.

As they crossed the great-hall, Ramona matched King Drake's long strides. Behind them, Amalia skipped to keep up.

When they reached the main door, Dunstan swung it open for the trio, allowing in the dim light of dawn and a chilled wall of morning air. Beyond the gatehouse and the raised portcullis gate, Reynard stood in front of his horse, the reins in his hand. A groom held the King's horse. Above, deep blue layers of clouds streaked the southern horizon.

A full day's ride to Evora's castle ahead of them, Reynard and King Drake were ready to depart for the war council.

Amalia watched as King Drake and Reynard mounted their horses. She caught Reynard's attention, and he hers; they exchanged private smiles. Reynard raised his head and glanced behind her. Amalia looked back over her shoulder to the two guardsmen standing by the portcullis gate.

"An accidental dragon kill need not lead to all-out war." Ramona, looking up at the King, stood next to his horse with one hand on the King's thigh, and one on his horse's withers.

"Yes, yes, I understand your concerns. We need to go. It's a full day's ride." King Drake too up the reins. "I'll be back in three days."

After the King's horse had only taken a few strides, Ramona called out. "Wait."

King Drake pulled the horse to a halt and turned with a harsh look of displeasure.

"Give my best regards to Saskia. Please."

"Of course." The King trotted his horse out unto the castle road, catching and passing Reynard.

At the edge of the road, Amalia joined Ramona. They watched their men ride down the castle road, through the rampart gate, left on the Village Road, and then right onto East Road. For a minute more, they watched until the riders disappeared.

Still looking ahead, Ramona spoke in a hushed voice. "I'm going on a trip of my own."

"When?"

"Today."

"Should I alert the guardsmen to be ready?"

"No, I'm going alone. And keep it quiet. The guardsmen are the last ones I want to know." Ramona looked briefly over her shoulder at the guards, still at attention at the castle entryway.

"Where are you going?" Amalia asked, now speaking in a whisper.

"I can't tell you. You wouldn't be pleased. We'll talk when I get back—if things go well—if I come back."

"If you come back? What do you mean by that?" Amalia couldn't help her voice getting louder.

"Shush," Ramona put her finger to her lips, "Try to act normally, please. I'm going to need your help. And it won't help if you give away my plans."

"How can I if I don't know what you're planning?"

"I'll need your assistance to make my escape," Ramona cast another glance over Amalia's shoulder at the King's guards. "That's all you need to know for now."

"Escape?" Amalia turned her head and followed Ramona's line of sight to the guardsmen, "From the guards, the King assigned to keep you safe?"

"Don't stare at them. Yes, escape from the guardsmen that the King assigned to keep TABS on me." Ramona's voice conveyed a sense of contempt.

"What is it you want me to do?" Amalia was beginning to suspect that this mission was more dangerous than the Queen's typical subterfuge.

"You're not going to like it. I'm afraid you won't approve."

"Have I ever refused you?" Amalia tried to appear hurt.

"I need you to tell some lies for me," Ramona took Amalia's arm, swung her around, and walked her back toward the castle, passing the guards who fell in several paces behind. The two women walked in silence across the great-hall, up the stairs and into the Queen's chambers where the guards stationed themselves outside the door.

A short while later, Amalia emerged from the chamber door with a bundle under her arm and the plan for Ramona's latest scheme in her head.

In an attempt to look natural, not suspicious, Amalia curtsied to the guards, who didn't seem to notice. She had to force herself to amble across the balcony and not skip any of the steps as she descended the stairs. Across the great-hall, past the throne, to the kitchen door, she moved faster. From a shelf in the kitchen, she grabbed a tie-string sack. Walking through the kitchen, she gathered bread, cheese, dried meat, and a few apples. Amalia did not ask the cook or the servants; the Queen's maid did not have to explain herself.

On out the kitchen back door and into the servant's quarters, Amalia scurried like a mouse pursued by a cat. In her room, a privilege of being the Queen's maid, she placed the Queen's package and food sack on a chair. She sat on her cot, intending to catch her breath and calm herself.

A quick moment later, too nervous to sit still, Amalia rose, took off her dress and put on her riding clothes, a tunic, and trousers, an outfit that still made her somewhat uncomfortable. She pulled her dress back over her head to hide the riding outfit. Next, Amalia took two blankets and a small throw from her bed and tied them up into a bedroll. Then she removed the food from the sack and placed it in a small basket. She repacked the sack with the bedroll, the Queen's package, and the food basket. Finally, she took a long-blade sheathed hunting knife from a shelf, a gift from Ramona, and slid it into the bag and tied it up with a stout cord.

Amalia's heart was pounding in her chest just as it had the day Ramona insisted on giving Amalia her first riding lesson. Ramona wanted a riding companion and saw no reason why it shouldn't be Amalia. Never having ridden a horse, Amalia was uneasy around them. She was afraid of large animals in general and most small ones as well. A merchant's daughter, living in town, had not brought her into contact with many animals or created any desire for it.

Her first summer as a Queen's maid, Amalia spent many hours away from the castle being taught how to ride 'properly' as Ramona called it. They always left the castle riding side-saddle as proper ladies, their dresses fluttering on the horses flank. But once out of sight and in the forest, they removed their dresses, revealing their hidden riding clothes. Now astraddle their horses, they were free to engage in the more robust antics of horsemanship, riding at a canter or gallop and jumping fences or stonewalls. By the end of that summer, Amalia had become an accomplished rider and welcomed every opportunity to go riding with Ramona.

Her riding skills will be of use today. She wondered if Ramona's insistence on riding lessons was secretly a ploy. It was to Ramona's advantage to have a maid who could ride and carry out clandestine errands.

Leaving her speculations behind, Amalia took hold of the sack cord and heaved the sack over her left shoulder onto her back, grasping the cord at her chest. For a moment, Amalia wobbled under the awkward load. She stepped out the door and strode across the courtyard to the castle's west-wall gatehouse. The sentry there didn't even seem to notice her as she passed through and outside the castle.

Along the castle wall, Amalia trudged westward toward the stables. When she arrived, she found Gaston in the tack room sitting in his chair, tilted back against the wall, napping.

"Gaston, wake up." Amalia spoke in a loud voice. She didn't care for Gaston, didn't mind waking him up, kind of enjoyed it.

Gaston and his chair flew forward, catapulting him to his feet. In a daze, he looked for the issuer of the command, his face showing contempt when he realized it was Amalia. "What's it ya want girl?"

"A horse. I am on an errand for the Queen."

Grumbling and swaying every other step or so, Gaston led

the way down the stable aisle, stopped midway, and gestured to a stall on his right. Amalia stopped but kept her load shouldered.

"Take this chestnut gelding. He's nice and gentle. Do ya wants a stable hand to tack him up for ya?" He was scrutinizing Amalia's bundle. Was he suspicious? Did he suspect something?

"No. I don't need help. I don't have time to wait for one of your lazy stable hands, and I don't want a slow mover. I'm not going out to plow the fields. I'll take Beauty." She was pointing at and walking toward a stall that held a black and white mare.

"If you knows what ya wanted and don't needs no help, why'd ya wake me?" Gaston said with disgust. He turned away and walked up the aisle the way they had come. Not to worry about Gaston, he was too lazy to care or to get involved.

Amalia dropped her load to the ground in front of Beauty's stall. She took up the halter and lead rope that hung from the stall door handle and stepped in with the horse. After slipping the halter on, she spent a respectful, but less than usual, amount of time stroking and talking to the horse. Without delay, she led the horse to the tack room, where Gaston was again asleep in his chair. Quietly she gathered up a saddle, a bridle, reins, and saddlebags and fitted them to the horse on the spot. As an afterthought, Amalia slipped back into the tack room and took a canteen off its wall hook.

Back at the stall where she had left the sack, she put the Queen's package, the knife, and food basket in the saddlebags, and then tied the bedroll to the cantle. Amalia led the horse from the stable and around the corner to the paddock fence, which she used to mount. She took a moment to take a breath of the clean, crisp air and pat the horse on the withers.

With a cluck from Amalia, the horse moved out, carrying Amalia along the castle wall, past the parade ground and reviewing stand, past the castle gatehouse door. After a hesitation for a look around, she walked the horse down the cobblestone road and out the rampart gate. In a few moments, they were riding north on Braga Road. The entire time, Amalia had gone unnoticed by all she passed (stable hands, servants, workmen, sentries). A mere maid on a Queen's errand. She took comfort in her invisibility.

Once out of sight of the castle, Amalia brought the horse to a halt at the intersection with the North Road. She scanned the surrounds, slid to the ground, removed her dress, immediately stepped back up in the stirrup, threw a leg over, and straddled the horse. Twisted around in the saddle, Amalia tucked her dress in between the cantle and bedroll. She looked back. Through the trees at the forest edge, the castle was partly visible. The trees, without foliage, only showed red flower buds (a promise of spring).

No going back now. It felt as if she had never made a decision for herself in her life. Under her father's roof, it was his will; in the service of the Queen, the Queen's will. Amalia wanted this to be her decision, but it felt more like fate. In front of her, the North Road snaked out ahead, vanishing over the next hill. Though its purpose was still unknown to her, Amalia felt that Ramona's venture would somehow affect the destiny of the Kingdom. This time, following Ramona would be her choice; she would commit to this path. She pushed Beauty into a canter departure, better to move with earnest into the unknown.

For two hours, moving at a trot most of the time, Amalia followed the North Road as it wound through forest and field, bordered by alternating pasture fences and stands of timber until she arrived at the hunting camp. This terrain was an excellent place for hunting birds (turkeys, pheasant, and grouse). From the camp, the King, Nobles, and their hunters ventured off into the fields and pastures, set snares and catching nets, hid in blinds, and tested their archery skills.

The hunting camp was a simple affair, a level clearing hidden from the road behind a stand of hemlock trees, 40 paces off the road. Central to the camp was a stone-ringed fire-pit surrounded by crude wooden benches hacked out of logs. On the south side of the clearing, the well-worn flat ground made an excellent area for pitching tents. On the west end, across from the road entrance, a roomy three-sided log lean-to sat nestled into the side of a hill, the edge of Calder Mountains, that rose abruptly behind it. At the far northern end, there was a small storage shed that the local sheepherders were tasked with keeping stocked with hay and grain for use by the King's hunters. Between the lean-to and the shed, a short wide path led to a set of hitching posts and a stone encased spring at the bottom of the steep hill where water flowed out of a pipe into a wooden trough. The surrounding maple trees provided shade in the summer and only filtered the sun in winter — an excellent camp.

Amalia slid from the saddle. Her feet touched solid ground with a sense of relief; the first half of her task was complete, successful, and undetected. She walked Beauty to the lean-to and unloaded the saddlebags and bedroll, then continued to the spring, where she tied the horse to a hitching post to allow a drink.

Back at the lean-to, Amalia unpacked, laying out things in order on the low plank bench, a rack for sleeping at the back wall. As she placed each item on the bench, Amalia reviewed a checklist in her mind, worried that something might have been forgotten in haste. She removed the Queen's package from the saddlebags and took out the Queen's riding clothes, a scarf, and a long wool overcoat. Next, she laid out the heavy blankets and a throw for a pillow. From the other side of the saddlebags, she pulled out the food basket that contained enough food for two days. The basket, she took to the shed and secured it in a grain barrel safe from wandering raccoons and bears.

On the way back to the lean-to, a horse whinny caught Amalia's attention and brought her focus to the canteen that hung from the saddle. Ramona would need it. After filling the canteen, she placed it on the lean-to bench. Amalia picked up the saddlebags, threw them over her shoulder and stepped out of the lean-to, but stopped and put them back down; she had forgotten something—the hunting knife. She found it at the bottom of a bag.

She pulled the knife from its sheath to examine the blade for sharpness, although it was too late to do anything about it. It was always too late. Without warning, violence struck her mind. Her hand tightened on the handle; her arm of its own volition with a downward thrust stabbed the knife-point into the wooden bench-top. Stunned, Amalia shuddered, then quickly and guiltily wiggled the standing knife out of the wood and laid it gently alongside the clothes. 'Oh, God,' she thought, 'what am I doing?' Not that God cared. Amalia looked to the sky. All the good praying did her mother; she died a broken woman.

Anger was a stranger in Amalia's mind; she didn't even curse when she stubbed her toe or stuck herself with a needle. Anger hadn't been a stranger to her father; he was always cursing someone (the servants, his clerk, or her mother). He could always conjure something, a reason, to bring his anger into the world. It was his way, the way to get what he wanted. Not hers, though, Amalia wasn't like him.

Still, here she was on a Queen's errand, involved in a dangerous scheme, of which Ramona hadn't shared the purpose. This was the last time for that. Amalia sat down and slumped forward, resting her elbows on her knees, her head in her hands. After a time, she straightened and took a few deep breaths; she was composed again, the anger had peeled away, leaving just simmering anxiety.

Calmed, Amalia got up and fetched the horse, ready to return to the castle. At a walk, the horse took her down the road with plenty of time for the next phase of the plan.

Hours later, on the path alongside the castle wall almost at the stables, Amalia leaned over and glanced at the sundial mounted on the paddock fence. More than an hour until noon, she needed to find ways to prolong her stay at the stable.

Trying to appear calm, she slowly removed Beauty's tack and dawdled with the grooming. She took the horse to the back of the stables and gave it the longest and most lavish bath the horse probably ever had.

It was difficult to resist the urge to check the time on the sundial. She was to wait for the strike of the church clock on the noon hour. The clock wasn't always reliable; sometimes, it failed, and Reynard was called to repair it.

After returning Beauty to her stall, Amalia stood petting and whispering her concerns to the horse. The horse listened patiently. She looked around, found no one was paying attention to her; invisibility played to her advantage still.

The first peal of the clock struck. A shock surged in Amalia; it pierced her chest and radiated down her arms. There was no need for haste, but she hurried to a groomsman at the front of the stables and informed him that the Queen required her horse at the castle gate immediately. He brought out the horse and tied her at the tack room door.

Unnecessary impatience made Amalia tap her foot, as the groom methodically tacked up the horse, first the saddle pad, then the saddle, then he ambled to the other side to pull up the cinch, and then back to the tack room for a bridle. He held two sets, looking from one to the other like he was weighing them.

"The black one. That's the one the Queen likes." Amalia tried to mask the hotness in her voice with a pleasant smile.

He tilted his head, smiled back, and returned the brown bridle to its hook, keeping the black set.

Finally ready, the groomsman with Amalia at his side led the horse from the stable along the castle wall to the gatehouse.

"I'll take her. You can go." She smiled again, hoping she was masking her nerves.

The groom returned the smile, turned away, and sauntered back toward the stables.

After the groom disappeared, Amalia led the horse forward until she was in front of the portcullis gate. From the entrance, she could see that the castle door was open, as per Ramona's request, under the pretense of allowing fresh air into the great-hall.

At the far end of the hall, Amalia could see Ramona seated at the central table facing the doorway, appearing to be at work with needlepoint. The two guardsmen stood behind her, against the wall, near the throne. Amalia put two fingers between her lips and gave a short, loud whistle. Ramona looked up, dropped her needlepoint on the tabletop, and then took a few quick steps to the table end. As she cleared the end of the table, to the astonishment of the guards, she pulled up her dress and bolted toward the open doorway.

As Ramona cleared the gatehouse door, Amalia dropped to one knee, the other raised to provide a mounting block. A moment later, Ramona was at the horse's side. She reached between her legs, grasped the back of her dress, and pulled it through and up, effectively creating baggy pantaloons. Ramona stepped on Amalia's knee; mounted the horse, her legs bare below the knee. Over her shoulder, Amalia saw the two guardsmen arrive at the castle door. Their faces registered shock and dismay at the sight of the Queen on horseback and out of their reach.

Ramona's feet were in the stirrups and the reins in her hands. Amalia pressed herself against the horse's shoulder.

"I'm worried about you. I wish you'd tell me what you plan to do in the North Woods." Amalia said, knowing there was no time now for the Queen to explain.

"Better you don't know for now. But if I'm not back by sunset tomorrow, you know where to send the search party." Ramona looked to the guards.

"Good luck." Amalia gave up her questioning and stepped back.

Ramona's horse leaped into a canter. The guards watching, panic on their faces, turned and ran toward the stables. Amalia remained at the gate, waiting to execute the next and most distasteful part of the plan.

The guards, jogging, leading their horses, arrived at the gate and confronted Amalia.

"Where's the Queen go'en?" said the head man in a stern voice and a face to match.

"I really shouldn't say."

"We's under the King's orders. Where's she go'en?" A forceful and louder voice.

Amalia held out a moment, trying to present both confusion and reluctance. "She didn't say exactly, but she mentioned something to do with a meeting in Morodon, a secret shipment, I believe." She tried putting on a submissive face. Boldface lying was easier than she had imagined.

Apparently satisfied, the guardsmen mounted their horses and rode off. Amalia watched their progress down the castle road, out the gate and into the village, the opposite direction that Ramona had taken. That should keep them busy for a while. Amalia wondered if she should have been more elusive, held out a little longer. Yet the ploy had worked; the guardsmen were on their fool's errand. She must have played it well. She was reluctantly pleased with herself.

In the late evening, after sunset, the guardsmen returned and sought out Amalia. They found her as she was coming out of the servant's quarters into the castle's courtyard. At some point on their ride along the Morodon Road, they must have realized they had been duped and turned back.

Standing ominously in front of her, blocking her path, they presented another opportunity for her to practice a manipulation. The headman's voice started out demanding and angry but soon shifted to pleading as Amalia presented a calm and unyielding front.

She explained that the Queen had promised to return by sunset the next day, long before the King returned the following evening. She pointed out it would be in everyone's best interest that the Queen's venture and their failure to keep track of her did not come to the King's attention. And the Queen could be counted on to look favorably on their discretion. Since they seemed hesitant, she again provided reassurance that the Queen would definitely be back by sunset, but she worried that her face might have betrayed her lack of conviction. She felt she had provided significant reasoning, promoting the idea of mutual benefit, plausible, if not quite entirely accurate, or guaranteed to work out.

Amalia watched the men's faces as they entered into whispering deliberations. Probably, they were considering the advantages of having done the Queen a favor. The commoners loved the Queen and went to extremes to protect her secrets and support her plans. And although most of the Nobles did not like her and her unconventional, less than Noble ways, they were careful not to cross her. It didn't take the guards long before logic and self-interest prevailed. The senior guard nodded their agreement, turned away, and left Amalia standing alone in the courtyard.

Things were going as planned, flawlessly. Maybe Ramona wasn't the only one with a talent for subterfuge. Despite her success, Amalia felt uncomfortable pangs of guilt, nagging worry for Ramona's safety, and the fear of discovery. Thoughts that tormented her throughout the evening and into the night disrupted her sleep. The next day was much the same, filled with increasing tensions as the day wound slowly on, ever so tediously, toward sunset.

An hour before sunset, Amalia took to the keep roof. She stationed herself at the west-facing parapets, from which she could see the Braga Road where it emerged from the forest, the place Ramona should first appear on her return. Amalia's heart was pounding, her skin crawled, and her breathing was short and quick. And then sudden relief as Ramona came riding out of the forest at a trot. Amalia watched Ramona ride along the road and around the castle's rampart wall, where she lost sight of her. Amalia left her station, descended the keep's stairwell recklessly, ran through the courtyard, out the west wall gate, and arrived at the castle gatehouse in time to see Ramona riding up the castle road.

At the gate, Ramona slid off the saddle to the ground. The sentry rushed forward and took up the horse's reins.

Amalia dashed to her side. "Did you accomplish your mission?"

"Yes," Ramona whispered through a brilliant smile.

"Tell me."

"Not here."

Ramona took Amalia by the elbow, and the two strode off into the castle. Inside the great-hall, they were alone.

Ramona's face beamed with excitement. "I have so much to tell you. It's fantastic, better than I had hoped. I know you won't believe me. But I swear it's the truth; I do." Ramona hesitated, and her face shifted to solemn. "I can't tell you now; it will have to wait. I want to show you instead. We will have to bide our time and find a way to sneak off to the North Woods. Then you'll see."

Amalia needed to protest, but she knew it was fruitless to try to thwart Ramona's will.

Returning Home

They had been riding hard, driven by the King's haste to return home. The horses' heavy hoofs clattered loudly on the wooden bridge with a staccato rhythm. King Drake always rode one of his black, heavy horses when he wanted to make a regal impression. The pair of matching horses were a magnificent sight, shinning black except for a white blaze on the face and white feathered front feet. Today, light horses would have been a better choice. The bulky beasts were laboring under the strain of a half-day of trotting that the King and Reynard had pressed since they left the Evora castle early that morning. The coolness of the air provided comfort for the men but wasn't sufficient for the horses.

Drake signaled for a halt as they reached the far end of the bridge. "We'll let the horses have a drink."

They followed a path off to their right between bare trees and yellow flowering bushes to the edge of the river. Side by side, the horses stepped into the water and lowered their heads. Rivulets of sweat were running down their bowed necks, and the white lather marked the edge of the saddle blankets. Reynard was not used to riding, and a heavy horse's broad back was like straddling a table. His inner thighs and butt appreciated the break. He would much rather be driving these horses than riding them. They were built for draft, plowing fields, and farm work, not riding long distances.

More than halfway home, the war council was behind them, and only God knows what was in front of them. They had passed the East Road tariff station and were now well within the boundaries of Enid. For hours, they rode through the Kingdom's eastern farmlands on the East Road that tracked alongside the Morodon River. It was these fertile bottom-lands along the river that produced Enid's grains and foodstuffs, adding to the wealth of the Kingdom. Now, they rested near the point where the turbulent Calder River flowed into and mingled with the larger Morodon River.

"As I see it, the council was of no value," the King said, "We learned nothing. All the other kingdoms have failed in their battles with the dragons."

"Agreed."

The Kings of the alliance who usually squabble and fight over most anything were driven by their fear of dragons to consultation and cooperation. In the compact that was formalized at the war council, all agreed to share information about the dragons and any tactics or strategies that proved useful. Elimination of the dragons was their priority, at least for now.

"We had the most to offer, one dragon killed." King Drake was undoubtedly pleased with himself.

"Yes, no one else offered anything of substance," Reynard said. In the meeting, King Drake was the center of attention. His telling of the killing was more in tune with Boetius' account than reality, as he avoided the role that luck had played.

"You met with Queen Saskia's weapon master. Anything come of that?"

"He shared the techniques he uses to produce those magnificent short swords and daggers."

The women of the royal court wore short, colorful tunics (reds, deep blues, or sea-green) with tan trousers underneath. A wide belt at their waist secured a dagger on the right thigh. The position made it readily available to grasp and raise quickly for a downward thrusting attack. On their left side, a short sword gave the women another option for a slashing defense or attack. The sheaths were of an open design meant to display the brilliant shine of the weapons' blades, a warning to any adversary. The unique coloration of the blades and the elaborately carved wooden hilts made for impressive weapons.

"Not much help with dragons." Drake sounded unimpressed.

Reynard chose not to respond. His interest in metalworking could not be restrained, even if the knowledge could not be put to immediate use.

From the reports at the war council, Reynard and the King now had knowledge of the surrounding kingdom's engagements with dragons. The other Kings had sent their Knights into battle armed with all manner of weaponry; lances, spears, arrows, and swords. Even large-scale Catapults capable of showering down a barrage of rock were tried. But they couldn't be maneuvered fast enough to get within range of the dragons before they flew off.

Fifty men at a time had been engaged in combat with small groups of dragons (three to five). Braga had deployed a full contingent against the dragons. Duren, a smaller force of Knights on horseback only, and Evora had attacked dragons in their northern wilds with archers. Despite the numbers thrown against them, the dragons always fared well, either by successfully driving the army back or by flying off at the noisy approach of an armed contingent.

The kingdoms of Chambold and Dacian to the south of Enid had not yet seen any dragons in their territories.

"I would like to go to Braga and meet with their weapon's master. He wasn't at the council," Reynard said, "I want to inspect the lightweight catapult he built." Reynard was thinking of the small, maneuverable catapult the Braga men had used to launch a spear.

"I heard that was a failure also?"

"It was, but I have some ideas of my own. Maybe with modifications, it might be useful."

"Didn't King Wilhelm use it when he launched the full assault he spoke of?" King Drake's counterpart in Braga was King Wilhelm.

"He did."

"Wilhelm pressed an attack similar to what Boetius has been advocating for," The King continued, "I believe Wilhelm said he sent 20 Knights, 30 men-at-arms and 40 archers against a group of five dragons and did not kill or wound any of them."

"With substantial casualties," Reynard said, "Four men were killed, and ten wounded, four of those critically. They may not survive their wounds."

"I see. He didn't offer that." The King looked surprised.

"I learned it from a friend, one of his men-at-arms. The injuries were mostly accidents, results of chaos and confusion, similar to our encounter. Several men were crushed to death when a dragon, trying to escape, trampled them.

"If we rush into battle without a plan for success, we can expect the same." Reynard hoped to elicit the King's concern. He wanted the King to proceed with caution.

"Yes, but we should be able to take advantage of our new knowledge of the Dragon's weakness," Drake spoke with obvious frustration bordering on anger. "Now that we know, we can kill them with a single arrow. We must try to replicate Boetius' success."

"Hard to replicate luck," Reynard said.

"Yes, just good fortune that Boetius' arrow struck the back of the dragon's neck," the King said, "Of course he says it was skill, his plan all along. Says he just knew about the dragon's vulnerable spot. Just came to him. The people are now calling it 'The Magnificent Shot.'"

"To be expected." Reynard was well aware of the King's frustration with Boetius' bragging. It was nothing new. Where the rivalry between Boetius and Feargus was out in the open, there had always been a subtle conflict simmering between Boetius and Drake, only kept in check then by Drake's rank.

"You were with the army, observed that fight. You saw nothing we could use to our advantage?" King Drake asked, "Keep in mind; we know their vulnerability now."

In Reynard's mind, the skirmish was vivid and horrible. In that chaotic scene, he could not imagine anything that the King's men could have done to kill a dragon. Reynard didn't have any ideas of substance, no new weapon, or new tactic. He was imagining how difficult it would be to maneuver on horseback behind a fire-breathing dragon and strike a blow to the back of its head with a lance, or for an archer to hit a moving dragon's vulnerable spot with an arrow.

"Not as yet, Sire. The dragons don't even fear us. We can't expect to corner them like Sir Boetius did in the ravine. Although slow and lumbering, they can fly off when they choose. If we had an effective weapon, something. They need to feed. Maybe they could be baited or lured to a spot of our choosing. But without a sure way to kill them ..." Reynard poured out random thoughts.

"I want you to meet with Boetius and Feargus," the King interrupted, "And fill them in on the war council and see if they have come up with anything of value. It's possible that while we were away, Boetius or Feargus have devised a plan to take advantage of the dragon's weakness."

"I will arrange a meeting for tomorrow morning." Reynard did not look forward to another meeting with Boetius and Feargus.

"What of Feargus? Do you think he can be persuaded to support the cause?"

"You have commanded it." Reynard knew Feargus would fall in line.

"I would prefer that his heart was in it."

"He's not unwilling, just cautious by nature. He will do his duty." Reynard stated what the King already knew, but he probably wanted to hear Reynard say it.

"He has refused to engage his men again unless he can be convinced that there is a possibility of victory," said King Drake, "I can't fault him."

"I have to agree that the full assault Boetius calls for would be reckless, especially now that we know what happened to King Wilhelm's men in Braga."

"After your meeting in the morning, I want all of you in the great-hall in the late afternoon. Say, four o'clock."

"Yes, Sire."

"The horses have rested long enough." A pull on the right rein, Drake's horse wheeled around and stumbled up the steep bank onto the road. Reynard followed, both men now on the road heading home.

Reynard had traveled little but preferred to stay at home and work in his shop. He had made only a few trips in his entire life. He was only briefly out of the Kingdom during the wars with Nendos, and a couple of times to Morodon, each time on kingdom business under King Drake's direction. The best part of those trips was returning home, the place he wanted to be. But today was different, trotting alongside King Drake, reluctance knotted his stomach. This was not how he wanted to feel about home and what lay ahead.

The Revelation

Ramona was surprised that Amalia didn't meet her for breakfast; she could be counted on every morning. She walked over to Dunstan at the great-hall main door and asked if he had seen Amalia. He said that she had been through much earlier, had her breakfast, and that he was to tell the Queen that Amalia had gone to the stables.

Ramona returned to the table intending to force down a breakfast.

She hoped that Amalia was being discrete; she did not want any of the King's guardsmen alerted. Today, she believed it safe to go to the North Woods, less chance of discovery. For the last four days, the men had been occupied at the training grounds, practicing their new battle tactics. Amalia and Ramona would travel on the North Road to the hunting camp and were unlikely to encounter the King's men.

Ramona wasn't sure if her guard detail could be trusted, so she challenged Drake to be rid of them. The guards he assigned for protection while he was away in Evora, a flimsy excuse, were no longer needed, she declared, now that he was home. He countered that because of the dragon war, they were still required. Ramona asserted that the idea she needed protection from dragons was absurd. She was perfectly safe here in her own Kingdom, and if he thought not, maybe she should take to wearing a dagger and short sword like the ladies in Evora. She understood that Reynard now knew how to make them. Deflated and with other pressing matters, Drake conceded; Ramona won the sham argument.

Her breakfast finished, the gloppy oatmeal was not mixing well in her nervous stomach. It was time to find Amalia and be off.

As she passed Dunstan at the great-hall door, he said, "Good day to you, Your Highness. Have a pleasant ride." Through the open doorway, he nodded to Amalia, who stood outside the castle gate, holding two horses.

"Oh, thank you, Dunstan, but I plan to spend the whole day in my chambers with Amalia." Ramona winked.

"A pleasant day to ya then," he replied, "I knows noth'en bouts a ride." He looked pale. Ramona touched his shoulder, and his habitual toothless grin returned to his aged face.

"Thank you, Dunstan." She needed to remember to have a word with the cook when she returned, make sure Dunstan got an extra portion of meat for supper, and one of those sweet scones he liked so much.

Ramona took the reins from Amalia, leaned in, and whispered, "You should have waited at the stables for me. We need to keep this trip a secret. The fewer people who see what we are doing, the better."

"Sorry, Ma'am."

Without another word, the women mounted and rode off down the castle road. They moved quickly out Braga road, stopping briefly at the forest edge to off their dresses that concealed their riding clothes.

During the first half of the two-hour ride on their way to the hunting camp, Ramona poured out her concerns with the coming war. Amalia was silent, listening, probably consumed by anxiety. Ramona considered the cost of this conflict, which appeared to be, to her mind, a futile endeavor. There would be casualties, deaths, and grief. So much pain and suffering, and to what end? What was to be gained, besides so-called glory and the satisfaction of egos?

In the latter half of the ride, Ramona fell into silence as well, occupied with her own consuming thoughts. Maybe she should speak with Drake; share what she knew of the dragons. Maybe she shouldn't keep it secret? No, no, no, he wouldn't listen to her. He'd call her crazy, say she was only a woman. She was sick of his condescension, heard it all before. She'd show him who was crazy. But then, maybe she was crazy. Could she be sure of her own senses? Perhaps it had been a dream or a hallucination. No, it wasn't. Amalia will confirm it.

Ramona revived from her trance as they reached the path that led into the hunting camp.

As they dismounted near the spring hitching post, Amalia said, "I was starting to worry that you didn't trust me."

"Come sit with me at the fire circle."

They tied their horses at the water trough and made their way back to the fire-ring in the middle of the hunting camp, taking up seats alongside each other on a log bench. Ramona brought along her saddlebags. "Of course, I trust you, but I wasn't sure what to do. I took my time to think it through, not wanting to involve you if it wasn't necessary. I didn't want to put you at risk. But the time has come to take action, and I need your help."

"What is it you want me to do?"

"I want to provide aid to the dragons, and I can't do it by myself."

"The dragons? Why help the dragons?" Amalia said, "The men are committed to hunting them down. We need to support the men, not the dragons."

"I believe that if we provide for the dragons, we can minimize the casualties on both sides."

"How is that possible? It's too late. We tried to stop the men from starting this war. What else could we do?"

"If we can get the dragons out of the Kingdom, we can avert the inevitable casualties." Ramona had not expected an argument from Amalia.

"How could we possibly do that?"

"What if I told you we could communicate with the dragons? Can you imagine the possibilities?" Ramona paused to let that suggestion sink in. Amalia's eyes shift back and forth, her brow furrowed.

"But that surely isn't possible," Amalia said, adding after a hesitation, "Is it?"

"Yes, but it is. That was the purpose of my trip to the North Woods, to find a dragon and find out what they were about. I had a hunch it was possible to communicate with them."

"You talked with a dragon?"

"Not talking exactly. It was as if we were exchanging thoughts, pictures really. It's hard to describe."

"So tell me what happened. Tell me the whole story. What happened those two days you were gone?" Amalia sounded as if she was giving orders.

"It's going to be hard to believe."

"Tell me already. I'll let you know if it sounds believable." Amalia was visibly losing patience, the first time ever that Ramona could recall.

"First, I want to thank you again for helping me that day. I couldn't have done it without you."

"RAMONA, please!"

"Sorry. This is what happened." Ramona began the narration of her story.

✿✿✿✿✿

I wanted to get to the hunting camp as fast as possible. I arrived two hours after midday. After changing into my riding clothes, I mounted my horse and started up the north road, heading for the place where the shepherds had their encounter with a dragon. They thought the dragon was threatening them, but it occurred to me that the dragon may have been trying to communicate. After all, if the dragon had meant them harm, it easily could have.

I found the spot they described near a pasture gate along the road. Sitting there on my horse, I felt ridiculous. What did I expect? That a dragon was just going to appear? I walked the pastures and surrounding woods. But of course, I found nothing. There was no place for a dragon to hide. I traveled up the road farther north, exploring side trails and paths as I went. With the sun setting, I knew I only had an hour of daylight left for my search, so I turned and headed back toward camp, exploring the same places I had earlier, hoping foolishly for a different result.

Back at the camp, it was just getting dark. I built a small fire to warm against the night chill and made a dinner of the food you provided. When darkness closed in, I crawled into the lean-to and curled up in my blankets, very disappointed and at a loss as what to do next. I thought it naïve to have expected a dragon to be waiting for me on the road.

I didn't sleep well and woke up the next morning still without a plan, so I made a fire and ate a leisurely breakfast of cold cheese and bread. I sat at the fire-ring reminiscing about the times I spent at the hunting camp with my childhood friends. We used it as a base of operations from which we launched explorations of the surrounding area. I remembered that at the top of the hill that rises behind the camp, there's a rock ledge that provides an excellent view of the territory.

Following my memories of childhood adventures, I went to the water trough. It's fed by a mountain spring that emerges from a rock crevice in the forested hillside. From the spring, I started up the hill. It's littered with moss-covered dark stones and lush patches of ferns. In the springtime, the rocky slope erupts with streams that cascade through the forest, but fortunately, the weather's been dry. I made quick work of the early gradual slope but was then slowed by the abrupt steepness and rugged rock outcroppings that confronted me. I used tree trunks as handholds and propelled myself up, scrambling up and over the ledges.

The hillside provided the same pleasure it did as when I was a child. It wasn't long before my youthful inspired energy propelled me to the top of the hill and edge of the cliff ledge. The view was dramatic, but not as vast as I remembered it.

As I sat there with my feet dangling over the edge, I combed the skies and the landscape for dragons. I had a marvelous view of the North Mountain twin peaks and the skirting foothills with their quilt-like patches of green sheep pasture. Short sections of the North Road that meandered through the hills were visible here and there, passing the horseman's camps and cottages. To the south, in the lowlands, the castle was just visible sitting on its little hill in the far distance.

But my new vantage point didn't offer any hope of finding a dragon, and I was feeling even more foolish.

I decided to give up and go home, but then I felt a rush of wind on my sweat-soaked back, and my body tensed with a jolt. In an urgent need to move, I twisted around, got to my hands and knees, and jerked my head up to see a dragon, not ten paces away. Later, I thought it amazing that such a huge creature could land right behind me with no sound except that rustle of the wind. But at the time, in my mind, the foolishness of expecting to find a dragon was replaced by the foolishness of actually finding one.

The dragon was, as Drake described, a strange creature, with sunlit glistening scales. The body was colored in shades of green with hints of blue, the belly in bands of amber, and the long neck and tail have a row of yellow fins from its head to the tip of its long tail. It squatted back on stout back legs, talons gripping the earth. Its front arm-like legs were poised in the air above me. Its head, mouth agape, displaying fangs and a slithering forked tongue, tilted ever so slightly from side to side. But it was its yellow eyes with black silted pupils that attracted and held my attention.

The dragon was much larger than I expected, more frightening than I could have imagined. Nothing could have prepared me for it.

Trying my best to control my building panic, I got to my feet. My heels on the cliff edge, my back to free air, and a fierce beast stood between me and any hope of escape. My heart was pounding in my chest, and my breathing had stopped.

It felt as if I was captivated by those penetrating eyes for a long time, but it probably wasn't; I don't really know. Then, unexpectedly, the dragon's eyes changed; the black slits opened into ovals of soft white glow. Then I was sensing something, seeing something, a dreaming vision. I can't explain it. I experienced an image of a foreign place, unknown, but peaceful and secluded. My body calmed; my heart slowed; my fear of the dragon faded; I was breathing.

I realized the dragon was transmitting the images to me: I don't know how. I couldn't help feeling my quest was justified, and of course, happy with the dragon's apparent benevolence.

A parade of pictures came into my mind, morphing from one image to another. I tried to maintain a focus, but I got disoriented and stumbled a few steps toward the dragon. Good thing too, I could have toppled backward off the cliff. Vertigo overwhelmed me, and I fell to my knees when they buckled. The dragon backed away several paces and waited, apparently, for me to come to my senses. I sat down, cross-legged. The best position, I thought, to continue doing whatever it was I was doing with the dragon.

The visions continued to invade my thoughts. I closed my eyes; that helped me focus. Gradually she conveyed what she wanted me to know—that the dragons were hunting for food and that their food resources at home had been depleted because of several harsh winters. I saw images of young dragons calling for food, infertile unhatched eggs. The dragons, at least 80 in their clan, are living on a subsistence diet, close to starvation.

The images stopped. I was myself again, in my own mind only. Everything around me was clear, distinct, and bright. The dragon emitted a graveled groan. I realized it was my turn to send messages to her, pictures of what I wanted to express. I tried to make up pictures in my mind, tried to hold my concentration on them, and failed. The dragon groaned. I tried again and again and then finally locked in for a moment, a scene of myself with a bow in hand hunting deer. The dragon groaned, but the pitch was higher. Pleased, I thought. She had gotten the message.

I continued working at it, creating, focusing, concentrating, trying to hold an image in my mind. After many hours, I got better at it, making pictures that she was apparently seeing in her mind. We continued exchanging images, getting confused at times, but gradually improving the clarity. Visualizing pictorials was the most effective way I found to transmit ideas and information, similar to ancient pictographs found in caves.

I let her know that I would help them avoid the army, find a way to provide food, and to get them back to their home.

❀❀❀❀❀❀

Ramona got a glimpse of Amalia's expression. "I know, an ambitious promise."

"I plan to enlist other people to help. I told her so. You're the first." Ramona smiled and waited for a smile in return, which Amalia provided reluctantly.

Ramona continued with the tale.

❀❀❀❀❀❀

I told her we needed a way to contact her, communicate at a distance, arrange meetings, and a way for the dragons to identify friends, those people recruited to help.

After one of the high-pitched growls, the dragon began searching the rocky clifftop, selecting loose stones, each near the size of a loaf of bread. She pushed them into a circle with her nose and then raised her head high above them. Onto the bed of stones, she shot a narrow stream of blue flame. The stones began to melt, shrink, and change color from dark gray to white. When she stopped the fire bath, the stones were now small, smooth, white, and relatively flat ovals the size of a robin's egg.

In the time it took the stones to cool, the dragon let me know that each of my friends should carry one of these stones. The stone acts like a beacon that the dragons can sense. Additionally, it can be used by a person to call to a dragon, project images to the dragons from a distance.

We agreed to meet again, on the clifftop, after I had time to develop a plan of action. She flew off, and I gathered up the stones into my shirt and tied it up to keep them secure during my descent back to the camp.

❦❦❦❦❦

Ramona paused, waiting for Amalia to digest the story, waiting for her to say something, anything. Amalia's face was blank, mouth slightly open, eyes wide and focused on Ramona. She didn't speak.

"I'm ready to meet with the dragon again." Ramona watched Amalia for a reaction. "I need to practice communications. And I need someone besides myself who can communicate with them."

Ramona sat quietly, waiting.

Finally, Amalia said, "That is quite a story. I'd have to say 'unbelievable' if I had heard it from anyone else but you."

"Thank you for believing me. You do really believe me?"

"Yes."

"I'm so glad to finally share it with someone. It's been a

difficult secret to keep, this last week." Ramona reached into her saddlebags and pulled out a black velvet pouch secured at the top with a blue ribbon, which she quickly untied. Unto a flat rock, a stone of the fire ring, she emptied the contents of the bag, a pile of small white stones.

"These are the stones the dragon's friends are supposed to carry?" Amalia asked.

"Yes, take one."

Tentatively, Amalia pushed the stones around with her finger before selecting one and taking it into her palm.

"I keep mine on a lanyard," Ramona said as she pulled a necklace of braided grass from her shirt that displayed one of the small stones attached at the bottom. She held out the stone and locked eyes with Amalia. "What do you say, shall we call her now?"

"Now?" Amalia's voice had an edge of alarm; the blood drained from her face.

"Yes."

"How do you call a dragon?" Amalia asked.

"Just think of a dragon. Think about asking her to come. Make it a picture in your mind."

"Me? You want me to do it?"

"Yes, might as well try it now, see if you can. I will help. Take my hand. Close your eyes."

"Okay." Amalia put one hand in Ramona's, closed her eyes and closed her other hand on the stone. A few moments later, she opened her hand. The stone glowed softly. "It's warm. What does that mean?"

"She's heard us." The stone at Ramona's neck was also glowing.

"What do we do now?"

"I was picturing the cliff top in my mind. We will meet her there. It's a safe place, out of the way," The glow of Ramona's stone pulsed a few times ever so lightly. "Are you with me? Are you ready to meet a dragon?"

Amalia got to her feet and stretched herself tall. "Yes, I'm ready."

Ramona stood as well. She was taken aback; this was too easy. She had rehearsed her arguments and counter-arguments, means of coaxing, inducement, and coercion even, to persuade Amalia to her cause. All not needed, apparently.

"The first time you talk with her, sit down and close your eyes. Don't want to risk you stumbling off the cliff." Ramona's attempt at humor was lost on Amalia.

"Yes, Ma'am." Amalia was visibly shaken. Ramona thought she saw her shoulders tremble.

The two women left the campfire circle and made their way to the hillside and began their climb.

Training for Battle

In the early morning sun at the westerly edge of the training ground, Feargus sat his horse, watching the King's army in their final day of training. The bay horse's neck arched down, its muzzle in the newly green tufts of grass. Feargus stretched up tall for a moment; the saddle leather creaked.

The men had been out every day of the last 25 practicing the tactics of Boetius' new battle strategy. They started their training exercises two days after King Drake and Reynard returned from the council. Boetius had lobbied for engagement within a week, claiming he could have readiness after only a week's practice. Feargus called for a full month of training. The King had sided with Feargus' argument. Drake also felt that they should wait for Reynard and his brothers to finish the manufacture of the newly designed shields and lances.

Perhaps now they had a chance, now that a dragon had been killed. Maybe Boetius' plan will be successful. Boetius was counting on the dragons being dimwitted, lacking even the cunning of a game animal. He took their slow-moving nature and slow response to threats as a lack of intelligence, something the men could use to their advantage. Feargus wasn't so sure. Even game animals learned to avoid hunters. Now vulnerable, perhaps the dragons will take heed and flee from the King's army. Feargus knew that was too much to ask for, a hope only.

Feargus shifted in his saddle. Over 100 paces away, King Drake was pacing his horse back and forth, a relief from standing most of the day. Astride his large, black horse, the King had the best vantage point, atop a hillock at the southern edge of the training ground.

What was Drake's assessment of Boetius' battle plan? The King came every day to observe the exercises. He could have just as easily watched from the roof of the castle keep with a spyglass. The training ground, an expansive flat stretch of land just west of the castle, was only a short distance away. It was easily reached by way of Braga Road. Kings had used the area for centuries to prepare their Knights and soldiers for battle. Combat skills and fighting techniques were tried, honed, and perfected on this field. And now, in Drake's reign, his army was preparing for what some were already calling the Dragon War.

Only the first regiment was on the field. The King had overruled Boetius and refused to call up the second regiment. He did not see the value in training old men and boys for this fight.

The field, for training purposes, was sectioned into three parts. As usual, Feargus and his Knights claimed the west side of the grounds; the archers the east side. Boetius and Hartmann were with the archers today, targets set up, practicing. The ground lancers currently occupied the middle, along with a peculiar, wobbly tower that sat dead center.

With his back to the tree line, Feargus watched his Knights riding back and forth in front of him, practicing their traditional jousting skills. They aimed their lances at the ring targets that hung by cords from a crossbar that extended out from the top of a pole. The target rings, hanging from each arm of the crossbar, varied in size from a three-hand width down to a half-hand width diameter. The rays of the low hanging sun streamed over Feargus' shoulder, making the Knight's dull armor glow orange. The older Knights insisted on using a full complement of armor for themselves and their horses. Whereas, the younger men only wore chest-plates and put no armor on their horses. Speed and agility were more important than protection, although the lack of protection from dragon fire concerned Feargus.

A Knight on a warhorse rode past Feargus in a thundering approach to the targets. Then suddenly, a man on a small brown and white paint—it was Cenhelm—flashed by on the Knight's outer flank. Reaching the target a moment before, Cenhelm swung his lance across in front of the Knight's lance, knocking it away, and took the target ring on its tip. The Knight pulled his horse up, lifted his lance straight up above his head, and let fly a series of loud curses. Cenhelm rode a trotting circle around the older Knight, extending his lance, displaying the ring on the tip. A chorus of laughter from the surrounding men drowned out the cursing.

Feargus should reprimand Cenhelm, but he had played similar pranks on the older Knights himself. The younger men opted for light horses, quicker and faster, that easily outmaneuvered the big horses on the battlefield. The Knights on warhorses had their advantages, suitable for setting up a solid line of defense. But Knights on light horses were superior on the attack. They had proved themselves in the battles in the wars with the Kingdom of Nendos. In those encounters, Drake sent out a customary line of Knights on heavy horses at a prodding charge. When the enemy committed in kind, the young men on their light horses, released from the rear and in flanking moves on both sides, were soon behind the enemy line creating havoc.

For this fight, Feargus hoped to persuade the old Knights

to use light horses. Knights on heavy horses would be useless in a fight with dragons. Regardless, the old men held to their traditions, to the familiar, and refused to change.

Just beyond the Knight's training area, squads of men-at-arms, commoners, were practicing with a modified lance now attached to a newly designed body harness. Also, each man was now equipped with a new shield. It had a U-shaped cutout in the middle to accommodate the forward extension of the lance while still keeping the shield directly in front of the soldier.

All the first regiment lancers, the men afoot, were on the field today, now formed up in rows and columns moving in the same direction from north to south. The regiment was composed of two platoons, the red and the green platoons, five squads in each, the men respectively wearing red or green armbands. The lancer squads consisted of eight men each. The squad leaders, corporals on the left end of each line, called out commands, the squads marched forward, then back, then right, then left, while trying to maintain a tight shoulder to shoulder formation. Feargus had been working his lancer troops hard. He wanted them to be in the best shape possible and as prepared as possible.

The drills had improved; lines were straight, formations tighter, and lances were not being dropped anymore. The lances, intended to prod a dragon, were more manageable, thanks to Reynard. He had designed a system of harness and straps that made it easier for the men to carry and maneuver the weapon. A strap attached to the balance point of the lance was connected to the top of the shoulder harness, allowing most of the weight to be transferred to the shoulder. A ring at the butt of the lance was looped into the waist belt, which put a man's weight behind the thrust of a lance.

Feargus turned to the pony-boy on his right, one of two with him at the moment. "Prepare the red platoon for the box drill."

The red platoon occupied the north-central part of the grounds, the green platoon in the south-central area. The boy, astride a black and white cob, bolted and charged across the grounds at a gallop. In seconds, he closed the 150 paces and was at Cenhelm's side, delivering Fergus' orders. These older boys, who made up the army's signal corps, lived to ride and ride fast. They were reserves, called up from the Horse Clan when needed. Six of them were attached to the army for this campaign. The Horse Clan did not submit men-at-arms for the King's army; in times of war, they provided logistics support and these boys, who, on horseback, acted as signalmen and message runners. This agreement, along with the Horse Clan's obligation to supply horses to the King's men, had been made in ancient times and never challenged.

The boys' riding skills were amazing. They rode better than even Feargus or Cenhelm, even though both Knights had been trained to ride by men of the Horse Clan. The boys rode without saddles, used a bridle without a bit, and rarely touched the reins even when moving at full gallop. The only way they could be more connected to their horses was if they were centaurs. The story was that they learned to ride before they could walk. Where Cenhelm could not resist showing off his skills, the pony-boys did not. They kept to themselves, and never left their horses, beautifully colored paints or pintos. They ate with and slept with their ponies. They could not be convinced to leave their horses to enter a shelter, not even in foul weather. Presumably, they liked horses better than they liked people.

"Ta-tahh, Ta-tahh, Ta-tahh," Short-long repeating trumpet blasts brought the red platoon to attention and a quick assembly into the attack formation, a line of three squads in front and two squads directly behind them. At the northern end of the grounds, Cenhelm was taking charge of the red platoon. The men of the green platoon jogged out of the way to the edge of the field.

Cenhelm, astride his horse, behind the lines, was barking orders to the pony-boy who issued the commands to the men with his drum. Each boy carried a trumpet attached to a shoulder strap and a flat metal drum that hung on his left hip from his belt. The instruments were used to convey orders above the noise of battle. Feargus had to credit Boetius for his well thought out signaling system, using drums and trumpets to command the army for the specific maneuvers his tactics required.

"Attack," Cenhelm barked.

"Boom—Boom—Boom." Lances swung down from vertical to horizontal, aimed at a currently invisible enemy as the men marched forward.

"Retire."

"Boom, Boom—Boom, Boom." The squads halted; lances returned to vertical at the shoulder.

"Defend."

"Boom, Boom, Boom, Boom." As the lancers dropped to one knee, they swung their shields off their backs and down in front of them.

"Begin the box drill," Feargus spoke to the pony-boy. The boy's horse jumped ahead several paces. The boy sounded three short blasts meant for Sir Cenhelm. "Ta, Ta, Ta."

Cenhelm called out his orders to his pony-boy, whose horse, a few steps away, stood like a statue as its rider banged out the command cadence. "Boom—Boom—Boom."

In straight lines, the platoon marched forward toward the dragon target, the wooded tower that occupied the center of the training ground. Cenhelm and his pony-boy fell in behind.

"Tahhh, Tahhh, Tahhh." The trumpet sounded a call for attack. Feargus could no longer hear Cenhelm's commands. They had rehearsed this maneuver so many times; however, everyone knew their roles.

The two squads on the opposite sides of the front line split off right and left and pivoted forward to form flanking positions, the center squad remaining in place. The two squads in the rear moved forward to fill the place created by the flanking movement. The platoon moved forward in this box-shaped formation, approaching and then containing the dragon target. Reynard had built a small tower of poles with a small red circular disk at the top to simulate the vulnerable spot on the back of the dragon's neck.

"Tahhh, Tahhh." The entire complement of men that formed the box rotated right.

"Tahhhhhh." The box rotated left. Once Feargus gave the attack command, the movement of the lancers was at Cenhelm's discretion.

Feargus watched with concern twisting in his mind. It was one thing to box in a wooden dragon target and another to surround an actual dragon. In theory, the lancer's task was to form a semi-circle to confront and flank the dragons. Then the men were to prod and threaten the dragons with their lances, turning the dragon's backs to a line of archers for them to have a clear shot at the dragons' vulnerable spot.

Feargus' Knights did not have a part to play in Boetius' strategy except to be held in reserve in case of an emergency, the rescue of casualties, or the like. For the Knights, this idea was repugnant in the least, and Feargus knew it would not stand. Although he did not officially encourage it, Feargus' Knights had plans to attack the dragons on horseback, with the intent to strike a blow to the back of the dragon's neck with their lances. He left them free to improvise if an opportunity presented itself. They and he did not relish the idea of all the glory of battle going to the archers.

As Feargus continued monitoring the lancers drills, a drumbeat called for a defensive position. Each man in line swung his shield forward and took a knee. The men were shoulder to shoulder, crouched behind the protective wall of shields. The development of the new shields was what made this battle plan acceptable for Feargus. At least the shields provided a measure of protection from the dragon fire.

Each man carried a tall new lightweight shield. The shields were a foot higher than the height of a man kneeling, flat on the bottom and pointed at the top. The frame was made of lightweight willow branches running horizontal and vertical and lashed where they crossed with jute cord. This framework was bent to make the shield convex. Thin, lightweight sheets of metal were attached in an overlapping fashion similar to the scales on a dragon. A diagonal strap on the back of the shield, when slung over the shoulder, allowed the men to carry them on their backs. When marching in formation, they looked like a line of metal clad turtles.

The metal plates were thinner and more durable than anything made before. A new forging technique and a new alloy formula Reynard had learned in Evora allowed for it. Reynard's two brothers, who were tinsmiths, already trained in forging thin metals, aided in the development of the forging method and the manufacture of the shields. They and their helpers had been toiling all day and into the night by lantern light. The weapon's shed attached to the west wall of the castle courtyard had been and was still a bustle of activity. All the ground lancers were now equipped with the new lances. The ground lancers and the archers had their new shields, and Reynard was working on building a stockpile of replacements.

Whether the shield could stand up to actual dragon fire was not yet known, but Reynard had tested it with success over the hot flames of his forge and with magnesium torches. The brightness of the new metal helped reflect the heat.

"Ta- ta- tahh, Ta-ta- tahh, Ta-ta- tahh." A trumpet command called for retreat. With their shields held in front of them, the men backed away several paces. Then shifting the shields to their shoulders, double-timed backward across the field.

"Ta-tahh, Ta-tahh, Ta-tahh." A trumpet-call from Boetius' pony-boy called the archers into the drill.

The archers jogged across the field and formed up lines

in a position opposite that of the lancers. In theory, they were now behind the back of the dragon target. The archers were organized into two squads, 15 men each. One squad made a frontal row, taking a knee, with the second squad standing in a row three paces behind. The plan was for the squads to alternate shots, delivering arrows in rapid succession. As they moved into position, most of the archers dropped their shields to the ground behind them. They complained that a shield on their back interfered with reaching their quiver when shooting from a knee. The first row let go a volley, a few arrows flew true to the red wicker circle on the dragon target's head, most missed and sailed over, striking the ground the lancers just vacated. A possible flaw in the plan that Feargus fretted over. It was likely that some errant arrows might find his men before they could retreat or protect themselves.

Cenhelm rode up. "Call it a day?"

The sun was setting; they wouldn't lose light for two hours, plenty of time for another drill. But with the dragon hunt set to start tomorrow, it was time to end the training.

"Yes, call an end to the training," Feargus said, "The men need to be well-rested for tomorrow." However, he knew it would not be a restful night; nervous energy would fuel the first day, like all the first days of battle.

"Cenhelm," Fergus called out. Cenhelm pulled up his horse and turned back to Feargus. "And close the tavern tonight."

"Yes, Sir." Cenhelm gave the command to the pony-boy who accompanied him. Without a word from the pony-boy, his pony reared, spun a quarter turn, and took off at a gallop. He raced along the outer edge of the grounds. He beat the drum that hung from his left hip and repeatedly blew the trumpet in his right hand. The other boys joined in the wild ride, and a cheer went up from the King's army. Charging around the training ground at breakneck speed was uncalled for, but apparently, they couldn't help themselves. Feargus thought to object to it, but he enjoyed watching, immensely.

Reports had come in that the hunting troop with their dogs was having success tracking and locating the dragons feeding areas. Early engagement with the dragons was likely.

The army would leave at dawn, march a half-day to the Western Hunting Grounds, and set up camp before noon. It was likely that Boetius would press to send out the troops immediately. They would have a quick uncooked meal and send the platoons out the Braga Road, heading north, toward the area where the dragons had last been sighted. The hunting troop had patrols out on east and west of the road. The army would move along slowly, waiting to be called out into the forests and fields in response to the hunter's summons.

Feargus sat and watched as the army disassembled and left the training grounds in a plodding procession back toward the castle. Where Boetius and Drake foresaw glory and success, Feargus imagined and ruminated on the flaws in the plan, all the things that could go wrong; from panicking uncontrollable horses, to dragons shooting fire, to shields that didn't repel fire, to overshot arrows wounding his lancers, to reckless Knights making foolish attacks. These specters that vied for Feargus' attention plagued his body with tension and his mind with unease. Most likely, a restless, sleepless night was ahead.

Dragon War

esterday morning on the march to camp, Drake's army was in high spirits spoiling for a fight. Drake had accepted Feargus' reasoning that it was best to wait until the next day before beginning the search for dragons. Now having spent an afternoon and night in camp and an entire morning of marching on the Braga Road, the men settled into a state of lethargic plodding in wait of battle. Drake would order a pause for a cold dinner soon.

Drake, Boetius, and Feargus rode three abreast at the head of the column. Behind them were Hartmann, Cenhelm, and Reynard, and two pony-boys. They followed the dirt road north as it meandered through the Western Hunting Grounds. No one spoke; subtle sounds reached Drake's ears; the clopping of horse's hoofs, the shuffle of boots in gravel, and birdsong from the enveloping forest. The ranks were quiet as well. Like Drake's, their minds were undoubtedly occupied with the anticipation of battle.

Behind their leaders, on this dry spring day, the lancers of the red platoon walked six abreast, filling the width of the roadway, scuffing up a cloud of dust that drifted around their feet. Behind them, the red platoon archers followed; and behind them 15 Knights on horseback. Farther back the green platoon in the same formation, the same number, brought up the rear. Glancing over his shoulder, Drake watched the upright lances swaying from side to side in rhythm with the marching cadence. There was no hurry; they had no destination as yet.

At dawn, before the army had assembled, the hunting troop left on their usual patrols, combing the area, looking for signs of dragons. The troop was divided into four scouting parties, four men and two dogs each. Each group took a pony-boy with them. The boys reported back every hour to Boetius, advising him of their hunting party's whereabouts. Boetius then calculated where to best position the army on the road near the areas where dragons were likely to be found.

Suddenly, the sounds of the plodding march were interrupted by the clatter of a galloping horse. Ahead, at the bend in the road, a pony-boy emerged, closing fast. Feargus raised a hand to halt the column. Boetius pushed his horse forward to meet the pony-boy. On Boetius' approach, the pony-boy slid his horse to a stop and spun right and waited for Boetius. They spoke for a moment. The pony-boy turned and galloped off in the direction he came. Boetius returned to Drake.

"Dragons, Sire, a half league ahead. Up a logging road to the left, then another half league. I will scout it out. I will post the boy at the logging road." Boetius, consumed with excitement, without waiting for a reply, turned and galloped up the road.

Feargus' arm went up to signal a quick march, jolting every member of the army to a state of alert. A murmur traveled down the line; the troops awoke from their drudging march. Drake and Feargus pushed their horses into a trot; the army followed at a jog. They headed up the road, deeper into the hunting grounds.

In a short time, they saw the pony-boy ahead, stationed at the logging road intersection. Upon reaching the boy's position, Feargus commanded a halt. Moments later, Boetius appeared.

"I've seen them, dragons. The hunters have them under watch. We must move quickly and attack before they have time to flee."

"How many?" Drake asked.

"Four—two adults and two juveniles."

"I'll ride ahead with Boetius," Drake said to Feargus.

"I'll follow with the red platoon. The green platoon will remain here in reserve." Feargus called for Cenhelm.

Boetius appeared to want an argument.

"Boetius, with me." Drake road out the road; Boetius fell in behind.

The two men rode along the rutted road under bare arching tree branches to a sharp break in the road, where Boetius signaled a halt. He dismounted and led his horse forward by the reins to a stand of oak trees and tied it. Drake did the same. From there, they stole their way, bent over, through open woods until they reached a waist-high stonewall. From a crouch, peering over the stones, Drake looked into an abandoned sheep pasture covered in tall dead grasses, a near square of 300 paces. To his left, at the far corner, the hunters, holding their dogs quiet, huddled behind the stonewall.

In the middle of the field, surrounding the carcasses of two wild boars, four dragons feasted. Their heads pivoted on their long necks, side to side, up and down, tearing flesh. They showed no concern with the men's approach. Didn't seem even to be aware they were being watched. Certainly, these were dim-witted, lethargic beasts. Drake was hopeful.

A muffled rumble behind Drake signaled the arrival of the red platoon. Back through the trees, he caught a glimpse of his men. Even at a silent march, it was not possible to move such a large contingent quietly. Drake looked back to the dragons, concerned that they might flee. They did not but were alert. The dragons circled their meal; they appeared to be defending it.

"Ta-tahh, Ta-tahh, Ta-tahh." Feargus committed his platoon.

Drake ran back to retrieve his horse. He was nearly knocked to the ground as he passed through the line of advancing lancers. The archers went by as he reached his horse. Mounted now, Drake saw Feargus, on horseback, leaping the stonewall as the lancers clamored over.

Drake cantered to a low rise at the west end of the field that offered a better view. He didn't like the role of observer; he preferred to lead his men, but could not envision a role to play between his men and the dragons.

"Boom—Boom—Boom." The lancers were in their double line, moving on the dragons.

"Tahhh, Tahhh, Tahhh." A trumpet command from Feargus' pony-boy sent the lancers into the box formation, much quicker than Drake expected.

The lancers, behind their shields, advanced with lances leveled at the dragons. The two adult dragons turned their attention to men. The small ones cowered behind.

"Tahhh, Tahhh." The lancer formation rotated right.

The archers were now over the stonewall in the field in their double row. The first row on a knee, the second standing, all with an arrow in the string, waiting.

The dragons, now alert, rotated on their haunches, following the lancer's movement as planned. It looked as if Boetius' strategy was working. But then, from his position atop the small knoll, Drake watched in dismay as the perfectly practiced battle plan dissolved into chaos.

The large dragon closest to Drake took several slow steps forward, confronting the lancers' flanking squad on the right.

"Boom, Boom, Boom, Boom." A signal from Cenhelm.

The dragon halted and sent a narrow stream of blue fire over the men's heads as they dropped behind their shields.

The other, largest dragon, turned in the opposite direction and trudged toward the lancer's left flank. Peering at the oncoming dragon from behind their shields, the men bravely held their position. The dragon smashed into their extended lances, the points breaking on its chest. The dragon spun around. The men scrambled away, running, crawling, averting the dragon, and its thrashing tail any way they could.

A moment later, the first dragon turning on the center squads. It spat a stream of flame on their shields, which flared orange and then dissipated, flowing to and dripping off the bottom. Thankfully, the shields were effective.

"Ta- ta- tahh, Ta-ta- tahh, Ta-ta- tahh."

The center and right flanking squads broke in retreat, running and stumbling backward, as the dragon continued shooting short bursts of flames over the men's heads.

On the opposite end of the field, the largest dragon plodded forward toward the archers. But rather than having a vulnerable target, the back of a dragon's neck, they were facing a dragon head-on. In desperation, the archers let a volley of arrows fly, all of which either missed or bounced off the dragon's scales. The archers pulled their shields from their backs or retrieved them from the ground, cowering behind them as they stumbled backward. Drake's men were defenseless. He instinctively drew his sword, intending to enter the fray.

But before Drake could move, the largest dragon halted, let out a deep gravelly sounding trumpet call that seemed to send tremors into the earth.

Panicked, his horse spun around. Quickly regaining control, Drake was again facing the battlefield. The archers were scrambling over the stonewall back into the woods, most of their shields and bows littered the ground behind them. At the same time, a cadre of Knights were coming through the trees, their horses leaping the stonewall, pouring into the chaos.

Once in the field, the Knights, following Cenhelm's commands, rode between the dragons and the King's men, around the dragons in a wide arc. It appeared he was trying to distract the dragons by riding a circle around them.

Both adult dragons trumpeted again. All four turned away and plodded west in Drake's direction. They moved in a formation of their own, the largest one in front, and the two small ones following closely behind. The fourth in the rear took up the remains of a boar in its front claws. It teetered back and forth on its hind legs.

Drake watched in alarm. Lancers and archers were scrambling away, over rough ground, in ragged waves, stumbling, falling, dropping their weapons and shields. Some men on their hands and knees. Two horses panicked, spun, reared up, and dislodged their riders. Others bolted out of control. In contrast, the dragons seemed to be moving in slow motion, as if they were a vision existing in a different time or different realm.

As the dragons bore down on Drake, the lead dragon raised its head and trumpeted. Drake's horse panicked and tried to bolt. Drake struggled with the reins, trying to keep the horse facing the dragon. The bit jammed hard in its mouth kept the horse's head forward. Even so, the horse backed at a furious pace, stumbling and crashing through the brush.

Only 20 paces from Drake, after several beats of their wings, the dragons lifted off. They flew over the knoll, directly over the King, only feet above his head. Drake felt the rush of wind on his face and the sting of defeat. Behind him now, the dragons sluggishly rotated in the air and turned north. Drake watched them fly over the trees and out of sight.

Battle Losses

hree battles, and in Feargus' opinion, three disasters; it couldn't continue; it was too dangerous; it was pointless.

He strode along the castle wall toward the parade ground to where, he had learned, Drake was meeting with Reynard. A meeting without Boetius, which would play to Feargus' advantage. As he walked, he was formulating what he planned to say. He must convince the King to give up this foolish pursuit of the dragons. He needed to be persuasive but diplomatic, put an end to these chaotic assaults.

In the two battles that followed the first, Feargus took charge and adjusted their tactics, abandoning the rigidity of Boetius' plan. The lancer squads moved in flanking the dragons as before, but kept a safe distance from the dragons at the limit of the fire stream, about 30 paces. The squads were given more independence and allowed to maneuver at their corporal's discretion. The overall task of the lancers was to distract and disorient the dragons. And now, each squad had two archers positioned behind the lancers. Without shields, the archers awaited the opportunity to duplicate Boetius' lucky shot. The so-called 'Magnificent Shot.' Feargus spat on the ground.

The Knights also served in a new capacity. They were sent ahead of the army column and attacked first instead of held in reserve. At a safe distance, the Knights on horseback circled the dragon group. When an opportunity presented itself, they charged in behind the dragons, intending to occupy and distract them. Several of Feargus' Knights, the younger men on their light horses, attempted brave attacks with their lances. But the tactic was dangerous and foolhardy, with little chance of success. In no instance had a Knight been able to maneuver his horse close enough to strike a blow, let alone a fatal one.

The archer platoon still set their double lines waiting for the opportune shot, but Feargus forbid a volley unless a true opening presented itself. They were to hold until he gave the command with a trumpet signal. He wanted no more lancers injured by arrows.

Despite the modification in tactics and even though the dragons were slow lumbering beasts, the army had no success. The dragons seemed to read the men's intent, apparently aware (if they had awareness) that the attacking army presented no real threat. In the second encounter with three large dragons, the beasts stubbornly stood their ground for a long time before each took up a turkey they had killed in its mouth and flew off.

In that first battle and the two that followed in quick succession only days later, none of the men were fatally injured. It was blind luck that no one had. In all the battles, only minor and recoverable injuries were suffered. In the third battle, they found one large dragon and two small ones, feasting on a deer carcass. It appeared to be the army's best opportunity: small dragons didn't seem able to shoot fire. But as soon as the lancers flanked the dragons, the large one picked up the deer carcass and ran straight through the lancer squad's lines, the small dragons following close behind. The dragons didn't take flight but crashed through trees and thickets. The men scattered, but not all in time to avoid the dragons. One dragon stepped on and shattered an archer's leg; another struck a lancer in the chest with its sweeping tail, breaking several of the man's ribs. Both men were expected to recover, but it was a close call. Boetius wanted to send the army in pursuit, but thankfully, Drake disallowed it.

Still rehearsing his arguments as he walked through the parade ground gate, Feargus saw the King and Reynard seated on the bottom step of the reviewing stand. They hovered over a scroll that lay on the top of a small makeshift table.

He quickened his pace and soon stood in front of the King. "Sire," Feargus said with a quick bow, "Reynard," with a nod in his direction.

Reynard nodded in return.

"Sir Feargus," King Drake replied. He sounded displeased already. The emphasis in the King's salutation was on 'Sir,' which let Feargus know he was not in the King's good graces. When his actions pleased Drake, he was 'Feargus,' when he didn't, he was 'Sir Feargus.'

"You have something to report?" Drake continued.

"No report. But I want to discuss our battles with the dragons."

"The battles that you have made clear, you don't approve of?"

Feargus chose not to answer.

Drake glanced at Reynard. "Reynard and I were just discussing the possibility of using new weapons in our attacks—crossbows, and a catapult."

A crossbow lay on the bench beside Reynard, and a circular target was positioned at the far end of the parade ground, apparently for demonstration. Feargus thought to comment on the crossbow but held his tongue. Crossbows were highly inaccurate and considered a toy, a curiosity. Despite the increase in power and range, archers scoffed at the idea of using them in combat.

Drake continued as he lifted the bow, "Reynard brought this back from his trip to Braga and Duren. They are in use by the Duren archers. They are more accurate and more powerful than what we have seen in the past."

Drake gestured to the target that sat 80 paces away. Feargus looked in that direction. Four arrows were in the outer rings and buried to the feathers. Still not accurate enough, but an improvement.

Drake seemed to read his mind. "Reynard believes he can improve the design, make it more accurate, and he has already designed a new arrow."

Reynard reached down to a quiver that leaned against the bench and handed an arrow to Feargus. "I'm hoping this will penetrate the dragon's scales."

Reynard picked up the bow. "As you can see, this crossbow is larger than what we've seen before. It's made of a different variety of wood, an ash from Duren. It's twice as powerful as the old bows." He returned the bow to the table and took up a short length of plank that had two arrows embedded in it. One penetrating only an inch and the other, obviously shot by the crossbow, extended a full six inches through the plank. He touched the point of the metal shaft arrow that extended through the board. "The arrow points are longer, more slender, made of the new alloy."

Feargus took the arrow in both hands and twisted it, examining it. The shaft was made of metal and twice the diameter of a standard wooden arrow. The point did not have a hunting blade, but a simple target arrow point. He slid his fingers along the shaft. "It's not true or smooth."

"It's the first attempt. Made from the new metal alloy, the process I learned while in Evora," Reynard responded, "My brothers think they can improve it. It's too big to work well with this bow. I plan to make changes to the bow to accommodate the size of the arrow. Hartmann has agreed to assist in the testing and final adjustments."

Drake beckoned Feargus to take a seat alongside him. "Take a look at this. A catapult design that Reynard is working on." Feargus walked around the table and sat down as Drake spread out a scroll and slid it in Feargus' direction.

Feargus could not make much sense of the sketches and looked past the King to Reynard for an explanation.

"The base is the same as the lightweight carriage used in Braga, easily pulled by two small horses." Reynard moved his finger across the sketch. "The throwing mechanism is the same but modified to throw for height instead of distance."

"I see, but the lance shafts the Braga catapult threw bounced off the dragons. Might have injured them, but didn't penetrate." Feargus had detailed reports from his sister and friends in Braga.

"The plan is not to throw a spear, but to launch a net."

"A net?"

"A square net made of heavy jute with a stone attached to each corner. The idea is to send it high into the air, spinning over a dragon, and then drop from above entrapping it."

"Good idea if it works."

"I purchased a catapult from the King of Braga, so Reynard won't have to start from scratch," Drake said, "I sent two guardsmen, and they returned with it this morning."

"How long before these new weapons will be ready for battle?" Feargus asked.

"It will be mostly a matter of trial and error to get the catapult working properly," Reynard said, "It could be several weeks."

"And the crossbow?"

"My brothers should be able to get the arrow straight and true soon with a little more experimentation. I need to divide my time between the bow design and the catapult. There's only so many hours in the day." Reynard was defensive; probably, the King had been pressing the same questions.

"These ideas have merit, but apparently, it will take some time to ready them. And since we don't have them as yet or anything else useful, tactics or otherwise, I think it wise we suspend our attacks." Feargus put forward his argument.

There, it was out, put a halt to the war. Not as diplomatically as he had rehearsed, but out.

"Suspend?" the King asked.

Shifting in his seat, Reynard was getting noticeably uncomfortable.

"We are wasting our time and resources attacking the dragons. We've had no success in battle. Not one dragon killed," Feargus blurted out.

Feargus paused, but King Drake did not respond. He was looking straight ahead, out over the parade ground.

"We are using the same failed strategy in each battle." Feargus continued. He felt it his duty to his men to challenge Boetius and the King. "The definition of foolishness is to apply the same solution repeatedly, expecting a different result."

The table toppled over as the King rose to his feet. He had the King's attention now. The two men were face to face. "So, what is your plan, then?"

"Stop the attacks now. Use harassing actions only to drive them away from the food source. Station groups of men, encampments around the West Woods, or wherever the dragons are sighted."

"Not acceptable."

"Boetius' plan for a frontal attack is a failure. It put the men at risk for no good reason. We had no chance of a victory."

"The changes you made to tactics reduced the risk. The light horses are quick; they were able to get behind the dragons. The Knights might have opportunities if Reynard made their lances longer."

Feargus thought he heard Reynard groan. "It would be blind luck for a Knight on horseback to strike a fatal blow. And there is the risk of the dragon's fire. The men and horses are completely unprotected."

"What if they had light armor made of the metal like on the shields?" Drake looked to Reynard.

"I can't foresee the possibility," Reynard said, "I could look into it, but I . . ." He was shaking his head.

Feargus interrupted, "We are putting the archers, the lancers, and the Knights at great risk. I don't believe our current plan has any chance of success. My Knights and lancers have little or no offensive opportunities. The lancers run the risk of being accidental targets. And should the dragons ever take the offensive, the results will be devastating."

Feargus paused and waited for a response from the King. Surely Drake couldn't argue with the obvious merit of the argument. Drake (in silence) was looking through him.

"I can't in good conscience send our men into another battle," Feargus asserted in as calm and as forceful a voice as he could muster. He hoped the King would see reason and not act out of pride or anger.

After a long pause, King Drake looked back and forth from Feargus to Reynard. He was angry but under control. "Very well, a secession then. Only a pause. Until these new weapons are ready, and we have a new plan to put them to use.

"I expect you, Boetius, and Reynard to get to work on it immediately. I want results, and soon." The King stepped from between his men, over the fallen table, and stormed away toward the castle.

The King's Dream

It had been four days since Drake agreed to the suspension. Unable to sleep, he had again taken to walking the keep's roof at night. For the last three days, he had seen the sunrise each morning from the roof. His ruminating mind would not let him rest. His subjects were living in fear; something needed to be done; it was his responsibility; he needed to take action; he needed a successful strategy.

The new weapons were not yet ready. The catapult was still being tested. The new arrows were perfected and in manufacture, but Reynard was not satisfied with the crossbow.

But despite those concerns and worries, all those nights without sleep finally took its toll. Last evening, just after midnight, his agitated mind relinquished, and Drake fell into a deep sleep.

The next morning, late in the morning, well after sunrise, the time when you fight to wake, but dreams take hold and pull you under, again and again, Drake awoke with a vision. He sat up in bed, swung his feet to the floor, and hurriedly stood up. His intent to take a step was immediately thwarted: the room began to spin. His mind darkened. He lost his balance. Drake's backside hit the floor with a thud.

Sitting there like a potted plant, he heard the creak of the Queen's chamber door.

In a moment, Ramona was standing over him. "Are you alright?"

"Yes ... yes, fine. I'm fine." Drake tried to dismiss Ramona with a quick wave of his arm, which jarred his head and brought back the vertigo.

"You don't look fine. Is this a new royal custom, of which I am unaware?" Ramona was smiling, reaching down to him.

"You're crowding me, woman. Give me some room." Obliging, the Queen took a step back.

As he attempted to pull himself up into the bed by grasping the bed covers, he sent a sour glare over his shoulder at Ramona. She looked away, which was unfortunate because she may have been able to catch him when his knees buckled. Instead, he was on the floor again.

"Let me help you, your Highness." Ramona moved behind him, slipping her arms under his armpits and locking her hands on his chest.

Again trying to take charge of the situation, Drake pushed hard with his legs, landing them both on the bed, on their backs, spread eagle, Drake on top.

The Queen made a sound somewhere between a groan and a humph.

After a few moments of wiggling and tottering, Drake righted himself and maneuvered to the edge of the bed and a somewhat stable sitting position.

Ramona's arm was around his shoulders, lending support, "Are you sure you're alright?"

"Yes." He stood, still reeling, but steadied by Ramona's embrace as she rose with him. "Let go: I need to get to my study. I have vital information that must be put to paper immediately."

"Alright then, good luck getting to your study. I don't want to get in the way of some vital undertaking."

"Know your place, woman!" Drake meant to call out in a stern voice but instead squeaked it out. Not to worry: no one could have heard him over the bang of the Queen's chamber door.

She, a mere woman, could not know the importance of the dream he just awoke from, a dream that demanded to be recorded. He needed to get to his study before the wisdom spirit took the vision away. Drake had great respect for the spirit, a voice that brought answers, keys to problems. His father had been a firm believer and told stories of how, in times of trouble, he had been rescued by a new idea or plan that seemed to come from nowhere. This was the first time Drake had the experience, an answer delivered in a dream, what he took to be a royal communication. Although he would not think to register a complaint, he could not help but wonder why the spirit chose to convey such a brilliant idea with a confluence of vertigo and nausea. Surely that was not necessary. But now he needed to write it down, a matter of recording providence.

Staggering like a drunken man leaving the tavern, Drake followed a serpentine path through the open door into his study, where he plopped down behind his enormous wooden desk. Drake took up paper and pen and began to write down his prophetic dream.

In the dream, King Drake was lying on the ground on his back in the middle of a field. He was staring up at the night sky as he had done as a child on starlit moonless nights. Many stars and constellations were familiar, like the Dog Star, but there were also strange ones, including one shaped like a dragon. Suddenly, the sky began to rotate slowly around the pole star. His eyes tracked the dragon on one side of the circle and the Dog Star on the opposite side. The rotation sped up, getting faster and faster. But instead of the two constellations staying in the same relative positions, the Dog Star moved faster and began to close on the dragon. Finally, in a spinning whirl of stars, the Dog Star reached the dragon's tail. This was the point where Drake woke up and tumbled out of bed. While sitting on the floor, he came to understand the meaning of the dream.

After hurriedly writing out the essence of the dream, he moved on to the practical application of the new ideas the dream had stirred. It wasn't long before he worked out the overall plan. He spent the rest of the morning hours sorting out the details and sketching designs.

By midday, he was satisfied. He was excited and eager to explain his plan. He sent a guard to summon Reynard; his skills would be essential in the implementation. He sent another for Feargus; his commitment would be crucial. Drake instructed both guards to keep the invitation a secret and to share it with no one, especially not Boetius.

Drake poured over his papers and rehearsed the presentation of his plan. He enjoyed hearing himself describe it.

The King's Plan

"Do you know what this is about?" Reynard said as he met Feargus at the castle door. He had approached from the village and Feargus from the stables.

"No, I was summoned in secret to a secret meeting." Feargus sounded annoyed.

"Why a secret meeting with just the two of us?"

"We'll find out soon enough." Feargus stepped through the doorway; Reynard followed.

Reynard expected the King to press him again to complete the catapult and crossbow. Drake asked of his progress every day. But why invite Feargus? There must be something else on Drake's mind.

The men entered the King's study and exchanged greetings with the King, seated behind his desk, the top of which was covered with papers and a scroll. The scroll was open and in place at their side of the desk, waiting for them. They took the two chairs in front of the desk.

"Gentlemen, we have a new strategy for battle." King Drake looked pleased, in contrast to his mostly sour disposition as of late. He leaned across the desk and pushed the scroll forward a few inches toward Reynard and Feargus, who both leaned in.

"What I have devised will change our fortunes. I am sure of it. This is a monumental moment. I have documented the plans to support my new strategy. Take a look." The King made a sweeping gesture over the scroll. Obviously, he wasn't going to make a direct presentation, instead, draw it out, and prolong the pleasure of it.

Of all the various sketches detailed on the paper, Reynard's eye was drawn at once to an illustration of a lance, a new design. It was longer and shaped differently. "A new lance?" Reynard's finger was on an item on the paper.

"Yes, for the Knights. Longer, to enable an attack from a greater distance and with a strap to connect to their armor at the shoulder. Like what you made for the ground lancers. I believe you can modify the old short lances, keeping the handles but replacing the shafts.

"Notice also the finer, sharper point, more so than what you put on the ground lances. It will more easily penetrate the dragon's vulnerable area. You can use the same alloy as you did for the crossbow arrow."

Reynard had considered using the new alloy for lance tips for the ground lancers. That was a good idea. But, not wanting to state the obvious objection that it was likely impossible for a Knight with an awkwardly long lance to maneuver his horse behind a dragon, Reynard did not and simply nodded. To move at speed with a long lance did not seem plausible. He expected Feargus to speak up and object, but he was silent. Perhaps he had lost his will for confrontation.

King Drake continued, "We know that the arrows Boetius uses are effective. He has the one dragon kill. Now his archers must practice hitting a moving target — the same for your Knights, Feargus. My instructions are in these papers. New movable targets need to be made and installed at the training grounds. You see, I have the designs worked out. But of course, it's at your discretion to make improvements." Drake looked to Reynard.

Out of the corner of his eye, Reynard glanced to Feargus, seated on his right. Feargus shifted in his seat, leaning back, but still no comment.

Again, his attention on the scroll, Reynard slid his hands along the parchment to the next set of drawings, which presented a variety of views of a complicated framework, an unrecognized design.

"I see this section puzzles you." The King was pointing to the same peculiar set of sketches that held Reynard's attention.

"Yes," Reynard acknowledged.

"It's a puppet." King Drake showed he was relishing the suspense.

"You must assign your best craftsmen to build it. Do you understand? We will commit our best to this new venture."

Reynard expected an explanation to follow, but the King continued without any clarification as to the need for a puppet in a battle plan.

Addressing Feargus, the King asked, "The hunting dogs from Duren, the ones they use for hunting elk, you're familiar with them?"

"Yes, my sister has a pair."

Because the Duren Kingdom was blessed with substantial herds of elk on its northern border, the hunters had bred dogs for hunting them. The dogs were large enough and fast enough to take down an elk, one on one. They were the size of a small pony; their heads stood above a man's waist.

"We will need to purchase at least ten," Drake said, "I want you to take on that responsibility. We need to have the dogs as soon as possible. Leave first thing tomorrow morning."

"That may not be possible," Feargus said, "It's rare for them to part with their prized dogs. My sister had a difficult time getting a pair of pups. They were very costly. Her husband traded an allotment of expensive imported jewelry for them."

"The cost be damned. Pay or trade whatever is required. We

need those dogs. I hear that they are aggressive and fearless."

"I will ask my sister to help find a breeder willing to part with the dogs. But I'm not sure I will be able to get them."

"Make it happen and be back in two days. And keep it quiet."

"Yes, Sire. I will leave at first light."

"Good." King Drake returned his attention to the scroll and the puppet sketches. "The puppet must be large enough for two men. They will operate it from inside, of course. It must look as realistic as possible. It must have, and this is critical, the dragon hide attached to it. Take down the dragon skin that hangs in the great-hall. The puppet must smell like a dragon; to fool the dogs."

The King in such an agitated state, Reynard worried about the King's mind. So far, the King's excited and erratic presentation of the plan was not making sense. He assumed Feargus was in the dark as well.

Reynard tried to contort his face into an expression that showed an appreciation for the King's grand idea, which at the moment alluded him.

"If I understand your intent, your plan is to use this dragon puppet to train the dogs?" Feargus asked. "And then use the dogs in battle?"

"Exactly, yes. We will use the dogs to encircle the dragons instead of lancers or the Knights on horseback. The dogs will be much faster and occupy the dragons—and also less risk for your men."

"And these dogs will be trained using fear and punishment?" Feargus said with no emotional tell. That was the opposite of how he trained his horses.

Reynard saw the picture now, understood the King's intention. The dragon puppet will be used to torment and harass the dogs, training them to hate dragons, to see the dragons as the enemy. Then the dogs could be released in battle to the King's purposes.

"We will need a hard man to direct the training, not

squeamish. He will have to be tough with the dogs. Any suggestions?" Drake asked.

Yes, it will take a hard man to abuse dogs in that way, Reynard thought. "Gaston."

"Gaston," Feargus said.

The Stable Master, Gaston, he was the man for the job. He certainly had a callous disregard for the horses in his charge, a hard man indeed.

Young for the post he held, only 25 years, and like his father, the stable master before him, he was set in the ways of traditional horsemanship. His father, also a hard man, had schooled Gaston in those cruel training methods. They had no reservations when it came to using harsh means to control a horse's behavior. In order to get a low headset, a strap was attached from the horse's bridle, pulled across its chest, and attached to the girth at the belly. It was left in place until the horse gave up the idea of lifting its head. The bits they used were twisted metal that the rider used to punish the horse to get the response they wanted. For Reynard, the worst of all was horse breaking. It was called 'sacking out.' The horse was tied up, and then repeatedly struck with blankets and sticks. This brutality continued until the terrified horse submitted out of complete exhaustion.

"Yes, then, I agree. Reynard, approach Gaston this afternoon, fill him in on our plan."

Reynard was sure that Gaston could be counted on not to care about the dog's well-being.

"What of Boetius?" Feargus asked, "He will be trouble if he finds out about the dogs."

"When he learns of the training, he will definitely object," Reynard said, "He cares more for his dogs than he does people." The dogs' hardship would offend Boetius' sensibilities.

"We must keep it a secret from him as long as possible. He need not know our plans, what the dogs will be used for or how they will be trained. Not yet."

"Train the dogs in secret," Feargus said, "That will be difficult."

"I don't want our plans for the dogs known, by Boetius or anyone else who is not directly involved with the training. Not until we are sure the dog training is successful. Anyone involved must swear an oath of secrecy on my royal seal.

"The longer it takes Boetius to find out the better," the King said, "Once he does, though, I will convince him that it's best of the Kingdom. We will all have to make sacrifices. I will remind him that he advocated for war with the dragons. And if needed, I will point out his lack of success so far. He will fall in line."

The King had his line of reasoning well thought out. If anyone could overcome Sir Boetius' objection to the abuse of the dogs, it would be Drake.

"My plans must be initiated immediately. Reynard, get to work on the new lances. Oh, but get the moving targets in production first. We will need the puppet by the end of the week. And the crossbow and the catapult must be completed soon as well. Feargus, the new training must start as soon as you return from Braga."

Reynard felt the involuntary roll of his eyes. He hoped that his exasperation did not show in his face.

"Yes, Sire, but what of a secret location for the training?" Feargus asked.

"I know of a satisfactory spot for the training, an out-of-the-way place," said Reynard, "the isolation barn."

The barn was used to isolate sick horses and unruly stallions. It rested at the bottom of the castle hill on the castle's north side, just inside the ramparts. The area with its paddock, run-in shed, and small barn was remote, removed from castle activities. It was an excellent choice for the secret training.

"I believe that will work. Good idea. The barn could be made into a kennel, and the paddock used as a training area. We should check it out." King Drake rose from his chair, rolled up the scroll, handed it to Reynard, and strode off toward the door.

"Gentlemen." He apparently meant now, this minute.

Both men followed the King out the door and on out of the castle.

Reynard's mind shifted, pondering the various concerns and challenges of his assignments, and trying to imagine a straight forward path. He could not.

Another Dragon Skin

Feargus, Drake, and Reynard were walking along the castle's western wall, almost to the stables, heading toward the isolation barn, when Feargus heard the clatter of a horse, approaching fast.

It was Cenhelm, who had just brought his horse to a halt back at the castle gate. He was about to dismount, but seeing the King ahead of him near the stable, he trotted up and dropped to the ground.

"Sire, news. A dragon. The hunting troop brought a skin in a cart."

"Just now?"

"About an hour ago. I just got word. Boetius took it to the village. He's at the tavern now with the men of the hunting troop."

"How?" Drake asked, "Did Boetius defy my orders for suspension? Did he order his archers to attack?"

"No Sire, it was the hunting troop, they. . ."

"The hunting troop killed it? How?"

"No, they didn't kill it. On one of their patrols, they came across it in the woods. It just died right in front of them."

"How is that possible? Was it wounded?"

"We don't know. I just came from questioning Berengar and the men that were with him. There's some confusion."

"Why didn't you bring Berengar to me?"

Cenhelm hesitated. "He's at the tavern, Sire. Drunk as a skunk."

"It's just past noon," This wasn't like Berengar, not the man Feargus knew.

Reynard spoke up. "But Berengar doesn't drink. I mean, not more than his medicinal dram of wine. I've never seen him drunk."

Feargus was puzzled. It was true; the old man was solid, nothing in excess, except for his charitable ways. In all his years as the leader of the hunting troop, he had always been held in high regard, especially by the poor and hungry.

"What did you learn from his men?" Drake asked, "They're not drunk too, are they?"

"No, Sire. They're at the tavern with him, keeping an eye on him. Berengar seems to have gone mad."

"Tell me what you know." Drake was undoubtedly losing patience with the mystery that Cenhelm was unfolding.

"The hunting troop was out on patrol last evening. Near dark, the dogs found a trail and led them a short distance to where they found a dragon lying in the path. It was lying on its side with its head up, thrashing about. It was trying to get up. Pushed its self up on to its back legs, flapped its wings, but flopped back to the ground. The men watched as it tried to rise over and over again until finally, it collapsed and died."

"Any visible wounds," Reynard asked.

"No wounds, they assured me. But Berengar said that he 'saw' that the animal was ill, starving."

"How could he 'see' that the beast was ill?" Drake asked.

"I pressed him on that. He kept saying over and over, 'I's saws it, I's saw's it.' That's all I could get out of him."

"A drunken hallucination?" Drake offered.

"His men said he'd started with that kind of crazy talk at camp last night. Said he was calling out in his sleep too. He'd nothing to drink at that point, not until he got back this afternoon.

"This morning, they skinned the animal and loaded the hide into the cart. They say Berengar didn't utter a word all morning, not on the ride home either. He went straight to the tavern and started in on the wine."

"What could have affected the old man like that?" Reynard asked.

"Has he gone senile?" Drake asked, "How old is he?"

"He's something over 70 years. Loss of mind shows up gradually. Never heard of it happening overnight," Reynard said.

"Maybe it was a fit? Something he ate or drank?" Feargus said, "I should go to the tavern and investigate, Sire."

"No, I need you here."

"I could go and take Berengar home, so his wife can look after him," Reynard said, "And I'll have Amalia fetch the Healer. She may be able to help him."

"You should have the priest look at him instead," Drake said, "That old woman doesn't have the medicines the priest has. He imports his from Dacian."

"Yes, Sire. But the priest's treatments are too costly for most commoners."

"Berengar's service should be rewarded. I will pay the cost," Drake said.

"I will inform his wife of your generosity," Reynard said.

"Reynard, while you're with him, see if you can get any sense out of him."

"Yes, Sire."

"Cenhelm, another matter. That dragon skin, have it delivered to the castle, put it in the weapon's shop. Reynard can use it to test the new crossbow." Drake gave Reynard a nod, and a glance to Cenhelm sent him on his way.

"Yes, Sire." Cenhelm sprang to his horse's back. He pivoted and rode away toward the castle road.

"Reynard, before you collect Berengar, a quick trip to the isolation barn." Drake turned and led Feargus and Reynard away, past the stables, and to the corner of the castle wall where he stopped. Drake looked down the dirt path that followed along the west-facing castle wall.

"We should post a sentry here on the corner to discourage anyone from discovering our training," Drake said.

"That would be too obvious," Feargus said.

Interjecting, Reynard said, "We can use my boys. They won't be as noticeable. They could relay a warning if someone approached."

Since Reynard had no son to inherit his business, some village families sent their sons to help at his shop, hoping he would select them as an apprentice.

"Can they be trusted?" Drake asked.

"Certainly."

"Good then, let's inspect the barn."

The path, a dead-end, led down the hill to the isolation barn that rested between the castle hill and the western ramparts.

Drake and Reynard walked ahead of Feargus, discussing their plans, Reynard asking questions, Drake expounding answers. Feargus fell in behind and into resignation.

Preparations

"With the King's new plan and the new weapons, we will surely have victory in our next encounter," Boetius said, "Things are going so well; a week more of training and we should be ready to launch our next attack."

Reynard had been with the army for the past three days, taking part in the training. Feargus had returned from Duren with the dogs. They were now in Gaston's charge, also in training, being schooled to hate dragons.

"No, a full two weeks of preparation. We all agreed. And the King approved," Feargus stated. He stared straight ahead out over the training ground from where he, Reynard, Cenhelm, Hartmann, and Boetius stood on the southern hillock.

The first regiment was assembled and in motion. The King's men had put the tactical elements of the King's new plan into immediate practice the day after Drake conveyed it to Reynard and Feargus. On the east side of the field, archers with longbows were testing their skills on moving targets that operated from ropes strung between two flat-topped towers Reynard had built. On the other side of the grounds, Knights on horseback were jousting at targets hung from a similar structure.

Boetius did not respond. Reynard was grateful for it. Everyone was committed now. Arguing and dissent was no longer an option.

"Hartmann your report," Feargus continued, still staring ahead.

"My men have been taking turns practicing with the five crossbows we have now. The bows are fairly accurate. They should be satisfactory for use with the new tactics."

In the King's new plan, the archers assigned to the lancer squads now had crossbows. Protected by the line of lancers, they, in theory, could concentrate on their targets.

"I've tried one myself. It is certainly powerful," Boetius said.

"I tested it on the dragon skin," Reynard said, "Although it won't penetrate the large scales on the dragon's sides or back, "it will if it hits at a slight angle, penetrate under the small scales on the dragon's underbelly. That's where the archers should focus. Aim for a glancing shot at the underbelly."

"It works on a dead hide," Hartmann said, "But will it work on a live dragon?"

"We'll find out soon enough." Feargus turned to Cenhelm. "Your report on the new lances."

"The Knights are having difficulty maneuvering the lance. They can hit a stationary, small ring, but it's difficult to hit a moving target. I doubt even our best Knights will be able to do it consistently. And I have other concerns. What will happen when a lance strikes something solid? The force will be transferred to the man's body."

Reynard had envisioned the same issues. The lance was attached to the Knight via the shoulder harness. Reynard feared men would be unseated or break a shoulder from the impact.

"Have the men continue practicing. Reynard, see if you can make some modifications," Feargus said.

"Yes, Sir. Maybe a break-away strap." The lances were made

to the King's design; Reynard saw no way to improve on a failed concept.

"Your report, Reynard."

"The catapult works as expected; the net throw is accurate for the most part. The catapult crew is doing well at hitting a stationary target. Tomorrow, they will start practicing the horse-drawn maneuvers." Reynard planned for the catapult to be maneuvered by the horses on the battlefield. There wouldn't be time to unhitch them. Cenhelm had provided two light horses that Reynard hoped would be calm enough to withstand the intensity of battle and respond to commands. One of Cenhelm's cousins, an excellent horseman, had volunteered to be the teamster.

Feargus walked away and mounted his horse, its head rising from the grass. "That will be all gentlemen; carry on." He rode off on the Braga Road, toward the castle, likely to make a report to King Drake.

The other men, also, rode away to pursue their duties, leaving Reynard alone on the hill, again envisioning another violent fray. Despite the warmth of the sun on his back, he shuddered.

Secret Discovered

"What have you learned?" Boetius leaned forward in his chair. He was seated at his usual table across from Hartmann and two men from the hunting troop.

Hartmann spoke. "People are repeating the same rumors about secret training, on the King's orders, training dogs for battle."

It was only a matter of time before the tavern's gossip grapevine unraveled any castle secret.

Hartmann and his conspirators, the hunters, had been spending evenings in the tavern, spying, listening in on conversations, and generously buying drinks.

"What would be the point of that?" Boetius asked, "We already have well-trained dogs for tracking the dragons."

"No one seems to know the details or location," Hartmann said, "But it may be what the King is waiting for. Complete the training before he commits the army to battle."

"Training to do what? We have tested and trained with the new crossbows. Reynard has demonstrated the effectiveness of the catapult."

Boetius had been pressing Drake to get the army into the

field. He was eager to put the new weapons to the test. He had had enough of the preparations for battle.

"Yes, my men are tired of just shooting at moving targets," Hartmann added.

To be excluded from the secret training was an embarrassment that Boetius took as a personal affront. He should have been in charge if there was a need for dogs to be schooled.

"It doesn't make sense."

"No, it doesn't." Hartmann said, "And they say the training has been going on for several weeks."

"I spoke with Reynard this morning. He's usually in on the King's plans. He wasn't sharing all he knows, he was holding back." Boetius was annoyed with Reynard. Reynard should have told him about this training. The idea that Boetius was not invited to lead the project was absurd. He knew more about dogs than anyone. All his hunting dogs were as respectful and obedient as his dog Riley, who rested under the table at his feet.

"I need to know more about what's going on and who's involved," Boetius continued.

"Last night, a couple of stable hands got to talking. They say that Gaston is training the dogs," Hartmann said with a hint of hesitation. "But it's so ridiculous; I put no stock in it."

"What?" Boetius said, "Gaston? Can't be. Nonsense."

"But that's what they're saying."

"The man doesn't even do a proper job training the horses he's responsible for." Boetius didn't like Gaston, and he had no respect for Gaston's horse training methods. Gaston got his way by brute force; he knew nothing of making a connection or bond between horse and rider. It was a shame that Gaston had been appointed Stable Master. He got results, but at what cost? And how much more a man could get from a horse with better methods. Only the older Knights accepted horses trained by Gaston. The younger men bought trained horses directly from the Horse Clan. It was too bad that the stable master's job wasn't a Noble's position. If it were, surely a better man could be found.

"True, he's a piss poor horse trainer. But if he is doing the training, could he be doing it at the stables?" Hartman said.

"Could be. Only one way to find out." Boetius stood up. "Thank you, gentlemen." He would confront Gaston. He turned away and left the tavern, bolted into the street and headed for the castle's stables.

Boetius should have led such a project, not Gaston. He didn't understand why King Drake had excluded him. He had always been included in Drake's ventures, ever since childhood. His agitated mind churned. He strode with determination along the Village Road to the castle rampart, and on through the gate without an acknowledgment to the sentry who had come to attention.

This intolerable situation provided the energy that propelled Boetius toward the stables. The heels of his boots clacking on the cobblestones. Taking long strides, he made short work of the road that wound up the hill to the castle.

Upon reaching the castle, Boetius continued walking along the lane-way between the castle's western wall on his right and the parade ground on the left. The stables were up ahead, where he expected to find Gaston.

At the stable entrance, the central doors fully open, Boetius stopped briefly and glanced in Gaston's tack room. He wasn't there. Boetius, standing in the middle of the stable entrance, called out for Gaston in a voice that commanded attention. Not getting a response, he walked down the runway through the center of the stables, checking the stalls as he passed. When he arrived at the far end of the stable, at the likewise-open doors, he came across two stable-hands. The pair claimed that they didn't know where Gaston was, but their nervous and awkward behavior suggested otherwise. Annoyed that the commoners dared lie to him, but with no alternative, Boetius would have to find Gaston himself.

A slight smile came to Boetius' lips: he looked to Riley, who was standing quietly by his side. Her ears perked up, and her head tipped from side to side, waiting a command. All black but for a white star marking on her chest, she was slender but muscular; her back stood just above Boetius' knee.

Boetius and his dog walked away, down the aisle to the other end of the stable and into Gaston's tack room.

"Riley, here girl," Boetius spoke as he touched Gaston's coat that hung from the back of a chair. The dog was quickly at the coat, nosing and taking up Gaston's scent. Boetius looked into the faces of the two stable-hands who had followed him. With an intentional sly smile, he swung his right arm out, pointed ahead, and gave the command. "Find."

With her nose to the ground, Riley made two full circles in front of the stable entrance, her head oscillating from side to side. After a sharp bark, she bolted toward the castle wall. At the wall, the dog hesitated, then turned left. She ran along the castle wall toward the northwest corner and disappeared. Boetius sprinted to catch up.

As Boetius rounded the corner, he caught a glimpse of a boy running ahead who disappeared on the path that led down the hill. Riley was halfway along the castle's north wall and starting down the same path. A shrill whistle, followed by, "Riley wait," Boetius called, "Not as young as I used to be."

The dog halted and looked back at her master, her black coat shining in the midday sun. She stood at the top of the narrow dirt path. He should have thought of it before. The trail led to the isolation barn at the bottom of the hill, the obvious choice to do something in secret.

Upon reaching Riley, "Find." Boetius gave the command with a wave of his hand. They started downhill on the winding path, Riley ahead at a jog, Boetius with a long-striding walk.

At the bottom of the hill, slowing his pace, Boetius walked along the back of the barn. From the other side, he heard dogs barking and men's indistinct, agitated voices in an argument. He walked around the corner of the barn to the paddock's open gate, where Riley sat waiting, her head tilted in his direction. The boy must have been a lookout and announced Boetius' arrival, which created the commotion.

A man not easily surprised, Boetius suffered a moment of shock as he took in the strange scene before him, and then lapsed into confounded puzzlement. Amongst the group of men, he immediately picked out Reynard, Gaston, and one of Reynard's boys from the blacksmith shop.

Boetius scanned the area. He noted that the paddock fence had been filled in solid with willow sticks. Two Duren hunting dogs were chained to a stake in the center of the paddock. In the run-in-shed (attached to the far side of the barn), Boetius saw a line of willow stick cages with dogs inside that sporadically barked and whined. But what captured his attention and held it was what appeared to be a life-size, but not too accurate, attempt at a dragon statue.

All the men were now quiet; their eyes were on Boetius. As he walked up to the front of the dragon image, his eyes were ranging in a top-to-bottom inspection. Twice his height, the figure had a relatively accurate head carved of wood, painted with appropriate colors. It had flopping wings made of canvas, outstretched on each side. The body was also of canvas, stretched over a frame that gave the impression of ribs showing undernourishment. Overall the contraption gave the appearance of an over-sized, awkward, tipsy goose whose intent, it seemed, was to topple over.

"Sir Boetius." Reynard was standing on the right side of the dragon, aided by another man on the left. Each had their hands on the body, steadying the monstrosity.

"Reynard."

Suddenly the dragon lurched left, then right, and settled to the ground.

Reynard moved to the back of the beast, flipped up a canvas

flap, exposing an opening from which two men, one after the other, hunched and stumbling, backed out, and in so doing, resembled the live birth of twins.

"What's going on here?" Boetius demanded.

Reynard calmly explained the purpose of the dragon puppet. He made it clear how the dogs were trained and how they would then be used in battle with the dragons.

"So this is what the King has been waiting for, these dogs. Trained so they will attack dragons in battle?"

"Yes,"

As images of this stupid looking apparatus in use conjured in his mind, Boetius felt his face flush with the heat of anger. He reached up and touched the dragon's back. He realized that a dragon skin was attached. "You're using my dragon skin for this training?"

"The King's dragon skin," Gaston interjected.

As Boetius turned toward Gaston, a hand grasped his shoulder. He raised his hand to knock it off but stopped when he realized it was Reynard. In that instant, he again caught sight of the dogs chained to the stake and the two men standing next to them. One of the men who had a switch in his hand tried to hide it behind his back.

Turning back on Gaston, "You had better not be harming these dogs." Boetius pointed a finger at Gaston's chest.

"Follow'en King's orders," Gaston replied, then adding, "Sir."

"He's doing what needs to be done." Reynard was interrupted by an eruption of barking from the cages.

"How long has this been going on?" Boetius asked of Reynard.

"Two weeks."

"Quiet," Gaston shouted at the dogs.

"I'll quiet you!" With violent intent, Boetius took a quick step toward the stable master.

Just as quickly, Reynard stepped in front of Boetius and restrained him by placing both hands on his shoulders. Gaston backed away several paces.

"He's following Drake's orders, Boetius." Reynard spoke quietly. "It's necessary for the King's new strategy."

"Why wasn't I informed? I should have been told about this."

"The King should answer that. He plans to call a meeting for tomorrow. We are satisfied with the training. He will present the entire strategy and authorize a renewal of the fight. Unless you would like to confront him about it now."

Boetius took a step back from Reynard. "This won't stand, I'll speak to the King and put an end to this cruelty." He turned away and stormed toward the paddock gate. "Riley," he called, and the dog snapped to heel at his side.

Boetius left the paddock and walked around the back of the barn and up the path toward the castle. His anger was pushing him toward a confrontation with Drake, which he knew was pointless. None the less, he needed to express his displeasure, but tomorrow would be soon enough.

Deployment

Drake had summoned the army's essential members to the great-hall for a meeting to launch the next venture into battle. All, except for Boetius, were now assembled, gathered around the central dining table. Drake stood facing the main door, his back to the throne wall. Feargus was standing to his right, Gaston and Reynard to his left. Cenhelm and Hartmann stood on the opposite side of the table.

The dog training had been going on for a fortnight. Reynard and Gaston reported that they believed it had been a success. The dogs, when released on command, circled and attacked the dragon puppet. Drake was pleased. He was confident that the attack dogs provided the final, crucial element of his battle plan.

Drake leaned forward and unrolled a scroll. "Gentlemen, this is a description and details of my new plan."

At that moment, Boetius burst into the great-hall through the main door.

Everyone, except Drake, looked in Boetius' direction as he strode across the room toward the group. Boetius took up a position opposite the King between Cenhelm and Hartmann, who shifted apart to make room for him.

"Sire," Boetius greeted Drake with a slight bow and then a nod to the others before turning a scowl on Gaston.

"Sir Boetius," Drake replied, "We were just about to start our discussions. This is a diagram of my new plan, which now includes the attack dogs."

"That's what I want to discuss, the mistreatment of the dogs in Gaston's charge ..."

Drake interrupted. "That's not what I'm here to discuss. The dog training is complete and successful. Gaston performed his duty, and now it's time for you to do yours."

"But I can't in good conscience ..." Boetius was cut off by King Drake's raised hand.

"If you like, we can take up your complaint in private after this meeting." Drake found it hard to understand Boetius' concern for the dogs. It seemed he cared more for them than the King's men.

Boetius did not respond; he looked defeated. Drake took it to mean that the conversation was over. Apparently, he didn't need his prepared arguments to thwart Boetius' objections to the harsh dog training. His strategy of excluding Boetius from the training until it was complete had worked.

Drake returned his attention to the scroll on the table. "As you are all aware, the battle plan and tactics are similar to those used before." Drake pointed to the diagram.

"As before, the Knights will be the first to enter the field, to encircle the dragons and distract them. This time though, five of the contingent of 15 will carry the new long lances. Your best horsemen, Feargus.

"Next, the lancers will execute the box drill maneuver as before." On the diagram, the lancer squad's lines formed an open rectangle, outlined with rotation arrows. "The archers assigned to the lancer squads will now, of course, have crossbows.

"Boetius, your longbow archers' responsibilities are the

same. But this time, only your best marksmen, 16 in total." Drake's finger tracked a curved arc on the paper. "Form up their lines as quickly as possible."

"My men will do their part." Boetius' posture stiffened.

"Gaston," Drake said, "We will initially only use four dogs. Get them in place behind the archer's line. Once the dragons are occupied by the Knights and lancers, Feargus will give you the command to release the dogs. Release them on the right side if the box drill is rotating counterclockwise, and the left if the box drill is rotating clockwise. Listen for the trumpet-calls.

"Reynard, while the lancers and Knights are engaged, that should give you time to get the catapult into position. The location will be up to you.

"What have you to report on the catapult? Are you satisfied with it?" Drake turned to his Weapons Master.

"It is easily and quickly maneuvered. The crew has been practicing and is now much more effective. I will continue to make adjustments and modifications as needed."

"Good. We will put it to use. Be prepared."

"Sire," Reynard said.

"Feargus, you will, of course, be in charge of the overall battle formations, field decisions are at your discretion." Drake looked to Feargus and then to Boetius.

"Yes, Sire." Feargus had clearly acquiesced to the need to fight the dragons. He was loyal and would play his part.

Feargus continued, "My Knights are having minimal success with the new long lances."

"Be that as it may, they are a potential tool in our arsenal. Just one successful strike could change our fortunes. Have them at the ready."

"My men will be taking a great risk moving into the dragon's range for fire. They have requested new armor made of the new lightweight metal, for thigh, chest, and arms and also the horse's face, neck, and shoulders. I want them to have some protection from the flame."

"It could probably be done," Reynard responded, "but it will take time. It could take several weeks to create a prototype. Crossbows and shields are my priority."

"We can't wait for it," Drake said, "I want to put my new plan to the test in two days. You have the day tomorrow for any final preparations. We travel the morning after and engage the next day."

"I am not sure if a lance attack is worth the risk," Feargus asserted.

"It's up to you, your call, but if the opportunity presents itself, I expect you to send them in."

"Yes, Sire. My Knights have been using Reynard's dragon puppet to desensitize the horses to the smell of the skin. My more able horsemen will be better able to maneuver closer to the dragons."

"Yes, Sire. It has been a big help," Cenhelm added.

"Anything else?" Drake looked to Boetius, Feargus, and each other man in turn.

There was no response.

"Alright then, we set out the day after tomorrow. Boetius, send out your tracking patrols tomorrow to locate the dragons."

"We do that every day, Sire," said Boetius.

"Good," Drake said, "I think we are ready, gentleman. This time I believe we are better prepared and have a winning strategy in place. May good fortune follow us into battle."

Each man, in turn, excused themselves and left the greathall in silence. Drake was disappointed with the lack of enthusiasm from his men. They left with only a nod and a bow. Only Boetius showed his usual eagerness for a fight. They did not react in the way he had hoped. He couldn't understand it. Surely, his new plan would produce success.

The Tale of Battle

Feargus followed Drake as the King burst through the main door and into the great-hall. The sentry at the door jumped to catch the weighty door before it swung back into Feargus' face. On Drake's heels, Feargus strode across the hall, with Boetius, Cenhelm, and Hartmann falling in his wake. The rest of the King's Knights straggled in, all the men still in battle dress, stinking of conflict. The King had left the battlefield with his Knights and rode hard to the castle, leaving the lancers and archers behind. Without a doubt, King Drake was eager to deliver the news and tell his story.

Alerted by a messenger, sent in advance, the Kingdom's Nobles had gathered in anticipation of the army's return. The King and his entourage advanced into the throng. The scene was illuminated by the late evening summer sun, streaming in through the western clerestory windows.

The Noblemen rose to their feet and broke into cheers and applause as the King moved across the room. Individuals in the crowd were easily identified by the colors that marked their clothing. Men wore sashes and armbands, and ladies wore waistbands and scarves that matched their family colors, the colors coordinating with those in the Noble family crests in the wall displays.

As the King, Feargus, and Boetius passed through the crowd, the Noblemen greeted them with back slaps, handshakes, and praising words. Upon reaching the far end of the room, King Drake turned and passed between the throne dais and the King's dining table at which Queen Ramona and the other ladies of the court were seated.

The King made a gracious bow to the women who stood, curtsied, and returned to their seats. The Queen remained seated, said nothing, but met the King's momentary expectant stare. He turned away, stepped up on the dais, and stood in front of the throne with his arms raised, facing the crowd. The gesture commanded quiet and attention. After a few moments, the chatter and socializing simmered to silence. Servants in the room came alert, waiting commands.

"Victory!" Drake shouted. Hands on his hips, he stood across the table from where Ramona sat. "We have victory at last."

There was a cheer and then a chant. "Hail King Drake, Hail King Drake, Hail King Drake . . ." It continued until the King raised his hands over his head, signaling again for quiet.

The chant died away; the room was silent.

"Everyone, take a seat, and I will tell the story," Drake said in a loud voice. He made a sweeping gesture in front of him and motioned to a servant, calling for a chair.

The Nobles, with the help of servants, began moving chairs and shifting tables to form a semi-circle around their King. Once the commotion quieted, and the Nobles settled in their seats, Drake dropped into his chair at the dais edge. He was facing the center of the great-hall. Boetius pulled a chair up near the King; the Knights mingled into the crowd. Feargus took a seat opposite Drake, near Ramona.

Drake looked satisfied with the arrangements and began the telling to his captive audience.

"Two dragons killed, a glorious victory." The King was exuberant.

A cheer from the assembly started but was promptly silenced by the King's raised hand. His expression made it known he wanted no more interruptions.

"Could have been more, but the beasts fled. My strategy worked perfectly. A grand day in the field." The King scanned the room, receiving the respectful nods and smiles from his audience now that they knew what response was expected.

Drake gestured with his arms flung wide, "You should have seen it. An excellent maneuver, executed perfectly. Couldn't ask for a better outcome." Drake dropped his hands to his knees and leaned forward. "A glorious day."

Feargus was not picturing the same event. What he had experienced was dramatically different from what the King was claiming to have witnessed from his hilltop station overlooking the battlefield. Where the King saw glory, Feargus had seen terror and chaos, a tormented struggle of men, horses, dogs, and beasts. Feargus looked to Ramona; her eyes appeared to reflect sympathy.

"We found the dragons in the hunting grounds, two leagues from the Warden's cabin, in a field to the northwest of the Braga Road."

Boetius, who was leaning forward in wait of an opportunity, said, "And finding them was easy; my dogs scented the trails, my hunters know their habits."

"Yes, yes, I get ahead of myself." King Drake acknowledged Boetius. "Fine work. The hunters and their dogs were instrumental in carrying out our plan. Allowed us to approach with stealth and mount a quick attack." The King looked perplexed for a moment. It must have been difficult for Drake to extend credit to Boetius.

"Where was I? Oh yes ..."

Leaning back in the chair with his legs stretched out long, the King continued, "We approached in formation just as we practiced on the training ground (the red platoon only) the green platoon held in reserve. The dragons were in a small pasture, a piece of flat land. Our first move was to send the Knights into the field. They encircled the dragons, keeping them distracted while the lancers and archers moved in. The lancers executed the box drill, approaching the dragons with great courage. They moved to the right, flanking the dragons, drawing their attention." He gave Feargus a congratulatory glance.

Feargus returned a nod. There is a fine line between courage and foolhardiness. Attempt an outrageously dangerous undertaking and succeed, you're called a hero—fail, and you're labeled a fool.

"Five huge dragons, there were. Truly dangerous beasts." King Drake paused to accept the nods of agreement from those seated around him. A servant approached with a tray from which Drake took up a goblet of wine.

Dangerous beasts, yes, Feargus agreed with that. But there were three adults and two small ones, the smallest he had seen as yet, obviously young-ens.

"The lancer squads were circling right," the King bent forward, his hand scribing a large circle in the air in front of him, wine spilling from his glass. "drawing the dragons' attention in preparation for our next maneuver."

The lancers were put at great risk, close in, prodding the dragons with their lances, retreating and ducking behind their shields for cover from the dragon fire that shot over their heads or dissipated on their shields. Thank the heavens that Reynard's shields provided protection and that the dragons were slow to use the fire. Feargus had concluded that the dragon's capacity for spitting flame was limited in some way.

Those near the King were also leaning in, obediently watching imagined events appear in the air in front of their King. "The lancers repeatedly advanced and withdrew, holding the dragon's focus." Drake leaned forward and back, the wine sloshing in his glass. "Then, from behind the archer's ranks, the attack dogs were released from the left flank. Just as I had envisioned, they circled the dragons, pulling the dragon's attention and spinning the lumbering beasts in a circle."

"And my archers, already in perfect position . . ." Boetius started to speak.

The King ignored Boetius, speaking over him in a louder voice, continued, "The archers had taken up their line ... And as the dragons spun in circles chasing after the dogs, the dragon's backs were available to the archers." With his left hand, the King was drawing a line in front of himself. "Only 20 paces from the beasts, a volley of arrows let fly, then another volley and then another. One of the dragons was struck in the back of his neck, the vulnerable spot. It fell to the ground dead. A clean kill."

Yes, a dragon was killed by the archers, one of the adults, but a clean kill it was not, not a heart shot made by a hunter. After the dragon fell, it writhed on the ground for an agonizing amount of time. The other dragons formed a circle of defense around it, holding that position until the final death cry, a horrible unearthly groan.

The King sat back in his chair, hands on his hips, waiting. After a pause, the room erupted in applause and cheering, the King basking in it.

"My men pressed the attack. The Knights circling on horseback. Two bold men attempted a strike with the new lances I designed, just missing their targets."

Two Knights had left the safety of their encircling position and, with long lances, attempted an attack. The first Knight, seeing an opportunity, approaching from behind a dragon, made a running pass alongside it. But at the last moment, the horse jumped away from the swinging tail. The lance point missed the dragon completely. The second man, following immediately after the first, made the same approach, keeping control of his horse. The lance hit the dragon's shoulder, broke in half, and dropped to the ground. And as feared, the Knight was unseated and landed roughly in the midst of the mayhem. It was Reynard who rushed in and carried the man to safety.

"The lancers also maintained the pressure on the stupid beasts. The attack dogs, the crucial element in my plan, continued to circle the dragons, disorienting them."

The way Feargus saw it, Drake was painting a flawless execution of a plan, and that was simply not the case.

What had gone according to plan—the tracking and approach, the lancers moving quickly into a position confronting and flanking the dragons, and the archers forming their lines, waiting outside the range of dragon fire. But the rest was a confusion of individual events and incidents in the control of circumstance and fate. Squads of lancers rushed forward and were repelled by dragon fire, ducking behind their shields just in time. The dogs were compelled by their own instincts. One attacked a dragon's underbelly as it would have an elk and was crushed underfoot.

"The archer's with crossbows behind the cover of the lancer squads took aim at the dragon's underbellies as we had planned. Unfortunately, none did any damage, but still, the bowman's assault added to our multi-pronged attack strategy."

"It was our execution of maneuvers, assault, and distraction that allowed for the deployment of the new catapult." Drake paused, took a long draft of wine.

"The catapult crew had followed us in. They positioned the catapult on the higher ground, maneuvering it with ease. It lay just to my left." Drake pointed it out on his imaginary battlefield. He rose from his chair, scanned the room for a moment, obviously looking for Reynard, wanting to acknowledge his part in the victory. "It was in the perfect position for a capture."

But Reynard was not in the hall. Of his own accord, he had stayed with the lancers and archers on their slow march home. He had the foresight to have brought along a wagon for the wounded who were now in his care.

Reynard had done more than command the catapult crew. After the first dragon was killed, another dragon lunged at a lancer squad on the left flank. The men held their ground as the dragon crashed into them. Lances shattered on the dragon's scales. Pieces flew in the air and fell to the ground. As the dragon pivoted away from them, men were swept over by the dragon's tail, tossing them about like rag dolls. Comrades picked up the fallen and scrambled away to safety behind another squad. Again, Reynard endangered himself, pulling another injured man to safety.

The King sat and returned his attention to his audience. "And then, one of the dragons sounded a trumpet-call, which we now know is the signal for retreat. Which plays into our hands, allows for a more predictable launch of the catapult.

"So, as it happened, as the remaining dragons tried to make their escape, the four of them ran across the field in an attempt to take flight. The first three were able to get off quickly and out of range, but the last one made a perfect target for the catapult as it took off. It was brought down in the net."

The lead dragon, who had sounded the call, started at a run at a right angle from the archer lines, the two small dragons followed, side by side, and the other adult dragon was last. They ran through two of the lancer squads; the men broke and scattered, trying to get out of harm's way. Despite their efforts, two of the lancers, trampled by a dragon, suffered broken legs. An archer broke his arm in a fall. Moments later, as the King described, Reynard's catapult crew launched the catching net, which snared the last dragon in midair, just after it left the ground. The net entangled a dragon's wings and head, bringing it down.

"While the beast struggled in the net, the archers formed up lines and shot volleys of arrows at it looking to connect with the back of the head, the vulnerable spot, the dragon's weakness, but to no avail. In the end, it was Sir Cenhelm who dealt the deathblow from horseback with one of the new lances of my design." The King stood and raised his arms over his head and shouted. "Two dragons killed. The others fled. And the victory is ours!"

More cheering, a chorus of hurrahs broke out that filled the great-hall.

The end was not as simple as Drake had described. The dragon had gone mad, thrashing in the net, becoming more entangled with each move. Without restraint, the archers began to shoot arrow after arrow, each man wanting to be the one whose arrow delivered the death blow. The melee was becoming increasingly dangerous as men tried to get closer to the thrashing dragon. A hale of arrows flew and ricocheted everywhere.

It became apparent that no one had planned for the eventuality of actually capturing a live dragon in the net. Feargus called for the retreat signal from a pony-boy. The archers quit their onslaught. Feargus saw Reynard take a crossbow from an archer and approach the beast. It was still thrashing but more constrained. Reynard was only a fair marksman with an inaccurate weapon. But as he closed in, a rider was coming from behind. It was Cenhelm, who had taken up a short lance from a man-at-arms, not a clumsy long lance. His horse brushed past Reynard. In that moment, the dragon went still, and Cenhelm plunged the lance into the back of the dragons' neck. The dragon collapsed, its body shuddered, a groan, and it was done.

Drake stood, his arms stretched out over his head, basking in the adoration from his subjects. The entire room stood with him. King Drake continued, "A celebration is required, a grand celebration. We shall have a feast. Tomorrow night we will celebrate our great victory." The crowd broke out in cheers again.

In an aside to Ramona, "Make up the invitations for tomorrow night. Spare no expense." Drake looked to the servants standing at the kitchen doorway and shouted, "For now, bring out the wine."

Another cheer. Servants scurried away and returned shortly with goblets and wine bottles on trays. Man-servants carried the trays to the tables, and maids poured the wine into the pewter goblets. Feargus noticed Ramona send Amalia to the kitchen. Not long after, servants appeared with platters of bread and cold meats. Then, two servants brought out a barrel of beer and wrestled it up onto a table. The beer and wine were distributed generously.

The commotion died down, and Drake's telling was replaced by clusters of conversation as the Nobles began to gather in factions around their tables.

Ramona, addressing Feargus, interjected into the descending calm, "Casualties?"

"No deaths. None of our men. Minor injuries to several Knights who fell from horseback. Two men were struck by a dragon's tail, only broken bones — an archer with a broken arm. One dog was killed outright. A horse broke its leg and was put down."

"I expected much worse," the Queen responded quietly.

"Yes. It could have been. Our greatest risk of injury is from accidents. The dragons are slow and lumbering. They seem reluctant to use their fire, and when they do, their timing is slow, missing their target, more of a warning."

"They may not be so slow in the future, now that you have struck a fatal blow," Ramona said.

"Possibly, if they have any intelligence."

"You should not engage with them again."

"The King has tasted blood; he will want more. Conflict is unavoidable."

"Still, if the army were to avoid contact with the dragons, that would be best."

Feargus nodded. Of course, that would be best, but not possible. As long as the dragons were in the Kingdom, Drake and Boetius would pursue them, wage their war.

The celebration dragged on late into the evening. King Drake was telling and retelling his story to anyone who'd listen and, in turn, was receiving their praise and congratulations.

Feargus was bored with it but felt compelled to stay. Looking around, he could see his Knights were of the same mind. No one dared leave until the King retired. Only the Noblemen showed an interest in continuing with the frivolous partying. But their women were beginning to make it known with whispers that they wanted to go.

Finally, Drake stood up, wobbled, and raised his drink in an effort to make yet another toast. Ramona stood with him, putting her arm around his waist for balance. She was whispering something in his ear. He smiled broadly.

"To a great day, a great victory," the King shouted, "and to the next—the next victory and to the celebration tomorrow."

A mumbled cheer went up from the assembly. The King began an attempt at a dramatic exit, staggering toward the staircase. With Ramona's help, he stayed upright. The couple stumbled up the steps, Drake's footfalls consistently missed the next tread, stubbing the toes of his boots. Finally, they reached the landing that ran in front of the royal chambers on the second floor.

Abruptly, Drake broke away from Ramona's grasp and stepped to the balcony railing, leaning over precariously. Ramona grasped the back of his shirt, holding him from plunging over the railing. At the landing rail, throne below, King Drake raised his clenched fists over his head to the jubilant cheers from his subjects below. He turned, stumbling, and disappeared through his bed chamber's door.

Weary and grateful for the end of the evening, Feargus rose and began to make his way out of the great-hall, interrupted on the way, by drunken Noblemen with back slaps and unintelligible praise. Feargus looked forward to the night and some rest, but not the future.

Rendezvous

Amalia couldn't rid herself of the jitters. It was a chilly morning, but her skin was damp. She had attempted a breakfast, but a queasy stomach rebelled. Two late nights of celebration, two nights of restless sleep, and an early rise this morning, Amalia was tired, desperately tired, and ridden with anxiety, all at the same time. Last night's banquet was not as raucous or long-lived as the impromptu celebration the night of the battle. Even so, Amalia was not getting enough sleep.

Ramona had called for a secret meeting this morning at the abandoned grain mill and had insisted they go separately. Ramona left first. Amalia was to follow by a circuitous route to the village and back to the East Road juncture and then on to Ramona's family estate, which bordered the castle estate. The extra distance, meant to dispel suspicion, was adding extra time to her journey in which to worry and conjure troubles.

She was at the bottom of the castle hill, facing the Village Road with no memory of walking down the castle road.

They could have had a conversation in the Queen's quarters as always. Amalia didn't understand why they needed to meet at a secret location. But she didn't question the Queen. Did

Ramona worry that someone might overhear them? No, that didn't make sense. Oh god, what did make sense these days?

The church clock tolled nine in the morning. The meeting was at ten. Why had she left so early? She couldn't sit still, so she was out walking, better to spend the time walking than sitting, walk off the nerves.

Maybe she wasn't cut out for a life of intrigue. She couldn't eat, couldn't sleep. At times, she wanted to crawl out of her skin. As the Queen's maid, Amalia had been involved in Ramona's intrigues and relished being Ramona's confidant, enjoyed the plotting and scheming. They had made her nervous but weren't as troubling as this conspiracy. But there was no going back, only forward, putting her life at risk to save the dragons and the foolish men who attack dragons.

In front of the tavern, Amalia stopped and made a U-turn on the village street to head back in the same direction she had just come. She looked around, felt silly, but no one seemed to notice.

It felt like forever since that first time when the dragon had dropped soundlessly out of the sky right in front of her and Ramona. But two months had passed since then, and Amalia had met with Alpha (the name they had given the dragon) on three other occasions, one meeting to warn of the army's intentions to initiate the hunt, another to inquire about injuries, and yet another to inform about the suspension.

That first meeting, Amalia was fortunate she hadn't wet her pants or backed off the cliff. Amalia's shoulders shuddered just thinking of it. There's something to be said for being scared stiff. Ramona had taken her hand; maybe that kept her in place.

How could Ramona have faced a dragon alone the first time? Amalia had always been impressed with Ramona's courage, something she saw lacking in herself. One time she asked Ramona how she did it, how she could do such courageous things. She remembered the simple statement

Ramona shared, 'Embrace the fear, and do it anyway.'

During the first meeting, Ramona spoke with the dragon for a period before it was Amalia's turn to try. Spoken wasn't the right word; it was a communication of sorts with pictures and images, accompanied by dizziness, vertigo, a sense of being lost in your own mind. Ramona said it would get more comfortable with more experience, less confusing, and it had; communications did get easier each time. Instead of being anxious, Amalia looked forward to the meetings. At least, she did until the last battle.

In the first three assaults, the King's army was no real threat to the dragons, and the dragons, of course, had no intention of harming the men. And then, during the suspension of fighting, the dragons could feed without harassment. Amalia had hoped that, given more time, the dragons would get enough food and be able to return home. But now, after this last battle, in which two dragons were killed and men injured, Amalia's hope was lost. She was plunged back into visions of a bleak future and the role she would have to play in this dragon war.

Emerging from her thoughts, Amalia was back at the castle crossroads, the junction of the major roads of the Kingdom—the castle road to the left, the Village Road behind, the Braga Road straight ahead, and the East Road off to her right. If she went right to the mill, she'd arrive too early. Better to walk up Braga Road to the North Road junction and then turn around to kill more time. Once passed the church, there would be few people out that way to worry about.

She wasn't afraid of the dragons anymore. Despite their appearance, there was nothing to fear. They were different looking, ugly—true, fierce—yes, and with intimidating eyes for sure.

In the beginning, based on what people said of them, Amalia had feared the dragons, thought them evil. The terrible things the dragons were accused of, and the crimes foreseen, had played on her mind. She had trusted the tellers of the tales:

they were her friends, her people. Now that she was intimate with the dragons, she knew the stories false, contrived opinions convoluted to serve personal agendas, and blatant lies to garner attention.

As she passed the church, she glanced at the sundial mounted on the gate post at the road edge. Still a half hour until the meeting time.

Amalia strode along the road, kicking rocks, more relaxed in the absence of people. No, she wasn't afraid of dragons anymore; it was people that frightened her, always had; she realized. As a child, hiding behind her mother's legs, in fear of strangers, she was called shy. As an adolescent, she was described as timid; as an adult, labeled meek. But now, her childhood fear of people felt justified; she had seen people do dreadful things. It wasn't only things they did, but what they said that did the damage. What they accepted as truth, the outrageous things they believed, drove them to harm.

After a few more minutes of walking in frustration with the subterfuge, Amalia turned around, hurried back to the castle crossroads, turned onto the East Road, and made her way to Ramona's family estate.

At the edge of the road, Amalia looked up the lane that led to the neglected mill. It ended in a roundabout, there for the convenience of turning wagons. Overgrown with weeds from lack of use, only the two old wheel tracks were still visible, barren alleyways in the knee-high grasses. Amalia made her way up the slight grade in one of the wheel paths and found comfort in the concealment of the over-growing trees and head-high brush that enclosed the lane. In front of her, the mill looked forlorn, a building no longer used or needed, on a slow decline to dilapidation.

Amalia walked past the wide double doors that, in the past, granted access for wagons to the smaller man-door on the right side. She raised her fist to knock, but her arm froze before it could strike; knocking was probably not appropriate for a clandestine meeting. Instead, she grasped and squeezed the rusty metal latch, which did not move and most likely never would. On closer inspection, the latch was frozen open. Both hands on the door edge, Amalia pushed, creating a small gap. With a solid nudge of her shoulder, the door creaked open, and she was in, in the darkness of the boarded-up old building. She leaned her back against the door, pushing it closed as she looked around the room, lit only by sunrays filtering through cracks in the old siding and slits in the window boards.

"Hello." A voice from nowhere announced.

Her mind knew it was Ramona, but her body didn't and startled. "Ma'am?"

"I'm at the far end."

Ramona's silhouette appeared with a simultaneous creaking and a burst of light. She was standing on a makeshift bench. She had pried an upper board from a window that cast a bright rectangular patch on the floor.

"That should help," Ramona said, "Don't want to be completely in the dark."

"Yes, Ma'am."

"Come here. Nothing to fear. Just dust and cobwebs. You're not afraid of spiders, are you?"

"No." Amalia cautiously made her way across the floor on well warn and sporadically creaking floorboards. As her eyes adjusted, the space was empty except for some wooden barrels, several dilapidated crates, and a few forsaken tools hanging on the walls.

Ramona's family, the House of Barin, was in the business of growing grain, milling the grain to flour, and exporting quantities of both. This old mill on the family estate, a half-mile east of the castle, was powered by the Calder River that ran through the family property. It was no longer used in favor of the new and more modern mill, located southeast of the village, built alongside the Morodon River. Where the old mill was powered by the unreliable flow of the Calder, the new mill had an ample reservoir pond that provided a consistent supply of water.

Ramona was at work. She rocked and twisted an empty grain barrel up next to the bench she had been standing on.

"Help me with this." Ramona moved to a cobwebbed wooden crate and grasped the top with her hands.

Understanding, Amalia was immediately at the other end. The two women, under Ramona's guidance, placed the crate top on the barrel, which became their makeshift desk.

As she took a seat, Ramona patted the bench. Amalia slid into place alongside Ramona.

From her travel pouch that Ramona retrieved from the floor, she removed and undid two small scrolls of paper. She smoothed them out on the rough wooden crate top. One Amalia recognized as an official document and another a sheet with a crosshatch table of rows and columns. The table squares were empty except for the headings spaces with letters and symbols.

"Okay. Let me explain this to you," Ramona said, "We're going to set up a network of people we can trust to help us rescue the dragons. We'll keep track of them on this chart I've made. So that we consider every possibility, we'll review this census report."

Amalia, studying the census paper, wondered how Ramona had gotten an official copy of a church census, but chose not to ask. To those kinds of questions, Ramona always said something like, 'you don't need to know, better you don't.'

Ramona, smiling, must have sensed the question. "One of the priests, the healer, owed me a favor."

Most everyone owed Ramona a favor. She liked it that way, others in her debt. It was why she granted so many. 'Keeps the wheels greased,' she would say.

"Get a marker from my pouch, please?"

While Amalia rummaged for a charcoal stick, Ramona positioned the report and the paper alongside each other, the paper with columns and rows in front of Amalia.

Ramona pointed to the letters PF at the top of the first column of the crosshatch table. "In this column, you will put the name of possible friends, people that I want you to approach."

"Me? You want me to ask people to help the dragons? Shouldn't that request come from you?"

"I can't move about the Kingdom as easily as you can. The King tries to keep track of me, has people watching. You must make the first contact."

"But I'm only a maid. Who's going to listen to me?"

"You're the QUEEN'S maid. You will be speaking for me, and you will make people understand that."

Amalia swallowed hard. She wasn't pleased with this task she was being charged with, but the Queen's tone made the request sound like a command, non-negotiable.

"Some will give you trouble: I know that. Should they need convincing, we can arrange a meeting. I will see them face-to-face if necessary. I won't be able to do it often, though. Be persuasive. Use my authority; use your charms, whatever it takes."

There was supposed to be mood lightening humor in Ramona's tone and quick smile, but a sense of panic was creeping into Amalia's chest.

"Why can't they leave the dragons alone? So what if they are taking a few deer or turkeys? Even if they took a few sheep or cattle, so what? The Kingdom has plenty to share." Amalia was certain the dragons hadn't taken any livestock; those animals were not part of their diet, and of course, they just didn't steal.

"Our men will not leave the dragons alone. You know that."

"Yes, I know." Amalia wished there was another way, a way that didn't require her involvement in this mission.

Another possibility crossed Amalia's mind. "Why not tell the King what we know of the dragons? Maybe you could convince him to abandon the fight and help the dragons?"

"Absolutely NOT! There's no way he would agree to that.

He's committed to this fight of his. He's so stubborn; he never changes course.

"And besides, he wouldn't believe me. I know how he thinks, how all the men think. I know what they'll say. They think the dragons are evil and thieves. 'You don't feed thieves,' they'll say. They blame the dragons for their troubles; they're not going to share their food with them. We will not approach any of them!"

Amalia diverted her eyes from Ramona's intense stare.

"What about Reynard, I'm sure he could . . ."

"NO, I said. He can't be trusted either; his loyalty is to, and always has been, to the King."

Amalia was first shocked and unnerved by the venom in Ramona's words, but then she flushed to anger.

"I trust Reynard with my life." Her tone of voice and challenge surprised herself.

"I'm sorry." Ramona put a hand on Amalia's. "I didn't mean he isn't trustworthy. It's just that it would put him in a very difficult position. To make him choose between the King and our mission. It's best to keep him in the dark for his own good. For now, at least."

Amalia considered for a few moments. "You're right. I see it."

Ramona took her hand away and returned her attention to her papers. "The first order of business, I want a record of each person you approach. In this first column, in each row, I want you to put in a symbol that will represent a person's name, something that only you will recognize."

"Why not their name?"

"In case this document should fall into the wrong hands. I don't want anyone else to be able to read it."

The thought of someone stealing this paper only increased Amalia's sense of unease.

"For example, you could draw a pear for Linza."

"A pear?"

"She's kind of pear-shaped."

Linza, the game warden's wife, had just had a baby, and her figure had not yet recovered. Probably more humor meant to ease Amalia's mind, but it wasn't helping. Amalia was envisioning the Queens' mission, and she was dreading it. Various ways of being found out and the consequences of being found out were haunting her mind.

"I see. Are you considering Linza?"

"Yes, but don't approach her right away. Hold off. There are others you should approach first." Ramona turned back to the papers.

"In the second column, you can record their response, and in the third any promises you make to secure their cooperation. I made several other columns, just in case, for other notes. But keep your notes cryptic. Use a code. You'll have to let me in on it, of course. We'll use this document to keep track of your activities and progress."

Despite her fears, ideas, methods, and means began to conjure in Amalia's mind as Ramona spoke.

"Let's go through the most likely candidates first. We can only approach those we are sure we can trust. Even if they decide not to help, and some may not, they will need to keep their silence."

The women's eyes met; Amalia nodded.

"For my plan to work, we need the cooperation of the people who live in the Kingdom's north, those along the North Road. Definitely the Sheep Clan and the Horse Clan. Without them, we don't have any chance of success. Ald is the leader of the Sheep Clan, and Eachan is the headman of the Horse Clan. You should approach them as soon as possible."

"Do you know them?"

"I've met them, but I don't know them."

That probably meant that they didn't owe the Queen any favors. Ramona was running her finger down the census report.

"See this. This lists the names of their wives, children, and grandchildren. You should memorize the names. It's good to drop names into a conversation. See, Ald's wife died last year. Valuable information to have."

"What am I supposed to tell them, besides help the dragons?"

"Put it as—to get rid of the dragons—end the war quickly and save our men from injury or worse. Many of the commoners are not in agreement with the King. They take the brunt of any war."

"Alright, but what am I going to tell them that we want them to do, exactly? What is the plan?"

"It's a work in progress; I have some ideas."

"But ..."

"Only give them the general idea. That we want a quick end to the dragon hunt; everyone should want that. Tell them they can help, but they need to keep things secret. If you can get that commitment, then we can present them with what we want them to do. Get agreement from the clans first, and then we can move forward."

Both the Sheep and Horse Clans lived in the northern territory of the Kingdom and could be reached by the North Road. The Sheep Clan's cabins were just north of the hunting camp; farther north, the Horse Clan lived in the foothills that preceded the Northern Mountains. Amalia could arrange to meet them at the hunting camp, only a short ride from the castle.

"What of the loggers and the quarrymen?"

"I will rely on you to approach the logger's families. I believe we will only need their silence. Ask them to turn a blind eye to any unusual activities. Tell them as little as possible. Create some story or other to keep them from reporting dragon sightings. Make promises that you know that I can keep. Never use a threat."

The Hirsch estate, Feargus' home, sat to the west of the Sheep Clan village, reached by the Stag Road. No Nobles were in residence, but the land was occupied by the loggers, the men who ran the sawmill, and their families, all of who lived in a small hamlet near the mill.

"And the quarrymen and Cenhelm's family? Their people traveling on business to and from the castle might come across our activities."

The Coner family estate, Sir Cenhelm's home, bordered the Hirsch estate to the west. There was a village for the quarry men's families on the estate. The mansion, the community, and the quarries the family-owned could be reached by following Stag Road west to its intersection with Braga Road. The Braga Road led back to the castle but was a longer route than taking the Stag Road shortcut to the North Road.

"Possible; good thinking. I will speak to Lady Conor. She and her husband are not friends of the King. There has always been bad blood between the King's family and the Conors over property rights."

Drake's family-owned and operated the iron mines and forges in the lands just north of and bordering the Conor estate. The rights to and location of quarries and iron mines were a source of contention going back generations.

"And Sir Cenhelm?"

"Best not to involve him. He's devoted to the King despite his father's wishes. I'm sure his mother will see the wisdom in my plan to bring the dragon hunt to a quick end. We won't involve any other Nobles; they can't be trusted. We will only reach out to commoners. The Nobles are loyal to the King. Loyal to the King when it serves their self-interest, that is."

Amalia looked to the census report, her interest peaked. "Who else should we consider?"

"One of the barmaids, perhaps."

"Not Dagny, she can't be trusted, she's the one to share a secret with if you want the whole Kingdom informed by morning. Elsa is the better choice: She's a friend of mine. We grew up together in Morodon." Amalia noticed the ease in her voice and calm in her chest, surprised that her fear was gone.

That didn't seem possible.

"She's the quiet one? Her reputation for being timid exceeds even yours. Excellent choice."

"People say I'm timid?" Amalia knew that they did, always had, didn't need to ask, but the question escaped anyway.

Ramona smiled. "Makes you the best choice for this assignment. If you are sure you can trust Elsa, approach her."

"We can trust her."

Amalia ran her finger down the list and stopped. "What about Renilda, the healer woman?"

"I'd rather not have people from the village; they thrive on gossip."

"She's not like that. She's not a gossip. My aunt used her services for years. I have too. We can trust her with any confidence."

"We only want people who will serve the plan. As few as possible."

"Her knowledge of medicine and healing skills could be of value someday. Besides, she's wise beyond her years."

"Your right. I can see that. Approach her."

"What of the priest who gave you the census?"

"He can't be trusted—manipulated, but not trusted."

The church clock struck ten chimes, interrupting the conversation.

"Time is passing. I need to go. Feel free to use this place for meetings. No one will bother you here. It's safe." Ramona, leaving the census report and the chart on the table, stood and gave Amalia a brief embrace and hustled off to and out the door.

"Ma'am," Amalia said to Ramona's back, too late for Ramona to hear her.

The servants and laborers on Ramona's family estate could be trusted; anything they witnessed would not be reported.

Now standing alone in darkness, Amalia realized that focusing on the task of planning had calmed her, but the calm eroded with the contemplation of actually carrying out the task.

What will I say? How will I convince them? I'm not Ramona. I don't have her courage. How am I going to do this? What if I can't?

In a storm of doubt, Amalia pushed through the mill door and stepped into the bright blinding sunlight.

Amalia
& the Witch

It had been four days since the second battle of the new campaign against the dragons, and Amalia was on the Village Road on her way to the Healer's cottage to get more medicine for treating burns. In this second encounter, only four days after the first, another dragon was killed, and this time, several men were severely injured. Three men had severe burns. A Knight had fallen from his horse and broken several ribs. Renilda believed the Knight had critical internal injuries, bad enough to pose a threat to his life, and his recovery will most likely be prolonged. The King ordered the use of burn medicine he purchased from the healer priest, but it had no effect. After one day of agony, Ramona ordered a switch to the ointment Renilda was now providing. Amalia deemed it a miracle that only three men had received burns from dragon fire. In the previous encounters, the dragons had restrained their use of fire, but now they were defending themselves.

Amalia, standing in the early morning light in front of the Healer's cottage, gave a quick rap on the door, stepped in, and immediately had to duck under batches of drying herbs that hung from the rafters.

"Good morning, child." From behind her worktable, Renilda glanced up, her hands moving diligently with a mortar and pestle, uninterrupted. The Healer made her own medicines, unlike the healer priest who imported his from other kingdoms. Most of her ingredients came from herbs, tree bark, and mineral clays that she gathered herself. To obtain some components (not locally available) for her salves, ointments, and tinctures, she bartered with Healers from other kingdoms.

"Morning."

"I have your ointment ready, but I need to finish grinding these herbs for another patient. Need to get them fresh into a tincture."

"Certainly. Take your time. I have something I want to talk to you about anyway," Amalia made her way through the room toward the workbench. The space was filled, every square inch put to use. "Is there anything I can do to help?"

"There's always something to do; you know that. I'd be grateful if you rinsed those bundles of comfrey and hung them up to dry." Her hands diligently at work, the old woman nodded to a pile of leaves at the other end of her work table.

Amalia was familiar with the Healer's cottage and the everyday tasks; she had frequented the place since she was a child. When she and her mother visited her elderly aunt Florence who lived in the castle village, Amalia went to see Renilda as often as her mother allowed. At the cottage, Amalia attended to the chores Renilda assigned. Helping Renilda had always been a joy. The inside of the cottage itself was a wonder. The walls were covered with shelves that held a variety of items; earthen jars, pots with soft leather covers bound by colored ribbons, corked blue and brown glass bottles, and an assortment of small wooden boxes. As Amalia crossed the room, fragrances competed for attention, sweet to sour to lemon to licorice to earthen must.

The interior was well lit, a necessity for the work, by glass pane windows on all sides but north. Glass, costly and unusual in a peasant cottage, had been installed by one of Renilda's predecessors. The cottage was handed down through the generations from one healer to the next. Renilda and healers before her never charged for treatments, only accepting in barter what the patient could afford. Possibly, an earlier healer had healed a king or a wealthy Noble, resulting in the installation of the glass windows.

From the pile on the table, Amalia took a few comfrey leaves at a time, inspected them, dipped them in a bowl of water, and placed them in the hanging baskets behind her. The worktable was on the south side of the cottage, along the wall with the most windows, where sunlight dried the herbs in stacked baskets that hung from the ceiling by braided grass cords.

The comfrey came from Renilda's herb garden located behind the cottage. Haphazard and wild-looking, the garden was organized in a way only Renilda understood, beds for annuals and pathways that meandered between plantings of perennials.

The garden had the usual cooking herbs (basil, thyme, chives, etc.). Renilda used them to barter with the castle cook. Amalia was particularly fond of the angelica that was used to flavor candies and cakes, giving them their licorice flavor. The bulk of the garden was dedicated to Renilda's medicinal herbs (feverfew, chamomile, valerian, and the like) she used in her healing treatments. Some plants were only for the benefit of insects, butterflies, and hummingbirds.

Renilda quit her work and looked Amalia up and down. "You've lost weight, haven't you? Are you taking care of yourself? Are you feeling ill?"

"I have lost some weight, lost my appetite, just don't care to eat. I'm thinking of taking in my clothes; they're getting baggy."

"Better to put some of that weight back on."

"Maybe."

"What's troubling you?"

"I'm having difficulty sleeping. I toss and turn most of the night and then wake up early."

"Does it have to do with what you want to talk about?"

"Yes."

"Out with it."

As she put the last of the leaves in the basket, Amalia glanced back at Renilda.

"Say what you came to say before you burst."

Amalia had been rehearsing over and over how she should start the conversation, revising it each time, but now she just blurted it out. "I wanted to talk about helping the dragons," she said as she pulled her necklace from her blouse, exposing the stone dangling at the end. "This is a dragon stone."

In the pause that followed, Renilda left her work, went to a shelf behind her, and returned with a small wooden box. Opening it, she withdrew a small stone similar to Amalia's.

"Yes, I know now, a dragon stone; I have one as well. I just recently came to understand what it is."

"How d'you get it? Did a dragon give it to you?"

"No, not a dragon, my mistress did. She gave it to me when she withdrew as Healer, leaving the Kingdom's practice to me and this stone as well."

"She didn't tell you what it was for?"

"She didn't know. Her mistress gave it to her with only the instruction that it was precious and that it may be needed someday. She believed the stone was passed down generation to generation from the original Healer, Ceridwen."

"Ceridwen, the witch in the Witches' Gate story? I thought the witches were just characters in legends. She was a healer?"

Tales of witches were common in the stories of the Raconteur.

"In the story, I was told she was the first healer, the ancient one who started the long tradition of Kingdom Healers."

Renilda's revelation was utterly unexpected. "Have you spoken with a dragon?"

"Yes, but from a distance, a communication of vague

pictures, but enough to know their intent. I know they're not malevolent. They're starving. But I believe you already know that."

Amalia nodded. As Amalia began to unravel her story, the old woman directed her to the other side of the cottage. They sat in the cottage's only two chairs at the small rough-cut table with a polished top, not by intent, but by many years of use. Amalia told of her recent experiences, Ramona's desire to help the dragons, and their goal to recruit people into a secret network of friends dedicated to helping the dragons and ending the war.

After Amalia finished, she paused and asked the question waiting in the back of her mind the entire time she had been talking. "Will you join us?"

"I believe I already have."

"Yes, clearly, thank you." Another question was poised on Amalia's lips, but it hung there.

"Well, go on, ask."

"Are you a witch?"

"That depends child, on what you think a witch is. The notion of a witch conjures up different images in different minds; imaginings of storytellers; apparitions in the night; evil, frightening creatures; or resourceful, helpful souls."

Amalia was taken back. Had she hurt this wise old woman's feelings? She considered her a friend, a patient teacher. Was Amalia's questioning taken as an affront? It was important to measure her words, and not say anything wounding, but the next compelling question expressed itself. "Do you have magical powers?"

"That depends on what magic means to you. How do you see it?" Answering questions with questions, maddening. But Amalia knew she would eventually get an answer.

"Casting of spells, making of magical potions, conjuring of ghosts and spirits. Like in the fairy tales, mothers tell their children."

"I've heard those accounts of witches' powers as well. And you're thinking that if I have them, and I am in agreement with you and the Queen, I could use them to the benefit of your cause?"

Another question, but to the point. That was what Amalia was thinking, only more specifically. "Possibly a potion that could change the King's mind, call off the hunt for the dragons. Or maybe a conjured spirit to threaten him—or just convince him to change course." The words sounded harsh as they came out.

"Those would be amazing feats of witchcraft, if they existed in the realm of possibility or prudence."

"I'm talking foolishness, aren't I?" Amalia was rejecting her fanciful moment. She was sure embarrassment was showing in the flush of her face.

"Let's just say you were entertaining a hope that there may be an easy way out of your difficult situation, something less challenging with less risk."

"I have to ask another question if you don't mind."

"Of course, as you like."

"Can you read my mind? Is that a witch's power, to read minds? Sometimes, it feels like you know what I'm thinking before I do."

"It's not a magical power, love; it's a simple practice. I pay attention, listen carefully, and make an effort to understand you. We've spent a great deal of time together. I know your mind and your heart."

"Intuition then, not witchcraft." Amalia showed a smile. She had let her conjuring mind create a belief and hope in witchcraft as a possible solution to her problems—brief and fleeting, thankfully.

The old woman returned the smile as she rose from her chair. She retrieved a reed basket, containing several cloth-covered, earthenware jars, from the other end of the table. "The ointments for the burn victims." She then walked to the far wall and returned with a corked square blue bottle with a dropping reed attached by jute cord and placed it in the basket.

As she took her seat, Renilda said, "This tincture, it's for the archer with the severe burns. There's no need to apply the ointment to his burns any longer; the application will only cause him unnecessary pain. Have the nurses give him five drops every hour of the tincture. It will ease his suffering. Tell them to double the dose if it doesn't last the hour."

Amalia understood: there was no hope for the man. In the last battle, he had been badly burned on the entire left side of his body. Two other men, lancers, had burns on their legs, which the ointment was expected to heal, a long process Renilda predicted. Application of the ointment to the burned skin caused considerable pain. Only Amalia and one other nurse had the stomach for it: the odor of infection mixed with the smell of sulfur that emanated from the wounds was retching.

Acting on the advice of Renilda, Ramona asked the King to build an open-air infirmary. It was located outside the castle walls in the courtyard, a roof with no walls. It was the best place for recovery with less chance of infection, away from people and molds. Bent willow stick frameworks were added to the beds, to support gauze tents that covered the patients. That way, nothing touched the burns, and the wounds were protected from dust and flies.

"Terrible, the burns, the worst possible injury," Amalia said.

"I expect the dragons will use their fire more from now on, more burn victims are likely," Renilda said.

"Reynard believes the dragons are propelling a fluid that they somehow ignite as it leaves their mouth. Fortunately, the flaming liquid doesn't penetrate the shields but drains off. That's how the lancers got burns on their exposed legs. It's extraordinary that a creature can spit fire."

"Maybe not so strange. Dragons resemble reptiles; they might be related to snakes and lizards. I've never taken you, but I sometimes hunt snakes and milk them for the venom. There's a drop of venom essence in the tincture I gave you for the archer. I trade for a lizard venom that comes from healers in the Dacian Kingdom. That lizard spits venom in the face of their enemies when attacked. We use the venom to make treatments for arthritis, and disorders like shakes, palsy, and fits. I think the dragons may have pouches similar to snakes that hold a flammable liquid, and they can regulate the quantity they release the same as a snake does when it bites. And like a lizard, they can spit it out, and somehow they can ignite it when they do."

"If you're right, that would explain the dragon's reluctance to use the limited quantity they carry."

"And starvation could influence their ability to produce it. You can share my ideas with Reynard if you like."

"I share as little as possible with him. I'm keeping our activities a secret from him."

"As you wish," Renilda said, "but I want to ask you a favor, dear."

"Yes, anything."

"I could use your help collecting herbs. I want to stock up on the ingredients for the burn ointment."

"What is it you need?"

Renilda twisted in her chair and surveyed the shelves on the back wall. "I have plenty of comfrey, enough dried elder-flowers. But I need witch hazel. Fortunately, it's abundant. If you were to collect a basket full of leaves and twigs, that would be a big help."

"I would love to do that. I'll do it this afternoon." Amalia was grateful for the opportunity to do something useful, something she loved to do. The search for witch hazel trees that grow on the edges of the farm fields would be a welcome respite.

"Another ingredient I'm completely out of, Saint John's Wart."

"Where is it found?"

"It's abundant in the sheep pastures; the sheep don't eat it. It's in flower this time of year. We need to gather as much as we can."

"Where should we go? To the southern sheep meadows?" The Southern Sheep Clan's pastures were just south of the village, not far away.

"The southern clan treats it as a weed and work at removing it. We'll have to go to the northern clan's pastures. Ald knows the value of it and saves it for me. And as much as I enjoy the long walk, if the Queen could lend two horses, we could make better use of our time."

"Definitely, I'll arrange it for tomorrow morning. I have business with Ald and Eachan. I can meet with them while we're there." This was the type of work Amalia cherished. She had always enjoyed her times with Renilda. Whatever it was, whether collecting herbs in the fields or working in her cottage, infusing herbs into alcohol tinctures, or grinding barks for oils and ointment, or mixing beeswax and oil for salves. All of it was a joy for the senses, the fragrances and textures, the warmth and chill, and countless shades and hues of color. It was good work.

"That will be fine."

"I have to admit, I'm looking forward to this afternoon, work with no risk. I worry someone will discover what I'm doing for the Queen and the dragons." Amalia was glad for the opportunity to tell someone how she felt, the things she couldn't admit to Ramona.

"I can see why that troubles your mind."

"Something could go wrong, someone makes a mistake, something might give us away, and the King would find us out."

"What you say is true. You can usually count on things going wrong in one way or another."

Amalia's heart froze; her body shuddered.

"But that's the nature of the task you've undertaken. It will be worth it though, I'm sure, when this dragon hunt is over," Renilda said, "But I know that doesn't help much now."

Amalia didn't feel like she had much choice in the matter; circumstances had thrust this duty on her. She took a deep breath and blew it out through her puffed-out cheeks. "I hope nothing goes wrong."

"You need not worry too much about the King; the King will see what the King wants to see, only what he wants to hear. I'm sure Ramona still has her powers over him. But if someone finds you out, with her skills, she will likely overcome it."

"You make the King sound the fool."

"I suppose he could be seen as a fool, but he is no more or less than anyone else who is unawares."

"What do you mean?" Amalia reckoned the old woman to be speaking in riddles, which was her way, one of the bothers of conversing with a wisdom keeper.

"Drake only sees the Kingdom as his, painted in the colors of his choosing, populated with spirits that serve him, the air filled with the music of his own royal orchestra.

"And like most people, most of the time, that's all he knows. Only his picture of the world, it makes him vulnerable, easily manipulated."

"You believe we are safe from discovery?" Amalia put great stock in the old woman's opinions.

"Yes, by the King, at least, unless he should awake, but that's unlikely."

Amalia didn't understand what was meant by 'awake'. "I wish you could put a spell on him to keep him from waking up?" Amalia almost laughed.

"I'm sure that's in Ramona's plans. The King has woven his own spell, his own trance; she only needs to feed it."

"I hope you're right," Amalia said, "But I should go. I need to get these medicines to the castle."

"It's always a pleasure to see you, Amalia."

"Thank you, Renilda. I will return this evening with the

witch hazel, and I will be here first thing tomorrow morning with the horses."

The women exchanged warm smiles and then a gentle embrace. Amalia took up her basket and left the cottage. She took long, urgent strides as she made her way up the castle road. The herb gathering tomorrow with Renilda would make a good cover story for her visit with Ald and Eachan. She could approach Ald with the request to help the dragons and do the same with Eachan at his home, which was only a short ride north.

Amalia had met with Elsa at the tavern last evening, and she had agreed to be the eyes and ears at the inn. Renilda was now a member of the friends. Next, Amalia needed to convince Ald and Eachan to join. It was in Amalia's hands now, up to her to make it happen.

Clan Leaders

Despite the tension as they waited for Ramona, Amalia enjoyed listening to the old men, their conversation lively and peppered with stories and reminiscing. Ald and Eachan had agreed to meet with her and Ramona at the hunting camp.

Yesterday, after collecting Saint John's wart as planned, Renilda introduced Amalia to Ald. They met at his cottage and presented Ramona's request. In turn, Ald, Renilda, and Amalia traveled to Eachan's home, where Amalia again set out the gist of the proposal. Renilda's mere presence facilitated the conversation. Better to have introductions from a friend than to approach as a stranger with a message from a queen they didn't know.

The men acknowledged that it was wise to aid the dragons, but they did not want to engage in what could be seen as treachery against the King until they had a face-to-face meeting with the Queen. Ending the dragon hunt as quickly as possible was in their interest, but they wanted assurance that the Queen's plan was solid, that their activities had a good chance of success, and there was little risk of detection. They voiced a concern that their activities might be discovered by the quarrymen or lumberjacks. Amalia assured Ald and

Eachan that she had a plan to take care of that.

Today, she and the men sat at the fire ring, waiting for Ramona to arrive, enjoying the lunch that Amalia had brought along (salted fish, imported cheese, fresh bakery bread—delicacies), a rare treat for these men. One strategy Amalia had learned from Ramona—food was a valuable tool in the art of persuasion.

From the stories they told, Amalia gathered that these elders had been childhood friends. And now their sons were friends and their grandsons as well. They must be around the same age, Amalia thought, but the years had treated them differently. Eachan was tall and straight; Ald bent and swayed from side to side with a limp. Eachan not handsome but attractive; Ald's face was aged with a wrinkled grin and missing teeth.

After yesterday's afternoon meeting, Amalia had approached the women of the loggers and quarrymen. They gathered together over a common dinner to discuss Ramona's proposal, which was accepted by consensus in short order. The women wanted their men out of the army and back home and back to work. Also, the burned man, the archer, was a lumberman; they buried him yesterday, the first death. He was one of those who refused to carry a shield, called it a hindrance; bravado Amalia thought—costly.

Keeping quiet about unusual activities and not reporting dragons sighting was all that was required of the families. Without risk, it was certainly worth it, to hasten the end of the dragon hunt.

"When do ya think the Queen will be here?" Ald asked. His perpetual toothless grin stood in contrast to his grumpy reputation.

"I can't be sure," Amalia said, "It's difficult to say." He had asked this question when they first arrived at noon and again an hour ago. He may have forgotten; he was an old man, possibly forgetful. In addition, a secret meeting with the

Queen may have unnerved him. Amalia had explained that the Queen needed to wait until she could get free and was sure she wasn't followed. The clandestine meeting and covert nature of the Queens' activities were unsettling for Amalia; it must be the same for these pragmatic men.

"Patience old man," Eachan said with a smile, "Have some grub. Not often, we sit at a royal feast." Eachan had a thick slice of bread in one hand and a wedge of sharp cheese in the other. Both men had tried the bread from the royal ovens, thanked her for it, but she could tell they didn't care for it. It was considerably different in texture and taste from the substantial sourdough bread they were used to. They were eating it to be polite.

"I's got's patience, got no hurries. Just ask'en." Ald gave his friend a stern look.

"I'm sure the Queen will be here soon." Actually, Amalia had no idea if Ramona would make it at all. Ramona had to avoid a scheduled meeting or contrive an early end to it. Then she had to make sure that the King's guards, who were still covertly trying to keep track of her, were given the slip.

"While we're wait'en, could ya fill us in a little more?" Eachan said, "So's we could be a bit better prepared when the Queen gets here."

"Yes, I could do that," Amalia said, "As we discussed yesterday, your opposition to the dragon hunt is in line with the Queen's."

"Not's opposed, no, we ain't opposed to nothing the King sees fit." Ald was nodding and looking to Eachan.

"Right," Eachan said, "Not against it, we just say's we don't see the usefulness of the project, is all."

Ald was nodding his head in agreement.

"I understand; the Queen understands—just the wrong choice of words. What I meant was that neither of you has a quarrel with the dragons."

Both men nodded. "Right, they never done us no harm,"

Eachan said, "Don't wish them no harm neither."

"The Queen sees it that way too." Amalia wished that Ramona was there; she was better at this. But she could give these men the outline of the plan at least, in case Ramona didn't make it. "Five days ago, there was another battle, and another dragon killed. A total of four so far, including the young one that Sir Boetius killed in the ravine. What the Queen wants to do is help the dragons, keep them out of harm's way, provide them with food, get them out of the Kingdom as quickly as possible and put an end to the dragon hunt."

"Miss, may I ask, what came of your meeting with them loggers?" Eachan asked.

"Everything is well on that front. The women will keep things quiet. They won't report anything having to do with the dragons or your doings."

"And what is it we'll be do'en, exactly?" Eachan asked, but was stopped short by Amalia's raised hand.

Amalia listened for a long moment. It was the beat of horse hooves. Both men were on their feet and looking down the path toward the road, from which they expected the Queen or the King's guard to emerge. Amalia's apprehension ended when she recognized the rider as Ramona.

Ramona rode up to the fire circle in the middle of the camp and dismounted. As Eachan took the reins, he and Ald tried their best to bow and address the Queen with proper courtesy, both of whom never had the opportunity before. Their discomfort was dismissed by Ramona's broad smile and greeting. "Gentlemen, I am so glad you're here. Thank you for accepting my invitation."

"Ma'am," Eachan managed to get out. Ald was nodding.

Eachan took the horse to the tie rail at the water trough and returned at a jog.

"We don't have much time, so let's get to it." Ramona gestured to the benches around the fire-ring, where Amalia was seated.

At the fire pit, Eachan caught his friend by the elbow as Ald was descending to the bench. Ald responded with a grunt and agitated look. A flick of Eachan's head let the old man know the Queen was still standing, and Ald returned to a standing position like a soldier to attention. Ramona sat down with a smile and an approving nod, which allowed the men to settle on their bench.

Turning to Amalia, Ramona asked, "What have you told them of our plans?"

"Just the basic idea, to protect and feed the dragons, and end the hunt."

"Gentlemen, for this to happen, I will need your help and your discretion. But first, I need your agreement to keep this conversation to ourselves. Do I have that commitment?"

Both men nodded.

"Our venture won't be without risk. It's important the King not find us out. That will be my job. To keep him in the dark." Ramona waited a long moment, giving them time to think. "Will you accept the risk and help me?"

The men looked at each other. Eachan said, "We'd like to help, but what is it exactly you want us to do?"

"I'll get to that. But first, Ald, the day you and your grandson saw the dragon on the road, what was it like? Were you frightened?"

"No, not's me, it's the boy that panicked, blew the alarm. The beast flew off."

"Did you experience anything unusual? Maybe a picture in your head, something you have never seen before."

"I thoughts there was something strange, a kinda fit like, let it be though. Didn't tell no one." The old man was clearly puzzled.

"That was the dragon trying to talk to you," Ramona said, "Were there any animals in the vision the dragon gave you?"

"Yes'm, strange ones, some I's never seen afore."

"She was showing you the animals the dragons normally

hunt for food, some with large, wide antlers and others that looked like they might be related to cattle, but heavy built and with short necks and woolly manes."

"That's what I saw." Ald looked relieved.

"The dragons are short on food. They came here in search of game. Where they live in the far north, they have had two harsh winters and several summers short on rain, which has diminished the herds they feed on. This spring has been good so far, plenty of rain. They are trying to live on a subsistence diet in order to preserve the herds. The dragons need to make it to winter when they can go into hibernation. If the winter is mild and the rains come in the spring, they can go back to a normal hunt next summer. But if the weather doesn't cooperate, we may need to help feed them again next year. That's far off, though, no need to think about that."

"Well practiced stewards, they are then," said Eachan.

"Yes, but they need our help to get them safely through this summer."

"How can we do that?" Eachan asked.

Ramona looked to Amalia. Ramona's confidence in her was something Amalia relished. As of late, she even dared to think of herself as an essential partner in this venture with Ramona. "We will need to provide them with food, share our game, and if need be some sheep," Amalia said, "And we're hoping you will be able to find hiding places for them around here in the North Woods."

Eachan and Ald exchanged worried glances. Eachan said, "That's doable mostly, to keep em hidden from people travel'en through, but I don't know what we can do about them hunt'en dogs Sir Boetius got."

"Our plan is to keep the army, and Sir Boetius occupied in the Western Hunting Grounds," Ramona said, "We have friends there that will keep them distracted."

Amalia knew that was not exactly true. They had hopes of convincing people to do just that, but it was not yet a reality.

"We don't got too much game in these woods to feed lots a dragons," Ald said, "And we got not that many sheep to spare either."

"The dragons will still hunt in the West Woods where game is plentiful," Amalia said, "Once they put on some weight, we'll send them here, feed a little more if needed and then send them on north to their home. And maybe we could get some cattle brought to you?" Amalia looked to Ramona.

"Some cattle would be a help," Ald said. Eachan nodded in agreement.

"I'm sure I can arrange it," Ramona said. "But there is one important thing you need to learn before you can begin your work helping the dragons. You will have to learn how to talk with them."

Neither man responded; they exchanged worried glances. Amalia retrieved a black cloth bag from her waist pouch. From the bag, Amalia poured dragon stones out onto a flat rock in front of the men. The men sat in quiet, exchanging quizzical looks as Ramona explained the purpose of the dragon stones. Then, as instructed, each man took a stone.

Ramona looked to the western horizon; the sun was dangling above it. "I need to get back to the castle before I'm missed," Ramona stood up.

After a moment's hesitation, both men jumped to their feet, nearly falling forward as they did. Both bowed awkwardly. "Your Highness," they said.

"I can't thank you enough for your cooperation and your willingness to help us and the dragons," Ramona said, "Amalia will be your contact if you need anything or have questions. She will take it from here." Again, Ramona assumed agreement and commitment even though neither man had voiced it. She gave each man a hug in turn, both of whom stood stiff. She hurried to her horse at the water trough and mounted. Passing the fire circle, the Queen waved. A moment later, she was on the road and quickly out of sight.

Eachan and Ald stood motionless. Eachan looked at the stone in his open hand. This must have been the strangest day of these men's lives; they looked bewildered.

Now for the best part. Amalia so enjoyed the idea of introducing someone to a dragon. It was terrifying her first time. But now, she couldn't help but feel the need to show off, to stand fearless in front of the scourge of the Kingdom, especially with these men by her side. Not gracious or meek, but she couldn't help herself.

"Gentlemen, follow me." Amalia started down the path toward the road. From there, they would travel a little way up the North Road to a pasture where she had arranged to meet Alpha.

The Warden's Wife

ore battles, more wounded, more deaths—dragons and men. Something needed to be done. Ramona had shared her ideas with Amalia. Amalia felt that she was doing her part, putting them in place. In an effort to recruit Linza, the game warden's wife, Amalia had met with her a week ago. It had been a few days after the third battle of the second campaign. In that fight, a lancer had been crushed by a dragon as it tried to escape. Three archers had severe burns (two not expected to live), one Knight broke his back in a fall from his horse, and many more men were injured; burns, broken bones, serious and minor. In addition, another dragon was killed after it was caught in the catapult net.

Amalia knew Linza had a brother and several cousins in the army and hoped that she would be inclined to support Ramona's efforts to bring an end to the conflict. If Linza and her husband could be convinced to join the group of friends, they would have a crucial role to play. Amalia had only given Linza the general idea of what she was proposing—that Linza and her husband could help Queen Ramona bring an early end to the dragon hunt. Linza had refused to commit: she was too angry, too frightened, and she sanctioned the prevailing hatred for the dragons. Linza refused to even consult with her husband, didn't want him involved, thought he might report Amalia. As she said, 'don't wants no troubles.'

Since that meeting with Linza, there had been yet another battle, just two days ago. Another dragon was killed, more men were wounded, and five men died; two lancers crushed, two archers killed by fire, a Knight thrown from his horse (he died of a head injury). One of the seriously wounded was Linza's cousin, a fact that Amalia hoped might influence her: she may now be more inclined to help end the war. Since Linza and her husband were so crucial to Ramona's new plan, Ramona thought it best to meet with Linza in person. Amalia went to see Linza at her cottage a second time yesterday evening to propose a meeting with the Queen.

It took from dinner time to near nightfall, an evening of persistent cajoling (Amalia stating and restating her case), which eventually overturned Linza's resistance. Linza agreed to go to the meeting the next morning.

Linza had kept saying, 'Don't never spoke to no royalty, and's don'ts want to.' Was Linza more afraid of dragons or a meeting with the Queen? It was hard to tell.

She grew up in the remote miner's village on the western edge of the Kingdom and then married the warden of the Western Hunting Grounds. A life of isolation, apparently, was what she was used to, and she wanted to keep it that way.

As Amalia approached the church, the morning of the meeting, the tower clock struck nine, perfect timing. Meeting Linza at the church was a good idea. It wouldn't create any suspicion. Linza went to the church often and had been planning to pick up colic medicine for her baby from the healer priest, a good cover story. Amalia didn't really need a cover story herself; she was invisible for the most part, no one would suspect her of being part of a secret plan to help the dragons. At least, that's what she told herself during her anxiety attacks.

Within sight of the church, Amalia stopped and waited; Linza was coming out the door. Linza, short and wide with the broad shoulders of a man, no distinguishable waist and close-cropped hair, was wearing a long brown tunic and black belt. "Hello, Linza. Glad you came. I was worried that you might have a change of heart."

Linza carried a small satchel and a worried look. Amalia was struck with a worry of her own; hopefully, Linza didn't confide in the priest.

"I said I would. I do what I say."

"Oh yes, I'm sure. How is your baby? How's he feeling?"

"Not much better, still got's the bellyaches. My cousin has em. She got's a baby bout the same age. We takes turns look'en after each other's babes." It was common practice for common women to exchange wet nurse favors.

"It's fortunate you have each other."

Linza smiled and nodded, then after a moment, her worried face returned. "I'm not sure I should be do'en this. Why's the Queen wants to meet with me?"

"Not to worry, she's very nice."

The women were walking now, on the road toward the castle. At the Kingdom Crossroads, Amalia guided Linza out the East Road, in the direction away from the castle toward the old mill.

"Where we go'en?"

"A secret place. I need your oath that you won't tell anyone about the meeting. Not even your husband for now."

Linza clutched the bag of medicine with both hands to her chest.

"Queen Ramona is a good friend to have. That's what she wants to talk with you about, friendship."

Linza slowed her pace, stopped, and looked to Amalia. "You has my word."

They walked the rest of the way to the old mill in silence. Upon reaching the mill, Linza trailed Amalia up the path to the main doors, followed her in through the creaking man-door, and across the big, open, darkened room to the bench on the far side. Amalia and Linza sat down to wait for Ramona.

This old mill was a suitable place for clandestine meetings. It was easy for Ramona to slip away from the castle to the old mill on her family estate without drawing attention to herself. A visit home did not arouse suspicion.

Amalia was glad that for this meeting, Ramona was involved with the recruitment. At first, like Linza, many of the people Amalia approached did not want to be party to the venture. Understandably, they were afraid. With persistence, Amalia had persuaded some. Others only agreed to keep silent and not report the Friends activities. Many of those living in areas where their silence was valuable; all they had to do was look the other way. But Linza was another matter; they needed her active support.

"I never talked with a Noble afore." The warden's wife sat on the bench next to Amalia, looking at her hands, clasped, and rubbing them together.

"It'll be okay, Linza. The Queen is a good woman," Amalia said, "Like you."

Linza looked up with a faint smile. "She wants to talk about them dragons, doesn't she? All I know is—one tried to take my son."

"We need to talk about that. That incident with your son was just a misunderstanding."

Linza was clearly puzzled. "How could ya know that?"

Amalia had her attention. Like with others, Amalia told the story of Ramona's first meeting with the dragon. She spoke of how Ramona learned to communicate with the dragons and how the dragon stones worked like a beacon. After which, she sat quietly for a time, letting the story sink in.

"I know it's hard to believe, but I talk with them as well."

"But a dragon tried to take my boy. Why'd it mean us harm?"

Not knowing when Ramona would arrive, Amalia decided

to tell Linza what actually happened the day the dragon appeared at her cottage. "The dragon you saw that day wasn't trying to take your son. She was protecting him."

"The beast was hover'en right over my boy, bout to snatch him up. If it didn't get distracted by somethin in the woods, I would'a lost him." Linza had a reputation for a stormy temper, and she was showing it.

With unusual felt calm, Amalia returned a smile to the angry woman. She had always thought of herself as timid, someone who dreaded confrontations. But meeting a dragon and Ramona's confidence in her had changed her, or maybe not changed, perhaps circumstances provided the opportunity to be herself. "The dragon didn't fly off because it was distracted; it attacked and drove off the wolf at the edge of the woods that had been stalking your son."

"I don'ts believe it," Linza said with defiance.

"Linza, think about it. If a dragon wanted your son, a distraction wouldn't have stopped her; you couldn't have stopped her. Queen Ramona will tell you the same."

"I don'ts wants to say I doubts you or the Queen, but I knows what I saw." Linza's voice trailed off.

Reaching into the pocket of her dress, Amalia pulled out a braided grass necklace with a dragon stone attached, which she held out to Linza. "When you join us, you can talk to the dragon yourself."

Linza took the necklace in her hand. "Talk to a dragon? Join you do'en what?"

Amalia knew it was presumptive when she braided the necklace to hold Linza's dragon stone, but Linza's agreement was essential, a negative response was not acceptable. Amalia went on to explain the dragon's predicament, why they were hunting in the game lands, that they were near starvation, and Ramona's plan to help the dragons avoid the hunt and end the conflict.

"It's a lot to take in. But the terrible stories you have heard about dragons are either misunderstandings like yours or simply not true.

"It's the dragons that are suffering terribly. Besides the five dragons that have been killed in the battles, three others have died. One was wounded in the belly by a crossbow arrow, got an infection and died of it. Two others, an old mated pair, chose to sacrifice themselves, give their allocation of food to the young; they flew off out to sea. It's a total of six killed if you include Alpha's young'en that was killed by Boetius in the ravine."

Linza rocked back, tilted her head.

"You have a question?"

"Miss, you said Alpha."

"That's the name of the dragon you saw at your cottage, the one that protected your son. It's not actually her name. We don't really know their names. They can't tell us. We just call her that because she appears to be the leader, the alpha."

The creak of the mill door opening interrupted Amalia and startled both women. It was Ramona. She hurried across the mill floor.

Linza jumped to her feet, curtsied, and bowed her head.

Ramona took up Linza's hands and noted the dragon stone necklace she was holding.

Ramona glanced to Amalia, "I see that you've shared our story with Linza."

"Please sit." Still holding Linza's hands, Ramona guided her down as they took a seat on the bench, side by side. "It's so good of you to meet us here. It's an odd request, the secrecy and all. But I'm sure you see the necessity for it knowing what you know now."

"I was just telling Linza about the harm and suffering the dragons have had to endure in the dragon hunt and how Alpha protected her son."

"Yes, true. And besides the harm to the dragons, as you well know, the King's army has also suffered many casualties."

Ramona said, "I'm so sorry your cousin was wounded. He seems to be doing well. Renilda tells me that a full recovery is expected."

"I heard's you be taken good care of our men. Thank you, Ma'am."

"You are so welcome. It's the least we can do.

"But what we want is to prevent any more casualties. And we need you and your husband to help put a stop to the hunt and the killing." Ramona was still holding Linza's hands.

"Me and my man? What could we do to help?" Linza showed signs of softening, her guard coming down, more at ease.

"First, by learning how to talk with the dragons." Ramona smiled at Linza; her eyes glowed. "Unbelievable, right? Just wait until the first time you talk with a dragon. A little frightening, but amazing."

Linza's eyes were wide; her mouth dropped open.

How Ramona approached people, so casually, with such delicate matters, amazed Amalia.

"Don't worry, Amalia will help you with your first contact." Ramona was patting Linza's hand. "Now that you have a stone, you will be able to call to the dragons when you need to. They're usually close by. They hunt in the West Woods near your cottage. That's how the dragon spotted that wolf that was threatening your son. She was out hunting." Linza looked like she had another question, Ramona paused. "I'm sorry, you have questions. Ask."

"Ma'am, beg your forgiveness, but you's say they be always about—watch'en us?"

"Yes, despite their size, they are very quiet. They fly at night looking for favorable places to hunt, and finding one, settle in till morning. During the day, they trail the game animals on the ground. Flying takes a great deal of energy, which of course, they need to conserve."

"That's why the hunt'en dogs can find them?"

"Yes, the trails they leave are easy for the dogs to follow, and the dragons have a rather strong and peculiar scent," Ramona said. "And that brings me to our reason for contacting you. We need you and your husband's help to set false trails."

"My husband?"

"Your husband is in the best position to help us. As Game Warden for the West Woods, he will be able to move around the woods without suspicion." Ramona nodded to Amalia, who opened a carry bag (left at the mill by Amalia early that morning) that was under the bench and pulled out a blanket. "This blanket carries the scent of a dragon. Amalia rubbed it on a dragon to pick up the scent. A bit strong, but not too unpleasant. Your husband can use the blanket to create false trails to fool the hunting dogs, send them in the wrong direction, and lead them away from the dragons hunting spots."

Linza was visibly overwhelmed.

"Do you understand what we are asking of you?" Amalia said.

"I understands. But my man wouldn't want no parts of it."

"I would like you to go home and discuss our proposal with him," Ramona said, "Amalia will go with you. She will help you through it, and if needed, I can meet him here and speak to him as well."

Amalia could tell from the look on Linza's face that this was too much, too sudden for her. She needed time to absorb it.

"We can't do what you ask. My man is good friends with the men in the hunting troop, especially Berengar. They been friends since my man was a young'en. Berengar taught em what he knows of hunt'en and track'en. He couldn't go's against them."

"In the long run, by helping us and the dragons, he would be protecting them from possibly being hurt or killed by bringing the dragon war to an end sooner," Ramona said.

Amalia asked, "Have you or your husband seen Berengar lately, since the day the hunters came back with the second dragon skin?"

"No, we haven't. Ain't seen him in over a month. Heard he took ill, something bad happened to him, a fit or somethin."

"After we are done here, I will take you to see him, so you can hear his story, his experience with the dragons," Amalia said.

Amalia was sure that hearing Berengar's story would help persuade Linza and her husband to take up the cause and accept their very dangerous part in the plan. Berengar wasn't ill, not physically; Renilda went to see him shortly after the incident with the dying dragon. She said he didn't so much need medicine but an explanation. He had been having nightmares, a case of the nerves, and the priest's medicines were making it worse, giving him the shakes. After Renilda made it clear what had happened with the dragon, and the drug was out of his system, Berengar regained his senses. He didn't rejoin the hunting troop though; Boetius took his place as leader. His sympathy for the dragons was part of it, but he also did not want to go into the woods and risk meeting a dragon again and having another vision.

"Yes, please visit with Berengar," Ramona said, "I'm sure that will be helpful."

"I think we should talk with Renilda as well," Amalia said, "She's the one who helped Berengar with his troubles. I'm sure she could help with your baby's illness."

Linza had complained of the cost of the medicine; it was taking too much of her husband's wages. Renilda could surely provide a more effective treatment and less costly.

"Another good idea, you must go see her too," Ramona said.

"Yes, Ma'am, I can go's along with those visits."

"I understand that you need time to think this over before you can commit to our plan," Ramona said, "But I'm sure you will see it our way once you have weighed the risks and benefits. Either way, no matter what you choose to do, you have a friend in me from now on."

"Thank you, Ma'am."

"After you visit with Berengar and Renilda, please let Amalia introduce you to a dragon. She can escort you home and call a dragon so you can hear—more accurately—see their story firsthand."

Linza looked as if she wanted to speak; her mouth hung open.

With that, Ramona finally released Linza's hands, stood, and guided her up by her shoulders, enveloping her in a warm hug. "I have to go, sorry. I don't want to be missed. Thank you so much for coming here to meet with me. You can ask anything of me, anytime—through Amalia—anything you need. Goodbye Linza." Ramona walked across the barn floor and disappeared out the door.

Amalia had gotten to know Linza well enough over the last week or so. She was sure Linza could be convinced to take part, and if she did, her husband would follow.

"Well now, we have things to do," Amalia said, "Let's go see Renilda first. Her cottage is just down the Village Road. I'm sure she will have something that will help with your baby's illness." It was best to put things in motion before Linza got over the shock and could protest.

"But's I just bought this medicine from the priest. I don'ts got's money to pay for more."

"Don't worry. Renilda never takes money. You can give her something in return. Something you have in surplus." It was the healer's practice to barter, to take anything she was offered. If she didn't need the item or have a use for it, she would pass it on to someone who could.

"My man got's lots a beaver furs."

"I'm sure that will do just fine. After we talk with Renilda, we'll head back toward your place. We can stop and visit with Berengar and his wife; their cottage isn't much out of the way. And after that, we can go to your home and call a dragon."

Linza looked at the dragon stone, cradled in her open hand. Her hand trembled slightly.

"Not to worry, it's going to be fine." Amalia wasn't sure how she could say that. She didn't know how things were going to go. There were lots of ways for things to go wrong. A plan, confidence, and hope—a page from Ramona's book was what she had.

Amalia put her arm around Linza's shoulders and guided her to the door and out into the bright sunlight, which portended a brighter future than the gloom of the barn.

A Stone
for Feargus

Feargus couldn't help but wonder. Why had Ramona invited her maid to this secret meeting? Could it be that she didn't trust him, or maybe she didn't trust herself to be alone with him? Sitting uncomfortably with the maid, he expected Ramona to dismiss her when she arrived.

"I'm sure Ramona will be here shortly," the maid said, breaking the awkward silence.

The maid sat calmly, too calm and too casual, on the bench next to where Feargus was standing. She hadn't addressed him formally when he arrived, hadn't done so when she delivered the invitation from Ramona either. She was impertinent. Admittedly, she was Reynard's woman, but that didn't give her license to disregard her manners. He didn't remember her being like that, but then he probably hadn't paid attention before.

Last evening, the maid came to Feargus' family manor house with the invitation. Located near the castle, Feargus lived there with his bachelor uncle instead of his family estate in the North Woods. Since Feargus was frequently engaged in some Kingdom business, the manor was more convenient. And these days, he was either in the field with the army or at home for quick respites.

Upon entering the receiving room, the maid declared that she had a message from the Queen and asked Feargus to dismiss the servants so that she could speak to him in private. Ramona wanted a secret meeting the next morning at seven o'clock, at the old mill. He was more than glad to receive a meeting request from Ramona, but not the brash manner in which her maid delivered it.

The creak of rusty hinges and a bright shaft of light penetrated the room as Ramona pushed through the old door.

"Amalia, Feargus, thank you for coming." As Ramona sat down next to Amalia, she motioned to a nearby crate.

He shook his head; he preferred to stand.

"Ramona," Feargus responded, "Why all the secrecy?"

"I wanted to speak with you privately. I have a request, a rather unusual request. It has to do with the dragon hunt, and it must be kept secret. No one can learn of it, especially Drake. I need your word."

"You're asking me to keep a secret from Drake? And you want my word before you tell me what it is?"

"Yes. I'm asking you to trust me."

Feargus glanced at Amalia.

"Anything we say can be said in front of Amalia."

Feargus didn't like the idea, but he was too intrigued to argue at this point. "Go on then."

"I believe we have a common goal—to end the dragon hunt as soon as possible, put an end to the killing and casualties." Ramona paused.

"True, I have always thought this venture foolish at least, but inevitable. I don't see any way out of it."

"There is a way. I have a plan, and I have a part for you to play in it."

"What is this plan of yours?"

"I can't give you the details of what I have put into play. I can only share what I want you to do, what I need you to do."

"So, you want me to trust you, but you don't trust me." Even when they were children, she always confided in Drake and not him. He didn't understand it.

"Other people are involved who are taking great risks. I need to protect them from discovery. I don't tell anyone more than they need to know. It's safer that way. You don't need to know what they are doing, and they don't need to know of your involvement."

"I'm not just one of your people; we have been friends for a long time. This secrecy is insulting." It was useless to argue with Ramona, but Feargus couldn't help himself. "Maybe I don't need all the details or names, but at least I need to understand the goal of this plot of yours. Possibly, I would have something to offer."

"The objective is to interfere with the army's ability to find the dragons—to reduce or eliminate encounters."

"That's well and good in the short run, but that doesn't get the dragons out of the Kingdom. That should be the goal of any plan."

"Of course it is, but you can help reduce the encounters. We only need a delay to buy time until I can get the dragons fed and escorted out of the Kingdom. They are only here for food; they're starving."

"So my hunch was correct: they are here searching for food because of the loss of game in their homeland, in the far north?"

"Yes. And once they get enough food, they will leave the Kingdom. It's just a matter of time. That's what I need you to do, buy time."

"Wait. How do you know this is true? How are you so sure of yourself?"

"I talk with the dragons. I know their thoughts."

"What? Impossible. No one talks with beasts."

Amalia shifted in her seat. Ramona folded her arms across her chest. She did not respond right away but stared at Feargus with a sourness that could curdle milk.

"Boetius communicates with his dogs; you communicate with your horses. Dogs, horses, dragons, are not beasts."

Feargus needed to backtrack. "Not that I don't believe you. I take your point. It's just hard to swallow."

"Well, it's true, I ... we," Ramona nodded to Amalia. "Can communicate with dragons. We can coordinate our activities, help them avoid the army, find food, and move them out of the Kingdom."

"Okay, but what is it you want me to do, exactly?"

Ramona looked to Amalia, who produced a small black bag from which she poured a handful of smooth white stones the size of a bird's eggs into her palm.

"Take one," Ramona said, "We use the stones to communicate with the dragons."

For a moment, Feargus' hand reluctantly hovered over the stones in Amalia's hand. He saw she was smiling and immediately snatched one up, giving her a look meant to wipe the smile off her face, which it did not.

"How's this work? What do I do with it?"

"You only need carry it with you when you are with the army. But keep it out of sight. It will glow softly when a dragon is nearby."

"So, if I get near a dragon, it will talk to me through this stone."

"No, not that, you won't be communicating directly with the dragons. The stone will act as a beacon. The dragons can sense it from a distance. It will alert them that the army is approaching and hopefully give them enough time to escape."

"So it's magical. You expect me to believe in magic."

"It's not magic; it's simply a different way of communicating with another creature."

Ramona had always been able to simplify the crazy. "So if I carry this stone with me, it will alert the dragons, and it could help bring the battles to an end?" Just what Feargus had wanted all along.

"Yes, that's the idea."

"We'll see if this magic works." Feargus could not resist the subtle tease.

"It'll work. And it's not magic, it's ... How else can I explain it?" Ramona's voice was tinged with agitation.

"Take it easy. I'm okay with this. I'll do it, can't hurt anything to carry a stone in my pouch."

"Fine. Thank you."

"Since you can talk with the dragons, maybe you can answer a few questions?" If Ramona could really talk with dragons, she should be able to clear up some things that had been bothering Feargus.

"I'll try."

"The dragons didn't use their fire to their advantage in our first engagements when we didn't have the dogs or the catapult. They used it as a warning?"

"Yes, the King's men weren't a threat then."

"And now they need to use it to defend themselves?"

"Yes."

"Thank god for Reynard's shields." Feargus glanced in Amalia's direction.

"Reynard is also working on metal-clad leggings for the men to wear," Amalia said.

"Yes, I am aware of that," Feargus said, "Hopefully, they will provide some additional protection."

"If my plan works, we won't have any more battles and no more burn victims," Ramona said.

"There's another thing I don't understand. Sometimes the dragons fly when we approach, sometimes they only fly after a protracted engagement, and sometimes they move off on the ground. Why not just fly off? It would seem the better option."

"For one thing, flying takes a lot of energy which they can't afford to waste since they are starving. And once they have a kill, they need to protect it. It's a matter of life or death; they need to eat."

"Makes sense. The dragons still don't use their fire that much."

"It also takes energy to make the fire, which is difficult for them because they're so weak."

"One last thing, the disappearance of the dead dragons, what of that." The bodies of the dragons killed in battle were left on the field. Feargus, as commander, had forbidden the practice of skinning them for hides. Boetius had argued for it, but the men were with Feargus. No trophies would be taken; the men saw the dragons as combatants, not animals.

"I'm not sure exactly why, but they return at night and perform a ritual obsequy, a cremation," Ramona said, "It was good of you to honor their dead and not let your men interfere."

Boetius had wanted to set a vigil over the bodies at night and launch an attack when the dragons returned for their fallen.

"An enemy's dead deserve the same respect as our own."

Feargus picked the stone from his palm and held it at eye level between his thumb and forefinger, twisting it for closer examination. "So this little stone will act as a beacon and alert the dragons when the army is near. Amazing. Hard to believe." He dropped it into his carry pouch that hung at his hip. "Even so, the hunting troop will still be a problem. Boetius has taken over the leadership since Berengar took ill. He thinks he's a better tracker than Berengar; he isn't. But with Berengar's dogs, he still finds the dragons trails easily."

"I have a plan in place to help with that."

"I'm sure you do, and I'm guessing you're not going to share it with me?"

Ramona only met his gaze.

"What of the other kingdoms? My sister tells me that the dragons in Braga and Duren mostly stay in the eastern wilds of both Kingdoms. The terrain is hilly, rough, very difficult for their armies to close in on the dragons. Their men only get a chance at them when they wander into the flatlands in the west to steal cattle."

"It's not likely they're stealing cattle."

"How would you know?" Feargus asked, "Oh, right, you probably talk with those dragons too." Ramona had always been so full of herself.

"One of the dragon clans has been living in the Northern Wilds. They roam the territories of Braga, Duren, and Evora following the elk herds. They sometimes pursue the elk out in the lowlands."

"What do you mean by one of the clans?"

"There are three clans in the dragon's tribe, with four to six families in each. The clans split up when they migrated south. One is in our Kingdom, one passed through to Chambold, and the other, as you know, is working the Northern Wilds of Braga and Duren and even Evora at times." Ramona paused.

"Any more questions?"

Feargus shook his head, "No."

After a few moments of silence, Feargus said, "I need to go. I'm expected at the encampment."

"Very well." Ramona stood. "Thank you so much, Feargus. I know it all sounds so strange."

"If it will help put an end to this war, it's certainly worth a try." Feargus bowed and turned away.

As Feargus approached the door, he considered the foolishness of accepting the idea that a little stone could be used to communicate with dragons. But then, the dragons were an impossibility a few months ago. Why not talk to them with a stone? And it had always been impossible to say no to Ramona. It couldn't hurt anything to carry this stone, and besides, no one would know what he was doing. And if this thing worked, it would foil Boetius' pursuit of the dragons; all the better.

He looked back, nodded to the two women seated on the bench, and pushed through the door. What would come of this? We shall see.

According to Plan

As Feargus left through the barn door, a burst of morning brightness momentarily flooded the barn. The two women exchanged a knowing glance.

"Well, that was easier than I expected," Ramona said.

"He's putty in your hands," Amalia replied, "He'd do anything for you."

Ramona's face blushed. The tables turned; Amalia was teasing her.

"How did it go with Linza and her husband?" It had only been a day since their meeting with Linza, and Ramona couldn't wait to hear how it went. Linza and her husband had a crucial role to play in the plan.

"Also better than expected. They didn't commit yesterday, but I think they will come around. They wanted more time to talk it over."

"Understandable. Tell me all about it."

"We went to visit with Renilda first. She gave Linza a treatment for her baby, talked with Linza for over an hour. Renilda has a way with people, put Linza at ease right off. She's like everyone's grandma. Linza asked Renilda if she knew about Alpha and the killing of the dragon's young'un by Sir Boetius. Apparently, it was troubling her mind, a mother's loss of a child. Renilda told her how she had sensed it when it happened; the pain of it came to her through her dragon stone. They both had a cry over it. Made me tear up too." Amalia's eyes were wet.

The skin around Ramona's eyes tightened at the thought, the pain of losing a child, also the pain of not having a child.

"After our visit with Renilda, we called on Berengar and his wife. Berengar hasn't left his cottage since the incident with the dying dragon. His wife says he's much easier to keep track of these days, a big change from spending most of his time roaming the woods. She made jokes the whole time we were there, saying how he was underfoot and all. He didn't seem to appreciate her humor. His situation must be intolerable for him, a man of the wilds, confined to a house."

"Did he share his story with Linza?"

"Yes, it was overwhelming, another sad story. It must have been a terrible experience to be in the mind of another being as it died; I can't imagine. I felt terribly sorry for Berengar— and Linza; she started crying again." Tears ran down Amalia's cheeks. Ramona couldn't stop her own and brushed a tear off her cheek.

"It was unexpected; it just didn't fit my image of Linza. I didn't expect her to be so—so emotional, crying openly like that. By the time we left, though, she wasn't sad anymore; she was back to her normal angry self, a good thing. Her sympathy is with the dragons now and wants to help them."

"Very good. Not good, she was upset. You know what I mean. What happened next?"

"After we left Berengar and his wife, we headed to Linza's cottage. When we got there, her husband wasn't home, but her cousin was with the babies and Linza's toddler. We visited with her cousin for a bit. Linza gave a dose of Renilda's medicine to her baby. We made excuses about having some errands and left her cousin and the babies and headed out into the woods to meet Alpha."

"She was agreeable? Willing to go that easily?"

"She was still angry, more angry than sad, and more angry than scared. One benefit of anger, I guess, it can override your fears."

"Go on."

"We headed up one of the old logging roads to a small clearing on a hilltop. I pulled out my dragon stone and told Linza to hold hers in her hand too. I let her know I was going to call to Alpha by making pictures in my mind, a picture of the three of us together in the clearing. I told her to try to keep her mind open. We needed to be patient: Alpha could be anywhere in the West Woods.

"After 20 minutes or so, Linza was getting nervous; her angry episode was wearing off. I worried that she might lose heart and change her mind, but then Alpha dropped silently out of the sky right in front of us."

"What did Linza do?"

"Nothing, she didn't move. She wasn't terrified, as you might expect, just overcome with the strangeness of the whole thing. As you know, Alpha's appearance is quite shocking at first. But it didn't take long for Linza to get her composure and start asking questions. She was eager to talk with a dragon and was making real attempts to exchange images with Alpha. She got vertigo, even threw up once, but kept at it, forcing herself to concentrate on the communication. I just stood back and watched. Once things started working pretty well, Linza got all emotional again. We were seeing pictures of the dragon saving her boy and the death of Alpha's young'un. For a moment, I thought she was going to give Alpha a hug. She didn't, though. I'm not sure how a dragon would interpret a hug."

"That's amazing."

"It seemed like the conversation lasted for a long time, but it was probably only minutes. Linza was exhausted. I let Alpha know the human had had enough. She flew off, and Linza fell to her knees, staring at the glowing stone in her hand."

"What about her husband? You spoke with him?"

"I did. After our time with Alpha, we returned to the cottage, and he was there. Her cousin left shortly after we arrived. Linza made tea, and the three of us sat outside at their fire pit. After I got her husband's agreement for secrecy, I let Linza tell her story, the whole story. It took a while, well after dark. At first, he argued with everything she said. He said he didn't believe her. At one point, he accused her of lying. Boy, did that set her off. I'm sure he regretted it, and she will make sure he regrets it for a long time to come. She's going to take him to visit with Berengar today to confirm that part of the story. But I'm sure he will see things her way. It might take a few days. I plan to go back soon and check in with them."

"Everything seems to be falling in place."

"I explained what we wanted him to do, to make false trails with the blanket to lead the tracking dogs astray. He was reluctant, but Linza asked that I bring the scented blanket to them as soon as I could."

"That's a good sign."

"Yes, her husband didn't object. I suspect he has accepted his wife's will. I don't think he has any real choice in the matter."

"Speaking of husbands, how are you progressing with Reynard? Set a wedding date?"

"Nothing as yet, the last time he proposed was over a year ago."

"He's asked more than once?"

"Yes, many times."

"You've turned him down, how many times?"

"I've lost count."

"Reynard is a patient and persistent man then. Should he ask again, you would say yes?"

"I would, but there's not much chance of that right now. The dragon hunt occupies all his time and mine as well."

"Once we bring this dragon hunt to an end, things will be different for everyone."

"So, it could end soon?"

"If things go according to plan, there shouldn't be any more battles," Ramona said, "And that will make it easier to feed the dragons and get them out of the Kingdom."

"I hope that's the case."

"And when that day comes, we can focus our attention on securing Reynard as your husband. I have influence with the priest to get a wedding date for you."

"I don't want to get married in the church; wouldn't waste the money." There was venom in Amalia's voice.

Ramona had been married by the priest in a church ceremony. It was obligatory for Nobles, and of course, a royal wedding was a rare and momentous event in Kingdom life. Most commoners weren't able or chose not to pay the high cost of a church wedding. They only paid the small registration fee to record the marriage. But Reynard was a man of high standing among commoners and did not lack the funds.

"Surely Reynard will want to be married in the church. His mother was religious. I remember that she was married in the church."

"True. But I just don't see the point in it. It's another source of contention every time the subject of marriage comes up."

Ramona knew how Amalia felt about the church and its priests, one of the things Amalia didn't keep to herself. She maintained that the priests had taken advantage of her mother. Late in her mother's life, when she was ill with wasting disease, they had overcharged her for medicines that had no effect.

"He sees marriage in the church as an obligation or duty. I, of course, disagree. I want a family ceremony. Anyway, it has always turned into an argument."

Most commoners had a family ceremony where the families of both parties came together for a day-long celebration. For those who live in or near the village, it's usually held at the common grounds, a flat, grassy area just off the Village Road between the castle and the village. The common grounds featured a grand pavilion with rough-cut tables and benches, a fire pit for roasting meats, a fire circle, and an expansive open field for sports and games.

Ramona was envious of Amalia. To have had a wedding with family at the common grounds would have been so much better than her stodgy royal wedding.

At a family wedding, the oldest woman from each family, or a surrogate, join together to officiate the marriage. The ceremony involves a series of rituals.

The matriarchs call for music and then take the groom and the bride to opposite ends of the picnic area. Holding hands, the women lead the couple in a serpentine dance, slowly approaching each other, which represents the fortuitous life-path they had traveled to find each other. They meet in the middle of the field at the fire circle. The women place the hands of the couple together and raise them high, and the couple is declared married, which is greeted by cheers from the crowd. The couple is then obliged to jump the flames in the fire circle, from their old lives into the new, after which follows; hugs, back-slapping, and congratulations. Other couples also jump the fire to renew their vows.

Next, the old women pour wine into the cup of each guest and make a toast that calls on their family's ancestors, recent and ancient, to bestow a blessing on the couple.

After that, each household sends a young child forward with a gift. The couple accepts each and lavishes gratitude on the child.

The women present the couple with a sack of seed packets collected from their family, a symbol of fertility.

Finally, the betrothed couple carves a specially prepared wedding roast and serves a piece to each guest to symbolize bounty and generosity.

"I'm sure you'll be able to work out your differences. Look at

Drake and me, who could be more different."

"I hope you're right."

"We need to get to work. What do you have planned next?"

"I will see Gerda later this morning. She has been very accommodating, providing food on the sneak."

"The kitchen servants likely know what she's up to, but they won't say anything," Ramona said, "Nothing to worry about there."

The kitchen staff most likely see the cook's activities as just one more ingredient in one more of Ramona's schemes.

"I need to check in with Renilda and Elsa sometime soon. And I'm going out to see Ald and Eachan later this afternoon."

"Be careful in your movements, not to arouse suspicion. You are traveling about the Kingdom more than usual. Someone might notice."

"I'll be careful." Amalia rose, started to bow, but was interrupted by a sudden embrace by Ramona.

"Off with you." Ramona planted a quick kiss on Amalia's cheek and released her.

Ramona watched Amalia walk away across the mill floor to the doorway. The confidence in that stride, Ramona hadn't noticed that before.

Suspicions

There was something afoot, something wrong; it was obvious, and Boetius planned to find out what and who was involved. He would start by confronting King Drake. Informed by the guard at the castle gatehouse that the King was at the stables, Boetius strode, double-time, along the castle wall. Drake was likely meeting with Gaston to arrange for replacement horses. Up ahead, he saw Drake, Reynard, and Gaston standing at the stable entrance. Along with a contingent of men, Boetius, Drake, and Reynard had returned to restock supplies. Feargus was in the field with the army, currently in camp, a brief respite from marching in a futile pursuit of the dragons.

As Boetius approached the men, he caught Reynard's eye first; Drake and Gaston had their backs to him. A gesture from Reynard and Drake turned around. Boetius stopped directly in front of the King. Drake looked annoyed; Gaston glanced at Boetius and then looked away; Reynard was expressionless.

"Sire, there's a problem I need to discuss with you."

"What is that?"

"The hunt for dragons, Sire. I haven't made contact with

any dragons in over three weeks. It's just not right. Something is going on. Something has changed."

"Not if there are no dragons to be found," Reynard said.

"Oh, THERE ARE dragons," Boetius said, "I know it. The hunting troop has found signs—tracks and remains of kills."

"How long has it been since you have found these signs?" Reynard asked, "Maybe they're old."

"Nonsense, the dogs are picking up fresh trails, but they lead nowhere, and I know why."

"Go on," Drake said.

"There must be people in the Kingdom that are interfering with the conduct of the war," Boetius announced, "I am doing my best to rid the Kingdom of the hideous beasts, but I cannot accomplish my goal if people are secretly aiding them."

"That can't be," Drake said, loud and angry, "Not my subjects. No one would provide aid to the enemy."

Boetius expected this reaction; any suggestion that the King's subjects were not loyal would be difficult for Drake to accept or even to consider. But the King needed to hear the truth.

"Someone must be helping the dragons," Boetius said, "It's like someone is warning them off or guiding them away. The dogs are being led on false trails, trails that end at stream beds; trails cross and fold back on each other like a man would do."

"That would require coordination between the dragons and the persons you think are helping them," Reynard said, "Are you suggesting that someone could be communicating with them?"

"Reynard is right; it can't be possible to communicate with a dragon—not with any beast. Absolute nonsense." Drake nodded to Reynard. "It's likely the dragons are in retreat, fleeing the Kingdom. You are most likely picking up the trails of the few remaining."

"Even if there are only a few left and in retreat, we need to track them down, follow them to their source, eliminate them

for good, so future generations won't have to deal with them."
A tightness was spreading through Boetius' jaw and neck. He
needed Drake to see the validity of his assertions, and he was
willing to press his argument to the limit of the King's patience.
Their years of friendship was probably the only thing stopping
Drake from dismissing Boetius outright.

"Only a few remaining and in retreat, our goal was to rid
the Kingdom of dragons." The King's voice carried an edge
of warning. "We have routed them. I am happy with that.
The people are happy. I believe we are near the end of our
campaign."

For some reason, the King did not understand the need
to track down and eliminate the dragons completely. Routing
them was simply not enough.

"Feargus has proposed reducing our contingent of lancers
and archers so that the men can have some time to attend to
the harvest. I am inclined to put a furlough system in place
of the commoners, rotating the men back home. The Knights
may also rotate duty if they so choose."

"Sire, I would ask that the catapult crew be given time off
each week, two days," Reynard said.

"Agreed," Drake replied.

Boetius glared at Reynard; he had taken Feargus' side.

"But, Sire, that won't do. Not at a time when we should be
expanding our search. We can't afford a reduction of force."

"There have been no reports of dragon sightings anywhere
in the Kingdom in many weeks. There's no indication as to
where to even begin a search," Reynard said.

"We should begin a systematic and thorough search of the
Kingdom, starting in the south and working our way north."

"I will not send our men out on a fool's errand. There's no
point in searching aimlessly for phantoms."

"We can't give up the pursuit now."

"I see no point in it," the King said, "But if your men should
actually make contact with the dragons again, I, of course, will

reconsider."

"But Sire. . ."

"That is my final word!" Drake's voice, his expression, and his posture all told Boetius not to press the conversation further. Drake turned away from Boetius. "Gaston, show us those new horses."

Gaston led the way into the stables; Drake and Reynard followed, leaving Boetius behind in the doorway.

Drake's decision to withdraw from the fight was a blunder, a miscalculation by the man people were calling the hero of the dragon war. Boetius was the one who brought down the first dragon with a single arrow—NOT Drake. Drake will regret not following his advice: there will be consequences, surely. There must be a way to counter the 'Hero of the Dragon War.'

Meeting of Friends

Ramona stopped walking, glanced back quickly over her shoulder; her heart raced. What was that, footsteps? Was there movement at that far corner in the road? Was someone following? She waited. No, it was her imagination again. Ramona stood on the East Road at the pathway that led to the old mill and waited a while to assure herself no one was following her. Besides that, she wanted her nerves to settle before she joined the meeting. It's best to show an air of confidence.

The old mill was a convenient meeting place for the Friends. It's what they called themselves, those who were providing aid, those who carried dragon stones. The crucial members of the Friends would be inside already, waiting for her.

Ramona hoped this would be the last meeting and that the dragon hunt would end soon, but there was still work to be done. The Friends had been protecting, feeding, and moving dragons north for the last two months. The end was in sight, another two weeks or so, and this undertaking could be concluded, their mission completed.

Despite nearing the end of their mission, Ramona was

on edge more than ever before, and her friends were as well. Amalia had warned her that some Friends might be losing their resolve. She wanted them together to discuss their concerns and bolster their courage. She couldn't afford to lose anyone, not when they were so near success. Ramona thought that bringing the Friends together for a meeting would be good for morale.

Settled now, Ramona walked up the path to the mill. She pushed through the creaky door into the barn and noticeably startled everyone in the mill. Those seated rose to their feet.

"I'm sorry. I didn't mean to startle you." Ramona felt guilty, always making people wait for her and now frightening them besides.

Everyone was quiet until Amalia broke the silence. "Good to see you, Ma'am. Any problems?"

"No problems. Caution takes extra time. I'm so glad all of you were able to make it. I know it's difficult to get away, but I thought we needed to get together." Ramona acknowledged each of those present with a nod and smile, Elsa, Eachan, Linza, and Ald, in turn. Each nodded and bowed in response.

"I want each of you to report your current state of affairs and your concerns." Ramona hoped to draw out any issues, so she could put her friends at ease and restore their confidence.

Turning to Eachan, "How many dragons are you still feeding?"

"Only eight Ma'am. I got's five and Ald's got's three. They'll be ready to go home in a few weeks."

"And the dragon clan from Chambold," Ramona asked, "What of them?"

"Most have all passed through and escorted home. I have eight in hiding and expect several more. We'll escort all of them home this week."

"That's good; less opportunity for discovery by Sir Boetius and his hunting troop," Ramona said, "Any problems to report?"

"No Ma'am, no problems. Glad it's the last of them, though.

Glad to see em go. Not that there's anything wrongs with em, mind ya. They just spooks the horses some." Eachan looked down; he appeared embarrassed.

"Ald, how goes it with you?" Ramona flashed the old man a broad smile, hoping to elicit one of his toothless grins.

"The same, Ma'am. Noth'en to worry bouts." No grin.

Eachan and Ald had concerns, sensed in their manner; they weren't yet sharing.

"Elsa, any problems?"

"No, Ma'am." Elsa was looking at the floor with her usual reluctance. Her 'no' wasn't convincing either.

"We appreciate what you're doing for us at the tavern. It's going well then?"

"Yes, Ma'am. I been keep'en a good ear out for any talk of dragons. Do'en like you asked, been spread'en the stories that the dragons are gone." Elsa was beaming in her subdued way.

Elsa was an instrumental part of Ramona's network, collecting information by eavesdropping on conversations. Amalia had asked Elsa to keep an ear out for any rumors of dragon sightings in Enid or the other kingdoms. It was also Elsa's task to contradict those stories of dragon sightings, to spread stories that the dragons had left the Kingdom. It would be to the Friends benefit if people thought the dragons were gone. It's what the people wanted to hear at this point anyway. Ramona got the impression Elsa was enjoying her newfound power to manipulate the course of events. Elsa was convincing and had a knack for presenting herself and her secret sources as trustworthy. It seems that quiet people get listened to when they do speak.

"Thank you, Elsa. Are you sure there's nothing else on your mind?"

"Well, I did hear a rumor that troubles me."

"What is it?"

"Some are say'en that Sir Boetius thinks there's people out there help'en the dragons."

"That's trouble!" Linza spoke up.

"Real troubles." Ald came to life.

"Let's not get ahead of ourselves. Sir Boetius may have his suspicions, but no one is taking him seriously, certainly not the King." Ramona needed to nip this in the bud.

"Sir Feargus and Reynard have dismissed Boetius' ideas as nonsense," Amalia said.

"Yes, true. He has no evidence. It's only a hunch on his part." Ramona looked around at her friend's distressed faces. "There's nothing to worry about at this point; I assure you."

"Sorry, Ma'am," Elsa said.

"No Elsa, it's fine. We need to hear about anything that concerns you. Thank you." Ramona turned to Linza. "Linza, what about you? How's it going?"

"My husband and me, we're do'en alright."

Getting these people to talk, to say what was on their minds was so difficult. It was exasperating sometimes.

"Amalia, have you anything to add?" Amalia had been spending time with Reynard; the days the catapult crew was on furlough. He was currently home coordinating resupply for the army.

"It's now a commonly held belief that the dragons are no longer in the Kingdom. We know that the men grow tired of the hunt and want it to end. We believe that Sir Feargus and Reynard will soon petition the King to declare victory."

Looking around, Ramona saw a sense of relief spreading across her friends' faces.

"The army is still in the Western Hunting Grounds, so it's important that we continue our work," Ramona said.

"Will the hunting troop soon quit their look'en for dragons?" Linza asked, "Sir Boetius is still out hunt'en the dragons every day."

"Yes, they are, but our tactics are still working as planned," Ramona said, "There's not much chance that he'll find the dragons."

"But there is a chance," Amalia inserted, "So we need to be vigilant. I heard that Sir Boetius is looking to expand the search to other parts of the Kingdom, including the North Woods."

Ramona wished that Amalia had kept that information to herself.

"That's bad for us if he does," Ald straightened up.

"The King has disallowed it. There will be NO expanded search," Ramona said.

"The longer this goes on, the more likely things could go wrong," Eachan said.

"You think'en things could be go'en wrong?" Elsa blurted out, addressing Eachan. But turning to Ramona, she lowered her head and eyes. "Pardon Ma-am."

"No Elsa, he didn't mean that. He just means we need to be careful, the same as always. We will be fine." Ramona's words and smile were meant to put Elsa at ease.

Turning back to the group, "We need to be cautious and vigilant," Ramona said, "Keep doing what we have been doing all along. We will get through this.

"The King will most likely bring this war to a close soon. And as I said, he has denied Sir Boetius' request to expand the search, and it's highly unlikely the King will change his mind."

"But if he stays in the Western Woods, that still makes troubles for me and my man," Linza said.

"Linza, are you and your husband having any problems?" Ramona asked.

"Our plan is work'en," Linza's words poured out, "Our friends are help'en, make'en up tales, send'en them hunters all about, but my husband's worry'en we might get caught. Last week was a close call. He was make'en false trails with the dragon blanket. The dogs got his scent and led the hunters to him, but he hid the blanket across a stream, talked his way out of it. He's hope'en to quit this game soon."

"He best not be quit'en, not anytime too soon," Ald

interrupted, "You's need to keep them hunters running abouts in your woods and out of ours." Ald's face and tone were stern.

"Ain't fair us take'en all the risk," Linza bristled with an angry tone of her own.

"Ain't fair us provid'en food for all them dragons." Ald raised his voice to match Linza's.

Ramona knew Ald didn't really begrudge the dragons; it was just talk.

"Now, let's be calm." Ramona intervened; Ald and Linza turned away from each other.

Ramona speaking to Linza, "I know this has been a burden for you and your husband, and I thank you both, but we need to stick to the plan until we move the last of the dragons on home. We should be able to keep the hunting troop off the track for the short amount of time we have left."

Amalia, speaking up, "You understand they're worried, very worried, afraid of getting caught."

"Yes, I ..." Ramona began.

"We're taking the risks," Linza interrupted, "If you get caught, it's exile. If we get caught," she gestured to the rest of the group, "we get beheaded."

"There's no reason to talk that way," Ramona said, "If something did happen, I would protect you. If someone were caught—and I'm confident that won't happen—I will tell the King you were acting under my orders. There wouldn't be any punishment for you." Ramona knew what she was saying wasn't likely true, but she needed to say what her friends needed to hear.

"I do appreciate the risks you're taking, I do. If there is anything I can do to help make things easier, less risky, you need to tell me." Ramona paused for a moment, waiting for a response. "If something comes up, you can always get in touch with Amalia through Alba."

Eachan straightened; a smile came to his face. He was obviously very proud of Alba, his teenage granddaughter, and the work she was doing. Over a month ago, she had joined the ranks of the friends as their messenger.

When the war broke out, Alba had tried to enlist in the ranks of the pony-boys; she could ride as well as the boys (her brothers and cousins and friends). But Feargus refused to accept a girl. So when the opportunity arose, she was more than happy to become Amalia's messenger. Ramona believed that Eachan had proposed this arrangement, not just as a practical matter, but as a way to assuage Alba's hurt feelings and disappointment.

Alba made for herself a hidden campsite in the woods a short way up the North Road from the castle. All Amalia had to do was sneak off, easy, to the camp with the message she or Ramona wanted sent, and Alba would deliver it. She made regular rounds to exchange messages between Amalia and the Friends. It was an ideal system; Alba flew about on her errands, inconspicuous, a young girl from the Horse Clan on horseback; no one paid any heed.

Ramona scanned the room. Her friends seemed to have dropped some of the worry from their faces.

"In any case, we need to keep up our work for a while longer, until the King proclaims victory. Success is within our grasp," Ramona said, "Thank you for all you've done and the risks you've been taking to help the dragons. We're near the end of our mission, I assure you." Ramona rose and strode to the door. As she pulled it open, she looked back, waved, and smiled. Outside she paused and caught her breath, hoping that her words had been enough to restore her friend's confidence.

Full Moon Ride

They had been riding for at least a half-hour, and the silence was growing awkward. Ramona wanted a conversation with Drake but wished he would start. She didn't want to dive into her agenda. For four long months, she had bitten her tongue and didn't want this opportunity to influence his decision thwarted by an argument. He wanted to talk too, she could tell, but he seemed reluctant.

"Beautiful evening." It slipped out of Ramona, small talk.

The temperature was between cool and warm, perfect for a ride; surely, the horses appreciated it. Both had blown out their nostrils several times, showing they were relaxed. The eastern sky ahead of them was clear except for purple streaked clouds resting on the horizon. A serenade of insect song emanated from the wood lots they passed.

"Yes, it is."

Silence again, except for the clopping of the horses' hooves on the hard-packed dirt road. As they leisurely rode along the East Road, they passed the free farmer's lands on their right. The Nobles' estates that lay to their left were connected to the road by bridges over the babbling Calder River, the river their constant companion.

There had been no dragon sightings in Enid for almost a month, and of course, there was no chance of encountering any on the East Road. Ramona surmised that Drake was aware of that as well. When she suggested they resume their traditional rides on the nights of a full moon, he feigned reluctance, but she could tell he was eager. They quickly came to agreement, a rare event these days, on the East Road, their favorite route, for their full moon ride.

The couple left the castle at half-past six this evening, the perfect time for a moonlit ride. The timing was determined by using the church's astrological charts. The priests were responsible for maintaining the calendar and timetables for celestial events, sunrise and sunset, moonrise and set, the equinoxes and solstices, and the movement of the wandering planets. In addition, they kept the records of periodic comets and heavenly firestorms.

The plan this evening was to leave the castle and ride east for an hour, the sun setting behind them. And then at the turning point, the sunlight extinguished, the moonrise would present its self in front of them. After they turned around, the moonlight streaming from behind would cast their long shadows, pointing the way home. Another hour of riding and they would arrive at the castle in darkness, with enough time for a light meal and drink before bed, which in the early days of their marriage would also lead to a sensational night.

The weather was cooperating; the conditions were right; the view and the atmosphere were enchanting.

"It's been a very good year. The fields appear to be ready for a plentiful harvest. The cattle look nice and fat," Ramona said.

"I can see that."

Ramona was inspecting the cows that grazed in a pasture used by the free farmers. These farmers rented land from the King to raise cattle, the pastures located on the southern side of the Calder River. The opposite side of the river was populated by the Nobles' farms. With the advantage of an irrigation system from the river, the Nobles' farms produced grains (wheat, oats, and rye) along with cattle and other livestock. The free farmers managed on the productive lowland pasture and what rain providence provided.

Stories circulated that dragons were flying into the eastern farmlands and snatching up cattle. But Ramona knew them to be false because she had instructed Elsa, at the tavern, to start those rumors. It provided the incentive for the free farmers to furnish the cattle she wanted them to supply to feed the dragons.

"I'm glad we were able to go out tonight." The admission was a concession that stuck in Ramona's throat.

"It's fortunate that I have been able to spend more time at the castle of late. Kingdom business needed attention, and of course, we will also be able to resume our rides."

It had been six months since their last ride and no acknowledgment from him that she was the one who asked for the resumption. Not him. What could she expect? She knew him well. He couldn't approach her for fear of rejection. Why was she the one to always acquiesce and accommodate his overbearing pride?

Drake spent most of his time over the last four months in the West Woods with the army. He only occasionally returned to the castle to take care of essential business, coincidentally, during times of the full moon. At those times, Ramona made sure she was either away or busy herself. She wanted a distant, silent, and tense relationship to show Drake she was not in agreement with his course of action, an unnecessary war.

"Do you think the conflict with the dragons is at an end?"

"Time will tell."

"How much time? It's been over three weeks since a dragon's been spotted and a month since your last fight with them?"

"True." Drake shifted his reins to his other hand and stared straight ahead.

"It's likely that you have driven them out of the Kingdom."

"Probably."

Ramona feared her questioning might antagonize Drake, but he was holding back, controlled.

There had been only one encounter between the dragons and the army since Linza's husband started his work in the West Woods, laying false trails. Since then, any chance meetings were averted by Feargus' stone.

The network of Friends was working well: the dragons were being fed, recovering from starvation, and then escorted out of the Kingdom. But if Drake declared an end to his war, the dragon's safety would be secured. With the army still active, there was always the possibility of another chance engagement.

"What was it like the last time the army found dragons?" A question Ramona knew the answer to.

"We routed them without a real fight. They fled before we had the opportunity to engage."

"No dragons were killed, no casualties, and there were only two dragons?"

"All true."

"Only two?" Ramona continued, "Only two seen and over a month, and there have been no other sightings anywhere else in the Kingdom in that time as well? And no sightings of dragons reported from other Kingdoms in a long while?"

Ramona knew the answers to her questions. In this, the fifth encounter, the dragons were alerted of the army's approach and had time to gather up the game they had killed. And when the King's men did arrive, now well aware of the army's tactics, the dragons, having the strength to fly, retreated in a direction away from the catapult and its deadly net before they could be surrounded.

"Yes. That's right."

She took the lack of an argument from Drake as a good sign. Maybe he was disposed to put his Dragon War behind him.

"You know, of course, we are in the harvest season. It's a hardship for the women to carry out all the work by themselves, not having their men at home." Ramona heard there was grumbling in the ranks, a point of pressure she hoped might influence Drake.

"Yes, I am aware."

Drake was surveying the farm fields that were visible across the river, full of golden wheat, dimly lit by the last glow of the sunset.

Keeping to herself, for now, Ramona turned her attention to the landscape. As they rode along, she took note of the pathways that led into the free farmers' households, marked by simple wooden signs with burned-in names or family symbols. On the opposite side of the road, Nobles estates were announced by elaborate signs decorated with carved family crests, mounted on stone columns, flanked by well-built, crafted stonewalls.

They continued riding easterly in silence, eventually reaching the turning point. Both gently brought their horses' heads around, pivoting back toward the west and the faded sky. The sun had sunk into the dark purple horizon.

For the next half hour, the quiet persisted except for the singing of insects announcing the end of summer. They passed a small stream and a marshy area with a solitary bullfrog still in hopeful chorus. From time to time, a barred owl called out with its distinctive melody; 'Who cooks for you?' A mnemonic for the owl's call Ramona learned as a child.

Farther along, they passed a field with at least a dozen deer (does, and a few fauns still with spots). Their heads popped up, ears twitching; they focused on the couple on horseback. After a moment, sensing no obvious threat, feeling secure again, they returned to grazing.

Ramona's horse shook itself from head to tail, rattling Ramona.

"I hate it when they do that," Drake said with a glancing smile.

Ramona looked back over her shoulder to the east: a few stars, faint points, asserted themselves there. Well after sunset now, the twilight gone, the moon hung overhead in the southeastern sky, having made some progress on its path to the western horizon.

Yet another quarter-hour passed without conversation.

The weather had cooperated. The full moon, a brilliant white-yellow disk, floated in a deep blue sky.

The heat of the sun gone, the temperature dropping, Ramona willed against it, but her body shuddered. Did Drake notice? No, he was staring ahead, seemingly lost in thought. Thinking of her coat, she twisted in her saddle and reached behind to the cantle where her warm coat should have been tied. It had been forgotten. She realized they didn't have their water canteens either. Hasty preparations, preoccupied, even their basic habits had been overridden.

Drake, noticing her movement, glanced at her saddle. "You're cold?" He brought his horse to a halt and removed his cloak. He side-passed his horse over alongside Ramona, leaned across, and draped the wide coat over her shoulders. "There, that should do it." He left his arm around her for a moment before tilting back to his seat.

"Thank you."

They started out again but had to wait for an opossum as it padded, in no hurry, across the road just ahead of them.

As they approached Ramona's family estate, she glanced to the left. At the end of a low cut grass field, a hay barn stood in silhouette, a shed used in common for hay storage by the free farmers. The hay had been taken from this vast field in midsummer. Ramona could picture the men walking abreast across the field, their scythes swinging in unison, waves of tall green grass falling into neat windrows behind them.

A short time later, they came to the path that led to the old abandoned mill.

Ramona thought of the assurances she had given the people at the meetings there, her network of 'Friends.' If things went wrong, if they were discovered, she would take care of them, set things right; she had promised. Although for that awful circumstance, she must admit, she didn't have a plan. She chose to put the thought out of her mind. From her childlike self, if you don't think about a problem, it can't happen. Magical thinking, her mother called it. She didn't want to depend on magic, or fate, or prayers, or the goodwill of the heavens. She wanted this 'War' to end before her luck ran out.

When she was a child, her mother told her she must have a guardian angel that rescued her from the many risky and dangerous situations Ramona frequently found herself in. She shouldn't push her guardian angel too far, test his patience—that is—if he really existed.

The angel or something had stepped in and saved them, just a week ago. Thank the heavens for Alba, Amalia's messenger. If she hadn't come across those kids from the logger's village who had spotted the dragons, it could have been a disaster. Ramona didn't want to think about that either.

As they approached the end of the ride, the King's horse whinnied, calling to its stablemates.

"Have you considered declaring victory?" Ramona asked while there was still time. She had put it off as long as she could.

"I am considering it. I will meet with my advisers soon." There was no resistance in his tone; he sounded almost agreeable. This was good, what she hoped for. Ramona knew that Feargus and Reynard were pressing the King for a withdrawal from the fight.

This outcome, Drake's response to the ultimate question, the one she expected to lead to an argument, instead gave her hope. It was not what Ramona was anticipating.

She had what she wanted and wanted no more from him.

This was indeed an enjoyable ride, a beautiful evening. The castle, now in sight, sat on the western horizon illuminated in pale moonlight. They rode in the quiet save the insect song, the hooves striking the road, the saddle leather squeaks, and the occasional hoot of a nearby owl.

Withdrawal

"It's been a month since our last battle with the dragons. And even then, we routed them; they fled before our advance. I believe you can declare victory," Feargus said, speaking to Drake.

"It's too soon for that." Boetius slid to the edge of his chair, hands on the tabletop.

Another meeting in the great-hall and Drake had been listening for a half-hour to Boetius and Feargus state and restate their positions on the issue, Feargus for withdrawal, Boetius for continuance. Reynard and Feargus had each approached Drake earlier with petitions to retire their men from the fight. Boetius, predictably, resisted even the suggestion. Drake had brought them together in the great-hall to discuss ending the war. Reynard hadn't said a word as yet, sitting between the other two, his arms crossed, leaning back in his chair, looking like he might doze off if they would only speak more quietly. Drake was waiting for them to play themselves out, which had never happened before, but it did give him time to formulate his thoughts.

"There have been no confirmed dragon sightings in the

Kingdom since the last engagement," Feargus said, "And I have heard the same is true in the other kingdoms. They don't report any dragon sightings either."

Drake could confirm Feargus' assertion; as of late, no dragon sightings had been reported by the other Kings. During the war, Drake had regular correspondence with his peers in the surrounding kingdoms (Evora, Braga, Duren, Chambold, and Dacian) via the circuit-riders.

The circuit-riders were official messengers, in the joint employment of the Kingdoms that rode a circular route from one kingdom to another. One rider was always riding in a south to west direction, another riding north to east, which guaranteed communication between kingdoms within two days. This communications system was only used by the Kings and Nobles, who can afford the fees to carry a message or package. Commoners sent messages between kingdoms through merchants and travelers. Who, out of goodwill, carried letters without cost between taverns and churches where they dropped the correspondence to be distributed.

The informal communication network of rumor and gossip, also provided by travelers and merchants, used by commoners and Nobles alike, brought the stories of dragon sightings. But for each such tale that came to the King's ear, it was followed by an equally strong rebuke, claiming the story to be nonsense.

"They're out there," Boetius said, "I know it. The dragons are still in the Kingdom, probably in hiding."

"There have been no signs," Feargus said, "Your dogs haven't found any valid trails. I, for one, am tired of tramping around in circles."

"No matter, we must continue the pursuit. We can't give up."

"Enough!" Drake interjected. "Reynard, your thoughts."

"I see no benefit in marching the army throughout the Western Hunting Grounds, day in and day out. The men are tired of the senseless pursuit of dragons that most believe have left the Kingdom. Besides, they are eager to get home to the harvest. The furlough system is not adequate."

"The harvest can be taken care of by the women, children, and old men," Boetius said.

"Only with hardship," Feargus said.

"It will be worth it to ensure the removal of the dragons from the Kingdom. Even better to pursue them, hunt them down, find their source and destroy them all," Boetius said.

"Pursuit of the dragons is needless and costly. There is no benefit to be had from scouring the Kingdom or beyond." Feargus made that last point to Drake.

From his seat at the opposite side of the table, Drake raised his hands, calling for silence. He did not speak for a long time as he considered his options. "Reynard, you may withdraw your catapult crew. Feargus, your lancers, and Knights as well. Boetius, withdraw your archers."

Boetius leaned forward, his mouth agape. Drake pointed a finger at his chest. Boetius sunk back in his chair.

Drake then added. "But, you may continue your search for dragons with the hunting troop." Drake hoped to appease Boetius.

Boetius brightened and came to life. "I believe we should extend our search beyond the Western Hunting Grounds. The last reported sightings were in the Kingdom of Braga.

"Sire, if you were to send an envoy to King Wilhelm and ask permission to send an expedition, a small force, into his kingdom, we could march up the North Road, investigate the north of our Kingdom, and then the wilds of Braga."

A few weeks ago, merchants from Duren on a trip into Enid had reported seeing a dragon flying above the Braga Road.

"My sister has assured me that Wilhelm's men have made thorough searches of the Northern Wilds and have found no trace of dragons," Feargus said, "But I have heard of sightings in the Chambold swamps. I believe those to be the more reliable accounts."

The swamps were other side of the Dark Forest on the northern border of Chambold. The only way to reach them was to go west to Morodon on the coast, follow the coastal road south, and then turn back east into the swamps, a two-day trip.

Drake had no memory of the report that Feargus alluded to, but the excursion might prove useful in support of an idea he had been entertaining. The King of Chambold, Adalharn, might be impressed with the voluntary offer to help with the dragon fight in his kingdom.

"It's unlikely that Wilhelm will allow it, but I believe Adalharn would be agreeable," Drake said.

"I will need a contingent of men, in case of contact with the dragons. Two squads of archers, the best men. Only one half of the hunting troop would accompany me. The remaining hunters will still search the Western Woods." Boetius then said with a surly voice aimed at Feargus. "And I will also need a cadre of Knights."

"I'm sure that Cenhelm will volunteer and could rally a group of the younger Knights," Feargus said, "And a few squads of men-at-arms, regulars, would be prudent."

"That is acceptable," Boetius said, with a puzzled look.

"You may pursue this campaign for two weeks," Drake said to Boetius. "You will return in two weeks' time."

"I will call up one of the pony-boys to take the correspondence today. They can make the ride in a day and can be back by tomorrow evening," Feargus said.

Odd that Feargus was now supporting Boetius' position, a very rare occurrence.

Drake looked to Feargus, "Drill the lancers, archers, and Knights once a week, keep them sharp in case the hunting dogs should make contact with the dragons again. Reynard, same for the catapult crew."

"I will have my expedition ready by tomorrow evening. We'll bivouac at Morodon and wait until we get word and then proceed south." Boetius was on the edge of his seat, ready to move and get underway.

"Fine, that will do." Drake addressed Boetius then Feargus, "Have the messenger report back to Boetius first at Morodon and then to me. I'm sure that King Adalharn will agree. Gentlemen make your preparations."

It was settled.

"You are dismissed." Drake didn't wait for a response. He stood and walked away, heading for the stairs and his chambers. He needed quiet; he needed to think. His men scrambled to their feet.

"Yes, Sire," they said in unison.

Drake paused at the foot of the stairs and pivoted and pointed in Boetius' direction. "Two weeks, no arguments. No dragon sightings in that time, and I declare victory."

Hunting
with Dragons

Under the protection of the lean-to, sitting across from Eachan, Amalia looked out over his shoulder at the persistent drizzle. It rained on her the entire ride, from the castle to the hunting camp. She was cold and damp but glad to see Eachan again. Amalia had arranged this clandestine meeting through Alba. She hadn't seen Eachan or Ald in over a month, not since they started using Alba as a messenger.

"The Queen sends her best regards and asked me to express her gratitude for the work you and Ald are doing—what all of your people are doing. You have shown great courage in this undertaking."

"It's the right thing to do, is all," Eachan replied.

Eachan and his fellow horsemen had been instrumental in the scheme to help the dragons, providing refuge and food. Also, after the dragons had gained a healthy amount of weight, horse clansmen escorted the dragons on their journey home. Acting as escorts, the horsemen traveled inconspicuously up the North Road, while maintaining contact with the dragons who followed in safety at a distance. On alarm from the horsemen, encountering other travelers, the dragons dropped into hiding in the forest. A sighting that could be reported to the King was avoided.

The horsemen and the dragons travel through Enid to the northern border with the Kingdom of Braga, a full day's ride, where they camp for the night. The following day, they continue through the eastern wilds of Braga to the Kingdom of Duren, another full day's ride. In the Northern Wilds of Duren, they are joined by the dragons from the clan who have been feeding in that area.

One real threat, although slight, on this trip is the chance encounter with a patrol from the Kingdom of Braga. Once through Braga, travel in Duren is safe since the King of Duren is not inclined to patrol the east of his kingdom; it would only antagonize the native tribes living there. And it's those native tribesmen who meet up with the horsemen and take on the task of escorting the dragons to their final destination, the Northern Mountains.

"I bring good news." Amalia reached out and touched Eachan's hand. "The King has withdrawn the army from the hunt.

"That is good news."

"But he has allowed for a portion of the hunting troop to remain in the Western Hunting Grounds to search for dragons. Thankfully there are only a few dragons still there."

"What of Sir Boetius?"

"Boetius has left with a small contingent on an expedition into Chambold in search of dragons. That's one of the reasons I'm here. Are there any dragons left in Chambold?"

"No, the last of em are en route north as we speak."

"Good, very good. We had hoped so. No chance of Sir Boetius finding any in Chambold. He's on a fool's errand."

"How long do you think he will be occupied chas'en his tail?"

"The King granted him two weeks."

"What's about when he comes back? We'll still be feeding some dragons. If he comes this way, he's our biggest threat. I worries mostly about them dogs of his."

"They haven't found a trail since the last battle, and no one has reported any dragon sightings anywhere in the Kingdom. And the King is still holding firm. He won't allow a search of the Kingdom."

"Let's hope Sir Boetius follows the King's orders."

"I'm sure he will," Amalia said, "You have more dragons than usual, are you having any trouble finding safe hiding places for the Chambold dragons?"

"We hide some in our hay barns, but most are in the deep woods out of the way, in a stand of virgin timber, just north of here. Ald hides em in a remote ravine, just up behind his place."

Behind Amalia, on the other side of the hills that rose behind her, the Calder River wound through the Calder Range, a narrow band of steep, rugged mountains that ran north to south through the center of Enid. Over the years, streams and rivulets flowing down the hillsides to the river cut deep ravines, perfect hiding places for dragons.

"How long do you think it will be before all the dragons are out of the Kingdom and on their way home?"

"Two, maybe three weeks."

"Good. Thank you. Do you have anything to report from Ald?"

"He complains a bit about the amount of sheep they eat, talks about how ugly they are too. Though his doings defy his complaints. I think he has a keen liken for the beasts."

"How so?"

"The dragons don't really eat that much sheep. Besides, it's Ald that slaughters the sheep for em. Butchers em too; he likes to hand-feed them. Especially the little ones. He had a female with two young-ens at his camp. He dotes on them. It's funny to watch the old man limp'en about, followed by two little dragons, growl'en for him."

"Yes, those noisy babies almost did us in. I assume Alba told you about it?"

"She did, a quick think'en young girl, my granddaughter."

"She's invaluable; she saved us."

It was on one of Alba's rides that she had rescued the whole endeavor from disaster, through a chance meeting. She was riding up the North Road, taking a message to her grandfather, when she came across four boys marching down the road full of bravado. The boys didn't need much encouragement from Alba to spill the story they were so eager to tell.

Those boys, young teenagers from the loggers' village, had been playing in the woods not far from Ald's homestead. On the hillside behind his cottage, they had cut a grapevine and were using it to swing off a cliff ledge. That's when they heard the dragon babies calling for food. The boys made a mission out of finding the source of the strange noise. They snuck through the woods, hiding behind trees and brush, and saw Ald feeding the baby dragons. At first, they were overwhelmed and frightened and carefully crept away, very grateful not to have been discovered. But once clear of the perceived danger, they decided that it was their duty to report what they'd seen to the King. Undoubtedly there would be a reward; they would be heroes.

Alba immediately turned around and rode back to warn Amalia.

After Alba told her story, Amalia sent her back to delay the boys, divert them to the hunting camp and keep them there until she arrived. Alba asked how. Amalia could only think to say to 'Get creative.'

Luckily, Ramona was free. She and Amalia road out to the hunting camp, where Ramona convinced the boys to keep the dragon sighting a secret. Amalia thought to grab a bag full of candy from the kitchen before she left, a useful item for bribing children. Commoners had honey and maple syrup for sweets, but only Nobles could afford imported sugar used to make a variety of flavored hard-candies. Between Ramona's persuasive abilities, Amalia's bag of candy, and a promise of more sweets to be supplied on a regular basis, the boys were inclined to keep the secret.

Since the incident with the boys, Gerda was kept busy making the sweets, using flavorings supplied by Renilda. Renilda had a variety of herbs in her garden used for flavorings (lemon balm, angelica, peppermint). Alba always carried a supply of candy and distributed it liberally to any children she came across, presented as a gift from the Queen.

"She's real popular these days with the kids around here, passing out candy hand over fist."

"It seemed like a good idea for her to have a supply of goodies on her at all times."

"Have'en one of them dragon stones though sure has gone to her head."

"She deserved to have one, and it could come in handy in case she comes across trouble again.

"The cattle we've been sending, has it been enough?" Amalia continued, "It's been difficult. We can't send too many at a time: they might be noticed. Queen Ramona is worried that you might not have enough meat for all the dragons in your charge."

"The cattle mostly goes to Ald. Takes care of his needs."

The cattle came from the eastern free farmers. Although she did not disclose what they were for, Ramona negotiated with the farmers to supply her with cattle. She could guarantee no dragon attacks on their herds if they provided, from amongst all the farmers, just a few cows each week. Even though no dragons had taken any livestock, the farmers were influenced by gossip and feared attacks.

Ramona told the farmers to think of the cows as sacrificial animals, like those they give the priests for prayers of penance or petition, or to look at it as a tax, one like others, that provides a service. Amalia thought it was more like extortion, very much like what the priests do, but Ramona, of course, didn't see it that way. And the farmers, trusting Ramona, seemed happy with the arrangement and played their unknowing part in aiding the dragons.

"Do the Chambold dragons need to be fed as well?"

"Them dragons came fattened up pretty good on those swamp boars they been feed'en on. We're do'en alright. We fills the gap with wild game."

"How's that?"

"My youngest son, Hubert, has been take'en the dragon's hunt'en with him."

"Takes them hunting, how does that work?"

"Hubert is an excellent hunter, an archer, and he knows the woods real good. He knows the animals' trails and feeding spots. Been tramp'en those North Woods all his life. Even as a boy, he'd be gone for days."

"What's he hunting for?"

"Elk. There's a big herd that sometimes travels down along the Braga border. It's a day's ride from here. Fortunate they're move'en in that area these days.

"On his own, Hubert can get one elk a day. When he goes off for a few days, he takes a couple of pack horses to bring back his kill. Hunt'en with them dragons; he can get four to six in a day."

"They hunt together? How?"

"You know how the Knights in the Kingdom of Brives hunts with falcons? Kind'a the same idea. Hubert knows where to look for the elk; he finds the herd. He's on horseback; the elk don't see him as a threat like they would if he were on foot. He gets up as close as he can and then calls the dragons in, who's been stay'en on the wing but well out of sight."

"The dragons are such slow beasts; I always wondered how they could catch wild game."

"Hubert thinks he's got it figured out. Even in flight, they's not so fast. But all they got to do is get close, maybe 30, 40 paces. Then they throws an image into their prey's mind, something that scares em stiff, paralyzed them with fear. That gives the dragon time enough to swoop in and snatch em."

"I wonder why they don't use that trick in battle with the King's men."

"Probably only works on prey animals; don't work on men, us being predators and all just like them. They might be doing it to the horses though, the horses being prey animals. Could be putting pictures into the horses' heads, Sends em into a panic."

"The dragons couldn't always attack from the air? I don't see how they could do that when they're starving."

"No, they hunt with Hubert from the ground too. They pick a spot before dawn, same as a hunter does, and waits in hiding in a blind, real still. Once an animal shows up, com'en along the trail, they comes out at em real slow, them pictures paralyzing them. Some of the animals in the herd panic and run off, but the dragons snatch up the still ones, and Hubert usually gets one with his bow too."

"Have you ever gone out with Hubert; seen how the image throwing works?" Eachan carried a dragon stone.

"Not me. Not again. Once was enough. I leave the dragon talk'en to Hubert. That's his job. He don't seem to mind. Seems to like being rounds the creatures."

"I understand; I like being with them as well."

Eachan rolled his eyes and smiled.

"Well, if there is nothing you need from me, I will be on my way." Amalia rose. Eachan snapped to his feet. "Before I go, again, I need to say that Queen Ramona sends her best regards to you, Ald and your clan folk. She greatly appreciates what you are doing for the dragons. She told me to say thank you from the bottom of her heart." Amalia gave Eachan a hesitant, awkward hug. "And of course, I do as well."

"Thanks for bring'en the news yourself."

Amalia, putting up her hood, head down, bowing to the drizzle, stepped quickly from the lean-to to her horse. Eachan was instantly beside her, stooped over with linked hands offering assistance to mount. As she put her foot in his hands, he raised up and vaulted her small frame into the saddle.

Her hood flopped to her back. She put it back in place and took up the reins. "Thank you, Eachan." She turned the horse away and headed down the North road, on her way back to the castle, another task complete. How many more? For how long?

The End in Sight

The autumn air was cooling quickly, the sun having set. Ramona and Amalia were out on the Braga Road on their evening stroll. Evening walks were the best time to exchange information, free from eavesdropping. Ramona turned her collar up to the brisk breeze. They had been walking for half an hour and were increasing their pace to create warmth.

The first report Ramona heard from Amalia this evening was about her meeting with Eachan yesterday. She was glad the dragons were out of Chambold.

"Boetius won't find any dragons in Chambold; nothing to fret over," Ramona said, "And it will be a relief for our friends while he's away," Boetius had started for Chambold that morning with a small contingent of the army.

"But he'll be back in two weeks, and we will still have dragons in the North Country," Amalia said. "And Reynard told me that Boetius wants to search in the Kingdoms of Braga and Duren. That would be a real problem if the King sanctioned it as he did in Chambold. Eachan's men are using the North Road to escort dragons, and some of the dragon clan in those kingdoms still remain."

"It served Drake's purposes to send Boetius to Chambold. Even if Drake wanted it, King Wilhelm certainly won't permit Drake's army to enter Braga. And the King of Duren will always follow Wilhelm's lead. Boetius will not be allowed to search in the northern kingdoms."

There was bad blood between King Drake and King Wilhelm, two men with inflated egos that fortified their uneasy relationship and rivalry. The Kingdoms of Enid and Braga had come close to war early in Drake's reign, a dispute over boundaries and hunting privileges. It was Feargus and his sister's allies in Braga who had negotiated a solution to the dispute.

"This war was such a useless venture. If people could have just seen the dragons' side." Amalia was shaking her head.

"Only if they had to overcome their fears."

"There's nothing to be afraid of; the dragons aren't dangerous. Well, only when provoked."

"Fear is usually a good thing; it keeps us safe from real threats, but sometimes it's just in the mind's eye. Confronted by something different, unknown, a stranger, the fear takes over. Remember when you first saw a dragon, your first reaction?"

"Yes, I was terrified." Amalia's eyes got wide.

"Took courage to get past it. And some help from a friend." Ramona turned a smile on Amalia.

"But," Ramona continued, "If your friends and family are dominated by the same fears, it would be very difficult to overcome that obstacle and act differently or even see the world differently in the first place."

"Why weren't you afraid of the dragons in the beginning?"

"I was afraid. I have the same instincts. My gut perceived a threat."

"So you felt the fear and did it anyway?"

"Right." Ramona couldn't help a smile. "That, and I was curious. I wanted to know what they were like, what I could learn. Also, I felt bad for them, being hated for no reason, their lives threatened. Putting myself in their place, had that curse since I was a child."

"But what made you think you could communicate with them?"

"I wasn't sure, but I was hopeful. I got the idea from the story of Ald and his grandson meeting a dragon on the North Road." Ramona knew now that the dragons had been trying to communicate, trying to let people know they meant no harm and that they needed food.

Ramona and Amalia walked along in silence for a few minutes.

"Elsa is concerned with some new rumors that are circulating," Amalia said, "Stories are going round about the Dark Forest. That the forest is full of beasts, large game animals, and the dragons have gone in the forest hunting for food."

"Does she know the source of these stories?"

"She says they're being spread by traders from Morodon. They claim they saw things come out of the forest as they traveled the Morodon Road, dragons and beasts."

"That's ridiculous."

Amalia nodded. "Also, she says these men have come into money, buying drinks, spending more than usual. One drunken trader hinted at 'how well it pays to be a tell'en stories.'"

"Very strange."

"She wants to know what she should do."

"Nothing, for now; sounds harmless," Ramona said, "We had better turn back. It's getting late."

"And cold."

Heading back, they were facing into the raw wind now. They both put their hoods up and heads down and pressed a quickened pace until they reached the castle hill.

In the shadow of the rampart wall, with a break from the wind, Amalia spoke again. "I can't help but worry about what might happen when Sir Boetius comes back. If he takes his hunting troop out searching in the north of the Kingdom, he's sure to find the dragons. Eachan is worried Boetius will convince the King to allow the hunt to continue."

"The King wants an end to this war: he won't allow it."

"But even so, what's to stop the hunting troop from just roaming where they want? He wouldn't need the King's permission to go out hunting."

"You're right; that is a worry." Ramona stopped and turned to Amalia. "Strange though, I spoke with Feargus about the same thing yesterday." Ramona and his paths had crossed at the stables.

"What did he say?"

"He told me not to worry about it. He refused to tell me what he meant. Said there was no need for me to be involved—real smug. Said Boetius would have other things to occupy him when he returns."

"That's mysterious."

"Yes. And I don't like mysteries. At least, not the ones I didn't create."

"What if Feargus is wrong, and Boetius does use hunting game as an excuse to go out and search for dragons?"

"We will deal with it if and when the time comes. We only need to hold things together for a few more weeks."

At the castle now, the women were at the end of their walk. And Ramona hoped, near the end of their adventure.

The Proclamation

"I have decided to declare victory," Drake said, "This is the order. The crier will make the announcement today." Drake looked to Ramona, hoping to see a sign of approval. He picked up the proclamation scroll as an offering. Sitting across the desk from Drake in his study, Ramona only nodded.

The King's clerk, besides assisting the King with his correspondence and record-keeping, was the crier as well. When a proclamation was decreed, the church bells rang an extra three tolls at each hour, to announce to those within earshot that a proclamation was to be read at noon that same day. People gathered at the castle gate, where the crier shouted out the King's message from an elevated platform on the gate wall. It was then the crier's job to travel the Kingdom to various locations to read the King's declaration repeatedly after announcing his intent with a horn blast.

"You have ordered Boetius out of Chambold?"

"I sent a messenger yesterday. He is on his way home."

"What of Boetius' request to expand the search to the north when he returns?"

"I will not allow it." He hoped she would accept this as a

concession intended for her.

"So this war has ended. And in time for the Veterans' Feast."

It was only two weeks away. Every year in the fall, a celebration was held for the army veterans, on the next full moon after the harvest moon, the Veterans' Moon. The celebration to honor the men who had served the King and the Kingdom started midmorning with a call to assembly at the castle parade-grounds. By noon a combat skills tournament was underway, competitions for the young bucks to show off their skills in archery, swordsmanship, and jousting. At the end of the tournament, the ribbon pinning ceremony was held at which each new veteran comes forward to have a scarlet ribbon pinned on his chest by the King. The games are followed by a supper held in the castle great-hall where the veterans, commoners, and Nobles alike feast, toast and boast together.

"We will need to start preparations," Drake said, "And we will have to postpone our ride. I'm sorry; maybe we could go the next night if the weather is good?" Drake intended to do everything he could to cement the positive relationship he now enjoyed with Ramona.

"A day or two of delay won't matter. There will be plenty of time for our ride.

"I will get to work on the feast preparations today. It will be a much larger feast this year; there are so many more veterans."

Ramona fell still; she cleared her throat; her eyes teared up. Drake presumed she was envisioning the casualties; the wounded and the dead. The number of veterans at the feast had dwindled every year. Of Drake's father's generation, there were less than a dozen men left. Drake's generation dominated the event in recent times, but this year a sizable number of young men would join the ranks.

"Yes, it will, and we must honor these men. Spare no expense."

Drake hoped that Ramona could now see his point of view

and come to understand why the war was necessary, why the dragons had to be driven out of the Kingdom. In contrast to this outbreak of tears, she had been in better spirits recently, much more agreeable and not as distant.

"I will need a headcount for the number of veterans. I believe we will need to have the supper in the courtyard instead of the great-hall to accommodate all the men and their families."

"Good idea. We should set up tents in case of rain."

"Also, I need the number of new veterans to plan for the ribbon ceremony?" Ramona sewed up the red ribbon badges herself.

"My clerk has the counts. I will have him let you know."

"I need to get started." Ramona rose to her feet. Drake jumped up, sending his chair sliding away. He rounded the old desk and took up both of her hands.

"Thank you for your support."

"You've always had it."

Drake didn't understand what she meant; she had consistently argued with him before the war. She had never accepted his decision to go to war with the dragons and was not supportive of his efforts to rid the Kingdom of dragons during the war. He thought maybe it was sarcasm, but he did not detect any malice in her tone. Her smile was genuine.

Ramona embraced him briefly and left the King's chambers.

Surely everything would return to normal. Drake saw a bright future. The war and the bad feelings were behind them.

A Proposal

"I knew you were keeping secrets," Reynard said.

"I knew you knew," Amalia said, "But it had to be that way. I felt terrible, not able to tell you what I was doing, but it was necessary. We didn't want to involve you." Amalia had just spilled out her confession that she had been aiding the dragons during the war. King Drake had declared the end to the war only two days ago; she couldn't wait any longer to share with Reynard all she had been hiding for so long.

"It's alright. I appreciate that you were trying to protect me." Reynard inched closer across the bench to Amalia and put his arm around her.

"You forgive me?" Her burden lifted, Amalia let her head fall on Reynard's shoulder. There was still evening light streaming in from the window behind them, throwing a bleached rectangle on the floor. Reynard had shown some puzzlement with Amalia's request for a meeting at the old mill, but he did not question her. It was her safe place to talk of secrets.

"Nothing to forgive. You were looking out for me. I see that." Reynard paused, waiting for something. "You know I couldn't openly oppose Drake. I had to go along with the war, had no choice. You understand that, don't you?"

Amalia lifted her head to face him. "Of course, my dear. I know you didn't want to take part in the dragon killing."

Reynard's face tensed, and his eyes closed for a moment. Amalia was tempted to continue that line of conversation but restrained herself. There will be plenty of time to talk out the traumas of war that must be torturing Reynard's mind.

"I know your true feelings. I do. Not to worry." Amalia smiled and changed the subject. "We haven't had much time for each other the last six months. I've been missing you."

"I've missed our time together too."

"Were you aware that someone was helping the dragons?" Amalia wondered how much he was aware of and how much he had guessed.

"Near the end, it became obvious that someone was. I was sure Ramona was involved, and if she were, you would be too." Reynard was smiling now.

"I'm so relieved that we're finally able to talk about it." Amalia had been dreading this conversation since this morning when she asked for this secret meeting. An uneasy feeling in the pit of her stomach had stayed with her all day until just now. She wasn't entirely sure how he would react to her confession.

But then a concern struck her. Amalia sat up straight and withdrew. "Is it common knowledge that Ramona was behind it?"

"I felt it had to be one of Ramona's conspiracies. If others thought the same, they kept it to themselves. I never heard anyone speak of it. In any case, you know how the common-folk feel about her. They will go to great lengths to support her."

"But so many people took the King's side, so many people wanted this war."

"At the beginning, yes. But as the war drug into the fall, they tired of it. They'd had enough of it. No one cared at that point if someone was providing aid to the dragons. Except Boetius."

"Does Boetius believe that Ramona and I were involved?"

"Of course not. He sees Ramona as a Noblewoman, thinks Nobles can do no wrong. He believes it's the commoners that were helping the dragons."

"Does he suspect me?"

"No, not in any way. Not you. No one would suspect timid little Amalia, the Queen's maid."

"Did he say that about me? Say I'm timid?" Her face flushed, recognized that angry tone, her father's voice in her head.

"No. No one did. I was teasing." Reynard said, "But Boetius did ask me to help find out who was helping the dragons."

"What did you say?"

"I told him I'd keep my eyes and ears open. Not a lie. I always do that," Reynard said with a chuckle.

"Not funny." In an angry tone again, she wanted serious conversation.

The smile vanished from Reynard's face.

"And what of the King? What do you know of his thoughts?"

"Ramona's conspiracy is safe from Drake. He can't even entertain the idea that any of his subjects could be against him or his ventures, not even Ramona. He knows she's had her schemes in the past but would scoff at the thought of anyone following a woman on such a daring venture. I believe he tried to have people keep an eye on her just in case. Not successfully, though, obviously."

"Did you know Feargus was involved?"

"Not for sure, but I surmised he might be. Near the end of the war, our conversations became somewhat awkward; he was hiding something. It made sense since it was clear from the beginning that Feargus was against the war. I wasn't sure if he was truly on the side of the dragons or if it was just another opportunity to be against Boetius."

"Near the end of summer, when things were going badly for the dragons, we gave him a dragon stone to carry so he could warn the dragons away from the army's approach."

"A what?"

"A dragon stone," Amalia repeated as she retrieved from her blouse her necklace with the stone. "We use it to communicate with the dragons."

"I don't understand."

Amalia was holding the stone out from her neck, between her fingers. "A dragon, we call Alpha, gave them to us. The dragons can sense the stones, like a beacon. They can find us that way, and we also use them to call the dragons to us. Then when we are with them, we communicate by reading each other's thoughts, not language, not words, but in the form of images."

Reynard's expression was a mix of disbelief and shock. "You can do that? You can talk to dragons through your thoughts?"

"Yes, it's like seeing pictures in your mind, visions that come from the dragon's mind. And we can create images to send back to them."

"That explains a lot. I could tell messages were getting to the dragons somehow. Feargus was talking with them through a stone like that?" Reynard nodded to the stone on Amalia's necklace.

"Actually, no, not Feargus. The dragons only sensed the stone he carried, a signal that the army was approaching. Feargus has never spoken with a dragon as far as I know. You have to be open to it, your mind open, to let the dragon's thoughts in. Ramona offered it to him once, but he never wanted to meet a dragon. He preferred a distance. Wise probably, they most likely would not have trusted him."

"He doesn't talk with them, but you and Ramona do?"

"Yes, and others, our friends."

"That's incredible. What's it like?

"At first, very confusing, makes you dizzy and sick, but after a while, you get used to it." Exuberance filled her voice in the telling of her secret exploits, the story she kept from him for so long.

"How did this happen?" Reynard interrupted.

She read the puzzlement on his face; these revelations would be difficult for Reynard to accept, for anyone really. She was sure his curious mind was conjuring questions faster than he could voice them.

"Ramona was the first to make contact," Amalia said, "While you and the King were away at the war council, she went looking for the dragons and managed to find one, Alpha the leader. She had a council of her own."

Amalia continued, describing Ramona's first encounter with a dragon and how she had gotten the dragon stones. She then recounted her own experiences with the dragons.

After she finished, Reynard was gazing into her eyes. "Really, you walked right up to a dragon, face to face, unarmed?"

Amelia sensed that Reynard was having trouble believing her story. He had never expressed doubt in her before. "Yes, I did."

Reynard's eyes were wide open. He shook his head, and a puff of air escaped his lips. "Wow. I don't—"

"What? You don't what, believe me?" Amalia pushed away from him. "You don't believe I have courage? You think facing dragons in battle with an army behind you is brave? Try walking up to one alone."

"I'm sorry, but it's hard to picture my little Amalia doing all this."

"The old Amalia, maybe, but not this one." She stood up, took one step back, and tapped her chest. "Oh, and how would you like to meet a dragon, one on one? I could arrange it." No tamping the anger down now.

"That's okay. Simmer down. It's going to take me a while to get used to the new Amalia." Reynard took both her hands and pulled her back down to the bench. "Sorry."

"I'm sorry too." His touch had a calming effect: it always did. She didn't understand how he managed such a gentle caress with those calloused and scarred hands. Nevertheless, she was compelled to set the record straight. "You should know; I not only spoke with dragons; I also helped Ramona recruit her network of friends. I made the initial contact and arranged the meetings. I was taking a great personal risk, more than even Ramona. If we were caught, she's a royal; not much would happen to her. But I would have been exiled, or worse." She was boasting, but couldn't help herself.

"Yes, I understand. It must've taken tremendous courage," Reynard said, "But you mentioned others, other people were involved?"

"Ramona put together a secret network, people we trusted, people willing to risk their lives. Each person or group had their responsibilities, some provided food, some hiding places, and other tasks."

"During the end of summer, Boetius' hunters weren't finding dragons anymore, but I was sure they were still in the Kingdom."

"We had people provide false reports of dragon sightings. Sent the hunters in the wrong direction."

"What of the hunting dogs?" Reynard asked.

"One of Ramona's more clever schemes. She had me take blankets to the dragons and rubbed them on their hides to pick up their scent. I gave the blankets to people who drug the blankets on the ground to create false trails." She held back the identities, feeling a reluctance to share too much, but he could probably guess.

"What of the dragons now?"

"Most of the dragons, those that have had enough food to sustain their hibernation, have traveled back north to their home. The friends are feeding and protecting the few that remain. We should have them fattened up in a few days, and then they can leave for home."

"So they do live in the north beyond the North Peaks? My grandfather's stories are true?"

"Yes."

"Strange though, there have been rumors surfacing

again about the dragons having come from the Dark Forest," Reynard said, "Odd, that old story should come to life again. When the dragons first appeared, the King questioned me about the Dark Forest. He asked about the time we saw the lights in the treetops."

"How do you think he found out we'd seen the Dark Forest lights?"

"Not sure, but we were young and told a few friends. A good story that people remembered, probably. No harm done."

Amalia and Reynard sat in silence for a short time.

"You know—those times we used to meet on the South Ridge Trail were a long time ago now, but it's like it was yesterday." Reynard's words turned silken. "They were the best times of my life. Clear summer nights, warm breezes."

He was smiling, entranced, she assumed, by the same memories that were moving through her mind.

"Those memories remind me of something I've wanted to ask you." Reynard moved closer and took up both of her hands in both of his.

"Oh, do they now." Over the years, many times, Reynard had voiced this reoccurring proposition, in the same manner, same tone of voice.

Reynard hesitated, waiting for Amalia, but she kept quiet. "You're not going to stop me from asking this time?"

"No, why would I?"

Reynard appeared to be taken back. One corner of Amalia's mouth turned up.

Reynard cleared his throat and straightened up. "Well then, my dear Amalia. Will you marry me?"

"Yes, I will." A part of Amalia was detached from herself, experiencing in amazement the assuredness with which she spoke. Over the last several months, she had been consistently astonished by herself as she executed one uncomfortable, frightening deed after another. The ease stood contrary to her mother's opinions and advice against men. Her mother's fears had no power over her anymore. Ramona's expression came to mind, 'Embrace the fear and do it anyway.' It was Amalia's mantra now.

Rising to her feet, she pulled Reynard up with her. She guided his hands to her waist, stepped into his embrace, and clasped her hands behind his neck. As he took a step back to maintain his balance, he bumped the bench, toppling it over.

For years, Amalia kept a likeness of this moment in a deep recess of her mind, one not allowed into consciousness often. Having turned Reynard away so many times, she assumed he would not ask again. Surely, a man could only stand so much rejection. It had been several years since he brought up the subject of marriage.

After a long hug, "How did you know to ask again?" Amalia put her hands on Reynard's chest and leaned back against his arms. "Wait. Ramona?"

Reynard smiled. "Yes, Ramona. Our Queen made a suggestion that I could not disobey."

"I must remember to thank her." It seemed Ramona was involved in everything. Another reason to be thankful for serving as the Queen's maid, no, as the Queen's friend, no, not serving. Amalia was still struggling with the idea that she and Ramona were equals, as Ramona had voiced and insisted on so many times.

"I'm so glad this war is over, and things will be getting back to normal," Reynard said.

"Back to normal!" Amalia stepped out of Reynard's embrace, shook her head, and wagged her finger in his direction. "No, No, No. We are getting married, you are the King's indispensable Weapons Master, and I speak with dragons. Things are NOT going back to normal. Things have changed."

Berengar's Words

The crowd noise that a moment ago had surrounded Boetius died away, table by table. The tavern was never quiet, especially in the evening. His hunter friends who sat across from him had their gaze fixed on the main door. Boetius, his back to the door, shifted in his seat and looked over his shoulder.

In the doorway, looking out of place but determined to be there, Berengar stood like a statue, frozen.

Boetius gestured with a head toss to the hunter seated to his left. The man got up and went to Berengar and guided him to the table, giving him the vacant seat. Berengar said nothing, made no eye contact. The conversations and clatter throughout the tavern hall restarted, but the awkward silence at the hunters' table remained until it was broken by Boetius.

"How are you, old man?"

It took a few moments for Berengar to respond. "I's good."

"You're not look'en so good. But then you never did." Boetius fell into his old habit of teasing the older man, his mentor. He expected a caustic response but got no response at all.

A barmaid appeared at the table. Boetius thought of

ordering Berengar a drink but thought better of it. He shook his head; the barmaid nodded and left.

Berengar was not the man he used to be, quick-witted and affable, as rambunctious as any of the younger men in the hunting group. This man sitting next to Boetius looked sullen, looked fragile. As far as Boetius knew, Berengar hadn't been out of his cottage since the incident with the dying dragon. Members of the hunting troop took turns visiting Berengar at his home, making sure he and his wife had provisions. He should have gone to visit, Boetius knew, but with the war, there just didn't seem to be time for it.

After waiting in an uncomfortable stretch of time, Boetius asked, "What brings you out?"

"To see you, son."

Another moment of silence passed. The men at the table appeared tense, shifting uneasily in their chairs.

"What about?"

"I gots word you's plan'en to go out hunt'en them dragons."

"No, not true; we aren't planning to hunt dragons. We are just readying for a hunting trip, looking for elk in the north of the Kingdom." Boetius gave Berengar a wink. "The King forbid hunting dragons." He looked around the table, wondering who had let the old man in on their plans.

With his small army contingent, Boetius had returned from an unsuccessful expedition to Chambold. They found no trace of any dragons. He had now turned his attention to planning a hunting party, in a guise of finding game, but secretly a hunt for dragons. Drake would have to change his mind about suspending the war once dragons were again found in the Kingdom.

Berengar spoke seriously; Boetius' jest was lost on him. "It's not the season for elk in Enid; the herds are mov'en farther up north this time of year."

Boetius leaned toward Berengar and spoke quietly, "Well, if we don't find any elk, we might find dragons—just by chance."

"That's not right. It's not what's you should be do'en." Berengar scanned the faces of the hunters around the table. His glare came to rest on Boetius. Berengar had been the leader of the hunting troop before most of these men were born, but Boetius was their leader now. These men would be in a tough spot if they had to choose who to follow.

"Noth'en good will come of it. Give it up," Berengar commanded. He pushed himself up from the table; his chair scraped the floor as it slid back. Silence fell on the tavern hall again. Berengar cast his gaze around the table; his arm swept out, his finger-pointing. His voice was loud and stern. "I's tell'en ya."

Berengar walked away, out the door, leaving Boetius with a dilemma. With that admonishment from the old man, no one would follow Boetius.

Victory & Peace

At dawn, Reynard was walking up the castle road serenaded by sweet birdsong. Last night, four days after Drake's proclamation, Reynard had been summoned to report to the King's chambers in the morning. The dread that had plagued him when he was required to meet with Drake during the war wasn't in play. He was enjoying the walk in the pale darkness and brisk early morning air.

With only a nod and smile (it would be a shame to spoil the silence), he greeted both the guard at the portcullis gate and then the guard at the great-hall door as he passed through the gatehouse into the great-hall. The room was lit by the orange glow of the sunrise, emanating in from the eastern clerestory windows.

Following the familiar route, he made his way through the great-hall and up the stairs to the King's chambers, where the door stood ajar. A rap on the door drew a quick response.

"Come in," Drake replied in a hushed voice.

Reynard passed through the chamber door. "Good morning, Sire."

The King stood looking out the chamber's west-facing

window, his hands clasped behind him, his back to Reynard. "Morning, Reynard. Yes, it is a good morning."

Now standing in the center of the room at the King's desk, Reynard looked out over the King's shoulder through the open window at the sky of yellow-orange streaked clouds. The hills of the hunting grounds in the distance, to ever hold in memory the stain of conflict, were visible as purple and blue mounds.

Reynard looked around the darkly adorned room where he had spent many hours in consultation with the King. The wall behind the King's desk was covered with floor to ceiling length dark red heavy drapes with black valances across the top. They were pulled back slightly above the middle by black sashes to make places for metal flat plate candle sconces that hung on the walnut-paneled walls. In the evenings, the sconces were lit to overcome (though not successfully) the darkness of the King's chamber. Reynard preferred it when their meetings were held in the well-lit great-hall.

Drake stayed at the window for a few moments and then walked back behind his desk.

"Take a seat." Drake gestured to the chair in front of his desk as he settled into his own.

"Thank you," Reynard replied as he took his seat.

The location of the meeting, Reynard knew, was a trivial matter. He was fortunate to be an adviser to the King. It afforded him a favored position in the Kingdom's hierarchy's society, not a Noble, but not just a commoner either. And the role he played in the war had enhanced his status.

"I have to say our fight has been a success. But I didn't expect victory so soon." King Drake stretched out his arms, hands resting at the edge of the desk, "Six dragons killed and the rest vanquished from the Kingdom."

"Yes, Sire. Unexpected, but grateful for the end of it," Reynard said, "Glad to be out of the field."

The King's army had been engaged in the Dragon War for a full six months, from mid-spring to mid-fall, tracking and attacking dragons. The last month in the field, although a relief from fighting, was nothing but a pointless pursuit of false alarms. Time after time, they had followed the dogs down trails that led to empty fields, not dragons.

"Now we will have time to concentrate on our trade deals with the other Kingdoms," Drake said, "What do you have to report?"

King Drake, taking advantage of the common belief in the other Kingdoms that he deserved the credit for vanquishing the dragons from all territories, had negotiated treaties with all the surrounding Kingdoms.

Although there were now no dragons in any of the Kingdoms, a fear remained that they could return at any time, next summer, the year after, years away, maybe. This worry motivated the other Kingdoms to enter into contracts that required them to pay a yearly stipend to Enid. The Kingdom of Enid, in return, was obligated to send its experienced "Dragon Soldiers" to the aid of a kingdom's army in case of an invasion by dragons.

The other Kingdoms during the war did not kill a single dragon. They didn't possess the weapons or dogs that King Drake had. During their confrontations with dragons, they only managed to harass the dragons and drive them away with a great cost in casualties.

The other Kings were also interested in procuring the new Dragon Weapons, Dragon Dogs, and training for their soldiers.

"My brothers are hiring men to help with the smithing. The materials for the weapon's shed arrived this morning. The masons and carpenters will start on the construction of the expansion tomorrow.

"Shields are the priority. I will start at once on the orders for shields for Dacian, Duran, and Chambold. We will stagger our deliveries; I think 20 for each would satisfy them. I will hold off on shipments to Braga and Evora until their full allotment of 50 each are ready."

The treaties contained trade agreements that required the purchase of set quantities of lances, dragon shields, and arrowheads, along with a catapult. The small Kingdoms of Dacian and Duran, along with Chambold, did not have the capacity or skilled workmen for weapon manufacture. Evora and Braga had weapon's masters and workmen capable of making their own weaponry and replicating the Enid weapons once they had the designs.

Reynard was grateful that Cenhelm and Hartmann were given the task of scheduling and training the other Kingdom's soldiers. He had enough on his plate.

"You're right. We shouldn't send a partial shipment to Evora or Braga and have them back out of their commitment. King Wilhelm is already complaining about my refusal to sell crossbows. He's still claiming that we stole the designs for the crossbow and catapult from him and owe him a better deal. The man thinks we should train dogs for him for free. He claims he arranged for the Elk Dogs to be delivered from Duren, which he didn't. The man is infuriating." Drake waved his arms in the air.

"It's wise to share our methods and weapons with the other Kingdoms," Reynard said.

"And it doesn't hurt to turn a healthy profit on the barter, either."

"After the shields, the men will work on lances and then arrows. A separate crew will work on the catapults. They will take at least two months to complete them. What of the requests for dogs or the training of dogs?"

"I don't see how we could supply trained dogs or train dogs they would send to us. I'm not sure how we will even take care of ourselves. The King of Duran says he won't part with any more of his elk hunting dogs. He has forbidden anyone in his kingdom from dealing with us. He is under the influence of Wilhelm. We will need to figure something out, so we will have a supply of dogs for the future."

"This is my written report of the weapons we will supply to the other Kingdoms." Reynard took a scroll from his waist bag and laid it on the King's desk.

"Very good, I will compare it with my notes. Some kingdoms will pay for what we supply, and to others, I will extend credit. It will be to our benefit to have those unpredictable Kings in our debt.

"What of our men's grumblings?"

"They've settled down. They were glad to serve when the Kingdom was under threat and even endure the casualties, but when harvest time came, they were not happy with what they saw as a useless pursuit of phantom dragons."

"I had to agree with Feargus' arguments. There was no reason to continue the hunt, with the hardships and sacrifices required, with no apparent benefit.

"Have you looked in on the wounded lately?"

"I recently accompanied Amalia and the healer on their rounds. We checked in on the men that are convalescing at home, and I visited the men at the healer's cottage."

The healer's cottage had a shed-like addition, a room that was used for housing and nursing seriously ill patients. It was attached to the south side of the cottage — tall south-facing windows allowed for the best light, east and west windows for the best ventilation.

"I want the men to have the best care. Do they have any needs? Any medicines?"

"I believe they are in good hands. Between Amalia, Ramona, and Renilda, we couldn't ask for better."

"The men's status?"

"The men at home have various injuries, broken bones and lacerations, a few men with minor burns. Some, at least five, have injuries that are disabling; they probably won't be able to return to their work."

"Get a list to me. I will assign pensions. And what of the men at the healer's cottage? Will they recover?"

Reynard had hoped the King would see fit to provide for these men and their families. The commoners had already banded together, providing food, and taking care of chores.

"The three men with serious burns, no, Sire, they will not. Renilda and the nurses can only try to keep them comfortable until their time comes. And Sir Anslem refuses to eat and will waste away. He has no will to live."

In the last battle with the dragons, Sir Anslem, a young Knight, had been thrown from his horse in the chaos and broken his back.

"I should visit him myself. I will call on his family as well."

"Yes, Sire, that's good of you."

"Fortunately, the dragons were inept in battle. Our loses could have been much worse if they were not so slow to react. And the fire, their most notable weapon, they couldn't accurately direct it. I believe that Feargus' theory is correct, that there was also a limit to how many times they could use it."

"Yes, Sire. Fortunate," Reynard said in agreement, although he was not. It was evident that the dragons fought a purely defensive battle in the beginning; flames were propelled over the King's soldier's heads. In later battles, the dragons directed their fire at the men, which flowed off the shields. The dragons' prime motivation was to escape, using their swinging tails to tumble men to the ground and create openings in the lancers' ranks. Once clear of the lancers, they had enough room to take flight or run off. But the King and Boetius didn't see it that way; they saw things the way they wanted to see them.

"Now, Reynard, we must look ahead." Drake left his seat and walked toward the chamber window.

Reynard started to rise but was stopped by the flat of the King's hand.

"The people can now settle back into the affairs of the Kingdom. All can celebrate our success. Our victory was won because everyone came together in the Kingdom's defense. We all had our part to play in the defeat of the dragons. It's not just my win, and my successful strategy, or even my fortuitous dream that should be celebrated. Everyone in the Kingdom can feel good about our triumph." Drake was staring out the window into a brightening sky.

"Yes, Sire. I'm sure everyone has a reason to celebrate the end of this war." Reynard doubted—actually, he was sure that not everyone in the Kingdom agreed with the King's assessment of his so-called victory.

"And the Veterans' Feast will be the ideal venue for our celebration."

Drake will undoubtedly be the center of attention at the Feast this year. He was being called the 'Hero of the Dragon War.' Amalia had shared the planning for the event, and it was extravagant. Over the next month or so, other kingdoms were also staging like celebrations. Duren, Dacian, Evora, and Chambold had sent invitations, requesting Drake's presence as the guest of honor. King Wilhelm of Braga, the only one who felt the need to slight King Drake, had not sent an invitation. Surely, Feargus, Boetius, Cenhelm, and Hartmann would be selected to travel with the King.

"I'm looking forward to the Feast. You should too, Reynard. You will get your ribbon this year. I'm sure Amalia is proud of you." Drake leaned back on the window seat, facing Reynard, a broad grin on his face.

"Yes, Sire." Reynard doubted it, doubted she appreciated the part he played in the war. He flushed with guilt at the thought. But they were reconciled now; she had assured him; they were to be married. He wished he could somehow avoid the ribbon pinning ceremony. He wanted all of this behind him.

"She must be more than proud, having accepted your marriage proposal. Congratulations."

"Thank you."

"And I was thinking, that before the celebration, I would like the dragon skin in your possession to be mounted on the throne wall alongside the first. I know this may upset Feargus and his sensibilities, but I believe the skins to be important exhibits that testify to our victory, a hallmark for future generations."

"That won't be possible."

"Why is that?

"It's not presentable for display. Testing weapons on it has caused some damage, and over time it has degraded significantly in appearance."

"Well, store it away, it may be of use someday,"

"Yes, Sire. I will take care of the hide, see to its proper care." He and Amalia had already taken care of it; they had sent the skin to Eachan. His horseman took it home for a proper obsequy. Not a lie exactly. And if Drake should catch him in the lie, so be it.

"Oh, and there's another thing I wanted to talk with you about."

"Yes, Sire."

"I've been thinking of old Samis again. With the war over, I believe I can find time to visit him. Remember we talked of it? I hope to see him at the Feast. That man can tell some stories."

Reynard hesitated for a moment. "I'm sorry, Sire, I didn't think to tell you. He passed away about two months back."

Drake slumped; a sharp breath escaped his lips. "Sorry to hear that. How? An old soldier like him deserved to die in his sleep."

"He was bedridden mostly for months. Only could get up and around with help. Uncle Munc's boys took care of him. The six of them took turns watching over the old man in shifts, rotating throughout the day. Samis used to call em his King's Guard. He said having a sentry by his side all day made him feel like a king. Always had someone to tell his stories to, though. The boys took to the story tell'en. Anyway, one night when no one was with him, Samis got himself out of bed and out the door. He took a bad tumble off the porch. Broke a couple of ribs, his leg, and hip. They asked what he was thinking, and he told em he had duty at the station. Stuck in bed, not able to move at all, he got pneumonia and died three days later."

"Let Munc know I was asking about Samis, will you?"

"I will," Reynard said, "I'll take my leave now."

"Yes, let's get about our business," Drake strode back to his cluttered desk.

Reynard bowed, turned, and stepped away, leaving King Drake to deal with the business of the Kingdom.

As Reynard passed out of the King's chambers and started across the balcony, Amalia and their upcoming marriage came to mind. It was only 20 days away. She had moved into his cottage, left her quarters at the castle. They had a family dinner planned for next week with his brothers. Yet they still hadn't spoken in any depth about his involvement in the Dragon War, the hunt as Amalia called it.

They had always had their disagreements, their divergent opinions on religion, her loyalty to the Queen, his loyalty to the King. Would their differences now, having played their parts on opposite sides of a war, be insurmountable? What did she really think of him? He was sure she wasn't proud.

Family Gathering

"Well, brother, how we go'en to live with him now? Our FAMOUS older brother." Maccus spoke to Donar but nodded at Reynard, with that familiar edge of sarcasm, obviously intended to mock Reynard's good fortunes.

Reynard's younger brothers sat across the kitchen table from him and Amalia, Maccus (one year his junior), and Donar (three years younger). It had been a long time since they had all sat together at this table for a family meal.

"Famous and getting married to boot. Attached to the old ball and chain." Donar nodded to Amalia. "Only ten days of freedom left, brother." He grinned at Reynard.

Since Reynard's proposal just a week ago, Amalia had been working on the wedding plans, a commoner's family wedding to which he had at last agreed. Reynard had decided to leave the wedding plans and decisions to Amalia, best to bite his tongue and stay out of it. The date, the food, the invitations, better that she handle it. But the choice of Renilda to represent his family concerned him; he didn't even know her. But he needed a matriarch to represent his family. And his mother and aunts were all gone; he had no sisters; his brothers were bachelors. None of the distant cousins (all churchgoers) were comfortable or willing to officiate at a family wedding ceremony. So Amalia arranged for Renilda to serve his family. Amalia's older sister, Adela, and Renilda would lead the couple through the wedding ritual.

"I apologize for my brothers," Reynard said, looking to Amalia, "A poor way to behave in front of the hostess of a family supper." He scowled his nastiest older brother look in their direction.

"Say you're sorry to the lady, Donar," Maccus said, "I want us to get more invites to family dinners, long as Amalia does the cook'en and not Reynard."

"Not to worry, I was trained by my four older brothers," Amalia said, "I can take it. And I can dish it out." She retrieved a wooden spoon from the stew pot and was pointing it at them with menacing intent.

Both brothers raised their hands in front of them in mock surrender. "Truce," Maccus said, "It's nice to have a woman in this house again. Got some feminine touches already. I mean, besides the good food."

"Yeah, makes me think of Ma." Donar's eyes scanned the room, the kitchen-common room of Reynard's cottage, their boyhood home. His eyes came to rest on the fireplace mantle behind Reynard. "There it is, the invite from the Queen of Evora." Donor elbowed Maccus and pointed to the placard resting in a place of honor in the center of the mantle, nestled in linen and ribbon.

To the surprise of everyone, Reynard had received a personal correspondence in the royal mail from the Kingdom of Evora. No common-folk ever used or got deliveries from the royal mail. It was the talk of the Kingdom, a letter from the Queen of Evora. Wrapped in linen cloth, secured with a red ribbon, a Royal seal in wax, it was a treasure no matter what the contents.

Summoned by one of the King's guardsmen to the castle,

Reynard had stood for a long moment in shock after Drake put the missive in his hands. The King stood waiting for Reynard to open it on the spot, but Reynard wanted Amalia to be with him when he opened it. He found her in the courtyard, and they took the letter to his cottage.

Sitting at the kitchen table, they examined the letter lying on the tabletop. Only after a long delay, reluctant to disturb the wrapping, did he finally break the sealing wax.

Inside, they found the placard invitation, written in an ornate script that neither he nor Amalia could read. They were only fluent in block print.

Together, they hurried off to find Ramona, to ask for help. Ramona read it out loud and then wrote out the translation in print on the backside of the paper. It was an invitation for Reynard to attend the veterans' celebration in Evora. It acknowledged his contribution to the dragon war and the elimination of the dragons from the Kingdoms.

"Imagine that," Maccus said, "A personal invite from the Queen of Evora. You must'a made a considerable impression on her. A guest of honor at their Veterans' Feast, along with old King Drake and his Knights." His tone turned serious (a rarity) and conveyed a hint of pride.

"He'll be going to two Veterans' Feasts, ours tomorrow and then the one in Evora. Theirs is just a week away, right?" Donar asked Reynard. Reynard nodded. "At our feast, Reynard being a hero, we'll be gett'en a place of honor at the Nobles' tables this year."

"I'll be damned to hell," Maccus added.

It was customary at the feast dinner for the King and Noble Council members to be seated on a dais at the front, the Nobles at dining tables near the King, and common-folk seated at trestle tables in the rear. For the supper tomorrow evening, King Drake had insisted that Reynard and his brothers take a place at the Nobles' tables, the first table in front of the King's dais.

"I'm not lik'en the idea of sitt'en at the Nobles' tables," Reynard said, "I couldn't talk King Drake out of it. He was damned insistent."

"You have to accept that the King means it as a place of honor," Amalia said.

"But the Nobles don't follow the 'empty chair tradition,'" Reynard said, "And I have to do it for Pa and Grandpa Samis. Not sure how the Nobles are going to take it."

"Do they pay your rent?" Maccus asked.

"Of course not."

"Then be damned with em." It was a saying they heard Grandpa Samis use many times.

"Besides, you're a veteran now and a war hero and the King's man," Donar added, "What are they go'en to do about it."

Reynard was uncomfortable with his new status. People nodded to him as they passed as if he were a Noble. Unlike most men his age, Reynard was not a veteran of the Nendos wars. He had not been in the actual combat but worked at the castle, making weapons, organizing provisions, and arranging for supplies to be transported to the army. Only occasionally had he seen the aftermath of battle when he accompanied supply wagons making deliveries and upon returning with the dead or wounded.

Now, though, he had taken part in the battles. He held himself accountable for deaths. His brothers had taken on the responsibilities of provisioner. They were left in charge of the weapon shop in his absence, while his catapult crew was attached to the army.

This year, as a veteran, he would be honored at the feast. He had received his official invitation from the King. At the end of the Veterans' Feast tournament, a scarlet ribbon would be pinned to his chest by the King along with the other first-timers, those mostly his junior.

"Pa would be proud, Reynard," Maccus said, "Grandpa too."

In the past, he and his brothers attended the feast as

guests. Each veteran could invite male members of the family to sit with him at the feasting tables, sons, brothers, nephews, grandsons. Reynard and his brothers had attended with Pa and Grandpa Samis for as long as he could remember.

"Pa and Grandpa Samis did their part for the Kingdom," Donar said, "They served their King, and now you've served yours."

Reynard had vivid childhood memories of sitting next to his father at the feast, listening to tales of war and adventure. It was noticeable that his father and friends didn't speak of battles or combat, but spoke of card games amongst themselves, stealing eggs from farms near their camp, and drinking parties after a victory. Also, glaringly obvious was the loud, raucous conversation at other tables where men were telling tales of combat, death, and glory.

Reynard remembered a time when he asked his father about a story he heard from one of the men at the feast. A story in which the man and his squad had been instrumental in a victory, destroying their enemies with vicious swordplay and crushing blows. Could such an amazing story be true? All his father said was, 'Men who talk of the fight most likely weren't there.' He said nothing more.

Reynard noted that Amalia was quiet. She had assured him that she made no judgments concerning his involvement in the war, but he had his doubts. Thoughts of the ribbon pinning ceremony were making him anxious.

"He served his comrades," Amalia said, "I know the stories of battles I heard from those who were there, those I trust with stories. Many times Reynard rushed into the fight to rescue the wounded, to get a broken man to safety. Many men are alive today, to his credit."

The three men were quiet for a long time, focused on their stew.

"So, gentlemen, I take it you approve of the stew?" Amalia broke the silence.

"Yes, Ma'am," Donar and Maccus answered in unison as they both raised their heads, clearly relieved that the tension of the moment had passed.

"Don't, Ma'am, me. I'm not a Noblewoman. Why don't you call me Sis? What's a couple more brothers, more or less?"

"Sis," Maccus said, "Sounds good to me. And you can call me Mac and," pointing to Donar, "You can call him dumb-ass."

"Mac, please. You're going to scare her off." Reynard shook his head.

"This stew is as good as Ma used to make," Donar said, ignoring Maccus, as was his custom.

"Better." Maccus delivered an elbow to his brother's ribs.

Amalia stood and took up the ladle from the pot, beckoning with a finger for Donar's plate. "More?"

"Yes, Ma-am—I mean Sis."

"Please. Manners." Maccus raised his eyebrows and delivered yet another shot to Donar's ribs as he raised his plate as well.

"Please," Donar said to Amalia with pleasant effect, while scowling at Maccus.

"Reynard." Amalia gestured to the loaf of bread on the table. He cut off two thick slices and handed them to his brothers. With another roll of her eyes, she told him to refill their tin mugs with beer. Obediently, he raised the pitcher.

"You haven't touched your aioli, Maccus," Amalia said as she sat down.

Everyone at the table had a small cup of aioli in front of them for dipping their bread.

"The garlic doesn't agree with me, Sis," Marcus said, "Sides, I wouldn't want bad breath to scare off the ladies."

"No fear. Your face does that." Donar dropped his arm to his side to protect his ribs.

"It is true, Amalia got the best look'en of the Smith brothers," Reynard said.

His brothers shook their heads and grunted.

"Well, no matter their looks, they are always welcome here," Amalia said to Reynard, then glancing to his brothers, "You all must have lots of special memories of this place."

"This was Ma's domain, the house," Reynard said, "She commanded this place, us boys and even Pa. I can still see her standing in that doorway, pointing a finger up in his face, from well below, telling him to get back out and get better cleaned up, for he dared cross the threshold."

Pa was a big man. Maccus took after him, tall and broad at the shoulders. Reynard and Donar were also stocky, but not so tall. They took after Ma's side. They resembled her father, Grandpa Samis.

"Ma kept everybody in line. She had the most trouble with Reynard, though. Us two was the good sons." Maccus gestured to himself and Donar. "Reynard, being the oldest, was supposed to look out for us."

"Reynard didn't do that job too good. Got us in trouble more than not. It was Grandpa Samis, who kept us out of trouble—mostly," Donar said.

"Those times at his farm were the best," Maccus said, "Some hard work, but damn good times."

"Has Reynard told you stories about's the times we spent at Grandpa Samis' farm?" Donar asked Amalia.

"I've heard some, but I wouldn't mind hearing your versions."

Reynard thought his brothers would probably different a slant on Grandpa Samis' farm stories, to their benefit, no doubt.

In the summer, several days a week, Reynard's Ma sent him and his brothers off to Grandpa Samis' farm with the stated intention of helping their grandfather with chores, doing day labor.

One of Reynard's favorite chores was milking the cows, first thing in the morning before sunrise. Reynard's job was keeping the feed buckets filled in front of the cows as they were milked. When Grandpa Samis was milking, the barn cats lined up against the wall waiting for him to turn a teat in their direction, splattering their open mouths.

After milking and breakfast, he and his brothers did barn chores. Late morning and afternoons were spent working the fields, doing what was needed doing. Picking rocks off the fields and building stonewalls was one of the toughest.

"There were lots of chances to get in trouble around Grandpa's farm." Maccus to Amalia. "Remember playing with the bear traps in the barn?" He said to his brothers.

"Yeah, lucky someone didn't lose an arm when we were set'en em." Donar flinched. "Those things would crush a three-inch pole. When they snapped shut, I believe my heart stopped. Do you think he ever found out we were play'en around with his traps?"

"Probably did, you couldn't get much past Grandpa," Maccus said, "Although, I don't think he ever found out about the whiskey."

Grandpa Samis kept his best whiskey hidden away from Grandma in the grain barrels in the barn, which the boys found in their exploring.

"Really?" Reynard said, "You don't think he noticed half a bottle of whiskey gone? Or that we were act'en crazy that evening, drunk as we were?"

"If he knew," Maccus replied, "I would'a expect'ed he'd a told Pa, and we'd a got a good lick'en—but we didn't."

"We should've got beat'ens for a lot the stuff we got into." Donar's eyes were wide.

"Grandpa was look'en out for us. He kept our shenanigans to his self," Reynard said.

"We ate good though, didn't we?" Maccus announced, "Grandpa and Grandma made sure of that."

Three squares a day, Grandpa insisted on it. 'You want to grow up big and strong like me, don't ya?' Grandpa Samis was guaranteed to say if someone suggested skipping a meal or didn't finish their plate.

After the milking, breakfast was a morning feast of slab bacon, fried potatoes, fried eggs, gravy (bacon grease) poured over the heaping plate, and Grandma's right out of the oven sourdough bread with butter.

"My best memory is Grandma's fresh bread slathered with butter at breakfast." Saliva squirted in Reynard's mouth, just thinking about it. "But I used to feel sorry for old Blue."

"Not sorry enough to take his place," Maccus said.

A big old dog named Blue earned his keep by walking for hours on an old rickety treadmill in the cottage basement that powered a butter churn.

"I did my share of chores," Reynard replied.

"Grandma made sure we didn't go hungry," Donar said.

"Dinner was my favorite." Maccus smacked his lips.

Dinner, at noon, was more of a quick snack where Grandpa Samis laid out the work plan for the afternoon. Reynard had to agree; everything always tasted so good after a morning of hard work, those sharp moldy cheeses, more buttered bread with a layer of rhubarb sauce, and tiny pickled fishes (bones, heads, and all).

"All these guys think about is food," Donar, nodding to his brothers, said to Amalia.

"Look who's talk'en, the littlest of us who could eat twice his weight in biscuits," Marcus said.

"The best times we had was when Grandpa set us loose in the afternoon. We had the run of the place till supper time," Donar said.

Late afternoons after a hard stretch of farm work, Grandpa Samis left the boys off to their own devices.

"Funny how Grandpa usually had an excuse for quit'en early; he needed a break; something need'en fix'en or an errand to be run," Reynard said.

"That's when we had our chances to get in trouble," Maccus said, "When Reynard was supposed to be keep'en his little brothers out of trouble, but he was mostly leading us into it."

"That's not the way I remember it," Reynard said to Amalia, "You can't believe their take on things. They got in trouble just fine on their own."

"There's truth in that," Donar said.

Reynard wasn't always with his brothers. Some afternoons Reynard, being the oldest, hung back and helped his grandfather with odd jobs, like butchering chickens. Grandpa Samis hung them by their feet in a tree by the barn. He let Reynard use the kill'en knife to slit the throat for them to bleed out. After that, they dunked them in boiling water, making their feathers pluck easy. Finally, they singed the pin feathers off with a flaming alcohol torch. During the butchering, Grandpa saved out the livers and gizzards for himself and the hearts for Reynard, their shared special treat for supper.

"Anyways, we had plenty of time for adventure, mischief, and pranks. The North Woods is a wondrous place for a pack of boys to run about in. There was the three of us and our six cousins, Uncle Munson's boys, who lived nearby and the kids from the lumber camp and the Sheep Clan and the Horse Clan." Reynard's mind was swimming in memories.

"Had to be back for supper," Donar said, "That was the rule."

"That was late, though, at dusk," Maccus looked to Amalia.

Supper was the late evening meal; the timing of which, Reynard later realized, was intended to give the boys as much playtime as possible. In good weather, they ate outside on a wooden table. They had baked potatoes that had been nestled in the banked up coals of the outside fire pit. They had more bread and generous portions of meats, ham from the smokehouse, or something freshly butchered. A variety of vegetables were set out in front of the boys, not their favorite, but which they ate because Grandma said they were good for them.

Best of all, the boys sat at table listening to Grandpa Samis' stories about the wars, his bear hunt excursions into the north woods, and more.

"That was Grandma's rule," Reynard said, "I think Grandpa Samis would have let us do anything."

"Your Grandma ruled over Samis then? And your Ma ruled over your Pa?" Amalia asked, "I like the sound of that."

"Me and Donar be'en bachelors ain't need'en any rules or supervision," Maccus said, "Reynard, on the other hand, could use some feminine guidance."

"That used to be Ma's job," Donar said, "Now it's your job, Sis."

"The house was Ma's domain; I'll give you that. But Pa ruled the shop." Reynard didn't like where this conversation was going and made a course correction. "We were lucky boys to have the run of the place."

"Yeah, when he was gone, we did." A smile crossed Maccus' face.

"All those tools, the forge," Donar said, "We made all kinds of things, weapons mostly. We were real popular with the other kids, supplying them with knives, swords, and the like."

"That's why those Nobles, Feargus, Boetius, and Drake took to Reynard," Maccus said, "He even made a pair of ice skates for Ramona. I think he had a crush on her."

Maccus was baiting him, trying to make Reynard blush, but Reynard was beyond that childish game.

"We liked to think we was sneaking round in Pa's shop," Reynard said, "But I don't think he minded. I think he was happy for it."

"Yeah, but remember the time Maccus throw Pa's war-hammer through the shop window?" Donar slapped Maccus on the back. "He wasn't happy that time."

"My backside still remembers that," Maccus said.

Maccus was the biggest, the strongest, and the one they had dared to try to swing Pa's war-hammer. It hung up high on the wall in the shop behind the forge. Pa had fought in the wars with King Drake's father, the only man to carry a war-hammer instead of a lance or sword, a weapon of his own invention. It had a chain thong attached to the bottom of the handle. The way Reynard understood it, in hand-to-hand combat, Pa grasped the hammer handle in one hand, no easy feat for the weight of it. But when confronting a group of foe or Knights on horseback, he swung it around him in a circle by the chain. Most could not even lift it. After a dare and a boast, Maccus had tried, and with some success, sent it through a shop window.

Reynard did not want the conversation or his thoughts to return to war. "Maybe my brothers could invite us to dinner next week?" He glanced to Amalia. "They could fry us up some fresh fish, and Maccus' home-brew is the best around."

The brothers' tin-smith shop was a converted farmhouse to the south of the village near the Morodon River. The brothers pretty much lived on the fish that Donar caught in the river. A modest spring near the farmhouse produced a trickle of a stream that ran through the cellar in the back of the structure. Years ago, a stone cistern had been built in the basement, fed by the stream, to store and keep milk cold. The brothers used it to keep beer cold. Donar put his live caught fish in also so they could have fresh fish whenever they wanted.

Donar and Maccus exchanged uncomfortable glances.

"Our housekeep'en, ain't exactly up to womanly standards," Donar said.

"Maybe we could help with that," Reynard said, "What do you think, Amalia? They could use the services of a matchmaker. For sure, they won't be attracting any women with their looks."

"I do have a couple of younger cousins that live in Morodon. Fine young women. Hard workers."

"A little on the robust side, not the prettiest girls in town, but just the same." Reynard exchanged a sly wink with Amalia.

Maccus' and Donar's faces slipped into shades of panic.

Reynard and Amalia sat back, laughing.

Reynard's Torment

eynard walked, in the crisp morning air, past the stables where the tournament participants were assembling for the parade. The whinny of horses, the clank of armor, and a cacophony of voices surrounded him. Pennants of various Noble colors hung limply from the ends of the lances. Banners, also, lay motionless from their poles in the still air.

As a final check, he walked along the parade-ground fence to where the procession would enter the west gate. Everything looked in order and ready; archery targets and jousting targets rested in wait against the rails near the entrance. Ground's-keepers were in position, ready for the tournament to begin.

He continued through the gate into the grounds, skirting along the stands on the southern side, greeting the common-folk who were taking their places on the benches. It seemed that everyone wanted his attention; his popularity was unnerving. People were calling and waving from the opposite side of the arena, as well. He felt like all eyes were on him.

The south and north sides of the parade-grounds were lined with benches arranged on three-tier platforms, the viewing areas for the common-folk. At the eastern end, a multi-level structure occupied that entire width. The first level was the King's dais. Two additional levels were erected behind, viewing platforms for the Nobles.

After a long walk of acknowledgments, a gauntlet, Reynard arrived at the east end of the parade-ground at the King's dais. Drake stepped down to meet him.

"Everything is ready, Sire," Reynard said with a slight bow.

"Excellent. What a beautiful day for the tournament." Drake scanned the bright, cloudless sky.

The temperature was perfect, not too cold for the spectators, and not too warm for the participants, an ideal day for the games.

"No doubt, my cousin will try to outdo my celebration, but I don't think she will top this; I have spared no expense."

Drake swept his arm out across his chest. He was referring to Queen Saskia and the Evora Veterans' Feast to be held next week.

"The invitation she sent you was a stroke of genius. It will add to the enthusiasm for the commoners. Just like here, you're held in high regard in Evora as well."

Reynard did not respond; he had no response, only angst.

"Also, you should know that I have been invited by King Adalharn to attend his victory celebration. I will take my Knights, and of course, you as well."

Reynard's breath escaped in a rasp; he hoped Drake didn't hear it. Reynard was aware that King Adalharn of Chambold had invited Drake and a contingent of Knights of Drake's choosing to attend that Kingdom's veterans' celebration. Until now, he didn't know; he too was on that list.

A smile crossed Drake's face, which Reynard took to mean he was expected to express gratitude for the unprecedented invitation.

"Thank you, Sire." It stuck in Reynard's throat.

A trip to Chambold was not in Reynard's plans, not another Veterans' Feast. When young, Reynard had considered it a privilege to be included in the gang of Noble children that surrounded Drake, the prince apparent to the throne. But now inclusion was not a felt privilege.

Grudgingly, he had taken part in a fight he did not want. But he couldn't very well disobey the King, having his duties as weapons master to fulfill. And he had always been loyal to Drake, even when they were boys, taking Drake's side, always choosing to follow Drake's lead.

"You're welcome. You deserve it; you made an outstanding contribution to the war effort. The first time, you used the catapult net to bring down a dragon—that was impressive. I will never forget it."

Out of Reynard's control, his body shuddered, his teeth clenched, and eyes closed tight, as the vision of the struggling dragon, thrashing in the weapon of his design, burst into his mind. He kept his eyes closed for a moment and tensed his whole body, trying to squeeze out that horrible image.

"Are you alright?"

"Yes. Yes. Just a headache, only lasts a moment."

"Nothing serious, I hope."

"You were saying, King Adalharn celebration, when is it?" He knew the date, but his mind was muddled. This celebration today, the Evora feast in less than a week, and now another obligation to add to the list. His wedding day was five days after the Evora feast; he hoped this new obligation wouldn't interfere.

"The banquet is in two weeks' time. Not to worry, it's well after your wedding day. And I won't keep you there long. I'll get you back to your bride as soon as possible." Drake clasped Reynard's shoulder, threw his head back, and chuckled.

Reynard nodded.

"We will have another opportunity to tell the battle stories and how we vanquished the dragons." Drake slapped Reynard on the back.

War stories, tales of the 'Dragon War' were on everyone's

lips. Since the King declared victory, calm and peace had returned to the Kingdom along with a good ration of gossip and boasting. Merchants and travelers carried wide-ranging accounts of King Drake's army's exploits to and from the other Kingdoms. Reynard received letters from friends in those Kingdoms, words of congratulation, and praise. Strangers confronted him, shaking his hand, slapping his back.

Reports of the army's encounters with the dragons took on a life of their own, stretching, exaggerating, and contorting into events unrecognizable to anyone who was actually there. The number of dragons killed doubled and more; the number of battles multiplied; the accounts of the action bore only a minimal resemblance to the truth. In some versions that emerged, King Drake, himself, engaged with dragons, sword against fire; the catapult net brought down two dragons at once; lances and arrows pierced dragons' hearts. It was all nonsense, but inextinguishable bravado fanned the flames.

The inflated stories had the effect of inflating Drake and Boetius. Even Feargus was enjoying the attention. None of them offered contradiction. At first, Reynard had tried to set the record straight, but it was useless. He had been there, but those who had not argued with him anyway. He avoided visits to the tavern anymore.

Reynard's thoughts turned back to the celebrations.

"Feargus and Boetius both will be going, the four of us?"

"Yes, they will."

"Hopefully, we won't have any problems with them," Reynard said, "I worry about the grudges they hold against each other. A celebration and too much to drink, it worries me?"

"They've always had an ax to grind," King Drake said, "You know it's been the same since we were children, always finding something to argue over. They'll behave themselves. They know better than to embarrass me with a public display."

"I hope you're right."

It was true; they had kept their conflicts in check, at least no argument had risen to the level of a physical fight, not since Drake's coronation. It was two days after Drake was made King, and he had appointed Feargus and Boetius as commanders of the army. The rivals were in the courtyard with swords drawn. Boetius had challenged Feargus to a dual over a perceived insult.

Reynard and Drake had arrived on the scene at the same time. Ramona, already on the scene, had positioned herself between the combatants, holding them off at arm's length, as she attempted to reason with them. Drake told Ramona to step aside and not interfere.

"Let them settle this, once and for all," he said. "It appears you have chosen to serve your egos rather than your King. So be it." Drake stood glaring at them. "You should know, at the end of it, I will bury the loser and banish the winner." Drake walked away.

They sheathed their swords; the truce has held ever since.

"If things are ready, let's get on with it." Drake was scanning the parade-grounds. The stands were full of people, standing and seated, conversing loudly. The din of voices hung in the air.

"Yes, Sire."

The King stepped back up on the dais, took his seat next to Ramona, putting his arm around her shoulders. Reynard's eyes met hers; she nodded. His tension eased.

Reynard walked back toward the commoners' stands. As he reached the end of the Nobles' grandstand, he pointed, an instruction for the trumpeter stationed there.

"Ta-Da, Ta-Da, Ta-Da." The call to assembly. The crowd quieted and hurried to their seats.

As Reynard took his seat next to Amalia, his thoughts leaped from his concerns about Feargus and Boetius to the pleasing expectation of the upcoming wedding. Blasted worry returned in a moment, the trips to Evora and now Chambold. He would have to tell Amalia about it, but later. Bad enough to leave home at all, but two long trips with Feargus and Boetius as companions, he was not looking forward to it.

Despite Drake's assurance that Feargus and Boetius would behave themselves, Reynard doubted it. Yes, they had always been in competition and always argued, but these days he sensed that the currents ran deeper. Feargus blamed Boetius for starting the war, and Boetius blamed Feargus for the end of it. Reynard did not believe in premonitions, but still, he had a bad feeling, a feeling that something grim was going to happen.

"Ta-Daaaaaa." One long trumpet blast, signaling the start of the tournament parade, brought Reynard back to the present. The King's nephews, at the head of the parade, were riding in through the west gate.

Immediately after the parade, the ribbon pinning ceremony would follow, the next ordeal to fret over.

Veterans' Feast Tournament

Even though she was expecting it, the three trumpet blasts startled Ramona. She had seen Reynard's signal that called for the tournament to begin. Drake, sitting next to her, placed his hand on hers. The couple sat in the middle of the Nobles' grandstand on the first tier, Feargus, and his family to the left, Boetius and his family to the right and her family directly behind her. Ramona was hemmed in, trapped. She wanted to be anywhere else but here, the parade-grounds, watching the Veterans' Feast Tournament. In the waiting, her mind was trying to take her away, visiting memories and conjuring futures. Her body shivered, but it wasn't cold.

One long trumpet blast, the west gate swung open, and the tournament participants poured into the parade-ground at the far end. To a roaring cheer, the young men and boys in the ritual procession waved to the crowd. The common-folk on both sides of the arena rose to their feet.

At the head of the procession, the King's two nephews sat astride their warhorses; their short legs stretched across the horses' wide backs. Their father's squire, following closely behind them, carried the house banner flag, red, with a white silhouette of a mountain-lion. Both boys, aged six and eight, were too small to carry the heavy flag. Without an heir-apparent to the throne, these boys had the honor of leading the parade, representing the royal family, the House of Lowe.

Drake's hand withdrew from Ramona's.

Following the squire, rode a group of boys in light armor, carrying lances with red and white pennants dangling from the tips. They were members of the royal family, offspring of Drake's aunts and uncles. Behind them on foot, more of the King's young male relations marched, each carrying his tournament weapon (bow, lance, or sword).

The King's clan was followed by a procession of the other Noble families, each cadre of boys headed by a junior Knight carrying the household banner. The order of parade was set by the rank of the Noble families in the Kingdom's hierarchy, determined by wealth, and the support offered the King.

When the royal contingent reached the King's grandstand, the boys presented themselves by spreading out in a line in front of the King's dais. At a command barked by the squire, each boy bowed as they tipped their lances, sword, or bow toward the ground. The younger of the King's nephews, attempting to bow in his ill-fitted armor, began to topple sideways. Quickly side-passing his horse up against the little fellow's horse, the squire grabbed the boy by the back of his collar and set him upright. Quiet laughter rippled through the crowd, followed by measured applause.

The boys moved off to the King's left and took up a position in front of the commoners' stands, facing the Nobles.

The next group of boys to approach the King was from the House of Hirsch, Feargus' family. Four junior Knights rode light horses that moved in high prancing action. The Hirsch family was very proud of their horsemanship. Near the age of maturity, the boy in the lead carried the house banner, a blue flag dipped at an angle to display the white stag emblem. Following behind them on foot were the other boys of the family, holding weapons above their heads in response to the cheering crowd.

In the line of boys in front of her, Ramona recognized two junior Knights as Feargus' bastards. It was common for a Noble bachelor to acknowledge his bastards and provide for them. Married Nobles took care of them in secret—or didn't. These boys had chosen the path to knighthood that provided a stipend and an honorable life. Ramona was grateful that Drake had no bastard sons: it would be unbearable for him to have a son he couldn't call his heir. She was confident in his fidelity. She had been since they were teenagers before they even talked of marriage.

The Knight with the banner was Feargus' sister's son, although, from Braga, his bloodline allowed him to enter the tournament. He shouted a command and lowered his flag in salute to the King. In unison, the other boy's horses took a step back. The horses dropped to one knee, lowering their heads to the ground in a bow as their riders bowed their heads.

Seated to Drake's left, Feargus, his sister, brother-in-law, and his uncle were on their feet saluting the boys. The crowd erupted in applause.

To her right, Ramona caught a glimpse of Boetius, who had leaned out to send a scowl of disapproval in Feargus' direction. The Hirsch family's higher status in the Kingdom than that of Boetius' family had always irked him. She heard him say many times that the Hirsch family contributed wealth, but the Eber family (his family) contributed men.

The Hirsch troop moved off to the right, leaving space for the next family to present itself, Ramona's family, the House of Barin. Her family (mother, father, brother, and sisters) seated on the next tier up behind her, rose to their feet with a cheer. Her mother poked her in the back; Ramona stood; Drake did likewise. He turned and shook her father's hand. The royal couple's fathers were great friends; they fought in past wars together.

She knew every one of these boys well, her cousins and nephews, six on horseback. Another group afoot, four with bows and three with swords, in line now, bowed to the King, displaying the family banner (half yellow, half white with the outline of a black bear in the center).

The boys of her family moved off and were replaced by Boetius' family's company. She counted 16 boys, the largest contingent to present itself today: the Eber men had a proclivity for fathering boys. They formed up in a semi-circle in front of the grandstand to salute the King, their banner flag, solid green with a wild boar emblem in white.

Next in was Sir Cenhelm's family, the House of Conor, flying an orange banner with a white image of a wolf. The group comprised only six boys on horseback with lances, wearing no armor, clad in bright orange and white tunics.

They pranced their horses into line. As the banner-man lowered his charge in honor to the King, the other boys to his left and right, their horses reared, hoofs pawing the air. The riders slid off their horses' rumps (they were riding bareback), stepped up alongside their horses, and planted the butt of their lances in the ground, lowering their heads as they took a knee.

Ramona could hear Cenhelm hollering his approval from somewhere behind and to her left. She wondered if he had been named men-at-arms' captain because of his ability to shout so loudly. As she looked back for him, she saw Feargus standing, twisted around, clapping his hands over his head in approval.

For Ramona, the procession continued in a blur of colored banners, cheers, applause, and shouting as the rest of the Noble families' boys presented themselves. She barely noticed when the commoners' contestants entered in mass, stopping at the far west end with raised weapons in salute to the King. Not until Drake stood to acknowledge them with a bow, did she regain her senses. Shouts rose up from the young men and boys assembled in lines on both sides and the far end of the parade-ground. "Hail King Drake, Hail King Drake, Hail King Drake."

Drake moved forward and stepped off the dais to the ground. His clerk carrying an ornate leather-bound book, having anticipated the beginning of the ribbon pinning ceremony, was with him and took his place on the King's left. A servant who had accompanied the clerk stood to Drake's right with an open oak wooden box in his outstretched arms.

The clerk called for the new Noble veterans to assemble in the center of the parade grounds. The ceremony proceeded with the clerk calling out names from his book. Newly acclaimed veterans, each, in turn, made their way to the King who pinned a red ribbon, taken from the wooden box, on the man's chest. After receiving their ribbon, the young men assembled to the King's right, some waving to their families in the Nobles' stands, others were solemn.

After the Nobles' portion of the ceremony, the clerk called for the commoners' veterans to come forward.

In the throng of commoners seated in the stands, Ramona looked for Amalia and Reynard. They were difficult to find; the stands were full this year. More benches were built to accommodate the multitude of new veterans. Attendance had been dwindling over the years as the old men died off, old veterans of old wars.

She caught sight of them, midway along the south side, Amalia, Reynard, and his brothers. Reynard, standing, moved off the bleachers and in behind the younger men, heading toward the King. Even from a distance, it looked to Ramona that Reynard was walking as a man to the gallows. Reynard lingered in the rear, possibly hoping to avoid the inevitable. The men organized themselves into a single line. The clerk called them forward one by one. Reynard was last, which made things worse; the commoners hailed a shout of his name and provided a standing ovation just for him.

The ceremony at an end, with all the new veterans

assembled in front of the Nobles' grandstand, King Drake stepped back up onto the dais and called for acclamation with raised arms. The gathering gladly accommodated with a roaring clamor.

As the veterans returned to their seats, the tournament participants left the arena by the west gate to wait to be recalled for their events. Through the same gate, the ground crew brought in the archery targets. Archery was judged by Hartmann, to be followed by jousting, judged by Feargus, and then sword dueling with Cenhelm as judge. For the competitions throughout the day, the young men and youths were separated into four age groups; 16-14 years, 13-11, 10-8, seven years, and under.

Watching the archery competition was bittersweet for Ramona; she loved archery, always had. At an early age, she had learned to shoot. She took lessons from her uncle, against her mother's wishes, but allowed grudgingly by her father after much pleading and whining. Her cousins teased her; the boys made fun of her—a silly girl trying to learn a man's sport.

The competition moved along. Now, the oldest boys were up for their turn, in position near the Nobles' stands, taking aim at targets at the far end of the arena. So near to them, Ramona was focused on their form. She felt the bow in her hand, the pressure of the string on her fingers. Muscles in her back were flexing in response; her shoulders squared up. She wanted to call out instructions to the boy nearest her: his feet were not in alignment with the target.

As a youth, Ramona had begged her father to let her enter the Veterans' Tournament, but he would not hear of it. Girls were not allowed in any tournament or competition. She promised him she'd win if he gave her a chance. But he only shook his head and laughed. He whispered to her that he was in enough trouble with her mother; he didn't need any more and to stop begging.

Had they let her compete, she would have won. She was

sure of it then and now. Everyone knew it. She was a better archer than even Boetius.

Boetius had won every archery competition he entered, competing against boys his age. Sometimes his father moved him up to the older brackets to compete, and he won there as well.

When they were in their middle teens, she had grown tired of his boasting, and the other boys teasing and challenged Boetius to a match. She shouldn't have done it: she regretted it still.

In a recently cut cornfield behind a barn not far from the village, they set up two makeshift targets of colored cloth stretched over old boards. A crowd of children gathered around as witnesses: they had heard of the challenge. The targets, at 30 yards distance, presented green and red checkered squares, three across and three down. Each archer had nine arrows; the goal was to put an arrow in each block. Ramona and Boetius took turns.

Boetius went first. His first arrow hit the top right square, acknowledged by cheers from the boys. Ramona's did the same, no cheers. His second to top middle, more cheers. Ramona did the same. The game continued, square after square; the third, the fourth, the fifth, the sixth, Ramona matched Boetius shot for shot, the cheering dying away, waning with each round.

The seventh and then the eighth, the same result. Ramona took one step back and watched Boetius ready himself for the final shot. He looked calm, but she could sense the tension in him. It was subtle, a different line in his shoulders. He released; the arrow struck the target. Was it in the last red square or on the line or in the green square to the left? They were too far away to tell. Drake and Feargus, the unofficial judges, ran to the targets. Feargus waved his arm over his head, a miss.

Ramona took up her stance for her final shot. A few boys in the crowd began to chant. "Miss, miss, miss. . ."

Boetius pointed his bow at them, and they went quiet.

Her final arrow struck the target with a loud twang in the silence. On target.

The regret, she should have missed. As she had drawn the bow, taken, and held her breath, the thought had crossed her mind. But pride won out; she was proved the better archer. Boetius shook her hand, and the crowd dispersed. She got no ribbons, no applause. Nothing good came of it.

Later on, she found out that Boetius' father had gotten wind of the contest. He was a harsh man, distant and demanding. He found ways to punish Boetius for the humiliation.

The sound of horses entering the grounds interrupted Ramona's thoughts. The jousting competition was starting. The youngest boys were assembled at the west gate, waiting to be called for their turn at the rings. The jousting targets, rings of various sizes hung form poles, were set up on the east and west sides so two horsemen could make a run at the same time.

Feargus had left his seat and was in the middle of the parade-grounds with the King's clerk. He was calling out scores for the clerk to record on a writing tablet. The smaller the ring, the boy hit with his lance, the higher the score.

Ramona's mind drifted unaware as the jousting continued to its conclusion, and the swordplay contest began.

The clacking of dull steel swords on armor from three pairs of dueling young men stung the air. Cenhelm and two other Knights were now in the arena with the clerk, judging the contests, counting points of contact, judged wounds or fatal blows.

In each contest, the younger boys took the field first, followed by the older age groups, the oldest last. But in the sword dueling, the youngest category (seven and under) was saved for last. The little boys were the comical highlight of the tournament.

A matter of tradition, Drake took over from Cenhelm to judge these matches. He was now shaking hands with the boys of the first match of three for the day.

As the two little fellows waddled and teetered about in their oversized straw-stuffed armor, whacking away at each other with oversized wooden swords, the crowd erupted in alternating bursts of shouts, applause, laughter, and cheers. At the end of the match time, the King declared a draw, as he did for all the matches, raising both boy's hands.

It was much the same for the second match.

For the third match, a King's nephew was a combatant, recognizable by his red and white tunic just visible under his straw armor.

The boys circled for the longest time, barely raising their swords off the ground, Drake circling as well, waved his arms inward, encouraging them to fight. Finally, apparently taking advice from his uncle, the King's nephew, with both hands on the hilt, raised his sword off the ground, up in front of him, over his head and behind, intending to strike a vicious blow. Instead, he tilted backward with the weight and fell on his back. His sword in the dust behind him, he lay like a turtle, thrashing his arms and legs about as he tried to right himself.

Laughter erupted. Drake stood over the boy for a moment and then circled behind, stooped over, took the boy under the armpits, and set him back on his feet to a rounding chorus of applause.

Since there was probably no point in letting the contest continue, Drake declared another draw.

The King raised the hands of both boys well above their heads. He turned them around in a circle, presenting them as winners to each side of the arena, their feet sometimes leaving the ground. The crowd of veterans sent up the last, most rousing cheer of the day. The cheer was for the boys and for King Drake. She knew he relished the adulation, but he was also sullen in it. There was nothing he wanted more than to have a son in the tournament, an heir competing in his name.

The sun was nearing the horizon; the afternoon was cooling. The commoners' families were moving out of the stands, lingering in scattered conversations. Most family members would go home now. The veterans and their guests, and the women and girls who would serve them at the feast-day dinner, would stay.

Ramona headed there next, the castle courtyard, to double-check the preparations for the feast (tables set, kegs of beer, stacked casts of wine, pigs on the spit, fresh-baked bread, platters of roasted vegetables, and torches and candles at the ready for a late evening).

Ramona had gotten through the tournament, now on to the feasting supper. One evening to get through, she could do that.

The Salute

Ramona stood with her back to the kitchen door and looked out into the crowd of men gathered for the veterans' supper, seated at tables under the giant tent. Drake had the tent imported from a distant kingdom she didn't even know the name of. It was made of sailcloth and was suspended from long ropes strung across the castle courtyard to provide protection from the possibility of rain. It had, though, remained clear. In the darkening sky, visible above the castle wall, the moon was rising. This night would have been perfect for a full moon ride. A moonlit ride was Ramona's preference over this onerous celebration. One day's delay, tomorrow will be fine: the pleasant weather will hold.

Under the protection of the makeshift shelter, the veterans had been served their supper by the women and girls of the veterans' families. Women now scurried in and out, between the tables, with pitchers of beer. Drake had commanded all the best this year; the choicest wine, scores of kegs of beer, and endless quantities of roasted meats, bread, and vegetables. The kitchen staff and servants had been preparing for two days and cooking since dawn.

At the end of the tent, the farthest from Ramona, a dais had been built for the King, his head Knights, and members of the Noble Council. Drake sat at the center of a long table with Feargus to his left and Boetius to his right. On down the table, the head of each Noble family sat in proximity to the King in order of their rank. In front of each Noble's place, a small family banner hung on display on the edge of the table.

In front of the King's dais, banquet tables and chairs, moved from the great-hall, were arranged in parallel to the dais for the council members' families and lesser Nobles of the Kingdom. Beyond those tables and perpendicular to them, makeshift plank board trestle tables for the commoners extended back to the far end of the courtyard.

Servants were moving about, lighting candles on the tables, and attaching torches on poles at the table ends. Outside the tent on the north end of the courtyard, four fire rings were being lit ablaze. They would provide an agreeable amount of warmth for those who choose to linger and gather around the fires.

The supper was at its end. Nevertheless, Ramona would have the servants keep platters of food, including sweets, circulating, and available throughout the evening. Wine and beer had been flowing for several hours, and the gathering was becoming raucous. Choruses of laughter rose and fell; men stood and held their mugs high in toasts, which were followed by shouts and pounding of fists on tabletops.

Stories were being told about the dragons, and how King Drake and his 'Dragon Army' had vanquished them from the Kingdom. The men's voices were so loud; it was easy for Ramona to eavesdrop on their conversations. Drake was even being given credit for keeping other kingdoms safe from harm. His success in Enid had saved the other domains from the dragon threat, it was said. Not true, but it favored the King for it to be believed.

In the flickering light of the torches, Ramona caught

Amalia's familiar form, weaving through the Nobles' tables with a pitcher of beer in one hand, held high to clear the men's heads.

Amalia arrived at the first Nobles' table where Reynard and his two brothers were seated. Drake had insisted on honoring Reynard's contribution to the war by moving him from the commoners' tables to a Nobles' table. An honor, which, according to Amalia, had made Reynard very uncomfortable.

Amalia planted a kiss on Reynard's cheek as she leaned over his shoulder to pour beer into his mug. To his right, his brothers were laughing and tapping their mugs together. To his left were two empty chairs. On the table in front of each chair was a plate and a full mug of beer. The commoners had a tradition of honoring the departed veterans of their families by placing an empty chair at the feasting tables. One chair was for Reynard's father and the other for his grandfather, Samis. The Nobles did not follow this tradition, which made Reynard's folk stand out, showing the only empty chairs in the section of Nobles' tables. Tears came to her eyes as she surveyed the gathering: her focus was on the many empty chairs.

Ramona was glad the feast was held in the courtyard this year and not in the great-hall. The dragon skin that hung on the wall behind the throne conjured angry thoughts and painful memories. Images, residuals from dragon communications, arose in her mind and then faded away. She was grateful that the last of the dragons had left Eachan's care two days ago. They were all safe now.

A child carrying a tray passed by her, and a bitter-sweet memory surfaced. Ramona remembered feeling such pride the first time she was allowed to serve her father during the Veterans' Feast. So carefully, she carried a serving tray of bread to his table, relishing his nod of approval. One of his last before falling from grace as she entered her teens and pursued activities in the world of men; archery, horseback riding, and such, leaving her needlework and fancy dresses behind.

In the kitchen behind Ramona, a commotion caught her attention. The King's steward was directing servants to assemble trays with bottles of wine and glasses. The wine was being distributed to the Nobles' tables for the traditional veterans' toast the King would deliver at the end of the meal.

In a single-file line, servants streamed out of the kitchen, heading for the near ends of the Nobles' tables. From there, a servant placed a glass in front of each Noble, followed by another servant with a bottle of wine, filling each vessel in turn.

Noticing the activity of the servants, the men grew quiet in preparation for the King's toast. Commoners were making sure their beer mugs were full. Nobles were shifting in their seats, making room for the servants to pour their wine.

Not knowing where it came from, a mysterious motivation compelled Ramona into action. From the kitchen door, she strode across the courtyard, skirting the ends of the tables. She passed the commoners, past the Nobles' tables, and stepped up onto the King's dais. Serving girls had already placed the glasses on the table, and two of them had wine bottles in their hands and were about to start pouring.

"Excuse me, Sansa," Ramona said as she took the wine bottle from the young woman's hand and a glass from a tray. With the bottle in one hand and a glass in the other, she picked her way along the front of the dais table, filling goblets as she passed until she reached the center. Standing in front of Drake, Ramona filled his glass and then the glasses of Feargus and Boetius. She put the wine bottle and spare glass on the table and took a few steps back, so she was no longer directly in front of the men (her childhood friends).

Hands clasped in front of her; she stood there waiting. The King waited. He glared at her for a moment. She was unaffected. She took in the worried gaze of Feargus and the surprised look of Boetius.

Finally, Drake rose and lifted his glass. Boetius and Feargus did the same, followed by the Noble Council, the lesser Nobles, and the commoners, all with glasses or mugs held high.

"We raise our glasses to salute all veterans assembled here today, to all those in service to the house of Lowe, and to all those who have fallen in service to the Kingdom of Enid. SALUTE."

"SALUTE!" the assemblage shouted in unison.

The Nobles drank down their wine. The commoners downed their beer and then took up the mugs in front of the empty chairs and poured the beer on the ground.

Drake shifted to take his seat, but the assembly remained standing, their eyes focused on Ramona, who had taken up the extra glass and was filling it with wine. Drake straightened up.

Ramona turned to the gathering, holding her glass up high. She caught the glance from Amalia, who was standing next to Reynard. The couple stood directly in front of her. Amalia's face pale and painted with worry; her concern was recognizable even in the dim light of torch flame. Ramona sent back a smile.

Everyone was still, quiet blanketed the courtyard. The clink of a glass, the scrape of a chair leg, a cough, each pierced the quiet like thunderclaps.

Ramona opened her mouth to speak, choked, and stopped. Tears streamed down her face. A moment later, her throat cleared. Her words came back to her, echoing off the courtyard walls. "To all our brothers and our sisters, to all friends lost, in all wars in all times, friends and foe alike. And to the empty chairs. SALUTE!"

Ramona brought her glass to her lips and threw back her head. Droplets of red wine trickled from the corners of her mouth. She wiped her mouth with the back of her sleeve, put her glass down gently, turned, and walked off the dais in the persistent silence. Servants moved aside as she walked through the tent along the ends of the tables in the direction of the kitchen.

From the back of the tent at the courtyard wall, a low rumble began. A crescendo, like distant thunder, came forward through the crowd; men leaned forward to pound their fists on the tabletops. The rumbling salute spread along through the commoner's tables and on into the lesser Nobles' tables, dying off in front of the King's dais.

As Ramona passed through the kitchen door, she heard a shout from the familiar, yet unfamiliar, drunken voice of Reynard. "SALUTE, Ramona, Queen of Enid."

The gathering erupted in cheers, faint now, as Ramona continued into the kitchen.

The End
of a Ride

"Well, that was worth the wait," Drake's hands rested on the balcony railing in front of the royal chambers. He and Ramona stood near the top of the stairs.

"Yes, a beautiful night, perfect for a ride," Ramona said.

Drake gazed into the dimness of the great-hall. Both east and west hearth fires blazed; a servant was loading wood into the east wall fireplace. Torches at the main and kitchen doorways flickered light up the walls.

"I always enjoy the ride on the East Road."

"I as well."

"The clouds obscured the view of the moon for the most part."

"It peeked out for a few moments. That was enough for me."

"It wasn't too cold for you, was it?" Drake stole a glance at Ramona. Her eyes cast downward.

"No, I was dressed for it."

"Fortunate that the cold snap held off for a day. Yesterday's weather for the feast was pleasantly cool."

"Yes. Very enjoyable."

Drake stood in front of the Queen's chamber door. It was

five paces to his bedroom door.

"The feast was a success. It couldn't have been better." Drake said, "Thank you for all the hard work you put into it." Drake thought to comment on the cheer the men had offered up for Ramona. It was good of them to acknowledge her contribution, the preparation of the feast, and of course, caring for the wounded.

"Your welcome."

The crackling of the distant fireplaces faintly imposed on the silence.

"What are your plans for tomorrow? A busy day ahead?"

"Not so much, a review of the larder and supplies and then give out the stipends to the household staff. And you?"

"I should spend the morning catching up on correspondence. And then a meeting with the Noble Council at noon. That confab will certainly take up the whole afternoon, maybe run into the evening. You can never tell with those blowhards."

"I'll arrange for supper if I see you're running late."

"I would appreciate that."

The door to the Queen's chambers opened. Sansa stepped out and curtsied.

"I tidied up your room, Ma'am. Do you require anything else this evening?"

"No Sansa, that will be all. Thank you."

Sansa hurried past the couple down the stairs into the hall and disappeared through the kitchen door. This girl was a better fit as a queen's maid. Drake wished Ramona would take her on full time.

Drake turned to face the royal chamber and leaned back on the banister, placing his hands on the rail behind his back. "It has been an exhausting few days. I'm a bit tired. And you?"

"Somewhat, all the preparation for the celebration, the tournament, the feast, and it was a late evening yesterday."

"And the freezing air this evening, excellent for sleeping."

"Yes."

Drake wanted to say more, draw out the evening, have it last a little longer. Instead, he said, "Well, goodnight then." He took a step toward his chamber door, turned to Ramona, and smiled. She returned the smile. He strode off into his chambers.

"Sleep well," Ramona called out as the door clunked closed behind him. Drake leaned back against the door, lost in disappointment for a long moment. He turned and put his hand on the handle, let go, and turned back, paralyzed while minutes passed.

A few steps, and he was at the Queen's chamber door listening. No sound, Ramona must have retired quickly, she must really have been tired.

Drake moved away from the door and took up a seat on the edge of his bed, looking into his fireplace, which was recently fed to blazing. A servant had recently attended it, probably Sansa. He would seek her out tomorrow, compliment her on her attentive service.

A brilliant fire, a warm bed on a frosty night, almost perfect, but Drake wasn't sleepy; he wasn't tired.

Blacksmith Shop Meeting

A shadow cast across the workbench; Reynard looked up. Someone was standing in the open doorway, a figure of a man, silhouetted by the early morning sunlight. Reynard had hoped to get through a whole day without interruption. His life had become busy lately, employed with work he enjoyed. He was putting the finishing touches on a new trivet. He planned to make all new cooking utensils and kitchen items to replace the old worn ones, the new with ornate designs. Others had also shown interest in his blacksmith work. It was welcome; he wanted to put his effort into creating something practical, not weapons.

As the intruder stepped into the room, his posture and walk gave away his identity. Boetius, with his dog Riley, his constant companion, was now standing on the opposite side of the workbench. Visits from Boetius were not unusual, but they were sporadic. He often used a pretext to visit the shop. Reynard was never sure if Boetius actually had an interest in Reynard's company, or he just liked to hear himself talk. Today though, Reynard was expecting him.

Reynard spoke first, trying, without success, not to express irritation in his tone. "What brings you to my shop today, Boetius?"

"I need your help with a refinement to my arrows." Boetius spoke with a hint of hesitation.

Reynard was well aware of the difficulty that Boetius had asking for help from anyone. Boetius was an independent man, did for himself, made his own bows and arrows, and proud of it. But metal-smithing was Reynard's specialty. If someone, even Boetius, needed skillful metalwork done, they came to Reynard. Reynard liked to think that given enough time and resources, he could do anything.

Reynard forced a smile. "What have you got in mind? I'd be glad to help."

"I need new heads for a newly designed arrow," Boetius began, seemingly put at ease by Reynard's encouraging attitude, "I want you to make two dozen for me. They need to have longer shanks and wider heads than what I use now. They need to fit a larger diameter shaft too. I've brought samples." Boetius reached to the quiver on his back and pulled out an arrow shaft, which he handed to Reynard. "This is the new shaft."

Reynard took the shaft in his hands, and rotated it in his fingertips, instinctively testing for balance and true.

Boetius took an arrowhead from his waist bag and laid it on the tabletop. It was a finely shaped piece of carved wood. "I want the same head design as this, NO changes to that." Boetius' tone had changed to a command.

Reynard, not appreciating Boetius' condescension, hesitated for an instant as a protest, but then took up the arrowhead and carefully examined it. "A slight increase in the curve in the blade will give you better penetration." He was holding the arrowhead up in the dusty sunlight streaming in from this workshop window. "But if you want to keep this exact design, I can do that," Reynard added with a shade of sarcasm that he could not stop from tinting his voice.

Boetius rocked back on his heels and folded his arms on his chest. "No, if you're sure it's an improvement, make the change."

Boetius' dog, who was sitting on the floor next to him, left her place and rounded the table and sat at Reynard's feet. She cocked her head and let out a barely audible whine.

Reynard put down the arrowhead and took a piece of meat from a plate that sat at the edge of the table. "Here you go, girl." He tossed the morsel in the air. Riley caught it with a quick snap of her jaws. She whined again.

"You need a sample of the cheese too?" Riley gently took the few morsels of cheese from the palm of Reynard's hand.

"Sorry about that; she's taught not to beg. I don't know what's got into her." Boetius was visibly annoyed.

"Don't worry. It's not begging. It's her due." Reynard bent down and scratched the dog behind her ears. "Good girl." When he stood back up, Riley looked at him for a moment, tilted her head back and forth, and then returned to her station at Boetius' feet.

Boetius gestured to the plate of cheese, meat, and bread. "Married life has its benefits. I don't remember ever seeing plates of food or a mug of tea in the shop before. The bread looks fresh. Baked this morning?"

"Yes. Have some."

"Thanks." Boetius cut a thick slice from the loaf. "Oh, and congratulations on your marriage. I couldn't be there, but—a— congratulations." Sentiment always came out of Boetius sideways.

"Thank you, Boetius" Reynard, with a pang of guilt, tried to speak with a more conciliatory tone.

Nobles never attended family weddings of the commoners. It was forbidden by the priest for anyone who had been or ever hoped to be married in the church. A Noble, as a patron, may attend a wedding of a commoner held in the church, a rare occasion. It had been one of Reynard's arguments for a church wedding, the hope that his childhood Noble friends would accept an invitation.

But Reynard and Amalia had been wed in a family ceremony at the commons, yesterday. His family, churchgoers, were at first reluctant participants, but as the day of celebration wore on and the wine flowed, they loosened and took part wholeheartedly. Since Reynard had no living adult women in his family, Renilda had assumed the role of elder. He was sure she was responsible for his family's change of heart. It was as if she had cast a spell over them.

"I thought you'd hold out to get married in the church."

"Pick your battles, my Ma used to say. I gave up on it."

"Surrendered more like it."

"Hmm." Reynard nodded and turned his attention to the arrow shaft.

"May I ask why this change? Why do you need such a large arrow and aggressive arrowhead?" Reynard was looking at the shaft and arrowhead that lay on his workbench. "Your arrows are sufficient to bring down a dragon. What do you need something this large for?" Reynard wasn't sure how Boetius would respond to questioning. Sometimes he was very defensive and secretive, and other times he couldn't wait to talk about his latest endeavor.

This time Boetius brightened. "My small arrows are perfect for targeting the dragon's vulnerability. But now I need something weightier to take down larger game." He paused, plainly encouraging Reynard to inquire.

Reynard expected Boetius to share his plans with him. He figured that the new arrows had something to do with the rumors he heard. It was said that Boetius was planning to go into the Dark Forest, hunting. If it were true, Reynard felt he had a responsibility to talk him out of it.

"Where will you find such animals?" Reynard asked, looking into Boetius' bright eyes and smile. Sensing the game was afoot, Reynard played along. His well-rehearsed arguments to change Boetius' mind were ready.

"In the Dark Forest," Boetius said in a hushed voice, his head nodding ever so slightly, a wink of his eye, and then pausing again, which called for the next question.

Trying not to express any great interest that could be construed as approval, Reynard replied, "What makes you think there's large game animals in the Dark Forest?"

"The stories Reynard, the stories," Boetius' hands where talking in front of him, out wide, palms up, fingers spread, "You know them as well as I do. We've heard them since we were children. I expect to find all kinds of animals in the Dark Forest, trophy game like big horned sheep, elk, deer, moose, and maybe even yet unknown animals. There have been recent accounts of sightings by travelers on the Morodon Road. There's talk of huge beasts on the edge of the river, and dragons flying above the treetops."

Reynard began to present his arguments, "No one knows what's really in the forest. It's just as likely that the stories of witches, sorcerers, evil spirits, monsters, or beasts could be true."

"Beasts, better yet!" Boetius' hands were making emphatic gestures. "I will return from the forest with grandest of trophies."

"But no one has ever returned from the forest."

"True—but I will be the first." Boetius said, "Just imagine that."

"And you mean to go alone?"

"Yes."

"Wouldn't your chances be better if the hunting troop went with you or a squad of archers?"

"Not necessary, I am perfectly capable of hunting by myself. I'm the most successful hunter in the Kingdom. In all the Kingdoms."

"That's true; you are the most renowned hunter of our time—probably of all time." Reynard thought the flattery might appeal to Boetius' ego. "Why take up this risky scheme? You're already famous and well-known for your prowess as a hunter, and your generosity with your harvest."

"Not enough. I can be so much more. My adventures will become legends. Someday your children will listen to stories of my exploits." Boetius was standing tall, feet spread apart.

Reynard was at a loss; you can't argue with a madman. "Your mind is made up then? Nothing I can say to dissuade you?"

"No, hell no!" Boetius said with a hint of a laugh.

"You're dedicated to this venture?"

"Yes, it's my destiny," Boetius replied. He came across as someone with unwavering conviction, possessed even.

Reynard realized that this might be the end of Boetius. And the thought that it might benefit the Kingdom made his jaw clench with guilt. Getting lost in that dark tangle of woods was assured as far as Reynard was concerned. Standing at the forest edge, you can't see more than a few paces into the dense mass of vines, thicket, and brush that fills the space between black tree trunks. It's as if the light that strikes the forest is not reflected back. It does not return; nothing returns, man or light.

"Well then, I will get to work on the arrowheads."

"I want to have them by the time we get back from Chambold. Can you have them ready by then?"

"I'll make a prototype and then have Donar work on them."

The war was over, but Reynard's life was still hectic, not as tranquil as he had hoped. 'Too many irons in the fire,' as his father used to say. First, it was the veterans' feast, then the celebration at Evora, his marriage yesterday, and the trip to Chambold just two days away. It was more exhausting than fighting. Things were moving fast; except for his time in the shop, life was a blur.

"I'm sure he can have them ready for you early next week."

Boetius nodded. "Thank you Reynard."

Reynard gave up the dissuasion. He was glad the conversation was exhausted. He stood patiently in the awkward silence until Boetius pivoted and left, disappearing through the bright sunlit doorway.

Reynard knew from the beginning he would oblige Boetius' request. His reasoning had no effect, as expected. It was best though that Boetius be armed as well as possible.

A moment after Boetius left, Reynard noticed the quiet. While in conversation with Boetius, crows, outside the cottage, had been engaged in a squawking dialogue that had escaped his conscious attention until now.

Reynard stepped out his door and looked up at the leafless oak tree in his backyard, in view above his cottage's roof. A band of crows, five or so, rested in stillness amongst its branches. An old saying, a bad omen, came to mind: 'When the crows go still, the fates bode ill will.'

The Gift

A sharp knock at the door startled Amalia.

"Were you expecting someone?" Reynard asked.

"No, I don't know who it could be." Amalia was seated opposite Reynard at the kitchen table.

Reynard rose and walked over and opened the door. Ramona was standing there with the biggest smile Amalia had ever seen on her friend's face.

"Ma'am, what a surprise," Reynard said.

"Reynard, surely, you haven't forgotten my name?"

"No, Ramona, I haven't. Enter my Queen." Reynard stepped back and made a grand sweeping gesture with his arm.

"Smartass." Ramona stepped in. Amalia propelled herself across the cottage floor and wrapped her arms around Ramona.

The women pushed away from each other while maintaining a hold on each other's arms at the elbow. They hadn't seen each other since the wedding. Ramona had insisted on a honeymoon. Tomorrow will make a full week that Amalia had been off duty as Ramona's maid. Amalia even accompanied Reynard to Chambold for its veterans' celebration, the first time she had ever been out of the Kingdom. It was King Drake who had insisted that she go, but it was likely that Ramona was behind it. While Amalia was away from the castle, Sansa, a competent servant, had taken over Amalia's duties and attended Ramona. Amalia didn't feel good about being replaced but had to accept it.

"Look at you, a married woman," Ramona said, "Married life suits you. Both of you." She glanced at Reynard, who was standing alongside them. Ramona let go of Amalia and embraced the unprepared Reynard encapsulating him, his arms still at his side trapped in Ramona's grasp.

Ramona released Reynard and scanned the room. "Very domestic. It looks like it did when we were children, when your mother had charge of this house. This suits you so, Amalia. I couldn't be happier—for your happiness." Ramona giggled. "You ARE happy with this fellow, aren't you? If not, I will have him sent to the dungeon."

"There is no dungeon in Enid," Reynard said.

"I'll have one built."

Amalia took the opportunity to gather up the dirty dishes from the table and put them on the wash cupboard. Looking back over her shoulder, "Oh, he's alright, he'll do as a husband. No need for the dungeon."

Amalia returned to the table. "Sit, please. Would you like something to eat?" The smell of fried bacon hung in the air.

"Thanks, but no." As she pulled out a chair, Ramona's smile faded. "I am sorry that I wasn't able to attend your wedding as myself."

It had been six days since the wedding and Ramona's clandestine appearance.

"That's alright, we understand," Amalia jumped in quickly, "It's convention, nothing to be done. We were glad to have you there in any guise."

Forbidden from attending a commoners wedding, Ramona did the only thing she could do: she went anyway, but in disguise, men's clothing and a hood. The ruse did not fool anyone, but it conveyed the need to keep the Queen's attendance a secret.

As Reynard and Amalia were taking their seats, Ramona jumped up. "Oh, oh, wait!" She bolted for the door. "I have something for you." She stepped one foot out the door, leaning out. Looking down the cottage path, she was waving someone to her. "In here, bring it in. I'm sorry; I didn't mean to keep you waiting. Bring it in."

Ramona stepped back into the cottage, leading two men, King's guardsmen, the first one walking backward. They shuffled into the cottage carrying a load between them, an item the size of a bale of hay, draped with a purple blanket with embroidered gold designs on the edges. "Careful, careful, don't bump the doorway." Ramona was walking backward, beckoning them to her with her hands.

The men placed the covered object on the floor next to the table between Reynard and Amalia. Both men took an awkward step back.

"Thank you," Ramona said, turning to the guards, "You may go."

"Yes, Your Highness," the older man said as they both, walking backward, bowing, trying to exit the cottage, bumping shoulders at the door.

Ramona called to them as they bumbled through the doorway into the morning sun's rays. "Don't forget to see Gerda. She has something special for you in the kitchen."

"Yes, Your Highness, thank you." They disappeared. A moment later, an arm reached back in and pulled the door closed.

Something special, Amalia thought, something meant to purchase the guards' silence, some treat (a pastry, a savory cheese maybe). The men looked familiar: they were the same two who had been assigned to keep watch of Ramona when the King was away.

"What is it, Ramona?" Amalia asked.

"A gift, of course. For the both of you. A wedding gift."

After a few moments. "Take a look!" Ramona beamed like a child.

Amalia reached down and took up the purple blanket in her arms, unveiling a wooden rocker cradle. There was one like it in the Queen's chambers; it was Ramona's when she was a baby. This one, like Ramona's, was solid white oak with carvings along the edges, vines with leaves and roses.

"It's beautiful." Amalia glanced at Reynard, "Don't you think so, Reynard?"

"Yes, the craftsmanship is excellent, fine work, the detail—and so solidly built." He always lent a practical eye to things.

"Thank you very much. We really appreciate it." Amalia threw her arms around Ramona again, held tight a moment, and then stepped away, wiping tears from her cheeks.

"And Reynard, my friend, I expect this cradle to be in use by this time next year."

Reynard's lips tightened, and he shook his head.

"That shouldn't be a problem." Amalia laughed, and Reynard turned a light shade of red.

"Reynard. Amalia and I have spent so much time together over the years that our fertility cycles are in mesh. If you need advice on the best time for sowing seed, I can help. It's around the time of the full moon."

"Ramona!" Reynard puffed out in exasperation. "The fire's dying out. I'm going out for firewood."

The fire wasn't dying, and there was a plentiful stack of wood at the hearth, Amalia noted as Reynard strode for the door. The door bumped shut behind him.

"Well, I guess we have time for woman talk," Ramona said as she took a seat at the kitchen table. Amalia sat down opposite her.

"All these years, I've been trying to get pregnant, and you've been trying to avoid it."

Renilda provided herbs to help limit Amalia's fertility. Amalia believed that Renilda could have also helped Ramona with whatever was interfering with her attempt to get pregnant. Ramona had rejected the idea in the past. Maybe now she would be more receptive to an herbal tonic. Ramona needed to get away from using that healer priest.

Amalia reached across the table and covered her friend's hands with hers. She didn't know what to say for comfort; she still believed Ramona would have a child.

"Well, now, at least, we'll be on the same page." Ramona's smile broadened.

Amalia was glad to see some confidence in that smile.

"How's Reynard doing?" Ramona said, an obvious change of subject.

"A little better."

"Is he still having the nightmares?"

"Yes, he cries out, tosses and turns. I sleep on the floor sometimes."

"Do you wake him out of it?"

"I did once, but he was up the rest of the night pacing, inconsolable. Renilda advised against waking him. She says it's the mind's way of healing, to let it take its course. She did provide an herbal tea to help with the shakes. He desperately wants to work in the shop, but sometimes his hands tremble, and he can't hold his hammer."

"Does the tea help?"

"Yes. I'm so grateful. If he couldn't work, I wouldn't know what to do with him."

"All the celebrations are behind him; that must help. I'm sure those Veterans' Feasts were like pouring salt in a wound."

Reynard and Amalia had returned from Chambold just two days ago.

"Yes, for sure. But what of the talk of another feast-day celebration in Dacian? What have you heard?"

"I understand it's in planning for the spring."

"Assuming I can get him through the winter with improvement, the last thing we need is another reminder, a possible setback."

"Don't worry; I will find a way to get him out of it. Leave it to me."

"Thank you."

"I wonder if our friends could help with the nightmares. Maybe a vision? A reconciliation of sorts."

"I don't think meeting a dragon would be good for him. Besides, they've all left the Kingdom, gone home thankfully."

"Even though they are far away, I can still communicate with them."

"Really?"

"It's not the same as when you're with them. The images are fainter. It takes longer for them to form up in the mind, and I need to be in a very quiet place. The old mill is the best place for peaceful, uninterrupted time. Talk with Renilda about it, please. If she thinks it would help, I'm sure I can call Alpha here if needed."

"I appreciate your concern, but let's put that off for now."

A bump on the door, it swung open as Reynard passed through with a bundle of firewood in his arms. He pushed the door closed with this heel.

The women were quiet as Reynard stacked the firewood. "Do you need more private time to talk?"

"No, we're done talking about you." Ramona provided a big grin. "Sit with us." She gestured to the chair next to Amalia. "She and I will have plenty of time for woman's talk next week."

Amalia was due to return to service at the castle to attend Ramona, a daytime schedule. The evenings reserved for Reynard.

Her tone turned serious as Ramona spoke to Reynard. "I wanted to thank you for the salute at the veterans' supper."

"Couldn't help myself."

"The DRINK couldn't help itself," Amalia said.

"I guess I—the drink—couldn't stand that Drake was getting all the attention and credit. Amalia has told me of all the things you both did to protect the dragons and bring a quick end to the war. Drake and Boetius on their high horses, I wasn't going to let it stand. You deserved a salute, even if only a few people knew what it was really for."

"Drake will go down in history, the 'Hero of the Dragon War,'" Amalia said, "Just not fair."

"Life isn't fair, they say," Ramona said, "Not to worry."

"Our friends will know the truth. They won't forget," Amalia said.

Reynard spoke to Ramona, likely trying to change the subject. "What of our friend Boetius, have you heard the rumors? He plans to go into the Dark Forest."

"Yes, I know of it."

"He visited me in the shop last week. Asked me to make new arrowheads. He wants them to hunt the big game animals he believes are in the forest. Donar delivered the arrowheads yesterday. Boetius is planning to go soon, in a day or two."

"Reynard tried to talk him out of it, but there was no reasoning with him," Amalia said.

"Boetius never could see reason. He's always been blinded by his desire to be famous and to be the best at everything he puts his hand to," Ramona said.

"He was the best archer until that time you beat him. He won all the tournaments but lost to a girl in a backyard contest. That was the day." Reynard shook his head.

"Not a good day," Ramona said with a down-turned smile.

"Yeah, especially for Boetius. He got a real beat'en when his father found out that you bested him."

"I never liked that man. Good rid'ens to him."

"You shouldn't speak ill of the dead." Amalia wiggled a finger at Ramona.

Reynard said, "My cousin has worked on the Eber farm his whole life. Boetius' father treated his workers like slaves. And the man was so tight; he made every penny squeal. Things changed for the better when the old man died, and Boetius' brother took over."

"So, Boetius didn't get his bent for generosity from his

father?" Amalia asked.

"No, that was Berengar's doing. Berengar took him under his wing, taught Boetius to track and hunt, and honed his skills in archery. Tramp'en around the wilds with Berengar, the generosity must've rubbed off too."

"I know you both have your differences with him," Amalia said, "But your lifelong friendship must count for something. Perhaps you could talk him out of it? Or maybe the King could be convinced to forbid it?" Amalia was asking Ramona.

"I could have a conversation with Boetius, but I have already spoken with Drake. He won't interfere, says it's not his place. 'A man's business is a man's business,' according to him." Undoubtedly that had been a difficult conversation between Queen and King, in contrast to their amicable relationship of late. Neither probably wanted to pursue the issue.

"We've heard that he's been talking it up at the tavern of late." Reynard said, "But the whole thing got started at the feast. He was boasting about not being afraid of the dragons, a natural thing for him. Plus the wine was help'en. And then somehow he got baited into bragging about having no fear of the forest, I don't think there's any going back for him now."

"She could try," Amalia said.

"I will. Tomorrow. I'll arrange a meeting for tomorrow evening."

"I wish you luck, I do. But I doubt he can be talked out of it," Reynard said.

"We'll see," Ramona said, "I can be very persuasive."

Amalia hoped Ramona's would be successful, not so much for Boetius' sake (she despised the man) but for Reynard's. Reynard had enough troubles without adding more. She knew Reynard would obsess over Boetius and his misguided venture. Bad enough that the Dark Forest existed in Enid, so close to the village and castle. Mostly, people put it out of their minds, but some people just couldn't let it be, had to stir things up.

The Queen's Reasoning

Ramona paused at the tavern door. According to her sources, she would find Boetius here, this late afternoon. It was early for him and his friends to frequent the tavern, but tomorrow was the day Boetius planned to go into the Dark Forest on his quest, a reason for a celebration, apparently. Foolish, she thought.

Ramona entered the tavern and headed for her customary seat at the corner table. Elsa arrived as Ramona sat down, placing a goblet of wine on the table. "Will there be anything else, Ma'am?" She nodded and smiled.

"Thank you Elsa, but no wine for me today. But please let Boetius know I want to see him."

Elsa scooped up the goblet and then crossed the hall to the center table where Sir Boetius, wrapped in boisterous laughter and loud conversation, was holding court with his companions. As she bent over, she touched Boetius' shoulder and whispered in his ear. He said something in return. Elsa continued back to the bar table.

After a moment more of conversation with his friends, Boetius got up, strode across the room, and took a seat across from Ramona. "Good evening, Ma'am. Lovely afternoon to be out for a walk. A bit cool. I think we'll have a frost again tonight."

Being addressed as Ma'am by her childhood friends still made Ramona uncomfortable. She had put an end to 'Your Highness' a long time ago, but she missed being just Ramona. "Good evening—SIR Boetius."

Elsa arrived, placed a mug of beer on the table in front of Boetius, curtsied, and hurried away.

"I've heard stories about you," Ramona began.

"Stories—this IS the place to hear stories." Boetius had mischief in his eyes.

On second thought, not appreciating the glib comment, maybe she should insist on 'Your Highness' to command more respect. "What I heard—is that you intend to go into the Dark Forest? I want to know if it's true."

Boetius smiled broadly. "Yes, it is. I am going tomorrow morning."

Ramona suddenly felt the urge to reach across the table and knock that smug smile off his face as she'd done many times when they were children. Unfortunately, being an adult and Queen had its limitations.

"Please don't do it." Ramona leaned forward. "You must know it's a fool's errand."

The smile vanishing, Boetius stiffened in his straight-back chair and crossed his arms.

Ramona knew she misspoke the moment the words left her mouth: Boetius' pride had been injured. If only she could take it back, implying he was a fool did not serve her purpose. "I'm sorry, but you must see what a terrible risk you're taking."

"I see it as a great adventure, one worth the risk. Besides, the risk is minimal. I am well-prepared." His chest expanding, he placed his hands on his hips.

"What could be worth such a risk?"

"Another dragon skin, one to hang here in the tavern hall.

I'm sure the Dark Forest is the hiding place for the last of those disgusting beasts." The loudness of Boetius' voice stilled the conversation in the tavern hall. Heads turned toward Boetius and the Queen. "It's likely that's where they came from in the first place."

Ramona leaned forward, speaking softly. "But there's no real evidence that the dragons are in the Dark Forest or ever have been." Ramona, of course, knew where the dragons came from and where they were. The last of the dragons had been safely moved back to their home beyond the North Mountains.

"There have been recent sightings." Boetius took a sip of beer.

"Are you speaking of the stories the traders are telling, that they've seen animals coming out of the forest and dragons flying above the trees?"

"Yes, enormous game animals have been seen drinking at the river on the forest's edge."

"You can't believe the stories those men tell." The sightings of dragons was simply a lie, sightings of game animals, surely another lie. Elsa had ferreted out the source, but she felt that the storytellers had an ulterior motive. There was something contrived in these reports.

"But it makes sense. Since we have driven the dragons out of our hunting grounds, they are likely pursuing game in the Dark Forest as a food source.

"In some Dark Forest stories, they speak of flickering lights in the treetops. It could be they are the flashing of dragon eyes."

"I don't remember any stories that speak of dragons in the forest, let alone that the lights are dragon eyes. It doesn't even sound plausible."

"It's not just me; it's widely believed that the lights are caused by the dragons," Boetius asserted.

"Widely believed or not, I know someone that has seen the lights, an eyewitness, someone I trust, not the rumors of strangers."

"And who is that?" Boetius had a smirk on his lips.

"Amalia. Amalia has seen the lights, and she assures me that the lights are small flickering multi-color flashes, not the large yellow eyes of dragons." Ramona was feeling guilty discussing Amalia's story about the Dark Forest lights, which was told in confidence. But she felt justified in using any information she had to dissuade Boetius.

"The word of a maid is not what I am going to rely on."

"Amalia is a more reliable source than that gossiping tavern pack you keep company with." Ramona nodded to the men seated and standing around the table in the center of the hall. Ramona's face was hot with temper; she struggled to stay calm. Dealing with the fragile pride of this man, so frustrating, it tested her patience. It was like that with all the men she'd had to deal with. Boetius was the worst though, no maybe Drake. No, they were both equally infuriating.

"I disagree."

"Well, Reynard was with her; he saw them too." Another pang of guilt, but Ramona knew Boetius had respect for Reynard. Reynard wouldn't mind the telling; he wanted this venture stopped as well.

"Reynard has never shared that with me." The conviction in Boetius' voice was dissolving.

"I think you have to admit it's not likely that you will find dragons in the forest."

Boetius had the look of a sailor floating in a boat that had just lost its anchor. His eyes were searching for land.

"If not dragons, then the game animals would be worth the hunt. The forest is probably full of elk, deer—all kinds of animals. Besides the recent sightings, look at those antler racks and horns on the wall." Boetius glanced back over his shoulder and gestured to the trophies that hung over the fireplace mantle. "Soon, it will be my trophies that hang there."

The Raconteur's stories did hold tales of beasts in the forest, and the trophy horns and antlers on the tavern wall were sizable, some from unknown animals testified to it.

"There's nothing that size these days." Boetius shifted his attention back to Ramona, and moved to the edge of his seat, put his hands on the table edge. "Think about it; I could feed the entire village with that kind of harvest."

And feed your enormous ego as well, Ramona thought. "You can't always rely on the stories people tell."

He leaned forward again. "But so many people are telling the same story."

"So that's where you're going to put your faith, in the stories people tell? Not your lifelong friend?"

"I'm sorry Ramona, but my mind is made up."

Ramona's arguments so far had failed. "So, tell me about your well-prepared plan?" She was ready to listen, hoping to find a flaw she could exploit.

"I will. I'm sure your mind will be put at ease." He placed his elbows on the table, arms crossed at the wrists with his hands under his chin. "The plan is to enter the forest at the Sheep Meadow gate."

The Witches' Gate, as it was called, was located where the southern Sheep Meadow boundary met the Dark Forest. It was the only option, really; except for the gate, the forest presented an impenetrable wall. All along the border with the Sheep Meadow, the forest presented a solid barrier of tall, dark trees with black trunks entangled with a mass of vines, brush, and thickets. This was true of the entire forest edge, on the west (bordering the swamplands), on the east (bordering the Morodon River). The opposite side of the forest, in the south (in the Kingdom of Chambold), the Chambold swamps intervened between the Dark Forest and civilization.

The Witches' Gate was formed by two bending tree trunks. It stood just wide enough and joined just high enough to create an arch-like opening that a man could ride through on horseback.

"I'll take a substantial pack of food and supplies, two bows, a double quiver with two types of arrows, the smaller arrows for dragons, and a new design for the larger game I'm sure to find." Boetius paused for a moment.

"And, of course, to secure my return, I will have Riley with me." He reached down and patted the dog's head. "She'll have no problem following our trail back out of the forest to the gate."

Many of the Dark Forest stories ended with some fool who had passed through the gate, never to return, or worse, his ghost returning with the whispering of witches, sorcerers, and monsters.

Taking his dog was the only sensible part of the plan. Boetius and his hunting dog, Riley, were inseparable, and she was well-known for her tracking ability. It was hard to imagine that the dog would let him down.

Besides the difficulty of finding his way out, Ramona's other concern centered on what he would find in the forest. "Riley. That's good. But what of your friends, your hunting troop, or the other Knights? Surely some of them have agreed to go with you? Wouldn't that be safer?" Ramona knew that his friends had declined, made their excuses.

"No. I have decided to go alone." Boetius sounded like he was trying to make a lie believable.

It was a result he was probably not uncomfortable with. More glory for himself in the triumph over the Dark Forest. This man was so easy to read.

Changing her line of reasoning again, Ramona asked, "What if for a moment we assume you're successful and you do return from the forest. What real difference will it make? What do you wish to gain?"

Boetius, with a guarded voice, said, "I will be known as the greatest archer that ever lived."

"Everyone knows you're the best archer." Ramona wondered if the sting of being beaten by a girl in his youth still lingered and had contributed to his decision to pursue this quest.

"The GREATEST archer—ever."

"Besides that?"

"People will praise my hunting and tracking skills." Boetius' voice was more assured.

"They already say you are the best hunter. No one disputes that. Something else?"

"People will be overwhelmed by the amount of extra game I will bring them."

"The people are already grateful for the extra meat you provide. There must be more to this venture than that?"

Boetius hesitated, then said, "Someday, Ramona, glorious stories will be told of my adventures, right here in this hall. I will be the hero of the Raconteur's tales."

"I don't see how it could be worth the risk." This can't be all there is to this man, the boyhood friend who defended her and looked out for her. Where was that boy? He defended the Kingdom against dragons as misguided as that was. How could he be so overwhelmed by his need for fame? He was already held in high regard. All the accolades that poured out for Boetius at the Veterans' feast and as well in Evora and Chambold, and more to come at the Dacian celebration, wasn't that enough?

"Nothing is more important than glory and a man's legacy," Boetius asserted, his voice rising.

Ramona, now, had to accept that Boetius was lost in his desire for glory and fame. A sadness shuddered her body. "You're dedicated to this venture? There's nothing I can say to dissuade you?"

"There's nothing to fear, my lady. I know what I'm doing." Boetius stood and bowed to Ramona. "Come see me off tomorrow."

She most certainly would not, but she did not respond. Words were lost on him.

He stood there for a moment, their eyes locked. He turned away.

"Boetius," Ramona called out softly, "Good luck."

He smiled and then returned to his table, where he was greeted with back-slapping and erupting laughter.

Hopeless, hopeless, hopeless. This quest would be Boetius' downfall, Ramona was sure of it. Foolishness.

Into the Forest

Reynard stood vigil on the Morodon River Bridge, hoping that Boetius would change his mind and not show. An empty hope, most likely. From his vantage point at the crest of the old stone arch bridge, Reynard could see the Sheep Meadow to the south, and in the opposite direction, the castle village to the north, both no more than 100 paces away. In the direction of the Sheep Meadow, people lined the road from the bridge to the field's edge. In the gathering were Knights, Noblemen, and Noblewomen, castle servants and common-folk, all waiting to send Boetius off on his quest.

King Drake and Queen Ramona, both not approving of this undertaking, were notably absent. But Feargus was there, standing well behind the people who lined the road, off in isolation.

The Sheep Meadow proper on the left side of the road was bathed in pale light by the rising sun. In the center, a group of men stood around the fire ring, warming themselves, members of the hunting troop, archers, and others, Boetius' comrades. Flames licked up several feet; smoke rose in a thin wavering column; mist from the river drifted past them like phantoms. In the background, the Dark Forest loomed at the far side of the meadow, the outline of the Witches Gate visible, but darkly, in the menacing wall of tall black trees.

Last evening at the tavern, these same men, waiting at the fire circle, had celebrated with Boetius, a raucous affair lasting late into the night. Now they were in attendance, awaiting his arrival, so they could send him off into the darkness of the forest. A new moon tonight, Boetius couldn't have picked a worst time to enter the forest.

Reynard pulled his cloak tighter to ward off the chill. The trees that surrounded him, adorned with their autumn leaves of orange and yellow, stood in contrast to the dark-leafed forest. The vegetation of the Dark Forest never changed color, always the darkest of greens, near black. The leaves of the trees, vines, and shrubs never fall, clinging through all the seasons. The prospect of the forest was always whispering a foreboding unwelcome.

The scene evoked his memory of the Witches' Gate origin story. In their youth, Reynard and his friends had sat spellbound in front of the tavern fireplace where the Raconteur held court, weaving stories, the Witches' Gate one of their favorites.

✿✿✿✿✿✿

In ancient times there was no entrance to the Dark Forest, no gateway at the Sheep Meadow or anywhere else. There were witches, though, and warlocks. It was reported that on nights of the full moon, they gathered in the Sheep Meadow at the stone fire-ring to conduct their ceremonies, ritual dancing, and chanting. At the time, the witches were not seen as frightening or evil. In fact, they were held in high regard as healers and wisdom keepers, especially their leader, the Witch Queen, a woman known as Ceridwen.

She was well respected and popular with the people of the Kingdom. Too popular for the Queen of the time, Queen Roza, who felt threatened by Ceridwen and the witches' high status.

Queen Roza set to plotting against the witches. She spread rumors, intending to discredit them. She confronted Ceridwen and threatened her with banishment, a power she did not have, which Ceridwen knew to be a bluff. Success came to the Queen through the King, a weak and easily manipulated man. She was able, with a constant stream of nagging, to convince him that the witches were a threat to his authority.

Queen Roza put in place a plan to rid the Kingdom of the witches. On a full moon night when the witches would be celebrating in the Sheep Meadow, a squad of the royal guard was sent to surround them, place them under arrest and escort them out of the Kingdom. This was to be accomplished under cover of night without the knowledge of the people. To pacify the Kingdom's subjects, the Queen planned to spread the lie that the witches had left on their own accord.

On the next full moon, the scheme was put in action. As the witches danced around the stone circle, casting long shadows by the light of a larger than normal moon sitting on the horizon, the King's guard arrived. In the soft light that flooded the meadow, the witches continued to dance, seemingly unaware of the guards who were slinking into the field from the road. When the guards were about to surround the witches, the dancing abruptly stopped. The witches began to chant with an eerie melody in a language unknown to the guards whose advance came to a halt. Ceridwen, from the center of the circle, turned toward the Dark Forest, extended her arms out high in front of her, and recited a chant, different from, but in harmony with the chant of the other witches.

The witches and the guards' attention was focused on the dark wall of trees and tangled vegetation that loomed in front of the Witch Queen. The tree trunks and vines were moving, writhing and twisting like a nest of snakes. At first, it appeared to be an optical illusion, a trick of the mind, or the shadows of moving clouds scattering moonlight on the forest wall. What happened can't be explained. But as the chanting continued, two large tree trunks bent to form an arch, undergrowth between them withered away, and the gateway materialized.

The guards froze in place.

As Ceridwen lowered her arms, the chanting stopped. She walked slowly toward the newly formed gate; the other witches fell in line behind her. The guards watched, grateful for their immobility, as the witches, one by one, disappeared into the mouth of darkness.

The witches were gone, what Queen Roza wanted, but the gate remained, a passageway into the Dark Forest. There was nothing to block the witches' return or block the release of whatever malevolent forces or creatures that may abide in the mysterious province.

Of course, that is only the story of the Witch's Gate's origin. There are many other stories involving the gate, tales of monsters, ghosts, demons, and of course, witches, coming and going through the gate. But the most widely held belief is that to this day, the witches on full moon nights come out of the Dark Forest to dance and celebrate in the Sheep Meadow. People say that on those nights they've heard chanting and singing, strange melodies, coming from the Sheep Meadow, a warning for sensible people to stay away.

❦❦❦❦❦

Reynard, his thoughts interrupted, heard a commotion behind him coming from the village and pivoted to look. Boetius was in the far distance, striding down the Village Road, dressed in his hunting garb, a dark green cloak, the sleeves and hood trimmed in white and light green, his family colors. Riley trotted alongside him. He ambled a weaving path, crossing the road from side to side to shake hands with villagers standing in front of their shops or homes. A group of children followed him, wiggling back and forth like the tail of a snake. Many of the villagers fell in behind Boetius, creating a ragged parade.

As Boetius passed Reynard on the bridge, he did not stop

but smiled broadly and nodded in acknowledgment. On his back, he carried a substantial pack, his bow and two quivers of arrows, one quiver full of arrows with the new arrowheads Reynard had provided. Reynard considered Boetius a friend. Not close, they had never been close, but he couldn't help feeling complicit in enabling Boetius' misadventure. Over and over, Reynard had reworked his conversation with Boetius, but in the end, he released himself of any responsibility for this foolishness.

Boetius continued on toward his friends at the fire ring.

When the parade reached the edge of the meadow, parents grabbed the arms of those children within reach and commanded those out of reach to stop.

At his position back behind the children and their apprehensive parents, Reynard felt a pang of embarrassment. He left the high point of the bridge and made his way into the midst of the gathering in the meadow. Boetius was with the men at the fire-ring. Their animated greetings and laughter, probably meant to show confidence and courage, were betrayed as swagger to Reynard. They must have the same distress in the gut.

The depths of Reynard's mind was conjuring images. At any moment, a long grizzly claw might sweep out from the gate, grab some innocent soul, and drag them into the blackness. The idea that someone was willingly and purposely planning to step through that wicked arch of trees was foolhardy at least. Reynard's heart was pounding.

As Reynard watched Boetius, who was shaking hands all around, a hand fell on his shoulder. He recoiled.

"Think this is the last we'll see of him?" It was Feargus, who had stepped up quietly from behind.

"Probably." Reynard glanced back to Feargus for a moment.

"This should be the end of the Dragon War as well—and the man's boasting," Feargus said, "Glad for the end of it." Drake and Boetius spoke with much bravado about the battles with the dragons. Feargus had let Reynard know how disgusted he was with their boasting and exaggerations, although Feargus did nothing publicly to counter it.

Boetius was now standing in front of the gate. From Reynard's outlying vantage point, Boetius' dark green clothing blended with the darkness behind him, making his face appear as a floating apparition. Boetius extended his arm in an arcing wave over his head, turned, and faded in the darkness of the arch. His dog Riley stopped at the threshold. After a whistle broke into the silence that had overcome the crowd, the dog placed one paw into the darkness, hesitated for a moment, and then jumped in.

"The sacrifice of one man should be worth the price of ending the dragon hunt," Feargus said.

Reynard's breath halted. That sentiment expressed out loud was even harsher than the thought of it. He turned to Feargus, but his attention was immediately drawn back to the fascination of the gate. The quieted crowd began haphazardly to disperse.

Reynard pivoted back to Feargus, but Feargus had walked away, turned his back on this disturbing episode.

But he was right, Boetius' likely misfortune meant that the Dragon Hunt no longer had a champion.

Berengar
at the Tavern

Earlier in the evening, when Amalia entered the tavern with Reynard, the tavern hall was already crowded; all the tables were full, standing room only. On their way to the Commoners Hall, they were stopped by Elsa, who reported to Amalia that the Royal Hall was full as well.

"Sir Boetius' friends have been make'en up excuses, none of them plan to go out there tomorrow night," Maccus said

"Ya can't blame em, no one with a lick of sense goes to the Sheep Meadow on a full moon night." Donar announced the obvious to those around the table: Amalia, Reynard, and Maccus. The family group sat at a small round table in a corner of the tavern's fully occupied Commoner's Hall.

"I sure as hell wouldn't want to be in that meadow tomorrow night." Maccus was shaking his head.

"It's a test of friendship for the volunteers, but for the King's sentries, it's a duty," Reynard said.

King Drake had posted sentries to maintain a vigil at the Witches' Gate. Two men of the Royal Guard, in rotations, three shifts, were at their post day and night. Drake had committed to maintaining the vigil for one full month until the next new moon.

Besides the King's sentries, friends of Boetius', hunters and archers had also committed to keeping watch, camping in the middle of the Sheep Meadow, six men always there, rotating shifts. Villagers and others generously provided food and supplies for the encampment. The men at the vigil had set up a tent and kept a fire going day and night, a towering fire, larger than necessary. They claimed the roaring fire was for Boetius, a signal light to help guide him out of the forest. It was known that the number of men attending at the meadow had slowly dwindled over the last few weeks. Only two to three men were now standing watch at any given time.

"The time is passed. He should'a come out by now." Donar said.

Boetius had promised his friends to return within a fortnight. That deadline had approached and passed. It seemed like everyone in the Kingdom was absorbed in chatter over the likelihood of Boetius' return. He had gone in on the day of the last new moon and was to return by yesterday. A few still held hope that he would prevail and expected him to come back, if not today, soon, maybe in another day or so, or a week. Most, though, thought him lost.

"Yeah, and his provisions must have run out by now," Maccus said.

"He could be liv'en off the land," Donar replied.

"In that forest?" Maccus said, "Not likely. What could be live'en in there, in that darkness?"

Amalia was sure that the conversation in the crowded tavern this evening was fixated on tonight's vigil at the Sheep Meadow. The question on everyone's lips; Who will have the courage to stand watch tomorrow night, the night of the full moon in the Sheep Meadow?

Amalia stood and reached across the table to light the candles: the sunlight had faded from the windows. Others in the room were lighting their candles as well, and Dagny, the serving maid, was lighting the wall sconces.

Amalia spoke in a hushed voice, which matched the conversational tone of everyone in the hall. "The guards should be relieved of duty. They can't be expected to stay out there alone. The fear of monsters or witches at the gate, it's too much to ask of them." The King's men would be left alone in the Sheep Meadow if the volunteers withdrew.

"Do you think King Drake will call off the vigil for the one night?" Donar asked.

"There's no chance of it," Amalia said, "The King and Queen will be off on their moonlit ride tomorrow. They're wrapped up in their own passions. The King is ignoring the whole affair, and Ramona says there's nothing to fear; it's nothing but superstition."

Elsa approached and bent over Amalia's shoulder, whispering to the group. "I have news. Berengar came in a short while ago. He took up a seat with the hunting troop. The word is—he told em he was gonna take the shift in the meadow tomorrow night, all alone, by his self. Then he went off to the Royal Hall. They tell me he begged Sir Hartmann to ask the King to withdraw the King's Guard. That he'd take their place too. Said to tells the King, he's the man for the job."

Maccus leaned in. "Berengar? I hear he ain't been to the tavern for months, not since spring. You know, when he went nuts."

Not appreciating the comment, Amalia threw him a scowl.

"I saw him." Elsa put her shoulders back. "I was serve-en the hunter's table. And Dagny was in the Royal hall. She heard every word he said. He was here a month ago too, for just a bit to talk to them hunters. I was serv'en by myself that evening."

"We believes ya. It's just we's heard he doesn't even leave his house no more," Donar said.

"Yeah, and that time in the spring when he was at the tavern, he got blind drunk. And then's, after that he swore off the drink. They been saying." Maccus looked to the others around the table.

Elsa glared and huffed.

Amalia knew that to be true. Berengar had been homebound for a long time, and he didn't drink anymore. She saw Berengar at his home a few times, months ago, when she tagged along with Renilda on her monthly visits. As of late, Renilda said that Berengar was doing much better, getting out, going for long walks in the countryside every morning. He was on the mend. But a visit to the tavern was completely unexpected.

"Is he still here?" Amalia interrupted.

"No, he's gone, just like that. Sir Hartmann left too."

"I guess that settles all the fuss," Maccus said.

Amalia didn't think so. Berengar didn't fear the dragons anymore; he had accepted the fact that they were gone from the Kingdom. Did he have no fear of witches or ghosts or monsters, either? No fear of the Witches' Gate or the Dark Forest? Where was his courage coming from?

Reconciled

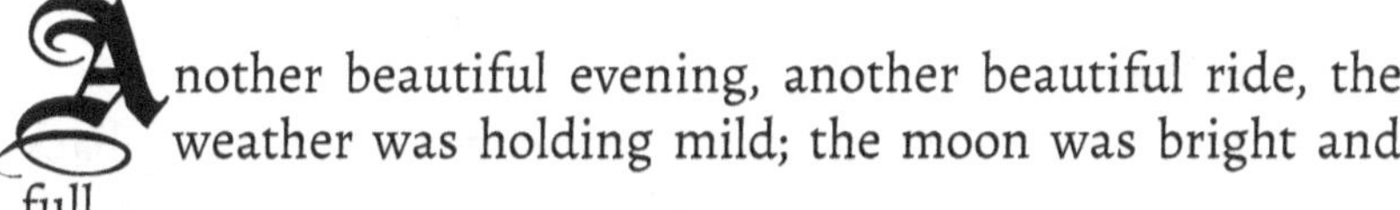

Another beautiful evening, another beautiful ride, the weather was holding mild; the moon was bright and full.

Drake, sitting atop his horse, looked out in a southerly direction over the village, the cottage windows dimly lit. The Sheep Meadow lay just beyond, too distant to see. Maybe he should order the guards back to their posts? He could ride with them to show there was nothing to fear. He looked to Ramona; she smiled; Drake decided not to go.

It was nonsense that the guards needed relief from their duty at the Sheep Meadow. But he allowed it; Hartmann had assured him that Berengar would take his guardsmen's place for the night. What a bunch of superstitious rubbish. It seemed that Berengar was the only subject in the Kingdom with a lick of sense. Drake appreciated the old man stepping in. That ridiculous story of witches appearing in the Sheep Meadow on full moon nights, not even as a child had that story disturbed him. He had challenged his friends to spend the night there to dispute the story, but no one accepted.

Drake and Ramona dismounted in the front of the castle

portcullis gate. The grooms stepped out of the shadows and took their horses' reins; Ramona acknowledged them with a nod as a giggle escaped her lips.

"Shhhh." Drake put his arm around her shoulder and guided her away through the gatehouse into the great-hall.

They were greeted by Dunstan and Sansa. Sansa gathered their riding coats in her arms and hurried away. Dunstan teetered to attention and swept an awkward arm across his body, "Evening Your Highness." He bent to bow but had to throw a foot forward to right himself.

Asleep on duty and now drunk on duty, Drake was distracted for a moment by the intent to discipline the man. But his mood refused to be sidetracked. "Good evening to you, Dunstan." He slapped the guard on the shoulder. Dunstan reeled from the blow. Drake caught him and guided him back into his chair.

Ramona was walking away, a few paces out, looking back over her shoulder. Drake closed the gap with a few quick strides. He fell in alongside her, his hands clasped behind his back.

Across the great-hall, they strode as slowly and with as much dignity as they could muster. Drake stayed close, almost touching her shoulder. Zig-zagging through the tables, they intentionally gave each other bumps for shifts in direction. Each touch was followed by giggles from Ramona and a flush of promise in Drake. They hadn't had any wine, but it must have looked as if they had.

Reaching the bottom of the stairs that led to their bed-chambers, Drake made a quick scan of the hall. "Race you to the top." He took long strides, two treads at a time, but not in haste. Ramona bolted up behind, stride for stride. She tried to pass, but his extended arm blocked her progress. Not to be deterred, she grabbed the back of his cloak at the shoulders and pulled down with her full weight. He, easily, crumbled on the stairs. Ramona bounded over him; he caught her trailing foot, halting her progress, flattening her on the steps. She twisted to face his grinning face.

"Got you."

"Think so?" Ramona wiggled, extracting her foot from her boot. She turned away and scrambled up the stairs on her hands and knees.

Drake crawled up behind her, making half-hearted attempts, grasping at her legs and coat. At the top of the stairs, she spun and took up a seat on the balcony floor. He reached her, and from his knees, grasped her thighs with both hands. She let out a high-pitched squeal.

"Shhhh." He released her and looked down into the great-hall.

Ramona took advantage; she bounded to her feet and dashed to the bedroom door, his bedroom door. She disappeared. The door was left ajar.

Night at the Gate

Brown leaves carpeted the road. The bare trees, the chilled air held the threat of snow, the signs of winter coming. The sun went down a half-hour ago, but there was still light enough to get there before dark. Reynard had no desire to be on this road at night, not where he was going. The idea entered his mind last night, right after Elsa had told them what Berengar was planning. He spent a restless night, the morning, and early part of the afternoon tormenting over it. Finally, he had brought Amalia into it.

"I been think'en of spending the night with Berengar."

"I know."

"You do?"

She twisted up her face, raised her eyebrows, and gave a half-smile.

"Well, anyway, what do you think?"

"It's up to you." Was all she said, no advice, no help at all.

By late afternoon he was still stewing in his own juices. He had nearly lingered too long in debate with himself; stay with Amalia and the warmth of the hearth or spend the frigid night with Berengar at the Sheep Meadow. Finally, shortly after sunset, he announced, "I'm going."

"Good," Amalia grabbed his coat from the rack, pressed it to his chest, and practically pushed him out the door.

Reynard hesitated at the edge of the Sheep Meadow. Berengar was sitting on a bench at the fire-ring, his back to Reynard. The ground in the meadow was soft, the leaves on the ground and grass were moist with dew. His approach would be muffled; he might frighten the old man. Should he call out?

As soon as Reynard stepped into the meadow, Berengar, bundled in the bearskin robe, turned and waved his arm, summoning Reynard. At the campsite where the old man sat, the modest fire wasn't providing much heat, but a considerable stack of wood stood ready to ward off the near-freezing night to come. The men who kept vigil had set up a tent, doubtfully ever used. Who could sleep confined in a tent out here at night with that gate so near?

"Evening, son. What brings you out tonight?"

"Thought you might want company." The last time Reynard had seen Berengar, he looked and acted like a man half his age. Now he looked his age, sounded his age. Berengar was near as old as Grandpa Samis.

"That seems to be what folks is pain'en abouts, that I'll be have'en some company tonight. They been say'en that my boots will be all that's left of me in the morn; OUR boots now." Berengar leaned back in a chuckle of laughter.

It was pleasing to hear him laugh, but Reynard wasn't sure it fit their situation.

"Looks like you were expecting someone." Reynard stood in front of a second bench next to the one Berengar occupied, a bearskin robe draped across it.

"I was expecting YOU."

"Me? How d'you know I was come'en?" No one but Amalia knew. She couldn't have told him. Reynard didn't know himself until a half-hour ago.

"You're Samis' grandson, ain't you? It's not like you had a

choice, is it?"

"No, I guess not."

"If Samis was alive, he'd be here. If your Pa was liv'en, he'd be here. Since they's gone, I guess you'll have to do." Berengar leaned away and twisted toward Reynard to show his big grin. "Take a load off." He pointed to the other bench with the bearskin.

"You and Samis were close." The two men had served in the army together, fought side by side.

"Yeah, I miss's him, our get-togethers."

"I miss him too."

"You reminds me of him, built like him, walk like a duck, toes point'en out. That's why he had to use traps to take bears; his big feet was too noisy to sneak up on em." Berengar was laughing again. So far, this wasn't the weighty evening Reynard had expected.

Reynard took pride in being compared to his grandfather, even if he was being made fun of. The memories of his times at the farm with Grandpa Samis flooded in, demanding a smile. Reynard thought back to the times when Berengar came out to visit with Grandpa Samis at the farm. They got together a few times a year. For those times, Reynard, his brothers, and cousins were let off their chores, so they could listen to the old men's stories.

"I wish he'd been around for the feast this year. Would've liked one more time together. Ah, but everything comes to an end. That's what us old veterans do; we die off. Not many of us left. Maybe next year, I'll be an empty chair. Pretty soon, you young bucks will have the feasts and battlefields all to yourselves."

"I wish it was Grandpa that was here with you tonight."

"You'll do son—just fine.

Time passed. How long? Reynard didn't know. They were too far from the church to hear the tower clock. He got up, put a few logs on the fire, returned to his bench, and pulled the bearskin up around his shoulders.

Amalia had assured him that no dragons were in the Dark

Forest. No dragons would come through the gate tonight; they were out of the Kingdom; he believed her; he did. Everything she'd told him about dragons now made sense.

He wondered. Could he ask Berengar about the dragon? Berengar would have told Grandpa Samis, to a fact, if they'd had the time together.

"I was wondering, that dragon you came across ..."

"You're wondering; they's all wondering."

"I don't mean to pry."

"Ah, don't worry, I'll tell ya about it." The old man paused, his eyes focused on the fire.

"I've killed our enemies, watched men die right in front of me. Never FELT em die a'for. Can't do that and be a good soldier. I felt that dragon die; I saw it." Berengar's eyes were on Reynard. "That's about all there was to it. No big story to tell. But you felt them dragons die too, didn't you, son?"

Reynard's eyes filled with tears; tension tightened in his jaw. He couldn't speak.

"Here, take a swig of this." Berengar withdrew a tin flask from within his robe.

"Not wine, is it?"

"Na, it's a tonic Renilda give me. It's helpful."

Reynard took the flask, took a sip, and then tried to give it back. It was a sweet syrup, not like the bitter herbal tea Renilda has proscribed for him.

Berengar put up the flat of his hand. "You drink it all. I've had my share. Not half bad, eh? That healer woman, don't know what me and my misses would've done without her."

"She's a good woman. She did the honors for me at our wedding."

"Sorry I didn't make it. Wasn't ready for no party. Wasn't ready to come out of myself. I wouldn't a made it out at all if it weren't for her."

"Out?"

"Ahh, it's hard to explain. It's kinda like Boetius in the forest, in the darkness, lost." Berengar nodded in the direction of the Witches' Gate. "I don't regret it, but I feels like I wasted my time on that boy; he's come to this. I'm not expect'en him."

Reynard didn't know what he could say to console the old man; he had no hope of a return either. He stared at the campfire, watched the yellow sparks escape up into the blackness. The flames, time, and the darkness slowed to a crawl.

Reynard opened his eyes and squinted; it was bright, well after sunrise. He remembered tipping over on his side, laying down on the bench, pulling the bearskin up around his chest.

Reynard pressed himself upright. The smell of frying bacon was in the air. Berengar, with his back to Reynard, was hunched over a pan suspended on a rack over the smoldering coals in the fire-ring.

"Bout's time yous'ed got up," Berengar said without turning around.

"I was dream'en. Couldn't get loose of it. I wanted to wake up. Ohh, what was in that flask?" Reynard stretched his arms over his head, and the bearskin robe fell away to the bench. That was the best night's sleep in a long while, not what he was expecting for a night at the Sheep Meadow.

"What was you dream'en abouts?"

"Witches, dance'en around the fire ring, chanting and singing. You were dance'en with em, go'en to town."

"Abouts what you'd expect from a dream in this neck of the woods. Cept me be'en in it a course. How was I doing though, the sing'en and dance'en and all?"

"Hold'en your own." Reynard tried to catch Berengar's eye, but he was concentrating on his cooking. "I was dream'en, right?"

"We all's in a dream, boy, all in our own dream."

He wasn't going to say more.

Reynard heard sounds, feet rustling dead leaves, coming from the Morodon Road. Over his shoulder, he saw Hartmann with two of the King's guards approaching across the meadow.

The Return

A commotion at the far end of the great-hall drew Drake's attention. Dunstan was standing at alert, speaking to a guardsman who had burst through the doorway. After a moment, Dunstan pointed in the direction of the King and his Noble Council, all seated at the center table near the throne wall.

The guardsman approached, walked a few steps, jogged a few, then back to a walk (an attempt at a dignified pace). Upon reaching the King, he bowed and announced. "Your Highness, begg'en your pardon. A trumpet-call, just now."

"You're sure."

"Yes, Sire."

"Very well, dismissed."

The guardsman hesitated. A look from Drake, he bowed and hurried away.

The hope growing in Drake's mind was also evident on the faces of all those present. No one moved. The members of the Noble Council, seated around the long table, waited for their King's response.

Drake wanted to leap from his seat, run to the door and

call for his horse and ride as fast as he could to the Sheep Meadow. He choked down the urge, sat rigid with forced calm, and continued with his narrative. "Gentlemen, I will take note of your concerns and promise to respond. I will decide each matter on its merits. That is, as soon ... I think we should break. We will reconvene tomorrow."

The two sentries posted at the Witches' Gate had instructions to alert the King of any activity. The guards outside the castle gate were charged with listening for the trumpet signal.

In the absolute silence of the great-hall, the scrape of the King's chair legs resounded as Drake rose to his feet, followed by the clatter his ministers made as they quickly stood and bowed. Drake briefly looked to his right at the displays on the far wall, the first of which was that of Boetius' family house. As he moved away from the table, Drake caught the eye of Boetius' uncle, a council member whose face mirrored the suspense churning in Drake. Boetius had promised to return within a fortnight with the tales of what he found in the Dark Forest. The end of the fortnight had come and gone a week ago.

"Gentlemen." Drake nodded to his ministers, turned away, and strode across the great-hall toward the main doors, struggling to maintain a slow, dignified pace.

Drake passed through the open doors, the castle gatehouse and out into the bright noonday sunlight. A groomsman who had anticipated the need for the King's horse stood by. Drake waved him off. He had to content himself with waiting and anxious pacing at the edge of the castle road. The pacing, he worried, was not fitting for a Noble either, but he could not help himself.

His ministers joined in the waiting, standing between him and the castle wall. Servants, Nobles, and others gathered, standing as close to the King as they felt was due their station. Drake halted for a moment as the tower clock bell called out twelve noon.

After an agonizing length of time, Drake finally caught a glimpse of one of the Sheep Meadow sentries on the distant Village Road. The man, running, was momentarily visible in the gaps between the cottages. The sentry passed the last cottage and continued at a steady pace toward the castle. A straggle of young boys had joined in behind him. As he approached the rampart at the base of the castle hill, he slowed to a jog. When he reached the rampart gate, he stopped and bent at the waist. The guard at the gate approached him. The runner waved him off as he righted himself and pushed off with long strides up the castle hill. The boys appeared to be cheering him on. Slowing, he plodded up the castle road, the hill taking his energy. His legs were pumping laboriously, but he seemed to be moving in slow motion.

As he neared the castle and the gathering, he picked up a jog again, finally arriving in front of the King with a bow. He looked to the King; his face flushed red, his breathing labored, showing the stress of his undertaking.

It was apparent that, in the sentry's haste to get his message to his King, he had not retained enough air to get his message out. With a show of patience, Drake raised his hand in front of the sentry. "Wait," and turning to a servant, "Fetch some water."

Listening to the rumblings in the crowd, it was clear to Drake that the people were expecting or at least hoping for good news of Boetius. Not sharing that expectation but fearing the worst, Drake was content to wait for the water to cool the messenger's throat.

After the tankard of water was downed and a few more moments passed, Drake felt that the sentry had recovered and nodded for him to deliver his message.

"Your Highness." He turned his head to cough. "Early this morn at first light we heards noises in the forest. Like someone was approach'en the gate. And then ..."

"Boetius?" Drake interrupted.

"No Sire, sorry, no, it was the dog. It come out of the gate alone." The sentry looked to the ground.

After a long pause. "Continue. Share the details with us." Drake thought it important that everyone heard the account.

"After we heard them rustling noises, there was a howl'en, pitiful and low. It kept gett'en louder and louder. We figured it was gett'en close to the gate. One of the hunters started whistle'en and a holler'en. Then the dog, Boetius' dog, stumbled out of the Witches' Gate, right in front of us. It was stagger'en. First, I thoughts it mad. Thought we mights need to put it down." The sentry paused; it was obvious he wasn't accustomed to addressing Nobles, let alone the King. He looked distressed, overstepping his place, maybe.

Drake understood his concern and nodded. "Go on."

"It wasn't mad though, cause it recognized the hunters, went right to em, and keeled over. The hunters got her now. They's taking care of her. Said they'd take her to Berengar. Pretty ragged look'en, I'd say." Again he paused and waited for permission to go on. With another quick nod from Drake, he continued. "We hoped for Sir Boetius to follow. We waited a good long time, but thoughts we should get the news to you, Your Highness. Should we stands our post?"

The dog would not have returned without Boetius—unless. It was what Drake had expected. Boetius, such a fool. If only he had been content, content with his accomplishments, his well-deserved fame, the loyalty of his comrades. He had more than most men could dream of.

Drake had already thought this through; he had to set a limit on hope. This matter must come to an end. Drake couldn't allow his people to focus on the plight of Boetius to the detriment of the Kingdom's affairs.

"Yes. Keep the watch for another ten days." Ten more days would complete the 30 days of vigil as promised. He turned and passed through the bowing crowd and into the castle, leaving his subjects to their mutterings.

The End of Watch

The summons today to meet with the King, Reynard was brooding over it as he climbed the stairs to the King's chambers. His left knee was clicking in response to each tread; stiffness was settling into his bones. Many of his joints were voicing complaint of late. A chilled breeze had tormented him for the entire walk from his cottage to the castle. In an earlier day, he would have shaken it off with long strides and warmed himself in short order.

Reynard hoped this late afternoon meeting wouldn't take long. A long walk home in the dark and cold had no appeal; although, on this new moon night, the stars would be brilliant in the black sky, a consolation.

Winter was making its icy grip known, the solstice approaching, only a month away. The solstice celebrations were something to look forward to. Yet Reynard's peace of mind was not yet secure, not with the Boetius and Dark Forest episode hanging over him. It was the end of the watch, the last day, 30 days since Boetius had gone into the Dark Forest, the end of the King's promise.

The sentries at the Witch's gate were probably anxious and

eager, their term of duty ending today. But they needed to wait for the King's command to release them. Someone would be sent with the King's order, and Reynard was afraid the task might be delegated to him. He knew he was borrowing trouble (his father's saying): he couldn't help himself.

Reynard entered the King's study. The room felt darker today.

From his seat behind his desk, Drake beckoned. "Reynard, take a seat."

"Sire."

As Reynard made his way to his chair, he thought of the many times Boetius, and he had met here with the King. He wondered if Drake did as well. Memories had dominated his day, flooding back, childhood pranks and jokes, games and childish exploits, arguments, and scuffles. Who could have envisioned then, this future? Who could have predicted a dragon war and Boetius' foolishness?

Reynard sat waiting. Drake shifted in his chair, moving papers about his desk.

Finally, after a long stretch, "I hear you have Boetius' dog."

A casual comment Reynard wasn't expecting.

"Yes, Berengar sent her to me. Amalia brought her home only a few days after she came out of the forest. She wouldn't eat for Berengar. He was afraid she might die of grief."

"I could see that; the dog was truly bonded to Boetius."

"Berengar told Amalia that Boetius would have wanted her entrusted to me. He thought she might recover in my care." At the time, Reynard deemed that to be far-fetched presumption on Berengar's part. Berengar had also conveyed through Amalia that Boetius had held Reynard in high-regard. That was something Reynard had not envisioned either.

"I'm sure Boetius would want it that way," Drake said, "How is the dog doing now?"

"Very well, I've had her a week; she's eating, and she's already gained some weight. Amalia calls her my King's guard.

She follows me everywhere."

"Good, glad to hear it." Drake looked puzzled. "Where is she?"

"With the sentry at the hall door."

"That won't due." The King stood up and started toward the chamber door. Reynard began to rise, but as Drake passed, he pushed Reynard back down with a hand on Reynard's shoulder. Drake went out the door and was at the balcony rail, commanding in a resounding voice. "Guard, bring that dog up here at once."

Drake returned, passed Reynard, and dropped back into his seat. Reynard didn't try to rise this time.

"Don't ever go anywhere without that dog again." It sounded like a command, but Drake was smiling. "Always keep her with you."

"I will." Reynard looked away, averting his attention from Drake's eyes. He did not want Drake to see his eyes.

The guard arrived at the open chamber door with Riley on a rope, which the guard attempted to untie from the collar, but the dog broke free and ran to Reynard. Her paws were on his thigh as he untied the leash. He coiled it up and put it in his waist bag.

"Won't need that anymore." Drake nodded to the rope.

Reynard returned a smile.

"The reason I called you here, Reynard, I have an assignment for you."

A slight gasp escaped Reynard's throat as he winced.

"It's about the Dragon Dogs. You know my concerns; we will need Dragon Dogs for the future. We can be sure the King of Duren won't cooperate and provide us with his Elk Dogs. The few dogs we have will be a start, but what we need is a breeding program."

Reynard nodded agreement in the waiting pause.

"And that's where you come in," Drake said, "I want you to take charge of it."

"You want me in charge of breeding dogs?"

"Yes."

After a hesitation, "But I've no experience. I know nothing about breeding animals. Smithing and weapons are what I know. There must be someone else more qualified."

"You don't think an old dog can learn new tricks?" Drake slapped his knees with both hands and sat back. "You're a married man now; you're tempered by battle. I am convinced you can handle it." Drake shook his head and came close to giggling.

Reynard dropped his hand and scratched Riley behind the ears.

"I think you're right." Surprising himself, Reynard was taken with the prospect. Confidence was setting in; he was comfortable with the assignment to raise and train dogs. Ideas were already developing in the back of his mind.

"I'm sure Berengar will help you get started." Drake nodded to Riley, "She may be of help as well. A cross between our hunting dogs and the elk dogs might prove of value. It's up to you, though. Just a suggestion."

The men fell into silence again. Long moments passed before Drake spoke. "This morning, I sent a guard with my command to end the watch at the Sheep Meadow."

Reynard nodded. A tension that he had forgotten was there, left his body.

After another long silence. "That will be all, Reynard." Drake slumped back in his chair, head, and eyes down.

"Yes, Sire."

As Reynard and Riley reached the door, Drake called out, "Reynard," a plea, not a command.

Reynard stopped and turned to Drake.

"Not a better man to have at your side in a fight."

Reynard nodded and turned away quickly. There would be no funeral, no memorial, only a nod between two men.

Friends Lost

Ramona shivered. She was far from the fireplace and its heat, seated at her familiar table near the tavern hall's drafty main door. Grateful for her hood and her warm scarf around her neck, Ramona stared at the flickering table candle. Her hands enshrouded in the folds of her cloak, she rubbed them together to generate warmth.

Feargus knew she was waiting. What was taking him so long? Sansa had delivered Ramona's message a while ago. Ramona had arranged for this meeting in mid-afternoon, so she could be back at the castle before dark, before the frigid nightfall. The winter darkness pressed a more than normal lethargy; it was bodily fatigue not experienced before. She was looking forward to the warmth of her hearth fire and the furs on her bed. Ramona did not want to linger.

The tavern hall was occupied by scattered clusters of men in quiet conversations. A few strangers sat at a table near the bar, probably traveling merchants. The calm was occasionally interrupted by the people who were filtering in for the solstice feast this evening. They passed Ramona, on their way to the commoner's hall or Royal Hall, dependent on their station. This, the darkest day of the year, was a cause for celebration, the promise of expanding daylight, and the spring season to come.

Across the room, Sansa sat in a chair near the bar conversing with Dagny, exchanging morsels of gossip, no doubt. Ramona was happy with Sansa, but it was not the same as always having Amalia by her side. Amalia's days were divided now; she spent her afternoons with Ramona, but her evenings, nights, and mornings were for Reynard. Ramona had to be content with what time she had with Amalia.

A burst of voices erupted from the commoner's hall, Amalia's laugh floating above it. Her maid, her friend, Amalia's happiness was her happiness. Ramona was to be a godmother. Did anyone notice the smile that crossed her face? No, no one was paying attention.

Reynard's voice was also recognizable in the chorus of laughter. Not since childhood had she seen him in such good spirits, the war over, married, to be a father next summer.

Ramona surveyed the tavern's common room. Nothing much had changed since childhood when she, Reynard, Drake, Feargus, and Boetius had gathered on the floor in front of the fireplace listening to the Raconteur's storytelling.

Ramona and her friends had had free reign of the Kingdom; the castle, stables, village, hunting camp, parade-grounds, anywhere their legs could carry them as long as they returned home in time for supper. Fields, hills, forests, streams, waterfalls, ponds and caves, all were their playground, filled with adventure and sport. Running down mountainsides, screaming and yelling, scaling rock walls, legs dangling from ledges, swinging off a cliff on a freshly cut vine, forts built of sticks and stones, campfires were built for fun and for cooking lunch. It's what they did all day long.

Each morning, they were off on secret missions; eggs borrowed from a farmer, bread borrowed from the baker, horses borrowed from the stables, all in good fun. Some ventures resulted in a good scolding, some a good thrashing.

Despite the reprimands, no restrictions were imposed; the adventures went on.

A loud metallic clang, Ramona jumped out of her thoughts. A barmaid had dropped a serving tray as she passed through the kitchen doorway. The aroma of roasting meat, drifting in from the kitchen, permeating the room, reached Ramona. Ordinarily pleasant, today, the aroma turned her stomach. Hopefully, not a sickness, but it was the time of year for it; the grip, fevers, the croup, all lay in wait. She resolved to go see Renilda tomorrow. Maybe an herbal would stave it off. The various tonics Ramona had been taking for the last two months had their positive effects. Ramona's energy level was up. She was relaxed and calm, compared to the stress and tension she had endured during the dragon hunt. She was even starting to put some weight back on.

A movement to her right caught her eye. Ah, finally, from the Royal Hall, Feargus moved across the tavern, weaving between tables. He took a seat next to her, with his back to the wall, as always. "Good evening Ma'am."

"Good evening Sir." Ramona intoned sarcasm.

Feargus returned an unconvincing smile.

"I asked you here to discuss Boetius."

"What is there to talk about?"

"He has been gone for two months. It's well past the fortnight. Do you think there's any hope that he will return?" Ramona asked the question, knowing the answer was no.

"When his dog returned without him, I was convinced he was lost. They were inseparable. Riley would not have left him unless ..." Feargus' voice trailed off.

"I still don't understand what would make him do such a foolish thing."

"He boxed himself into a corner with all the bragging he did at Veterans' Feast and then later at the Tavern."

Ramona had reports from Elsa. Once the stories of dragons and beasts in the Dark Forest stared circulating in the Tavern,

Boetius couldn't help but get involved.

Maybe Ramona should have done something. She could have confided in Boetius, told him about the dragons, her secrets. The claim that dragons were in the forest was false. She may have been able to convince him the stories of game animals were false as well. No, couldn't be done, too risky. The outcome of that conversation would have been ill-fated.

Ramona looked to the central table where Boetius used to sit. "There must be something we can do? Is there any talk of a rescue attempt?"

"Go into the Dark Forest looking for him?" Feargus' voice was loud. He looked around and then in a whisper. "That would be insane. No one is going to do that."

He was right, but she had to bring it up, talk with someone about it. Ramona started to speak, but Feargus interrupted.

"No one, not me, not Drake, not Reynard, not the hunting troop, or the archers. No one." Feargus leaned in toward Ramona. "Even Berengar has accepted it, Boetius is lost. You need to accept it too."

"I understand, I know it's hopeless, but I feel we owe him something."

"I don't understand your concern. He was your enemy. Tried to kill off the dragons you were trying to protect." Feargus was whispering.

"What of our friendship, we were friends since childhood."

"WAS our friend. You don't make sense, Ramona. He wasn't on our side. It was his choice to hunt the dragons, his choice to go into the forest. The fault is his; he shouldn't have tempted fate."

Feargus sat back and folded his arms across his chest.

"I don't see it that way. Things aren't black and white. I can't turn off my feelings. I can't just forget. If everyone else wants to forget about him, fine, that's just fine, but I can't." Ramona crossed her arms as well.

They sat in awkward silence, staring at each other. Feargus

shook his head.

Ramona relaxed. "Before he left, people were calling him a hero; he was celebrated. I can't believe he's forgotten so soon by his friends." Forgotten, for now, but someday he'd be the stuff of legends and stories like he wanted, but not the way he wanted. He would be known as just another fool who entered the Dark Forest.

"People don't even talk of him." Ramona knew from Elsa that the gossip no longer focused on Boetius.

"People want to put misfortunes behind them. Especially if it doesn't affect them or there's nothing to be done about it. You can't think of him without thinking of the forest. No one wants that malevolent place in their mind. They want his misadventure behind them."

Ramona was well aware of that. People don't want to dwell on what frightens them. Life goes on, but, "I just don't understand people, don't his friends miss him?"

"Oh, some people will. They'll miss the extra food he used to bring them from his hunts. With winter upon us and less meat, they'll think of him then."

"Won't the other hunters bring in extra game?"

"They don't have the hunting prowess of Boetius. They rarely have excess game. And if they did, they don't have Boetius to prod them into sharing. They will only take care of themselves."

"What of Berengar? He holds sway over the hunters. Won't he lead the hunting troop?"

"No, he's taking his veteran's pension. Says he's too old; says it's a younger man's job."

Again the two friends lapsed into silence. The glare of the low hanging afternoon sun had faded from the western windows, leaving them tinged with the orange of sunset.

"I keep wondering if there was something that could have been done to stop Boetius. I tried to talk him out of it. He wouldn't listen," Ramona said.

"He was sure of himself. His mind was made up. Even

Berengar couldn't talk him out of it."

"I suppose he wouldn't listen to you either."

"I didn't try."

"What?" Ramona withdrew. At the same time, nausea struck another blow.

"Why would I? His disappearance served our cause," Feargus placed a hand on his waist pouch. Ramona knew it contained his dragon stone; strange, he still carried it. "Between Boetius and his dogs, it wouldn't have been long before they tracked the dragons to their hiding places, maybe even to their home, and destroyed them all."

"Drake forbid him from hunting the dragons."

"You know that wouldn't last. Drake would tire of saying no, and Boetius would have found a way to get around Berengar's objections. He would have figured out how the dragons got out of the Kingdom, where they went, and who helped them. It would have been just a matter of time."

He was right.

"Maybe, but ..."

"Besides, what goes around comes around," Feargus interrupted.

"What do you mean by that?"

"Rumors brought on the Dragon War; rumors put an end to it. Rumors promoted Boetius' cause, and rumors did him in." After a pause. "It's even likely that he started that gossip that fueled the call for war in the first place."

"I don't see Boetius making up a pack of lies."

Feargus coolly shook his head; his brow wrinkled.

Another few moments of awkward silence.

"Wait, YOU didn't start those rumors about the dragons and trophy game animals being in the Dark Forest? Did you?" Ramona asked, fearing the answer.

A smile passed across Feargus' face.

"How could you do such a thing?" How could he justify such a terrible deed?

"What? Spread a few false rumors, create a little misdirection. You of all people have a problem with that. The pot calling the kettle black, don't you think," Feargus scoffed.

How dare he compare what he did to her conduct? "It's not the same thing; there are rules."

Feargus' face flushed. "There are no rules in war, no rules to start a war, no rules to end one." He abruptly stood up, scowled at her briefly, and then stormed off toward the tavern door. At the doorway, he jostled through several men who were entering the tavern, bumping shoulders with two of them who were trying to lean out of his way.

The table candle's flame flickered in the icy draft that enveloped Ramona. Her eyes scanning the room, settled on the fireplace, the blazing fire. The pleasant memories were consumed. Fatigue overtook her. A heat-less tear ran down her cheek; two friends lost.

Winter's Ride

"I've enjoyed our rides as of late." Drake shifted in his saddle and glanced toward Ramona. The royal couple had gotten back in the habit of their monthly rides, gone out on the full moon for the last four months.

"As have I."

Drake and Ramona were riding on the North Road through the northern foothills, the route chosen by Ramona. Their horses followed the tamped paths in the snow that merchants' wagons had made earlier in the day. The sun was near the horizon, soon to drop below the low mountain ridge on their left that would keep them company the entire ride. Occasionally, as they passed high points in the hills, the sun touched the barren treetops.

"It was unfortunate you weren't able to attend the Solstice feast, a shame you were ill. You're feeling well now?"

"Yes."

The Solstice was two weeks behind them. Drake felt he had detected a change in the daylight: days were only a fraction longer, or maybe it was just wishful thinking.

"Such a beautiful afternoon," Drake announced, still hoping

for a more enthusiastic response from Ramona. She had offered no conversation since they left the stables, only curt responses to his comments and questions. Her silence was unnerving. She usually used these rides to voice her opinions and express her displeasure with his decisions. Although of late, since the end of the war, she was much more agreeable. As a matter of fact, in that time, she hadn't offered one criticism that he could recall.

"I could have done without this robe," Drake continued.

Drake opened his fur robe; it was unseasonably warm for a midwinter's afternoon. Today's blue sky and sunshine were brilliant in contrast to yesterday's clouds and snowstorm. Bare tree branches dripped away the melting snow. On evergreens, snow still clung stubbornly to the drooping boughs.

Tomorrow, without a doubt, winter will continue; its grip will hold for months. This dark season, Drake welcomed it, a respite from the hustle and bustle of the other seasons' occupations. The early darkness that forced leisure evenings, the warmth of a generous fire, it was to be embraced, especially after this year's long summer of battling dragons.

"I very much enjoy this time of year."

Drake caught a glimpse of Ramona's smile and nod.

"I have decided to change the family emblem from a mountain- lion to a dragon." He expected Ramona to erupt. He had been putting off his announcement, not wanting to upset her or their current gratifying relationship.

"I see."

That was it, all she said. Drake was baffled. Aware of her lack of commitment to the war and her attitude toward the dragons, he foresaw objections. Odd that she accepted a symbol of a defeated dragon as the totem for her house without an argument.

They continued to walk their horses in silence. The road was now in the mountain's shadow, the sun has set. Nightfall was not far off. Drake's horse's footing had changed: the snow trails they were following were icing up. The air had chilled.

"We'll have to turn back soon. It will get dark in an hour or so."

They were nearing the hunting camp, a two-hour ride back to the castle from there.

"I don't mind riding in the dark; let's go a little farther."

So they did, in the winter silence, with only the crunch of snow yielding under the horses' hoofs. Strangely, he was not enjoying the quiet. Ramona's reticence was not at all satisfying.

Minutes later, they arrived at the trail that led to the hunting camp and paused.

Drake nodded to the trail. "Lots of good times spent there."

The hunting camp played a significant part in their lives, ever since they were children. It held many wonderful memories: royal hunts, camping overnight, feasting at a campfire, all in the company of good friends.

"Yes, a very special place." She was looking up the trail. Drake appreciated her agreement. Ramona trotted her horse into the lead.

As they continued up the North Road, in silence again, they alternately passed stretches of pastures and woodlots separated by snow-topped stonewalls. Some walls were works of art and others tumbled rubble, dependent on the builders' available time and talent. Brush thickets or willow fences at the boundaries of the pastures contained the sheep. The forest growth was varied with patches of big old-growth trees mixed in with the new growth saplings, the result of timbering.

"There's something to be said for a leisurely ride in the country on a warm winter afternoon." Drake kept up the one-sided conversation.

"Safe and secure now since we banished those beastly dragons." Drake looked to Ramona for a reaction.

"Surely, the decision to go to war with them was the right one." Now she would have to agree, see things his way.

"With Boetius' skills and my decisive strategy, we could

not have expected anything but success. It's unfortunate that Boetius isn't here to receive his accolades. I, of course, always try to mention his contribution when the people pay me honor. There's always a banquet or celebration I'm required to attend. It's difficult to keep up with it all. I have received the invitation to Dacian's Veterans' Feast. And I also expect—."

"I suggest you prepare yourself for even more celebrations," Ramona interrupted.

"What do you mean?" It took her long enough to engage in conversation, and she had to start it with a mystery.

"There's something I've been meaning to tell you. I've been waiting for the right time."

"And of course, now is the right time," She had to interrupt his train of thought.

Drake waited. "Alright, please tell me your news." He knew he had to ask her for her to continue.

"I'm pregnant."

Drake's horse halted by a command he did not consciously give. Ramona came to a halt. The King and Queen swiveled in their saddles to face each other.

Drake felt as if he had been struck a blow to the chest, sat silent, staring at Ramona.

"I said, I'm pregnant."

"I, I understand ..." Ten years, he had given up. He was going to be a father. There would be an heir to the throne. There would be celebrations.

"Oh good, I hoped I wouldn't have to explain it to you."

She always managed to take a good thing and make him angry about it. He resented the sarcastic interruption to a bright future that was dawning like a spectacular sunrise. But this new future pushed his anger aside.

"Hero of the dragon war and father of the new heir to the Kingdom."

"Hero of the Dragon War," spoken so softly by Ramona, Drake barely heard her. And then with conviction, "And father of the new heir. I'm glad we can agree on that. Our daughter, the Princess, heir to the throne. The first woman monarch."

"What are you talking about? A daughter? How do you know you're carrying a girl?"

"A seer told me."

"A seer? Not that old healer woman in the village? I don't believe it. You can't trust her. They say she's a witch."

"No, not Renilda. Although, if I asked her, I'm sure she would confirm it.

"We should pick out a strong name for our daughter since she will be Queen someday. Brianna, I think. What are your thoughts?"

"The word of a seer or that witch does not make it so, a girl child or a woman as monarch."

"Renilda is a good woman; you shouldn't call her a witch."

"Whatever, that healer woman or any other seer, fortune-teller, whoever you've consulted, whatever you call them. I call them charlatans, fakers." Drake put no stock in fortune-telling, no stock in the prophets or oracles. He prided himself on being a practical man, down to earth. No one sees the future, no one. A man makes his own future.

"I've seen it myself. I've seen visions of our daughter in my womb and on the throne."

"Your dreams don't make it so either."

"They weren't just dreams."

"Nonsense. Now you're saying you're a prophesier?"

"I thought you might not accept it, that our first child will be a girl."

"Our first child?"

"Yes, the seer says we will have a second, a boy."

"Well, that is good news ..." Drake began, "No. No one knows the future. Except that, I know our first male child will be the heir to the throne. I will not be the first king to abdicate to a woman."

"Since, as you say, we don't know the future, we'll have to

wait and see, won't we?" Ramona pivoted away from him and set her gaze back to the road in front of them.

"I don't have to wait. I know that a son of mine will be the next monarch, not a daughter. And it's just as likely that the baby is a boy."

"I thought you might feel that way. Maybe I can convince you otherwise."

"There's nothing you can say that will change my mind. I don't—" Drake interrupted himself as he followed the Queen's concentrating stare, her attention fixed on the western horizon where the moon floated in the light blue sky. A trick of his imagination, briefly, a dark object passed in front of the moon.

Drake returned his attention to Ramona; she appeared to be in a trance.

"Ramona, are you alright?"

A rush of wind, bitter on the face, and then, 20 paces away, a dragon landed softly on the road. The retracting of its wings sent another blast of wind. Then, stretching out its neck, mouth gaping, a gravelly trumpet call assaulted Drake.

In that moment, his horse reared and pivoted on its hind legs to his left. The horse continued to circle as its front feet returned to the ground. Drake instinctively reached for his sword at his hip. But leaning too far, he tipped off the right side of his saddle and pulled hard on the left rein for balance. The horse made two complete revolutions. Drake's sword flailed in circles above his head.

When the horse stopped, it was facing the dragon. The horse backed up furiously, until she collapsed on her haunches, spilling Drake over and off her rump onto the ground. His sword flew through the air and landed in a thicket at the edge of the road. The horse regained its feet and galloped away, down the road, the way they had come.

Sprawled out flat on his back, Drake pushed himself up to a sitting position, to come face to face with a dragon looming over him. Choking on a sense of panic, Drake was again staring into the yellow, black silted eyes of his enemy. The dragon's tongue slithered in and out of its closed mouth.

"She won't hurt you."

The dragon lumbered back a few steps. Drake did not look to Ramona but kept his focus on the dragon.

"Let her show you."

"Show me? Show me what?" Drake's voice was quiet; his eyes still locked with the dragon's eyes.

"That's it. Just keep your focus on her. Try to stay calm." Drake felt anything but calm. And how could he help from focusing on the beast so close, dominating his senses?

"I don't know what you want me to do ..." Drake's vision began to blur. The dragon's eyes, then head, disappeared into a haze of colors, a dull yellow, shades of green, without shape or definition. The kaleidoscope that was now Drake's world vibrated and twisted back and forth. From the center, an image started to form, growing larger and larger, taking a recognizable shape, a baby, curled up on its back, floating in the air, revolving slowly. He saw it was a girl child. And with that acknowledgment, the image disappeared; the palate of colors evaporated, and Drake's senses returned rapidly to normal.

Drake was overwhelmed with disequilibrium and nausea. His arms, unconsciously extended behind himself for bracing, abruptly buckled. He fell back to the ground, his arms and legs spread eagle. For a worrisome amount of time, Drake lay there, waiting for the horrible sense of vertigo to slack off.

Finally, Drake struggled up to a sitting position. Ramona was standing in between him and the dragon, her back to him. Her horse was standing calmly off to the side. He wanted to rise, to protect her, but his legs weren't ready to move. From his snowy throne in the middle of the road, Drake could only watch as the menacing dragon's head rose over his Queen. As it looked down on her, the dragon's head slowly tilted from side to side, coming to rest too near her face. And then the dragon's black vertical pupils widened, radiated a soft white glow for a moment, but quickly faded. A trick of the mind most likely, but his fear and the dragon's fierceness also somehow faded. A calm settled in his chest as he took a long breath.

After a long moment, Ramona bent forward slightly as if to bow and then took a few steps back. The dragon spread its wings and lifted off, hovering in front of her. With each beat of the wings, the Queen's clothing ruffled in the gusts. The icy breeze washed over Drake. He fixated intently on the dragon as it rose into the sky in widening circles. At a height equal to the treetops, the dragon's flight straightened out. It disappeared behind the mountain ridge.

Drake's trance was suddenly broken. Ramona was bending over him, her hand outstretched. "Do you need a hand up?"

As he twisted to rise, he brushed her hand away with a sweep of his arm. She recoiled, and a braided grass necklace with a dangling white stone slipped out of the fold in her cloak. Halfway to his feet, one knee on the ground, Drake froze in place. The stone was glowing softly. Ramona turned away, the necklace gone from view. Must have been the fall, Drake thought, must have hit my head.

Drake got his feet under him. Bent over, he wobbled and then tentatively straightened up.

"It's not so bad once you get used to it," Ramona said.

Drake thought to ask what she meant but decided against it. Did she see what he had seen? What had just happened? His mind was a muddle of disbelief and confusion. A voice told him that Ramona could clear this up. He wanted to ask her, but he could not.

"Did you say something?" Ramona asked.

"No."

"Your lips were moving."

"No, nothing, I didn't say anything."

As he spoke, the dragon appeared overhead, skimming the

treetops. It flew over the couple as it set its direction north. The King and Queen watched as the dragon became smaller and smaller until it disappeared over the tops of the North Mountains.

Drake turned away from Ramona, stumbled across the road, collected his sword from the thicket, and started down the road toward the castle. Ramona followed behind him on horseback. She was humming an unfamiliar melody that oddly inspired an image of dancing, which in this moment, he found annoying.

He looked over his shoulder with the thought of silencing her but saw the necklace stone glowing on her chest. He thought the better of it.

Epilogue

Ramona's predictions were correct; her firstborn child was a girl, and she was named Brianna. Two years later, a second child came into the world, and he was called Bardolf.

Drake's desire to have a son succeed him, and Ramona's desire to see Brianna made the first woman monarch of Enid guaranteed a continued contentious relationship between King and Queen, and also between sister and brother.

Amalia had two children as well, a girl first, Emmalinde, and a year later a boy, named Durst.

The lives of the women's children would become entangled. Controversy and conflict were inevitable; the throne of Enid was at stake.

How it all plays out, though, is the subject of another story.

About the Author

Raymond G Dennis is a grandfather, writing stories for his grandchildren, great-grandchildren, and if things go according to plan, maybe even great-great-grandchildren. His interest in genealogy led to research of family historical records, which provided basic data (dates of birth, marriage, death, etc.) about his ancestors but lacked the most hoped for and interesting information - what those distant relatives thought, what interested them, what they believed, and what they valued.

So to that end, hoping to someday be a subject of ancestral research by future relatives, Raymond has incorporated in his fantasy stories moral dilemmas, parables, and thoughts on the sciences of most interest - psychology, sociology and neuroscience.